The Truth Circle

by

Cameron Ayers

D1409212

The Truth Circle by Cameron Ayers

For Stephanie

— Because I keep my promises

ACKNOWLEDGEMENTS

Writing a novel is very much as people imagine it: a solitary figure hunched over a computer screen, pecking feverishly at the keys for hours on end. But taking those reams of words and shaping them into a coherent product requires help. Lots of it.

I'd like to thank my early readers, all of whom provided valuable insight and gave selflessly of their time. Without these eagle-eyed individuals, numerous mistakes and leaps in logic would still be stinking up this book. Thanks go to: Michael Cipriano for all of the above plus translation help, Greg Salvatore, Tamra Sami, Wesley Elmore and Elizabeth Hollis.

Proofreader Jessica Filippi deserves props for catching tons of typos, as does Unesh Saini for creating a pinwheel text effect.

Lastly, I'd like to express my gratitude to graphic designer Andrea Orlic for producing the remarkable cover.

ON THE E-BOOK EDITION

Portions of this novel employ experimental formatting techniques to enhance the reading experience. Due to the limitations of the Kindle publishing platform, these are presented as non-scalable images embedded in the story.

So what's all that gobbledygook mean? If you purchased the paperback, absolutely nothing. But if you bought the e-book, parts of the story will be locked into a single font and size.

For this reason, the digital edition is best read in Bookerly with a Kindle font setting of 3 or 4. If you're using a tablet, don't muck with the device settings and you should be fine.

Here's a simple way to tell: if this section appears on a single page, you should be fine. If it's two pages, consider changing your settings, as some sections may prove jarring otherwise. And if it's three or more pages, then get ... off ... your ... phone!

SATURDAY

"Ugh, what is this place?"

"It's the same address on the brochure."

"This can't be right."

"Says so on the sign: 'Mystic Tours.'"

"I don't like the energy of this place."

"I can't believe I shelled out $900 for this."

"You paid in advance? Sucker."

Six strangers stood in the parking lot of a rundown strip mall in the foothills of rural Pennsylvania. The complex housed only five buildings, two of which — a boarded-up Blockbuster and a hardware shop whose sign had faded past the point of readability — were abandoned. The nearly empty parking lot was similarly neglected, with weeds poking out of numerous seams in the uneven asphalt.

The morning sun still had yet to produce any real warmth, leaving the group chilled and anxious on this blustery day in mid-October.

On the end of the row was a stucco-encrusted, single-level building that looked like a repurposed convenience store. The stenciled logo over the display window identified it as "Mystic Tours," with the words separated by the image of a bald eagle in flight. Parked beside it was a late-model

Chevy Astro being loaded by an older man whose silver hair spilled out across his shoulders as he worked. A feathered dreamcatcher decorated the vehicle's rear window, its crimson frame glinting dully in the sunlight.

Behind the group, the shuttle bus that had ferried them from the airport closed its doors and sped off down the tree-lined highway. More than one of them looked back at the bus longingly, wondering if they hadn't made a terrible mistake.

The offer had sounded irresistible: a fun-filled week of rugged adventure and spiritual growth in pristine mountain country, all under the tutelage of a Native American guide. The brochure showed smiling participants living off the land during the day and performing ancient purification rituals in a sweat lodge at night. That promise rang decidedly hollow in this dreary shopping center marooned in the backwoods of nowhere.

One of the strangers, an attractive woman in her mid-30s whose dark complexion and curly black hair revealed her Hispanic heritage, cupped her hands together and blew on them for warmth.

An older woman standing nearby — her taut face and frosted blonde hair said 50, but her prominent crow's feet and liver-spotted hands grudgingly admitted to 60 — fished into her jacket and offered a pair of expensive-looking calf-skin gloves. The Hispanic woman gave a small smile of gratitude but shook her head no.

Behind the pair stood a small and wiry man whose open-toed sandals and long, flowing robes seemed better suited for a sultry summer night than a nippy autumn morning. He adjusted the tortoiseshell glasses on the bridge of his nose and flashed an uneasy grin at the man to his left, a surly-looking fellow sporting a woolen Cowboys cap and a serious case of sunburn. The smile was not returned.

Standing off on his own was a heavyset black man whose scraggly goatee did little to disguise the fact that he was barely out of his teens. He stretched his back, causing his T-shirt to ride up, exposing his potbelly to the others. Embarrassed, he hastily sucked in his gut and the shirt descended on its own.

At the sound of the shuttle bus's departure, the old man loading the van looked up and spotted the six. He smiled and waved them over.

The last member of the group, who stood a head taller than the others, took a drag on his cigarette before dropping it to the asphalt and stamping it out with the heel of his hiking boot. He gave a resigned shrug as he exhaled and said what all of them were thinking.

"Well, too late to back out now."

* * * * * *

As the group drew near, the old man loaded the last of the supplies and turned to greet them. He looked to be around 70, with skin like worn leather, marred by deep furrows and pockmarks. His Native American heritage was evident in his sun-reddened cheeks and the gossamer strands of his thinning silver hair.

Despite his advanced age, he showed no signs of infirmity. He moved with the speed and grace of a man 20 years his junior, and his only protection against the chill morning air was a pair of navy blue dungarees and a light camelhair jacket. His eyes twinkled with irrepressible enthusiasm, like he had a secret that he couldn't wait to share.

"Greetings everyone, gather around," he said with a broad smile. "Bezon and may the Earth Mother smile on you. My name is John Lightfoot. I am a pure-blooded Shawnee of the Chalakatha tribe and will serve as your spiritual guide for the next week."

It was immediately apparent from the ease of his delivery that John had given this speech many times over the years and had honed it to perfection, pausing at all the right points for dramatic effect.

"For those of you familiar with my peoples' history, I am a distant relative of the great Tecumseh, who stormed Fort Detroit during the War of 1812. And as anyone who's been to Detroit will tell you, not much has changed in 200 years."

John waited a beat for the usual polite laughter from his audience, but when none came, he continued as if nothing was amiss.

"Over the next week, I will train you in the ways of the Shawnee, teaching you how to commune with nature and helping you discover your true selves, stripped of all the 9-to-5 stresses and excesses of modern life."

The tallest member of the group, whose breath still stunk of cigarette smoke, rolled his eyes.

"Now, I know you all have a lot of questions," John continued, "but because we're on a schedule, I'll tackle the most obvious question first: What kind of spiritual retreat operates out of a crappy strip mall in the middle of nowhere?"

That finally broke the tension and his uneasy audience

lightened up a bit. One or two of them even chuckling.

"Two very simple reasons," John said. "First, the middle of nowhere is precisely where I'm taking you. Our campsite is a 90-minute drive into the heart of the wilderness. You can look forward to 75 square miles of rustic beauty, occupied by nobody except the people you see here."

The slight man in the ankle-length robes clapped his hands in delight.

"And second," John continued, "my brother-in-law owns this mall and cuts me a deal on the rent. This enables us to put the money where it really matters: your experience."

"Now, seeing as how you folks will be spending a lot of time together this week, how about introductions?" the guide suggested. "We'll start off easy for now: tell us your name and something about yourself. Who wants to go first?"

"Me! Me!"

The bespectacled man in the robes shot his hand into the air and started waving it excitedly, like a student desperate to impress his teacher. His flowing pink robes looked like something from a Hare Krishna rummage sale and contrasted jarringly with his two-toned Patagonia windbreaker and full head of curly red locks that bounced as he waved his hand in the air.

"Hey everyone, I'm Coop!" he exclaimed in an oddly high register for a man. "And I've been looking forward to this all month!" He punctuated his obvious enthusiasm with garish hand gestures as he spoke, making him seem vaguely cartoonish.

The tallest member of the group shook his head in disdain.

"We know," he groaned. "You wouldn't stop talking about it on the ride over."

Coop went on, seemingly oblivious.

"This will be my second spiritual journey this season," he said, fiddling with an amethyst crystal that had been fashioned into a necklace.

John motioned toward the man's strange attire.

"I take it your last one was to an ashram?"

Coop nodded happily.

"I can locate your heart chakra, if you like."

John politely declined before continuing.

"And how about you?" he asked the tall 30-something standing beside Coop.

With his aviators and brown bomber jacket, he looked like something out of a 1960s Marlboro ad, right down to the uneven part of his wheat-colored hair, as though he were too busy being manly to use a comb properly.

"I'm Ken, Ken Berman. I run a brokerage," he said in a baritone voice brimming with self-satisfaction. "If anybody here has a Roth or 401(k) with one of the Big 10 investment banks, chances are I manage your money. You're welcome."

Their guide turned next to the sunburned man in the Cowboys cap.

"Why don't you go next?"

He looked to be about 40, though it was hard to tell because his face was a patchwork of raw, pinkish flesh growing alongside dead skin peeling off in clumps. Piercing blue eyes studied the others cautiously from under bushy black eyebrows as his tightly balled fists quivered with nervous energy.

"The name's Wade," he said in a raspy voice that held a touch of Texas twang.

John waited for Wade to volunteer something about himself, but after several seconds of uncomfortable silence, he took the lead himself.

"The strong, silent type, am I right?" he joked, playfully ribbing Wade, who didn't react.

"I'm sure he wouldn't mind me telling you that he came cross-country to be with us today. And although he doesn't look it, Mr. Rollins must have been excited when he booked the trip, because he did it just two days ago."

The others murmured in surprise while Wade maintained his sullen silence.

"Who's next?" the guide asked.

The Hispanic woman stepped forward. Even among such a diverse group, she stood out with her easy smile, dusky skin and semi-curly raven locks that gleamed in the sun. The body-hugging turtleneck she wore showed off her athletic figure.

"I'm Gabriella Moreno," she said with a pronounced roll of each "r." "My friends call me 'Gaby.' I'm a personal trainer."

At this the older woman standing beside her spoke up.

"You're the one who does all the tapes, aren't you?" she asked.

Gaby's smile quickly faltered and she looked flustered by the question, which piqued the others' curiosity.

"Tapes?" Coop asked. "Like mixtapes?"

"Workout tapes," Gaby said, her cheeks reddening with embarrassment. "I've done a few but ..."

"She has a whole line of them," the old woman interrupted. "'Abs by Gabs.' My niece swears but your routines."

"I'm flattered," Gaby said self-consciously. "But I've been out of that racket for a few years. I'm just a personal trainer now."

"Nice to have a celebrity with us," John said with a wink before pointing to the older woman. "Why don't you introduce yourself, ma'am?"

The older woman gave a lazy half-wave to the group before stuffing her hands back in the pockets of a wine-colored designer jacket that came down to her knees. Between her woolen leggings and heeled ankle-boots, she looked better suited to a night at the theater than a week-long camping trip. Her pixie-cut frosted hair and heavy pancake makeup gave the impression she was doing everything in her power to turn back the clock.

"My name's Beverly Sutton," she said, in a tone that came off as equal parts amused and disdainful. "I'm not exactly what you would call spiritual, so I'm not entirely sure I'll fit in with this … crowd," she said, her eyes drifting toward Coop and his robes.

"Not to worry, I know you'll make the best of it," John said with sunny optimism.

"Yeah, sure," Beverly responded noncommittally.

After a few moments, everyone's eyes naturally gravitated toward the only person still awaiting introduction: the overweight black youth. He looked almost embarrassingly young, an impression reinforced by his "Pwned U" T-shirt, which was styled like a university emblem but with the trollface meme in the center.

A pair of old-school headphones dangled from his neck,

fed by a wire snaking its way into a hunter-orange bubble jacket, which was too small to cover his ample midsection. These hipster trappings contrasted jarringly with his obvious aversion to attention. He assiduously avoided eye contact with the others, shaking like a lost lamb at a wolves convention.

"I'm, uhm … Lamar," he said haltingly in an embarrassed mumble that trailed off the longer he spoke. "And, I'm uhm … I'm into computers and online culture."

"What?" John called out, tilting his head as he strained to hear him.

"I said I'm into computers," Lamar repeated in a louder voice, his eyes glued to his feet.

Ken roared with laughter.

"Well, you're *uhm* a long way from Kansas, fat Dorothy!"

Lamar visibly stiffened but did not look up from his feet.

"Lay off the kid, pendejo," Gaby said dismissively as she fished her phone out of her pocket and started tapping out messages one handed.

Just as Ken opened his mouth to respond, John clapped his hands to get everyone's attention.

"Before we get underway, there are a couple more things we need to address. First, the baggage," John said, pointing at the mountain of luggage in front of him. "I can see that some of you may have overpacked for this trip. None of you should need anything more than the essentials: six days' worth of comfortable, warm clothes, a bathing suit for the sweat lodge, toiletries and personal effects. Everything else we supply."

Beverly, whose four-piece matched luggage set was lying

at her feet, wrinkled her nose at the news.

The guide glanced at his watch.

"We leave in 10 minutes," he said. "You can leave your excess baggage in the office and pick it up when you return. If you need to 'go' before we do, there's a bathroom to the left of the entrance. And if you're anything like the young lady here," he said, motioning toward Gaby as she pounded out another text on her phone, "then I'm going to collect your cell phones and other electronic doohickeys before we go."

Gaby took a step back in alarm as John reached for her phone, cradling it to her chest protectively.

"No way!" she exclaimed, her eyes flashing in anger. "I'll participate in whatever ritualistic mumbo-jumbo you want, but you are *not* taking my phone!"

John looked at her with a mixture of amusement and pity.

"I'm not trying to rob you, ma'am," he explained patiently. "There's a charger in the office. It'll be waiting for you when you return."

Gaby didn't budge, clearly unsatisfied with this explanation.

"There's no electricity where we're going," he pressed. "And the nearest cell tower is 80 miles away. Your phone won't work out there."

At this she slowly relented, and with a great display of reluctance, handed the phone over.

"Oh," she replied awkwardly.

John smiled warmly, registering how difficult that must have been for her.

"It'll be safe in the office, I promise you," he assured her.

One by one, the others fished in their pockets and handed over their devices, except for Lamar. John motioned toward the headphones around Lamar's neck, but the young man silently shook his head and reached into his jacket to produce a vintage battery-powered Walkman.

John acquiesced and went into the office to plug everything else in.

Ken shot Gaby another dirty look before stalking off to the van with his luggage. The rest of the group slowly dispersed. Coop and Wade followed Ken to the van, while Beverly started sorting through her luggage to see what she could leave behind. Gaby followed John into the shop to ensure her phone would be safe. Only Lamar remained, his head bowed low as he contemplated a full week of this. With fumbling fingers, he slipped on his headphones and retreated once more into the world of music.

* * * * * *

The Chevy Astro sent its occupants careening from side to side as it skidded its way down an uneven dirt path in the forest.

"Could you please keep it on the road?" Beverly intoned from the front passenger's seat as their guide swerved to avoid a downed birch tree, nearly sending them into a ditch.

Even though John was only doing 30 mph, the serpentine nature of the dirt track, with its winding loops and tight corners, made it feel like twice that speed. Its pitted surface was marred by protruding rocks and bowing potholes, like someone had taken an expert-level ski slope and painted it a particularly ugly shade of brown.

"You can't even call this a road," Coop remarked as the van whipped around another corner, unseating his tortoise-shell glasses for the tenth time in as many minutes. "It's more like a deer trail."

John stole a glance back at his passengers through the rearview mirror.

"Sorry about that, folks. Some of the trails out here aren't really meant for vehicles. We'll be back on the main road in a bit."

The van was already deep in the woods. The group hadn't seen a person or house for the last 45 minutes, as lightly populated towns had quickly given way to farm country, which gradually receded to uninhabited scrublands before plunging into the heart of Quehanna. Most of that time had been spent on a freshly paved two-lane highway, but 15 minutes ago John had taken a sudden detour down this tooth-rattling nightmare of a path.

While Beverly rode up front with John, clutching anx-iously at one of the monogrammed bags on her lap, Ken and Gaby sat in the mid-passengers' seat, each clinging to the safety handles on the roof. Sandwiched between them was Lamar, who compensated for the lack of a safety handle by bracing his feet against the back of the gearbox. Coop, who was sitting in the very back, steadied himself by gripping an armrest. Beside him sat Wade, who quietly picked at the skin peeling off his sunburned cheeks, seemingly unfazed by their current predicament.

Ken polished off the last of his Coke and tossed the empty can to the floor. He looked around the cabin for something else to slake his thirst and spotted Gaby's partially drunk Sprite in her cupholder.

"You gonna finish that?" he asked as he reached across Lamar and snatched the drink, not bothering to wait for an reply.

"Hey! I was saving that!" Gaby protested.

"You snooze, you lose, babe," he replied.

Just as Ken tilted the can back for a sip, the Chevy lurched violently to the left, sending most of Gaby's drink rolling down the back of his neck instead of his throat, soaking his bomber jacket and seat cushion.

"Goddammit!" Ken roared, flinging the now empty can to the floor and peeling off his jacket. "I'm soaked to the skin!"

"Sorry," John said, stealing a quick look back at Gaby and giving her a knowing wink. "These roads can be unpredictable."

Gaby snorted with laughter and quickly covered her mouth as Ken glared at her. Sensing the tension, Lamar slunk down in his seat and did his best to avoid eye contact with either one of them.

The dirt trail gradually widened and straightened after reaching the bottom of an expansive gully. The jostling slowly subsided.

As the van chugged along, the passengers noticed that the banks of the gully were starting to close in. The interior gradually darkened as the looming gully walls blotted out most of the light from the windows. The encroaching banks were so close that scrub plants growing along the edges started scraping against the van's exterior. Claustrophobia began to set in.

"You sure you know where you're going?" Ken asked nervously as he wiped the last remnants of Gaby's drink off his jacket.

"We'll be on the road again in a minute," John assured him.

The floor of the gully rose precipitously as they reached its outer edges. John floored the gas pedal as the van sputtered and wheezed its way up the slope. Ken's discarded soda cans rattled their way to the back of the van as it slowly climbed. As the van crested the slope, the group saw it connected to a narrow dirt trail, and just beyond it lay a paved, two-lane highway.

"Well, I'll be," Coop said, clapping appreciatively.

Lamar loosened his death grip on his seat cushion as John steered the van onto the highway and the dirt path quickly faded in the rearview mirror.

"In case you all were wondering, that little excursion was a shortcut," he explained. "The main highway through Quehanna loops east and then south about forty miles out of our way. That shaved about an hour off our travel time."

"And about a year off our lives," Beverly muttered.

A thought occurred to Lamar.

"I thought you said this was a wild area," Lamar offered timidly before trailing off into a nearly imperceptible murmur as the others turned to look at him. "So why are there roads here at all?"

"Huh?" John replied.

"Why are there roads in a wild area?" Lamar responded louder.

"Oh, this wasn't always a wildlife refuge," John explained,

keeping his eyes on the road. "Back in the '50s, an Air Force contractor built a research facility out here. Wanted to test out nuclear-powered jets, if you can believe it. They spent years setting this place up, built a working reactor, miles of roads, an airstrip, the works. But the project never got off the ground — so to speak — and they eventually abandoned it. That dirt path we just left actually leads to the facility; they cleared the land but never got around to paving it over. If you check survey maps, you'll see it listed as Reactor Road."

Coop gulped at the name, as Gaby and Lamar exchanged worried glances.

John sensed their discomfort and chuckled good-naturedly.

"Relax, the facility's been shuttered for 60 years, and anyway, our campsite is five miles north of the plant," he said. "Take my word for it: I've been coming here for over four decades, and I don't glow in the dark."

"Is that why we haven't seen anyone else out here?" Ken chimed in. "Fear of glowing in the dark?"

John shook his head.

"Nope, it's just the wrong season. Quehanna gets its fair share of backpackers, but you never see any after Labor Day," he explained. "And only the most adventurous stray this far north; all the popular hiking trails are in the southern block."

"What about campers?" Ken continued.

"Hardly ever get 'em," the old Shawnee Indian replied. "'Wild area' means no permanent structures allowed, so you won't find any cabins or campgrounds out here. When palefaces hear that there's no hookup for their RV, no Wi-Fi and no porta potties, they look elsewhere for their vacations. Present company excepted, of course."

"So, what's that mean for us?" Beverly asked, dreading the answer to come. "Are we sleeping in the van?"

"I call shotgun!" Ken blurted out.

John roared with laughter, momentarily startling the others.

"No need for anything so drastic. You're getting all the amenities you were promised: running water, a shower, out-houses, firepits, and of course, the sweat lodge."

Beverly looked confused.

"But you said ..."

"Everything at the campsite predates the construction ban," John explained, anticipating her question. "It's all grandfathered in."

This news cheered the group as John turned off the main highway and onto another dirt track, this one identified by a wooden post with trail markers painted on it. Unlike the last dirt road, this one was well worn and wide enough for two vans to pass.

"The sweat lodge. Is that where we'll perform the purification ceremony?" Coop called out from the back row.

"That's right," John responded.

"And you'll teach us how to do it?"

"Think of it more as me guiding you along the path," John answered.

"The path to the spirit realm?" Coop asked earnestly.

Ken rolled his eyes contemptuously.

John studied Coop in the rearview mirror for a long moment before responding.

"Look, Coop … it is Coop, right? I'm concerned that you have the wrong idea. I'm not here to help you commune with your dead ancestors. I'm here to help you rediscover yourself."

"But it's titled 'Mystic Tours,'" Coop insisted, clearly unconvinced.

"You watch too many movies," John replied good-naturedly. "Mysticism isn't hocus-pocus and channeling other realms. It's spiritual. Just like believing in the divinity of Jesus makes you Christian, not a sorcerer. And while it may be a different take on spirituality, the end goal is the same: spiritual rebirth."

"Are we gonna have to listen to this New Age bullshit all week?" Ken fumed, pounding his armrest in frustration. "I came for survival training, like the brochure promised. Living off the land and all that. If this is gonna turn into some touchy-feely, Kumbaya-chanting nonsense, then drop me off here!"

"The quest for a new you is both spiritual and physical," John explained patiently. "Just give it a try, and I promise that by the end of the week, you will be a changed person, guaranteed. That goes for all of you, by the way."

"Guaranteed?" Beverly chimed in. "As in, money-back guarantee, like it said on the website? Because if I'm going to live like a savage for a week, I expect results."

"What sort of results were you expecting?" Lamar asked mildly.

The question was harmless, but Beverly took immediate umbrage to it. She spun around in her seat and glared at Lamar, who withered under her intense gaze.

"My reasons are my own, and that's all you need to know," she responded haughtily, crossing her arms protectively.

An uncomfortable silence descended on the van as John steered it into a clearing the size of a soccer field where five dirt paths converged.

For 10 agonizing minutes, the only sound was the hum of the motor and the whoosh of tree limbs scraping along the edges of the van. During this time, John guided the van through a veritable maze of converging and diverging trails, most of them unmarked and overgrown with weeds. The feathered dreamcatcher hanging from the rear window undulated wildly as the van hopped from one trail to the next, switching from dirt trails to gravel roads and then back again at seemingly random intervals. How John kept this leafy labyrinth straight in his head was a mystery.

The silence in the van was growing oppressive. Coop shifted uncomfortably in his seat. The minutes seemed to drag on interminably, with nothing to mark their passage.

"You got any grub in here?" a raspy voice called from the back, piercing the stifling silence. "I'm starving."

It was Wade, who hadn't spoken a word since the trip began. The others looked back in stunned silence. If the sudden rush of attention bothered him, he didn't show it. He continued peeling layers of dead skin from his sunburned face, occasionally pausing to idly flick the balled-up remains to the floor.

"We won't be eating a proper meal until sundown," John responded, sounding relieved to have some interaction. "But I have snacks in a storage container just below your feet."

Wade leaned forward and spotted a clear plastic container under his seat. It was overflowing with chips, beef jerky and chocolate bars.

"Yeah that's the one," John said, watching through the rearview mirror as Wade hefted the container onto his lap. "Help yourself."

Wade needed no further encouragement. He popped the lid off and tore into the snacks like a man possessed. He devoured a Milky Way in two bites, pausing just long enough to swallow before he ripped open a bag of Bugles and poured them unceremoniously into his mouth. His next victim — a Twinkie — was barely out of its wrapper before he crammed it down his throat with abandon. There was no attempt to savor his high-calorie meal; it was a frenzy of feasting.

The others watched this gluttonous display with a mixture of disgust and fascination.

"You must really be hungry," Coop said diplomatically as Wade polished off some beef jerky and moved on to a tin of buttered popcorn. "Do you want a napkin?"

"Or diabetes," Ken muttered under his breath.

The gravel road was starting to thin out in patches as the van followed its course beneath a natural limestone bridge and then ascended to the bridge's level before banking left around a muddy escarpment into an ankle-high cluster of thistles. The overhead tree canopy had thinned out considerably, allowing light to stream into the area as the van finally stopped at a fork in the road.

The right fork ended after 30 feet in an open field, while the left fork was a dirt trail that traced a steep hill out of view. The right fork was flanked by two eight-foot-tall totem poles on either side.

"We're here," John said as he idled the van between the two totem poles.

Hand carved, each pole bore three distinct faces: one on the bottom, one in the middle and one perched on top. While the faces on the bottom and the middle differed between the two poles, both were topped with the same image: a beaked creature with blood-red eyes. The creature's outspread wings extended out a foot in both directions.

"These are the welcome posts," John explained, anticipating the others' questions. "Each face represents a different creature that is special to my people."

"What are those eagle-like things on top?" Gaby asked.

"Those are thunderbirds, the spirit animal of my tribe," John said, giving the van some gas as it followed the left fork up the hill. "It's said they possess the sacred eye of the Beholder; those who fall under its gaze have their failings exposed and cleansed. As you can probably guess, the thunderbird represents self-knowledge and transformation."

"Like the transformation we'll be undergoing," Coop mused as he adjusted his glasses.

John nodded.

"Remember these welcome posts, folks," he said. "The next time you see them, you'll be very different people."

* * * * * *

As the van crested the hill, the passengers leaned forward to catch a glimpse of their home for the next week. Through the windshield they could see the van was on the cusp of a bowl-shaped depression some four miles wide that dipped 10 stories downward before reaching the bottom.

The bowl was ringed on three sides by hills to the north, east and south. The van clung to its southern lip, which was the shortest of the hills; the northern and eastern slopes were far steeper and too overgrown to allow passage except on foot. There was no western lip; instead, the base gave way to a lower-lying floodplain that stretched out of view. The group could make out a creek in the sparsely wooded floodplain and several large rock formations nearby.

Near the depression's western edge, right beside the floodplain, was a circular campground some 30 yards in diameter, dotted with structures too small to discern at this distance. The dirt road led straight to the camp, cutting a swath through a sea of deciduous trees awash in seasonal hues of yellow, orange and red.

As the group drew closer to the camp, they started to make out more details. It was laid out like a clock face; at the center of the dial was an open firepit overlaid with a mesh cooking grill. All the remaining structures were on the periphery of the circle. In the 2 o'clock position was an un-covered log rack holding neatly stacked piles of wood; at 4 o'clock was a pair of single-seat outhouses with doors facing the center of the campsite; the dirt road ended at the camp's 5 o'clock position; in the 7 o'clock position was a well-worn footpath leading downhill to the floodplain; 8 o'clock was occupied by a cabana-style shower; at 10 o'clock was a tin-roofed storage shed; and at the 12 o'clock position was the campsite's largest structure, a 12-foot-tall domed wigwam with an open roof. It was situated beneath the boughs of an enormous pine tree that towered fifteen feet above every other tree in the region.

"This is it?" Beverly asked contemptuously as the van slowly descended into the depression.

"Yep," John replied with a hint of pride. "She's a beauty."

The van did a partial loop around the circular campsite before stopping in front of the storage shed, giving the group a closer look at the amenities. Many of the buildings were in dire need of repair. The tin roof of the storage shed was badly rusted, and the shower door sagged, thanks to a busted hinge. One of the outhouses showed evidence of a recent repair job to its outer walls, with several unevenly spaced boards nailed diagonally over a hole. Several boards on the front of the second outhouse had separated with age; even from the van, the group could see between the seams inside.

"So, what do you all think?" John asked as he killed the ignition, causing the Chevy to choke and wheeze momentarily before shutting off.

"It's very ... rustic," Gaby offered charitably as she opened the sliding panel door and scooted out.

John was already out of the van and darting around the front to help unload the group. His movements were so swift and nimble that it was easy to forget his age.

Beverly opened the passenger's door just as John came around to her side. As he helped her out of the van, she sniffed the air and wrinkled her nose in disgust.

"What is that odor?"

John paused to inhale deeply.

"That's just the outhouses," he replied nonchalantly. "I cleaned the traps on my last trip, but I guess that wasn't enough. I'll throw on another layer of lime before dinner."

Beverly looked like she wanted to retch.

The others started piling out of the Chevy one by one. Ken exited cradling his bomber jacket, which was still sticky with spilled soda. Coop stepped out gingerly, careful not to catch the hem of his ankle-length robes on the sliding side door. He paused just outside the door to drink in the surroundings before being shoved aside by Wade, who was too busy munching on the last remnants of the snacks to bother with an apology.

The weather had warmed considerably since they left the strip mall as the sun was nearing its apogee. Gaby peeled off her down jacket to reveal a pale-green turtleneck underneath. Lamar quickly followed suit, unzipping his bubble jacket and tucking it under his arm. Wade stopped shoveling Pringles in his mouth just long enough to remove his threadbare Cowboys cap, revealing a military-short crew cut that accentuated his rapidly receding hairline.

Despite the dismal state of the campsite, the surrounding wilderness more than made up for it. The surrounding maple and elm trees were nearing peak bloom and had yet to shed most of their leaves. In the distance they heard the chattering of squirrels, busy stocking their larders. Several dozen monarch butterflies swooped overhead as they winged their way south for the season. It was picturesque in a way that only a bright fall morning can seem, radiant and serene as nature revels in its last days before succumbing to winter's withering bite.

Coop breathed in the crisp forest air and exhaled contentedly.

John clapped his hands together to get the group's attention.

"Let me give you the five cent tour."

He led them to the other end of the campsite, past the central firepit and the three wooden stools surrounding it before stopping at the outhouses. The one on the left with the recent repair work had a sign over the door that read "Squaws." The one with two visible seams in the front was labeled "Braves."

"Mrs. Sutton has already pointed out the facilities," their guide continued, motioning to a humorless Beverly, "so this seems a good place to start."

He opened the door to the "Braves" to reveal a single wooden seat, several rolls of toilet paper on a spindle and a pail on the floor.

"For those of you who've never used an outhouse before," John said, "there are two rules to remember: first, don't put anything down the hole that isn't biodegradable. Second ..." He paused to tilt the pail toward the others so they could see its contents: finely grained sawdust. "Make sure you sprinkle a handful of this in the hole when you're finished," he continued. "It helps with the smell. Oh, I almost forgot. Ladies, an unruly guest broke the door latch for your facilities on the last trip, and I haven't had a chance to replace it. Just knock on the door before you enter."

Beverly absorbed all the information in wide-eyed horror, as though she'd just received instructions on how to deep-fry newborns.

"Now, once you've done your business, you'll want to know where the water pump is so you can wash up," John said, leading them back across the campsite and over to the shower.

As they walked past the storage shed on their way to the shower, Ken's roving eye fixed on the steel latch to the shed door. It had been smashed loose, judging from the warped hinges still dangling freely, and replaced with a bungee cord looped through a hole in the door. He paused several moments to consider the implications before rejoining the others.

The wooden shower stall resembled a cabana, with seven-foot cedar walls on all sides. The hinged door had a gap at the bottom to allow for drainage.

Behind the stall was an old-fashioned hand pump extending from a concrete block in the ground. It had two lines: one curved downward several inches before ending in a spigot, while the other extended five feet upward before disappearing over the rear wall of the shower. Both lines were coated in rust, as was the pump handle.

"All you need to do is prime the pump a few times," John said, grunting with exertion as he demonstrated, raising and lowering the handle several times before turning a knob on the spigot. A thin trickle of water emerged from the nozzle. "And presto! Creek water, without the bother of walking to the creek."

"Does this also feed the shower?" Lamar asked, looking at the second line that snaked across the back of the cabana wall.

John nodded.

"Naturally, you have to prime it a bit longer for that," he explained.

Their guide walked around to the shower door, opening it gingerly and motioning for the others to have a look.

The group peeked inside and saw that the second line ended in a shower head. A small caddy containing soap and shampoo hung from its neck. John called the others' attention to a large button on the side of the line.

"Once you've primed the pump, press this button to activate the shower," he explained. "When you're done, just press it again."

Lamar looked confused.

"But how do you heat the water?" he asked, trailing off once again.

"You don't," John answered evenly. "It's not like we have a boiler up here."

"There's no hot water?" Gaby asked, dumbfounded.

"It'll be fine," John replied unhelpfully. "Just think warm thoughts."

Beverly opened her mouth to protest when Coop interrupted her.

"Where does this path lead?" he asked, pointing to a foot trail that exited the campsite about 10 feet from the shower before turning sharply right and following the slope of the ground downward and out of view.

"That leads to the floodplain and Deer Creek," John replied. "I also have an archery range set up down there. Well, had," he quickly corrected himself. "The last group tore up the targets to use as ponchos and raincatches. I don't know what they did with the bows and arrows, but replacing the targets was a royal pain."

"That must have been a wild bunch," Ken said. "They

busted up an outhouse, the archery range, and the lock on that shed, from the looks of things."

John brightened and touched his finger to his nose.

"You have a keen eye," he replied. "Yes, some visitors can be, shall we say, rambunctious. I guess it's not all that surprising."

He noticed the group's quizzical stares and elaborated.

"This is a journey of self-discovery. It's not always an easy process," he explained. "And just like any journey, sometimes people can get ... lost," he finished cryptically.

Coop and Lamar exchanged worried glances.

"But there'll be plenty of time to discuss that later," John said breezily as he motioned toward the wigwam on the north side of the campground. "Right now, I want to show you the main attraction."

Everyone started to follow John except for Wade. He had polished off the last of the snacks and was in the mood for a little exploration. Gaby watched as he turned on his heels and started to follow the trail westward into the floodplain.

"Hey, don't you want to see?" she asked.

Wade dropped a Slim Jim wrapper and belched to show the depth of his concern. He followed the trail around a grove of maple trees and quickly disappeared from view.

"Such a strange fellow," Beverly observed. "We're probably better off without him."

The pair quickly joined the others, who were already gathering around the wigwam. It stood some 12 feet tall and was nearly triple that in circumference. Nearly every inch of the exterior was covered in stitched-together animal pelts, with only a small gap near the base to accommodate a round wooden door facing the camp center. John opened the door outward, revealing that its interior was reinforced with wooden struts to maintain its shape.

Their guide stooped low to fit in the narrow entrance before disappearing into its dim recesses. The others exchanged glances, wondering if they should follow. After a moment, an arm emerged from the entrance, motioning for the others to follow.

Lamar shrugged and went in after him. As he crossed the threshold, Lamar was immediately struck by how little headroom the teepee afforded. Despite standing over 12 feet tall, the teepee's walls sloped inward dramatically after only six feet, forcing taller visitors to stoop when walking around the perimeter. Even someone comparatively short like Lamar — who barely stood 5 foot 6 — found the lack of headroom stifling.

As his eyes acclimated to the dim lighting, Lamar noticed that the interior walls were lined with a lattice frame that gave the wigwam its distinctive shape. Overlaid on top of that was some kind of canvas-like material; probably whatever all those animal skins were attached to.

The sloping overhead ceiling was also made of this material, but in place of the wooden lattice, it rested on a network of evenly spaced aluminum poles, each set at a 50-degree angle. The poles joined in the center, connected to one another by steel springs to form a funnel shape. The canvas stopped at the edge of this ring, leaving a three-foot-wide gap in the ceiling that allowed outside light to stream in. Hanging from this elaborate system of poles and springs was a pull chain.

Looking down, Lamar saw that the hole in the ceiling overhung a large central firepit, ringed by two rows of river stones. The combination of the firepit and its stone girdle took up nearly a quarter of the floor space in the wigwam, with the rest given over to dirt flooring and little else.

"Hey, Fat Lives Matter, you wanna make way for the rest of us?"

Lamar looked back and saw Ken waiting impatiently behind him. He quickly stepped aside as the others began funneling in one at a time, all stooping low to fit through the narrow entrance.

"This is where you'll be spending most of your time this week," John said.

"You mean *we'll* be spending," Beverly corrected as she came in behind Gaby. Ken stood up to make room for them and promptly clipped his noggin on one of the aluminum poles overhead. The last in was Coop, who closed the door behind him, shutting off the only light source apart from the hole in the ceiling. Everyone squinted as they struggled to see in the gloom.

"What is this stuff?" Coop's thin and reedy voice called out in the dim light.

The others turned to see him running his finger along the canvas walls of the wigwam.

"It doesn't feel like animal skin," he said.

"It isn't," John replied. "Fire-resistant polyethylene. Sixty dollars a yard on Amazon."

"And why is it so dark in here?" Gaby asked, taking baby steps forward to avoid tripping on anything unseen in the shadows.

"Forget the darkness," Ken complained as he rubbed his sore pate. "Why is it so cramped?"

"Your questions have the same answer," John replied evenly. "It's a sweat lodge. The more light we let in, the more steam escapes. And since steam rises, we want to keep the ceiling low to get the most out of it."

While the others stewed over the accommodations, Lamar fixated on the pull chain dangling from the rafters. He tugged it out of curiosity and watched as the aluminum poles overhead bent downward and inward several inches. This pulled the canvas lining the roof taut, constricting the three-foot diameter gap to less than a foot. An audible click sounded as the springs holding the poles together locked into place.

"It operates like the flue to a chimney," John explained, seeing Lamar's puzzled expression. "For the ceremony, you light a fire and pull it tight so that it traps the heat and steam in."

"While still allowing the smoke to escape," Lamar said, beginning to catch on.

"Exactly," John said. "And when the ceremony is over ..." He gave the pull chain a firm tug, raising the poles once more and expanding the gap to its original size.

"That releases all the steam and heat into the sky, making it just another wigwam," John continued. "After all, no one wants to sleep in a sauna."

This jolted the others out of their collective reverie as they watched the two play with the convertible roof.

"We're sleeping in *here*?" Beverly asked, her voice rising an octave in alarm. "All of us together?"

"Of course," John Lightfoot said. "Where else would you sleep, outside?"

"Uhm ... ever heard of cabins?" Lamar groused.

"Yes, and I've also heard of four-star hotels, but you won't find either in a wild area," John responded, the tiniest hint of aggravation creeping into his voice. "No permanent structures allowed, remember? The only reason you have all these amenities is because they predate the ban. I had to get a special permit just to maintain them."

"I don't care, this is simply unacceptable," Beverly said with a stamp of her foot.

"What are you so afraid of?" Ken teased. "Worried that we'll catch you snoring?"

"I ... I don't know any of you people!" Beverly spat back. "One of you could be some kind of rapist!"

"I think I speak for everyone here when I say, 'No one wants to get in your pants, granny,'" Ken said with a look of revulsion.

"It's not just that," Lamar said, unexpectedly standing up for the older woman. "What if someone kicks in their sleep and their foot is by my head? What if someone rolls into the fire? There's all sorts of problems with this," he said, once again trailing off.

John chuckled.

"I've seen some crazy things in four decades of doing this, and yes, that includes people smacking each other in their sleep. But no one's ever rolled into the fire."

"Be that as it may, the black boy is right," Beverly said as the others gawked at her casual racism. "This is not what we paid for. You said this was a satisfaction-guaranteed trip.

Well, I'm not satisfied."

John looked at her impassively.

"That guarantee stands," he answered slowly. "But only at the end of the trip, and *only* for paying customers."

Beverly momentarily went wide-eyed before regaining her composure.

"Just … just what are you implying?"

John stepped toward Beverly and leaned in uncomfortably close, until his mouth was right by her ear.

" Don't make me call the judge. "

The others strained to hear what he'd whispered, but couldn't make it out. The older woman's reaction, however, was impossible to miss.

"You … you … you," she stammered with rage as the half-light of the wigwam turned her facial contortions into a truly frightening display.

John stood there calmly, waiting for her response.

Unable to come up with a truly cutting remark, Beverly abruptly turned on her heels and stormed out of the wigwam.

"You'll be hearing from my lawyers," she said icily as pushed open the door and rushed outside.

The others watched in confusion.

"What was all that about?" Coop asked, reseating his glasses.

John shook his head slowly in disappointment.

"I don't think anyone's stood up to her in a long, long time," he said.

* * * * * *

"Beverly? I know you can hear me. Just talk to me. We can work this out."

Gaby stood by the Chevy's passenger door, trying to coax the older woman out. After her confrontation with John, Beverly had locked the van from the inside and become completely unresponsive. She simply sulked in the passenger's seat with her arms crossed and a scowl affixed to her face.

While Gaby tried to reason with Beverly, the others were busy cleaning up her mess. Beverly's last act before shutting herself off from the world had been to dump all the luggage and supplies out the back of the van. Now the men sifted through the untidy heap, trying to salvage what they could and determine what belonged to whom.

Most of the food had escaped unharmed. Two coolers loaded with fresh meats and veggies had survived the fall, as had most of the canned products, although a couple of containers of beef stew were badly dented. A bag of potato chips had torn open and was a total write-off, but the other packaged foods —dried apricots and trail mix — were undamaged. Nearly all of the drinks were a loss, however. Only two water bottles had come through intact, while the ground greedily lapped up the shattered remnants of the rest, forming a small mudpile beneath all the suitcases. A two-liter of Coke shared a similar fate, punctured by the corner of Ken's metal suitcase.

"Maybe we should go back into town for supplies," Lamar mused, trailing off as he picked up shards of broken plastic.

"There's a pump 20 feet away," Ken reminded him.

"Drinking H_2O for a week won't kill you."

"But that's creek water," Coop protested. "We can't drink that stuff."

"Grow a backbone, already," Ken sneered as he set the undamaged canned goods on a hanging rack at the back of the storage shed.

"Animals defecate in creeks," Coop explained, his already high voice reaching falsetto tones as his exasperation grew. "A guy on my last Shinto harai got a mouthful of river water and spent the next month in the hospital."

"Hey, if you'd rather drink your own piss," Ken said dismissively.

"Gentlemen, I think it's a little early to resort to urine drinking," John said drolly as he sorted through the luggage. "And there'll be no going back. The water pump has all the water you could ever want."

"Told you!" Ken gloated.

"*After* we boil it, of course," John finished with a sly smile.

Gaby poked her head around the side of the van.

"Guys, she's not coming out."

"Let her be," John advised. "She'll come out when she gets hungry."

That answer clearly didn't satisfy Gaby. She trotted over to John and crouched in front of him.

"What did you say to her?" she asked in a conspiratorial whisper. "I mean, she's acting like a teenager."

"She's acting like what she is: pampered and spoiled," Lamar said with uncharacteristic conviction. "You see it in a lot of old-money types. They think they're uhm ... superior because people like us kiss their ass all day long. When one of us stands up to them, like John did, they don't know how to react."

The others all stared wide-eyed at Lamar.

"What?" he asked self-consciously.

"Listen to Malcolm Manifesto over here," Ken said in a tone that was almost complimentary.

"That's the most you've said all day," Coop agreed.

"People like that just burn me up, is all," Lamar said, retreating once again into his embarrassed mumble.

"Can we get back on track here?" Gaby asked as the others switched from cleaning up to rummaging through the coolers. "What do we do about Beverly? Suppose she tries to take the van?"

John, who was busy laying out seven fish fillets to thaw in the sun, looked up from his work.

"She won't get very far without these," he replied, pulling the keys from his pocket and jingling them for effect. "Now, let's get the rest of the perishables down to the creek before they spoil."

John led them past the shower and down the trail leading to the floodplain. Lamar and Coop struggled to carry one of the heavily laden coolers between them, while Ken easily hoisted the other by himself. The trail hooked right shortly after exiting the campsite and quickly reached the outer edge of the plateau, which ended in a two-story cliff overlooking the floodplain. Coop peered down and gulped, imagining what would happen if someone stumbled over the edge. Fortunately, someone had carved a narrow channel into the dirt cliffside that started at the foot of the trail and sloped sharply downward before ending in the floodplain.

The trees were sparser and smaller down here, making room for thigh-high wild grasses interspersed with patches of barren, rocky soil and the odd huckleberry bush. Large stretches of the pitted landscape were barren, however, home only to moss-covered rocks eager to snag unwary feet.

Two hay bales had been set up at the cliff's feet. Ken spotted several broken shafts jutting out of them at odd angles and concluded that this was the archery range. Laid beside the bales were white tarps with hand-painted targets on them; presumably the replacements John had mentioned earlier.

"Hey, look everyone!" Coop called out excitedly. "Deer!"

The others followed his gaze to find a doe and buck quietly grazing on the edge of the overlook some 50 yards away. The creatures raised their heads, more curious than concerned. Shafts of sunlight streamed through the tree canopy overhead, bathing the majestic animals in a shimmering, golden light.

"Bellos," Gaby whispered in awe. She instinctively reached for her cellphone, intent on capturing the moment, only to come away with nothing more than a few wads of pocket lint. It was a sharp reminder that she had no way to memorialize this or anything else over the next week.

The creatures moved on and the moment slowly passed.

"Are there many animals here?" Coop asked John.

"You'll see all kinds," their guide replied matter-of-factly, his eyes trained on the path ahead. "Snowshoe hare, beavers, black squirrels, several species of deer; you'll also see grouse and ducks congregate down by the lake. One year, I had a wild turkey walk through the camp, bold as brass. Everyone ate well on that trip, let me tell you."

"What about predators?" Ken asked. He sounded weirdly excited at the prospect. "Are there any dangerous creatures around?"

"Some black bears," John replied nonchalantly. "But most of them are already hibernating. We get coyotes, too, even the occasional bobcat, but they know their place in the food chain and won't hurt you."

Lamar and Coop exchanged worried glances.

John led the group downhill for several minutes, across an open field and through a thicket of scrub bushes on the other side. They began to register a faint hissing noise, like a record player with a worn needle. As the group crossed between two rock formations, it grew louder until it was unmistakable: the sound of rushing water. They followed a rocky path through another dense brake of scrub plants and emerged several feet from the water's edge.

The creek was some 10 feet wide and fast moving, although it was barely knee-deep. The water was surprisingly clear for such a shallow body of water; Gaby could see the pebble-covered bottom of the creek despite the churn of the water. John motioned for the men to set the coolers down as he lifted a downed tree branch beside the creek. Beneath it they could see a T-shaped metal cleat planted in the ground with two nylon cords tied to each end.

"Welcome to Mother Nature's icebox," he said as he fastened the free ends of both cords to the coolers and lowered them into a slower-moving pool on the creek's fringes until they were nearly submerged.

"Now, let's get back to camp," he insisted as he stood up

and wiped his hands on his dungarees. "We need to prepare for tonight's ceremony."

* * * * * *

The next couple of hours were a whirlwind of activity. Lamar and Coop gathered kindling and dead leaves for tinder, while Ken was tasked with splitting logs, using a hand axe and stump behind the log rack. John filled two pails with water — one for drinking water and the other for the evening's ceremony — before teaching Gaby how to start a friction fire using a bow drill.

The only ones not contributing were Beverly, who was still pouting in the van, and Wade, whose continued absence sparked more curiosity than concern.

Gaby gritted her teeth as she furiously worked the bow next to the central firepit, sawing it back and forth, watching as it rotated a spindle on top of a fireboard. She'd been at it for 20 minutes, and although the spindle had already bored a groove into the fireboard, Gaby had yet to see the telltale wisps of smoke that signaled the makings of a fire. John was kneeling beside her, holding the fireboard steady.

"My arm feels like it's about to fall off," she said, growing frustrated.

"We could trade places," John offered.

"No," she insisted, holding up her hand to dissuade him. "If I could get Missy Elliot down to a size 6, I can start a fire."

"Give up already," Ken said as he dropped off another load of split logs beside them. "Women don't have the upper body strength to work a bow drill."

"You're doing fine," John reassured her. "It's about friction, not strength."

Incensed at Ken's casual misogyny, Gaby took out her frustration on the bow drill, working the spindle so furiously that it slipped its perch and launched itself into the firepit.

"Hijo de puta!" Gaby shouted in frustration, throwing the bow drill at Ken's feet, where it threw up a small dust cloud.

"Did we miss something?"

Coop's bespectacled face poked out from behind a tree on the eastern fringes of camp. He and Lamar were dropping off another load of kindling, each of them carrying an armful of twigs, dead leaves, bark and anything else potentially flammable.

"Nothing a little time and Bactine won't cure," John assured him as Gaby nursed her blistering fingers.

"Hey, big man, what time you got?" Ken asked Lamar as he dropped the kindling beside the firepit and wiped his hands on his rotund belly.

Instead of answering, Lamar turned his wrist outward so Ken could read it himself.

Ken stared at the watch face in utter confusion. Instead of two rotating hands on a marked field, Lamar's watch contained three columns of eight lights, with the lights aligned vertically.

"What the hell is that?" Ken asked.

"4:51," Lamar replied. "Hours, minutes and seconds," he explained, pointing to each column in turn.

Ken just stared uncomprehendingly.

"Dios mío, eres estupido," Gaby muttered to herself as she

watched the exchange. "It's binary. Didn't you learn basic programming in school?"

"A binary watch?" Ken sneered. "You pretentious fag!"

The rest of the group blanched at his language.

"I close million-dollar deals before lunch," he continued, oblivious to the others' reactions. "I don't have time to learn that crap. Success means delegation, as my father always says. I leave the techie shit to basement-dwelling pimple pushers like you."

Ken's words hung in the air for a moment.

"Is there anyone you don't discriminate against?" Coop asked quietly, shaking his head sadly.

Ken grew flushed as he looked from one face to the next. All of them registered varying degrees of contempt and pity.

"This is a new era," Ken lashed out. "Trump's in office and P.C. is out! Best get with the program, Jehovah's Witless!"

He stalked off in a huff to find more firewood while the others shook their heads or clucked their tongues in annoyance.

When he returned 20 minutes later with a final stack of split logs, Lamar was explaining hacktivism to a bewildered Coop, while John and Gaby had switched to a more modern fire-starting technique: a magnesium stick and a pocket knife. After scraping magnesium flakes onto the tinder pile, Gaby ran the blade's edge on the flint backing of the stick, producing a spark on her second try. Coop clapped politely as John presented Gaby with the pocket knife and the magnesium stick, christening her "Chief Pyro."

Within minutes they got a good fire going, and John set the thawed fish fillets on a mesh grill over the firepit. Coop added two cans of baked beans to the mix; he didn't even bother taking them out of the can, he just heated them up on the grill top.

The smell of grilled grouper and beans quickly permeated the air. As John had predicted, hunger ultimately overcame Beverly's deep-seated sense of grievance, luring her from her self-imposed exile in the van. She grabbed a plate without saying a word to the others and sat alone, glaring daggers at John as she ate.

It was already late afternoon, and the shadows were growing long. The sun was starting its slow descent toward the western edge of the floodplain as the roaring fire staved off the encroaching cold. The group had finished eating, and John started collecting plates as Coop detailed his first experience with transcendental meditation to a less-than-enthused audience. Lamar handed his plate to John and wiped his hands on his shirt appreciatively. Ken stood off to the side puffing on a cigarette and staring at the sunset. John had just set one of the pails of creek water on the grill to boil when a tree branch snapped in the distance.

Coop paused midstory when he heard the sound, and he had just started up again when another branch snapped from the same direction, only closer. Whatever it was, it sounded large, and it seemed to be coming toward them.

They heard a rustling noise in the undergrowth just outside the tree line.

"Should we be concerned?" Coop asked John.

A dense thicket of rhododendrons on the southwestern edge of the campsite started to shake and out came Wade. His jacket was torn and tattered, as though he'd spent hours crawling through thickets like the one he'd just emerged from. However, the group was more focused on his face and arms, which were streaked with dried blood. In his left hand he held a freshly skinned and dressed duck carcass. In his right he held an eight-inch serrated hunting knife covered in blood and feathers.

"Ah, there he is!" John said with an inviting smile, as though this were perfectly normal behavior. "Sorry, but you just missed dinner."

Gaby tried to force a weak smile, while the others made no attempt to hide their discomfort. Beverly's eyes were fixated on the knife, whose blade glinted dully in the slowly fading light.

Wade held up the duck carcass.

"I've brought my own," he drawled.

Wade stalked toward the group, knife still in hand. His grim, unshaven visage was unreadable but his eyes were wild, reflecting the dancing flames from the campfire.

As Wade approached, Beverly hastily stood up and walked to the other side of the fire. Coop and Gaby — who were sitting on log stools — scooted their seats away from him. The only one left in his path was Lamar. Wade strode forward while Lamar quivered in fear, like a deer caught in the headlights of an oncoming car.

Wade stopped a foot from Lamar and reached out. Lamar squeezed his eyes closed and waited for the inevitable to happen. After several uneventful seconds, he hesitantly opened one eye.

Wade towered over him, staring at the grill. Lamar could heard the sizzle of cooking duck and realized Wade wasn't going to throttle him today. Not that Lamar wanted to tempt fate by sitting beside him. He got off his stool and slowly backed away.

"You can, uhm ... have here seat," he stammered as he backed away, so flustered that he didn't realize how garbled his words were.

Wade didn't acknowledge the gesture, he just continued warming his hands over the fire and staring at the grill. The only person he acknowledged was John, who offered him a dinner plate.

A guttural "no" and a small shake of the head was the best Wade could manage.

After a few minutes of cooking, Wade plucked his kill off the grill with his bare hands and raised it to his mouth.

"Hey, I don't think that's fully cooked yet," Ken cautioned.

Wade ignored the warning and proceeded to scarf the duck down in under two minutes, pausing only occasionally to wipe away bloody juices with his shirt sleeve and to spit larger bones into the fire. The smaller bones he ate right along with the barely cooked meat, crunching them viscerally. Beverly looked like she was going to faint.

When he was done eating, Wade belched contentedly before throwing the remains into the fire. He then stalked over to the water pump on the other side of the shower, presumably to clean up.

The others exchanged uneasy glances.

"Anyone else super uncomfortable right now?" Coop asked in a hushed tone, eliciting affirmative nods from the rest.

"That man is a savage," said Beverly, who was so shocked that she'd momentarily forgotten her own indignation.

"The process starts differently for everyone," John muttered as he removed the now-boiling pail of water from the grill and set it at his feet. When he noticed the others staring at him blankly, he elaborated.

"Remember our earlier discussion about how this is a journey of self-discovery? Wade's off to a bit of an early start, and it's jarring to the rest of you because you're still thinking of this as a vacation."

"You expect us to act like that by the end of the week?" Ken asked. "Running around in loincloths, beating our chests and saying, 'Me Tarzan, you Jane?'"

John smiled enigmatically.

"Like I said, the process is different for everyone. You'll experience it at your own pace and in your own way. As for Mr. Rollins over there," he said, using Wade's last name, "while his transition is ... accelerated, he also looks to be heading down a dark path."

"You mean, like the last group," Gaby said. "The ones that wrecked the place."

John nodded.

"And he's going to need everyone's help to avoid falling into the same trap," the old man said.

The group quickly fell silent as Wade returned, looking cleaner but no less savage, like a lion that has groomed itself after a particularly bloody kill. He stood beside the fire with the setting sun to his back, casting a long shadow across the others in the fading light.

John stood up and banged his fork on a plate to get everyone's attention.

"Now that everyone's together and we've all got a good meal in us, I think it's time to begin the sweat lodge ceremony," he said. "I still have some preparations to make, so I'll attend to those while the rest of you change into your swimsuits."

"I forgot mine," Coop said.

John sighed.

"Anyone else?"

Gaby raised her hand.

"I didn't forget, I just don't have one modest enough for this," she said. "I'll wear normal clothes."

John shook his head no.

"You'll get heat stroke," he warned. "The temperature can spike over 140 degrees. Wear a towel and undergarments."

"Thanks, but I'm a big girl," Gaby replied in an uncharacteristically dismissive manner, "and you have a signed waiver proving it."

The old man threw up his hands in exasperation.

"Suit yourself."

He looked to the setting sun, which was slowly retreating behind the western ridge in the distance.

"Since we're a little pressed for time, ladies, why don't you each use an outhouse to change, while the men can use the back end of the wigwam as a changing area? It's large enough to accommodate two at a time."

With that, John selected the leftover wood and kindling beside the still-roaring bonfire, along with the unused pail of creek water, and entered the sweat lodge.

* * * * * *

The brilliant red and orange hues illuminating the horizon were starting to fade, replaced with streaks of pink and purple as Ken, Coop and Lamar sifted through their luggage for swimwear. The ladies had gone ahead of them and were currently changing in the outhouses as the men decided how to pair off to do the same.

The deepening shadows made it harder for them to locate their belongings in the mishmash of baggage.

"So, how do we pair off?" Ken mused as he located his Speedo.

He looked up after several seconds when neither of them answered. They were both staring at Wade, drinking from the water bucket like a barbarian, tilting it back until almost as much liquid was spilling down his front as down his throat. Ken found their wide-eyed reactions amusing until he remembered that not 15 minutes ago, that bucket had been sitting on a red-hot grill; both the water and the container must be scalding hot.

Wade exhibited no signs of discomfort. He polished off more than a third of the bucket before placing it on the ground and wiping his mouth on his sleeve. With that, he stalked toward the group, grabbed his duffel bag from the top of the pile and went around the back of the wigwam without a word to the others.

Coop and Lamar exchange worried glances before Coop plucked up the courage to speak.

"I'll go with Lamar, you can go with ... him."

Lamar fervently nodded his agreement.

Ken snorted derisively.

"You guys are pussies," he said with a laugh.

The pair stared at their feet, embarrassed and emasculated, as Ken walked away, twirling his swimsuit nonchalantly on his index finger.

Ken was still chuckling to himself when he rounded the corner and nearly stumbled into the back of Wade. As John had indicated, there was little room behind the wigwam, only a few feet of space on either side before the ground sloped sharply downward into a depression some 12 feet down lined with brambles and bushes. This natural shelf was large enough to accommodate two people, but little else.

Wade turned to face him. There was something profoundly unsettling in Wade's stare. It seemed less of an acknowledgement and more like a warning.

"What are you laughing at?" he asked gruffly.

"No, it's nothing," Ken hastily assured him, sounding uncharacteristically apologetic. "Just those clowns back there. They seem to think you're some kind of psycho killer just because you bagged a duck. It's just ... funny, is all," he finished lamely.

"Funny," Wade said slowly, as though he were trying to process an unfamiliar word. He shook his head and went back to changing.

Ken followed suit, sitting on a moss-covered rock and unlacing his hiking boots. He could see a faint orange glow emanating from the wigwam as John started the fire.

"So, what part of Texas you from?" Ken asked.

Wade paused as he was taking off his shirt, looking at the

younger man searchingly.

"The drawl and the Cowboys hat kinda give you away," Ken explained.

"Fort Davis," Wade replied haltingly after a moment.

Ken brightened at this.

"I've been there before," he said. "That's like West Texas. Most arid place I've ever been. I was there for an endurance run in the desert a few years back, and the wind just seemed to suck all the moisture right out of my body within the first two miles."

Wade was unlacing his own boots while Ken kept talking.

"The desert had a funny name, a Mexican word," Ken reminisced as he stripped his jeans off. " I think it was 'Chihuahuan,' sorta like the dog. Does that sound right?"

He looked over at Wade, who was shaking out one of his upended boots.

Wade froze at the word. Slowly, his icy glare gave way to slack-jawed astonishment.

"You do know it!" Ken said, delighted that he'd found something they had in common. It was then that he noticed what Wade had been shaking out of his boots.

A thin trickle of sand fell from the heel of Wade's upturned boot.

"I take it you've been there pretty recently," Ken said, putting two and two together. "That would explain your sunburn."

Wade said nothing.

Ken had a thought as he stripped off his briefs and swapped them out for the Speedo.

"Hey, you know what? You should tell those pussies back

there that that's where you bury all the bodies. As a prank, you know? That would be so ..."

"Shut it," Wade muttered.

"Say what?"

"Shut your mouth right now if you know what's good for you!" Wade spat, his expression going from shocked to grim to wrathful all in the space of a few seconds. His hands slowly balled into fists.

Ken stood up, showcasing that he had at least six inches and 40 pounds of muscle on the older man.

"I don't know who you think you're threatening here, but ..."

Time seemed to slow down. Ken watched, fascinated as Wade tensed himself up before lunging at him. He watched Wade floating lazily in the air toward him, spittle flying from his lips. He had just enough time to observe the murderous rage in Wade's eyes before he was tackled to the ground, knocking the air out of him.

Time sped up again, and Ken found himself flailing ineffectually as Wade's hands encircled his neck and started squeezing. Those hands, those impossibly strong, suffocating hands. Ken tried to plead with him but could only get out a small gurgle. Wade's face started to get hazy. As the image went further out of focus, Wade's face doubled and then quadrupled. Ken could feel himself blacking out.

A sound. From an impossibly far-off distance, Ken could hear a voice calling out, as though from the bottom of a well.

"Hey, you guys almost done back there?"

Wade loosened his grip and clambered off him.

"Say nothing," Wade warned him.

Ken's eyes refocused. He felt a searing pain in his chest. He took a deep, gasping breath and the pain slowly subsided. He took another and started coughing uncontrollably. He rolled onto his stomach until the coughing fit slowly subsided.

When he looked up again, he saw Wade calmly changing into a pair of black swim trunks as though nothing had happened.

Coop poked his head from around the corner.

"Guys, what's the holdup?"

Coop's expression changed when he saw Ken on his hands and knees, struggling to breathe.

"Hey," Coop asked as Wade passed him, "is he OK?"

"He's fine," Wade grunted. "Food went down the wrong pipe."

Lamar and Coop exchanged puzzled looks.

"But uhm ... we finished dinner 10 minutes ago," Lamar said.

* * * * * *

"What do you suppose all that was about?"

Lamar and Coop were taking their turn behind the wigwam, but were more focused on what they'd just witnessed than on changing clothes. Lamar faced one direction and Coop another, to avoid locker-room-style embarrassment.

Lamar fished a set of Bermuda shorts from his backpack. He looked over his shoulder to make certain Coop's back was turned before he unbuttoned his cargo pants.

"The same thing that happens whenever two alpha dogs meet," Lamar replied.

Coop chuckled.

"You think Wade and Ken were sniffing each other's butts?"

An absurd mental picture formed in Lamar's head, and he burst out loud laughing. It was the first good belly laugh he'd had all day, and badly needed after the tension of the past couple of hours.

"The *other* thing that happens when alpha dogs meet," he said, still chuckling.

Coop located another set of full-length robes in his travel bag, only these were a different color and made of a lighter material.

"A fight?" he said, weighing the possibility. "Nah."

"Ken finally pushed the wrong guy's buttons and got laid out."

Coop paused a few moments before responding.

"Wade scares me," he said hesitantly, as though he were revealing a dark secret.

"Wade frightens all of us."

"I don't mean it like he intimidates me," Coop explained. "He does, obviously, but it's deeper than that. That man's aura is … dark. I think he's done terrible things."

"With that knife, I believe it," Lamar responded. "I still can't get over the size of that thing."

"It's like the one from 'Crocodile Dundee,'" Coop said, nodding in agreement.

"That's not a knife, *that's* a knife," Lamar said in his best faux Aussie accent.

Coop smiled and stole a glance over his shoulder.

"Is it just me, or do you seem a lot less nervous? No stammering, no mumbling."

Lamar thought about this.

"I don't do so well in group settings," he explained. "Too many alphas, particularly in this group," he explained. "You, Gaby and John — I can talk to you people. You're all right. Those others, they're so in your face, I just clam up."

Lamar pulled on his Bermuda shorts and laced them up. His protruding belly, which poked out from beneath his T-shirt, overhung the waistband of his swimwear. He tried sucking in his gut when he noticed Coop looking over his shoulder at him.

"Hey, I thought we agreed: no looking," Lamar said, annoyed.

"Sorry," Coop said, turning his head back.

The two changed in silence for a while. The temperature had dropped sharply in the last 30 minutes, and Coop found himself shivering involuntarily as he removed his robes. Overhead, a wren chirped its presence, happily unaffected by the cold.

Lamar removed his shirt and was stowing it in his rucksack when he spied something metallic glinting in the fading sunlight near Coop. Momentarily forgetting their no-peek pledge, he looked over and saw it came from something attached to Coop's leg.

Coop had propped his right foot up on the same moss-covered stone that Ken had used earlier. The glint came from a black bracelet wrapped around Coop's right leg, located between his shin and his ankle. It was bulky, like a fitness tracker, with a metallic object the size of a pager in the center reflecting the waning light. Coop noticed Lamar's stare and hurriedly lowered his robes, hiding the bracelet and its exotic decoration.

"What gives?" Coop asked, as Lamar quickly turned away with a "Sorry."

"It's ... it's fine, it's just this is ... sacred jewelry," Coop said, sounding uncharacteristically flustered. "I'm not supposed to show it to anyone to avoid material attachment."

"Yeah?" Lamar asked, sounding unconvinced.

"It was a gift from the preceptor of a monastery in the Qinghai Province, as a reward for reaching the second stage of enlightenment," Coop explained hastily.

"That sounds pretty cool," Lamar said as he stowed his shirt and zipped up the rucksack. "You know, my uncle has something similar, only he didn't go to Tibet for it."

"How'd he earn his, then?"

"He robbed a liquor store," Lamar said quietly as he slung his bag over his shoulder and walked off.

* * * * * *

Coop opened the door to the wigwam and immediately flinched at the heat radiating from the interior. He had been expecting the sultry warmth of a sauna, but instead was greeted with the oppressive heat of a blast furnace. Coop took a moment to adjust to the temperature change before making his way into the wigwam, duckwalking to fit through the narrow entrance.

The firepit in the center was greedily consuming most of the tinder and logs they had spent the afternoon gathering, and radiated incredible heat in return. At points the fire rose to three feet in height, which was all the more impressive considering the bottom of the pit was a full foot below ground. Coop looked up and saw that the ceiling's venting hole was fully open to accommodate the inferno John had unleashed on the group.

Most of the others were already here. Lamar sat to the right of the entrance in a pair of turquoise Bermuda shorts. He seemed ashamed of his near-nakedness and kept positioning his arms at odd angles to hide his sagging man boobs. Beside him was Gaby, who was uncomfortable for a wholly different reason. Despite her earlier assurances, the heat was clearly getting to her. Her long-sleeved T-shirt and checkered harem pants were already coated in a thin layer of sweat, and she had taken to fanning herself to keep cool. Their guide was on the other side of the fire, wearing a pair of brown swim trunks that had probably been very fashionable in the early '70s. The shimmering haze of the fire's heat exaggerated his features, making him appear almost mystical. Beverly was to his right, wearing a simple black one-piece. Her makeup was already beginning to run. Last was Wade, who sat immediately to the left of the door, staring passively into the fire.

Coop crossed in front of Gaby and Lamar, holding up his hand to shield his face from the fire, before taking his place between Gaby and John. He noticed that John had surrounded himself with a host of accoutrements: on his left was a large metal funnel, to his right was the water pail with a ladle in it, and in front of him were about two dozen lava rocks.

John leaned in toward Coop, his expression uncharacteristically anxious.

"Have you seen Ken?"

Coop shook his head.

"Not since we were changing," he replied.

The old man's eyebrows knotted in worry.

"What's the problem?" Gaby asked.

"We can't start the sweat without him," John explained. "And like I said earlier, we're running out of time."

"Why do we have to wait on Ken?" Gaby asked. "If the roles were reversed, he wouldn't think twice about excluding us."

"Everyone has to participate," John said firmly. "Otherwise, the circle will be incomplete."

As Coop's eyes acclimated to the room, he noticed a dreamcatcher hanging from a nail over the door. Unlike the ornate ones found in curio shops, this one was monochrome and had a fairly simple design: an eight-petalled crimson flower with a corresponding number of feathers dangling from the bottom.

"Is that the same dreamcatcher from the van?" he asked, pointing to the trinket.

John nodded.

"I brought it for the ceremony," he explained. "Only it's not a dreamcatcher. It's a mandala. It acts more like a guidepost than a ward."

"What are you guiding here?" Coop asked.

John ignored the question and stood up.

"I'm going to go search for Ken in case ..."

Before he could finish his sentence, the door opened and Ken thrust his head in.

"There he is," John said, sounding immensely relieved.

Ken immediately squinted and turned his face away from the intense heat of the fire. It was then that Gaby noticed the purple welts forming on his neck.

"Ken, what happened?" she asked in alarm.

"Oh, this?" he replied, stealing a glance at Wade, whose back was turned to him. "It's nothing. Tripped in the woods and caught a tree branch in the throat."

Coop and Lamar exchanged knowing looks but said nothing.

"Hurry up and come in," John said. "You're letting the heat out."

Because of his height, Ken had to walk through the tiny opening hunched over. Gaby and Beverly noticed he was wearing a Speedo and fought to stave off a wave of revulsion. Ken closed the door behind him and looked for an empty space.

"There's room beside Wade," John said.

Ken walked right past the open spot, giving Wade a wide berth before planting himself between John and Beverly. He nudged Beverly to make room, earning a dirty look from the older woman as she scooted over.

"Comfy?" Beverly asked sharply as Ken sat in her former spot.

John clapped his hands.

"Everyone, this is the moment you've all been waiting for," he said loudly, to ensure everyone could hear him over the roaring fire. "The circle is now complete, and we can begin the ceremony."

John reached beside him and grabbed the metal funnel. It looked a mutant pairing of a pot lid and a kitchen funnel, except it was four times larger than either, with a foot-wide spout at its center and a raised exterior. Their guide upended the funnel and laid it gingerly over the roaring fire, covering it completely. The bright orange light that had illuminated the teepee was now reduced to a few wisps of flame emanating from the funnel's conical center. The room was immediately enveloped in darkness.

Black smoke started belching forth from the funnel's opening; between that and the dim reddish glow of the funnel's interior, it looked like a miniature volcano. The funnel started to glow faintly as the metal heated up. John began placing fist-sized lava rocks along the outer rim of the funnel, walking around the teepee as he did so.

"My ancestors referred to this space as the truth circle," he said as he moved around the edge of the fire, placing lava rocks at evenly spaced intervals. "They believed that once the circle is formed, a sacred bond develops between the participants, one that cannot be broken until the truth comes to light."

"What truth?" Coop asked, entranced.

"Your truth. For each of you. What drives you, what haunts you. What makes you ... incomplete. Each of you must face your own truth over the next seven days. And when you have all faced your truths, you will no longer require the circle, and will go forth as whole people."

"Face our truths?" Ken sneered. "What's the penalty for refusal? Scalping?"

John merely smiled and placed another stone on the rapidly heating funnel.

"No penalty," he said. "Because the truth will find its way

into the circle, one way or another."

John leaned in uncomfortably close to Ken before suddenly bursting into song.

"One way, or another, it's gonna find ya, it's gonna getcha-getcha-getcha-getcha!" he sang, making pistol fingers with each "getcha."

The others all laughed; even Wade cracked a faint smile.

"My ancestors performed this ceremony — the Inipi — at the start of every vision quest," John continued, turning serious once again. "It's a rite of passage for my people. Children would enter the truth circle, then emerge seven days later as adults, having conquered their demons. You shall all undergo a similar process, and will learn, as they did, that it isn't the experience that shapes you: it's the truth. Tonight, we call upon the weyekin — the spirits of the forest — for their assistance in the cleansing to come."

He placed the last of the lava rocks on the now-sizzling funnel and took his place at the head of the circle.

"Is everybody ready?" John asked.

Hearing no objections, he pulled the chain tied to the rafter poles, and the ceiling's opening shrank to less than a foot. An audible click confirmed that the "flue" was effectively closed.

John grabbed the pail and started ladling water on the lava rocks and the funnel. An ear-splitting hiss echoed throughout the small structure as the water came to a boil, enveloping the room in a cloud of steam. The hazy mist only further obscured everyone's vision; people whose features were barely visible in the darkness were now distorted and twisted, rendering them as hideous approximations of people.

"So, do we start saying our mantras?" Coop asked earnestly, wiping condensed water from his glasses.

"All you have to do is relax and breathe deeply," John advised. "The circle will do the rest. The only thing I would suggest is that you keep an open mind."

"You putting the knock on critical thinking?" Ken asked.

"Not at all," John replied evenly. "A critical mind is still open to persuasion, if the evidence presented is strong enough. But a skeptic rejects anything that challenges his worldview, no matter the proof. Over the next six days, your worldview will be tested. All of you will encounter things beyond your experience. It's up to you to decide whether to close your minds ... or change your outlook."

Through the hazy darkness, Beverly could just make out Ken making a jerk-off gesture toward John.

The sizzling in the funnel had started to abate as the water boiled off. John applied another ladleful, and the air was again alive with steam and that deafening hiss.

As the tumult tapered off, Lamar could hear another sound, faint and indistinct at first, but growing in clarity as the hissing gradually subsided into a dull sizzle. It was John.

"Heya-heyo-heya-heyo-heya-heyo-heya-heyo-heya-heyo," he chanted with his eyes closed. John started tapping out a rhythm on his legs in time with the chanting.

The combination of John's voice, the cadence of his chant and the finger-drumming had a drone-like quality. Lamar found it oddly soothing, like ASMR relaxation. His shoulders slowly started to sag. That made Lamar's discomfort from sitting seiza, with his legs under him, all the more acute. He could already feel the pins-and-needles sensation that told him his legs were going numb.

"Heya-heyo-heya-heyo-heya-heyo-heya-heyo."

Lamar could hear another voice joining in the chant. He looked to his right and through the swirling mist he could just make out Coop, who was mimicking John's chant. The harmony between John's potent baritone voice and Coop's higher-pitched tenor enriched the experience, even though Coop had to pause frequently to catch his breath.

"Heya-heyo-heya-heyo-heya-heyo."

Lamar stared at the flames creeping up from the interior of the funnel. There was something indescribable about the way they moved and shifted in the haze of steam. It was almost like they were dancing in time to the chant. He was starting to feel light-headed. Lamar raised his hand to rub his eyes; it felt like his hand was made of lead. He no longer felt his legs going to sleep. In fact, he couldn't feel his legs at all.

"Heya-heyo-heya-heyo."

Lamar basked in the caressing warmth of the steam. He could feel his head start to nod in rhythm to the chant but was powerless to control it. His eyes closed and his mind began to wander.

"Heya-heyo."

He felt impossibly light, like he was floating. No teepee, no fire, no Lamar. Only that floating sensation.

Lamar's eyes shot open. He was back in the teepee, right

alongside the others. He involuntarily shivered, despite the heat. He must have nodded off for a moment.

"Heya-heyo-heya-heyo-heya-heyo-heya-heyo."

What was that? He'd felt so peaceful, so free, so light. He was 16 again, floating on his back at the YMCA pool, watching the clouds lazily float by. And then a sudden wave of darkness, empty and all-consuming. Lamar realized his heart was jackhammering. He closed his eyes, trying to calm down.

"Heya-heyo-heya-heyo-heya-heyo."

Lamar concentrated on the chanting, trying to remember that remarkable sensation of floating. His heart rate slowed. Before he knew it, he was breathing in time to the chant.

"Heya-heyo-heya-heyo."

The steam's heated embrace caressed him lovingly. Lamar welcomed the sensation.

"Heya-heyo."

It was coming again. Lightness. Floating.

Beverly came to with a start. She looked around, momentarily disoriented. Everyone was still there; or at least, she thought they still were. It was so hard to see through the steam. She could still hear their guide chanting.

"Heya-heyo-heya-heyo-heya-heyo-heya-heyo."

She mentally chided herself for nodding off like that. She could just imagine how smug the rest of the group would act if they'd seen her drift off like some blue-hair who hadn't gotten her afternoon nap. She wouldn't give these brats the satisfaction.

"Heya-heyo-heya-heyo-heya-heyo."

It had been such a strange dream, too. She was 36 again, back in the Hamptons on vacation with her second husband and their daughter. Little Darcy had begged her to go para-sailing. It had seemed scary at first, as the wind lofted them higher and higher, with only a narrow bench and a metal brace bar between them and certain death. But once they'd reached 400 feet, the winds calmed, and Beverly was struck by how serene it seemed. While Darcy went on and on about how tiny everything looked, Beverly put her arm around her and basked in the wonderment of this one, perfect moment.

"Heya-heyo-heya-heyo-heya-heyo."

But the dream had been interrupted by something. An overwhelming sense of isolation, as though she were cut off from the world. Beverly could feel a migraine coming on. Her head was throbbing in time with the chant, the kind of pounding headache she always had the morning after she ...

"Heya-heyo-heya-heyo."

Beverly could feel herself getting dizzy. Her eyelids drooped and then snapped shut. It was happening again, and as before, she was powerless to stop it. That chanting voice beckoned to her younger self, asking if she and Darcy wanted to take another ride. And she answered eagerly in the affirm-ative. Beverly could feel the bottom drop out of her stomach as they rose higher and higher into the sky, Darcy's little hands clasped tightly in her own. Sailing on the wind's cur-rents. Such bliss.

"Heya-heyo."

Together. Tranquil. Free.

Coop opened his eyes hesitantly. He was afraid of what he would find. He was back in the teepee — the steam and John's chanting made that clear — but he couldn't see anything on account of his fogged-over glasses. He ran his index finger across the front and back of both lenses, but both fogged up again within a matter of seconds.

"Heya-heyo-heya-heyo-heya-heyo-heya-heyo."

Had he been daydreaming? One minute he was chanting, trying to keep pace with John, and then the next he was ... elsewhere. The steam; it sapped his concentration, made it hard to focus. His breathing was ragged and uneven, like he'd just experienced a violent nightmare. What was it? Coop couldn't remember.

"Heya-heyo-heya-heyo-heya-heyo."

To calm himself, Coop focused his inner chi and concentrated on his spirit animal: the majestic bald eagle. That's when the dream came flooding back. He was an eagle, soaring over the canyons, watching his shadow trying to keep up from impossibly far below. That feeling of the sun beating down on his wings as he rode a crosswind higher into the sky, gliding along a flyway among the clouds. So exhilarating. So different from the nightmare. There was no confinement, no shame, no guilt at 10,000 feet. Only the open sky and the wind at your back.

"Heya-heyo-heya-heyo."

Coop could feel his mind start to wander again. He strug-

gled to regain control, but that impossibly blue sky called to
him. He could feel himself slipping gravity's iron grip, tracing a spiral pattern as he rode an updraft high into the air.
Coop could hear another voice join in the chant, very faint
and far below. It took him a moment to realize it was his
own. He couldn't stop. He wasn't sure he even wanted to.

"Heya-heyo."

He was one with the sky, soaring higher and higher. He
was wind rider.

Ken sat bolt upright. He was suddenly back among the
weekend warriors and that old fraud, all praying to … whatever. Well, them and that psychopath Wade. It still hurt to
swallow.

"Heya-heyo-heya-heyo-heya-heyo-heya-heyo."

He must have zoned out for a moment. Weird. He remembered a dream; it had been so vivid at the time, but now it
lingered on the edge of recollection. It had something to do
with the twinkling lights of …

"Heya-heyo-heya-heyo-heya-heyo."

Space! That was it. Not that sci-fi nonsense, but the real
thing: NASA. His father used to take him down to Cape Can-
averal on the weekends to show him what dreams were
made of. Every time they watched the rockets launch from
the viewing platforms, the old man would give some corn-
ball speech about making something of yourself, so one day
you could live your dreams, just like these astronauts. Ken
didn't mind. That windbag could have recited the phone

book for all he cared. All he wanted was see the spacemen.

He used to fantasize about what it was like out in space. He imagined how exhilarating it would be to experience zero G. To spin endlessly in that weightless environment with no impediments. He hadn't thought about those simple, boyish fantasies in decades. The dream brought them back with stunning clarity.

"Heya-heyo-heya-heyo."

But something had interrupted the dream. He struggled to remember what it was. It was scary. He remembered it made him feel naked and afraid. And anything that could scare Ken Berman was …

"Heya-heyo."

His mind start to wander again. That sense of weightlessness returned. He was heading back into space. All he had to do was reach out and …

You tell him but you'll be a dull dolt it's your dusk dolt him dull because him him think he's a star your eye you rake a rim of it rusacio

Gaby flinched reflexively. She opened her eyes and saw that she was shielding her face with her arms as if warding off a blow. Everything around her was lost in swirling clouds of steam. She was still in the teepee. It couldn't have been a dream. It was so powerful. Gaby touched her hand to her cheek and realized that tears were streaming down her face. Or maybe it was sweat; it was hard to tell in this environment.

"Heya-heyo-heya-heyo-heya-heyo-heya-heyo."

Something had threatened her. She remembered that much. It had tried to hurt her. Only, she couldn't recall what.

And almost as bad, it had it intruded on a wonderful fantasy. She saw herself as a child growing up in Little Havana, bouncing on the backyard trampoline for hours on end during tranquil summer days that seemed to last forever. Only this time, when the trampoline launched her into the air, she stayed up there, hovering for several precious seconds before descending. It was so ... liberating.

"Heya-heyo-heya-heyo-heya-heyo."

She closed her eyes and could smell chorizo cooking on the grill, could hear papa calling her to dinner. She felt safe up here, like nothing could touch her. Maybe if she jumped higher, she could even escape the sinister presence that had threatened her earlier.

"Heya-heyo-heya-heyo."

Gaby could feel her mind retreating back to the comfort of that trampoline. Bouncing higher and higher. Her head began to loll. Her arms sat limp and motionless in her lap. The air clung to her throat, slowing her breath. Her fears melted away as each bounce sent her higher.

"Heya-heyo."

Bouncing. Levitating. Safe.

Wade's eyes fluttered open. He felt a prickling sensation as the steam and heat irritated the raw skin on his sunburned face. Wade studied his surroundings. Years of working in crawl spaces had given him excellent night vision, and his eyes easily pierced the curtain of steam and gloom. The others had fallen under the old man's spell.

"Heya-heyo-heya-heyo-heya-heyo-heya-heyo."

On his left, the crone was gently swaying to and fro, like she was riding the world's slowest roller coaster. Her eyes were closed and her expression radiated pure bliss. Beside her, the mouthy man sat with his arms outstretched limply like a zombie. His countenance conveyed the same joy. To Wade's right, the fat one was rocking slowly back and forth as though he were reclining on a waterbed. Like the other two, he was off in his own little world, a smile plastered across his face. The pretty woman beside him was curled up in the fetal position, having passed out from the intense heat. Directly across from Wade was the strange little man in the robes. His arms were extended to either side, like he was mimicking an airplane. Same expression, same ear-to-ear grin.

"Heya-heyo-heya-heyo-heya-heyo."

Wade had seen this before. Years ago, Ginny had dragged him to see one of those hypnotist performers, the ones that brought people on stage and made them start clucking like chickens. He'd gone up on stage at her behest but was quickly weeded out of the process; he was simply too strong-willed to go under. The trancelike, blissed-out expressions on the others' faces reminded Wade of the participants in those shows. He could light the fat one's swim trunks on fire and he'd just smile contentedly as the flesh was seared right off his waist.

Wade suspected something similar had happened to him earlier. His eyes had closed momentarily and he had experienced a brief but violent nightmare about Ginny.

"Heya-heyo-heya-heyo."

Wade couldn't understand how the old man was manipulating the others. Had he added some chemical to the fire? Wade noticed that the colors emanating from the cone of the metal funnel periodically changed, and not all of them were natural. It might be the chanting. Wade had trouble concentrating with it; he couldn't get the singsong rhythm out of his head. It whispered ideas into his ears. Dark ideas.

"Heya-heyo."

Wade shook his head emphatically. That was in the past. He tried to leave. Only, his legs wouldn't obey him. They remained fixed in place as though they were encased in stone. He blinked and his eyes refused to open again. He could feel himself losing consciousness. He was returning to the nightmare. Ginny would suffer once more.

* * * * * *

John clapped his hands loudly three times, snapping the others out of their reverie.

"The sweat is over," he proclaimed before giving the pull chain a sharp tug, which reset the rafter poles and expanded the roof's opening. The omnipresent haze of steam quickly dissipated, revealing a group of soaked and deeply disoriented participants.

Beverly came to and started looking wildly around the wigwam in a panic, until she remembered where she was and what she'd been doing. Ken awoke to find his arms splayed out in front of him and quickly lowered them in embarrassment.

Lamar's first conscious thought was of pain. He awoke to find his legs — which he'd been sitting on this whole time

—had started cramping up. He rolled onto his side and frantically massaged his spasming calf muscles, desperate to relieve the pain.

Coop momentarily panicked when he awoke to find everything blurry and indistinct. A moment of reflection and a quick wipe of his glasses restored his vision. He noticed Gaby lying on the ground beside him, curled up in a ball. He shook her shoulders several times until she groggily came to.

"Stop ... Bill," she murmured woozily. "Don't ... don't touch me."

Coop lifted her to a sitting position as she feebly batted her arms at him, still disoriented. He saw Lamar staring quizzically at him. Lamar's eyes seemed to reflect the same questions Coop had, as though they were silently confirming each other's experiences.

The departing steam was quickly replaced with the chill night air, and the perspiration pouring off the participants began to turn cold. John pulled out heavy gloves and began collecting the still-smoking lava rocks from the outer rim of the funnel.

"What the hell was that?" Beverly exclaimed.

"The start of your vision quest," John replied, tossing the lava rocks one after another into the pail, where they sizzled in the last dregs of creek water. "You've all just taken your first steps into a larger world."

John motioned to Lamar, who was still massaging his oxygen-starved calves.

"Can you get her some water?" he asked, pointing at Gaby, who was still only semi-conscious. "The drinking bucket is right by the entrance."

Lamar nodded and rose unsteadily, his legs still barking after so much neglect.

"How did you do that?" Coop asked in wonder.

"Do what?" John asked as he gingerly removed the metal funnel, which was glowing from the heat. Fire leapt from the embers as he peeled back the cover.

"Give us that experience," Coop gushed, his curly red locks bouncing in excitement. "I don't even know how to describe it. It was magical, like my first tarot card reading."

The old man simply smiled as he fed the fire.

Lamar returned with the water and offered Gaby a ladleful. She was fully conscious now but still dizzy, and needed assistance getting the ladle to her mouth. Gaby found the liquid to be remarkably restorative. After several more ladlefuls, she was able to sit up unassisted.

"Feeling better?" Lamar asked her.

Gaby nodded slowly.

"Okay folks, it's time we prepare to bed down for the night," John declared, studying the sky through the opening in the roof. Stars were visible between the branches of the enormous pine tree that sheltered the teepee, and the sky was an inky shade of indigo. "I figure we've got 15 more minutes of light, so I recommend everyone towel off, change your clothes, and if you have any 'business' to attend to, now is the time. Once night falls, that door stays closed," he said, pointing to the entrance.

"What if I have to 'go' in the night?" Beverly protested.

"Hold it," John replied casually. "Nobody leaves the truth circle after dark."

"Why, does the boogeyman come?" Ken asked teasingly.

"I'm perfectly serious," John continued, his tone turning uncharacteristically stern. "Nights out here can be dangerous. From dusk to dawn, we all stay in here. No exceptions."

"What's so scary out there?" Coop asked. "You said the bears were hibernating and the coyotes wouldn't bother us."

"There's things out there besides coyotes," John replied cryptically. "Now, unless you want to sleep in soaked clothes, I recommend you all go change."

* * * * * *

Lamar emerged from the Braves outhouse in a T-shirt and sweatshorts to find Ken and Coop outside the teepee, arguing about what they'd just experienced.

"I'm telling you, the only power that old phony has is to hoodwink rubes," Ken insisted loudly, not caring whether John heard him or not. "He keeps talking like we've just entered the Twilight Zone. Well, I don't feel any different. Nothing happened."

"Something *did* happen in there," Coop replied with equal conviction, albeit at a lower volume. "To all of us. I saw you nod off."

"Pfft!" Ken sneered. "Yeah, out of boredom!"

"And you didn't have any visions?" Coop probed.

"If you mean 'a dream,' no, CEOs don't dream," Ken responded derisively. "We live our dreams."

"He took you to a higher state of consciousness," Coop insisted. "Like in Jainism; he showed us a world free of material possessions. You're just too proud to admit it."

As Lamar approached, Ken co-opted him into the conversation.

"Yo, Cake and the Fat Man. Did you have any magically splendiferous visions back there?" Ken asked.

"N ... no," Lamar lied. "I don't remember anything after I fell asleep."

"See?" Ken said, as though browbeating Lamar into submission somehow proved his contention. "Just admit it: the geezer slipped us some of Bill Cosby's roofies and made up a story to explain it. I'm sure you can't wait to taste his Pudding Pop, but the rest of us would just as soon pass."

Coop threw up his hands in frustration and stormed into the wigwam.

"Can you believe that guy?" Ken asked with a triumphant smirk.

Lamar was about to protest but Ken was already partway through the entrance. Lamar decided that complaining would have to wait. In truth, he was relieved to avoid another confrontation with Ken.

The fire was lower now, still emitting sufficient heat to stave off the night's chill, but not so much as to make things uncomfortable. Lamar could see that everyone had changed after the sweat; Gaby was wearing a long-sleeved turtleneck and loose-fitting jeans, while the others were dressed more comfortably, in short-sleeved T-shirts and shorts or pajama bottoms. Half of them were already in their sleeping bags. John, who had situated himself to the right of the entrance, had taken a slightly more modern approach: an inflatable mattress paired with a down comforter and his bedroll as a pillow.

Lamar found his belongings, including his vintage Voltron sleeping bag, on the opposite side of the entrance, in an open area between Gaby and Wade. He made his way through the minefield of arms and legs before slipping into the sleeping bag, pausing just long enough to remove his shoes. He watched as John tied off the top and bottom of the door with nylon drawstrings attached to the wigwam's lattice frame. Beside him, Coop appeared to be off in his own little world, staring quietly at a photo in his wallet.

On the other side of the teepee, Beverly was complaining about the accommodations.

"This is just so primitive. And the light from the fire is so distracting. It's a pity I didn't bring my sleeping shade with me."

Wade, who was laying by her feet, grunted his annoyance and sat up suddenly. He reached into his bag and produced his hunting knife, still stained with duck blood. Beverly shrieked in wide-eyed horror and immediately started scooting backward.

But instead of attacking her, Wade pulled off his woolen Cowboy's cap and sawed a two-inch band from the bottom, leaving just enough material for the cap to still fit on his balding pate. He tossed the band at Beverly.

"There, your own personal sleep mask," he barked. "Now shut the hell up."

Beverly sniffed the material to ensure it was clean, and satisfied that it was, warily pulled it over her eyes and lay back down.

"We all could use some sleep," John said. "You've got a long day ahead of you."

"You mean *we* have a long day," Beverly corrected.

John ignored her and continued.

"One final thing," John said. "Don't let the fire go out. If you wake up in the night and see it starting to ebb, just throw some more wood and kindling on it."

Lamar curled up in the fetal position and slipped on his headphones. Bob Marley quickly drowned out the others, and little by little, Lamar started to relax. As he grew more comfortable, he started to drift once more. Lamar welcomed the sensation. Before long, he was floating again.

SUNDAY

You're worried about money
at a time like this? Stop hurling
charges! How do we know he won't
return? Did anyone see him leave? All
we have to do is follow the tracks. They'll
lead us back home. Face facts, this jerk played
us for suckers! 'Satisfaction guaranteed' my ass!
The only satisfaction I'll get is from wringing his
shriveled neck. Calm down, you're not helping. Don't
tell me what to do! He's obviously coming back at some
point. He probably went to fetch supplies. Without telling
anyone? Let's just calm down and take a deep breath. I *am* calm!
Well, I'm sure not! How can anyone be calm when John's vanished?

Lamar's eyes fluttered opened. It was morning. He could see fragments of blue sky peeking through a dense patchwork of pine tree branches and needles overhead. He was in a building of some kind with an opening in the ceiling. A multitude of poles and springs lined the interior of the opening. He sat up. Empty sleeping bags and luggage covered most of the dirt floor except for a central firepit and a bare spot to the right of the entrance. Outside, muffled voices were quarreling. He removed his headphones and the voices grew clearer. They were arguing about someone named "John." Did he know anyone named …

WigwamQuehannaRetreatForestVanCampWadeBeverlyCoopGabyKen … John!

All of Saturday's events came flooding back. Lamar sat up

in his sleeping bag and hastily unzipped it with fumbling fingers. What they were saying, it didn't make sense. He must have misheard.

He made for the entrance, which was partially ajar, and thrust it open with such force that he nearly fell to the ground.

The others were all standing around the remnants of last night's campfire, arguing. He could see Gaby and Ken mixing it up, while Beverly stood to the side, ranting mostly to herself. Coop was on the other end of the firepit, sitting crosslegged with his eyes closed as though he were meditating. Wade and John were nowhere to be seen.

"John's gone?" Lamar asked anxiously.

Gaby and Ken stopped arguing long enough to acknowledge Lamar's presence.

"Well, look who's decided to grace us with his presence," Beverly said, her voice dripping with sarcasm.

"What did you mean by 'John's vanished?'" Lamar pressed, his breath visible in the chill morning air.

"What do you think it means?" Ken spat, plainly annoyed at having to bring Lamar up to speed. "He made tracks and abandoned us here."

"We don't know that for certain," Gaby hastily interjected when panic started to creep over Lamar's face. "All we know is he isn't here."

"Did you check down by the creek?" Lamar asked, growing increasingly concerned.

"Nobody takes their bedroll and air mattress with them to do some fishing," Ken sneered.

Lamar flashed back to the bare spot near the entrance of

the teepee, the one where John had bedded down the night before. Lamar had been so preoccupied by the arguing that he'd scarcely noticed.

"We checked everywhere," Gaby said, her concern evident in her quavering voice. "But that's not the worst of it. The van's gone, too."

If Lamar wasn't fully awake before, he was now. He looked to his right, where the van had been parked in front of the shed. Nothing. He noticed tire tracks leading out of camp.

"Did he leave a note or anything?"

Gaby shook her heads animatedly, biting her lower lip in anxiety.

"Can we skip the Rip Van Winkle routine?" Beverly said, her impatience starting to catch up to her anxiety. "We need to get out of here!"

"I wish you all would relax."

In contrast to the others' frantic clamor, Coop's voice was serene and contented.

Coop opened his eyes and untangled his legs from the lotus position before sitting up and dusting off his ankle-length robes.

"Like I said earlier, he'll be back," Coop said confidently.

Ken responded with a dismissive wave of his hand.

"Ignore the Dali Llama Humper over there," Ken said derisively. "He thinks this is all some kind of practical joke, like that old fraud is going to jump out of the bushes at any moment shouting 'Smile, you're on *Candid Camera*!'"

"What's a candid camera?" Lamar asked, his voice trailing off in embarrassment at a reference that everyone except for him seemed to understand.

Beverly rolled her eyes skyward, like she was pleading for heavenly patience.

"I don't think he's toying with us," Coop continued, walking around the firepit to join the others with a beatific smile on his face. Ken looked like he wanted to punch him. "I think he's testing us."

"What?" Lamar asked, growing more confused by the second.

"Don't get him started again," Ken said with a groan of resignation.

"Think of what he told us yesterday: this trip will be a challenge for us physically and mentally," Coop reminded them. "What better way to challenge people than by making them think they're stranded in the woods? I guarantee you, he's going to come strolling back into camp in a day or two, seeing which of us adapted to the situation and which of us *panicked*."

Coop's stress on that last word finally got through to Lamar, who slowly realized he'd been shouting this whole time, trying to hear himself over the sound of his own heartbeat jackhammering in his ears. The young man took several deep breaths and the sound gradually subsided. As it did, he started to become aware of a new sensation: cold. He could see the others had all dressed appropriately for the weather, while he was wearing only a T-shirt and sweatshorts. He started bouncing around from one bare foot to the other in an effort to keep warm.

Unlike Lamar, Beverly willfully ignored Coop's insight.

"If panicking is what it takes to get us going, I'm all for

it," she ranted as her anxiety started to feed on itself. "I can't understand why you're all just standing around! We need to go! We could die out here!"

Gaby and Lamar exchanged worried glances.

"Go where?" Gaby gently probed.

"Anywhere!" Beverly practically screamed. "Civilization is in every direction! All we have to do is leave!"

"Let's just all calm down and think things through rationally," Gaby insisted, despite giving every appearance that she was also succumbing to fear. "If we panic, we're liable to make a mistake. Is there any chance he went back into town for supplies? I know we discussed it."

"John's the one who shot that idea down," Ken replied. "Besides, why would he leave without telling anyone?"

"Where's Wade? Did he leave with John?" Lamar asked, finally calm enough to take another stab at contributing.

"Wade was with us when we woke up," Gaby explained, her distaste for him evident in the face she made. "When he saw John was gone, he left without saying a word. That was about 20 minutes ago."

"I'm sure he's just doing whatever it is that serial killers do in their spare time," Ken said. "Probably pulling the limbs off of small critters and masturbating to their screams. Point is, we can't count on anybody except ourselves."

"I still say John's testing us," Coop volunteered.

"And we're still ignoring you until you have something useful to contribute!" Ken shot back.

"What if we follow the tire tracks? Let's just follow the tire tracks home!" Beverly said, the words now tumbling out of her mouth as fast as she could open it. "They'll lead us back to the highway. Let's do it now!"

"Part of the trip was on gravel roads, remember?" Gaby said. "No trail to follow. And we'd still have to negotiate that maze of paths John took us down. We're more likely to get ourselves lost than find the highway."

"We *are* lost!" Beverly wailed.

"Then forget the road," Ken said. "We can save time by cutting across the woods. The strip mall we started out from was northwest of Quehanna, right?"

The others looked at him blankly.

"Am I the only one who checked Google Maps before booking this trip?"

Judging from the others' blank expressions, he was.

Ken sighed and pointed to the mid-morning sun, which was towering over the hills fencing the campsite in to the east. "That direction's east, so that means the floodplains lead west. I say we pack up what we can and follow the floodplains until we reach civilization."

"Forget it," Gaby said, rejecting the idea out of hand. "That's even worse. John said this was … how many square miles? Sixty-five?"

"Seventy-five," Lamar answered. "That's a lot of walking."

"And that's assuming we don't get lost," Gaby added.

"If you two have a better idea, I'd love to hear it," Ken challenged.

"I think we should stay put," Lamar volunteered.

Ken studied him for a moment before bursting out laughing. Lamar's cheeks grew flushed and he looked away, embarrassed.

"Are you shitting me, Urkel?" Ken guffawed. "That's your

master plan? Just do nothing?"

"Uhmm … I watch a lot of survival shows," Lamar continued, embarrassed but refusing to back down. "*Man vs. Wild, Naked and Afraid, Survivorman*. And they all say the same thing: if you're lost, stay put and wait for help to arrive," he finished, growing more confident as he spoke.

"Exactly," Gaby said, siding with Lamar.

Ken opened his mouth to respond when Beverly unexpectedly erupted.

"I'm not trusting my life to your viewing habits!" she shouted, her shrill tone catching even Ken off guard. "What's wrong with you people? We need to get out of here!"

"Take it easy, Beverly," Gaby said, placing her hand on the older woman's shoulder to calm her.

"We can't waste daylight discussing this!" Beverly persisted, though at a lower volume. "We need to go now!"

"What she said," Ken added unhelpfully. "Sitting on our asses is *not* a solution."

"All of us have family and friends expecting us back, right?" Gaby said. "All of whom know where we are. So when we aren't back by Friday night, they'll know something's up. They'll file missing persons reports."

"Lady, nobody knows where we are," Ken retorted. "Hell, we don't even know where we are!"

"John knows," Coop said, still unperturbed.

"Then you can ask him the next time you see him!" Beverly snapped.

"They know we booked with Mystic Tours and they know that we were headed into Quehanna," Lamar said. "By Saturday, these woods should be crawling with state troopers."

"Oh, so all we have to do is not starve to death and not get mauled by wild animals for a whole week?" Ken replied sarcastically.

"We have the canned food and the coolers," Lamar replied evenly.

"Lamar's right," Gaby chimed in. "If we ration the food carefully, we should be able to hold out."

"And what if it doesn't last?" Beverly challenged, her voice rising in panic.

"We're in a forest. We can hunt and fish," Gaby said, trying to comfort the older woman.

"I can't be stuck here with you people," Beverly mumbled, rubbing her arms for comfort. "I won't do it."

"What'll we do for warmth?" Ken asked, looking askance at Beverly. Her behavior was starting to concern even him. "A week out here, we could freeze to death."

"Gaby still has the fire-starting kit," Lamar jumped in, avoiding eye contact with Ken. "John gave it to her. And we have all this wood," he added, pointing to the woodpile situated between the wigwam and the outhouses.

"I still don't like it," Ken said. "CEOs don't just sit on their haunches. As dad would say, 'a leader who doesn't attack the problem is no leader.'"

"Tell you what, why don't we go down to the creek and take an inventory of the food?" Gaby said. "And if it doesn't look like there's enough to last us, we can come up with another plan."

"I also agree about staying put," Coop spoke up. "But only because John won't know where to find us when he returns."

Ken stewed for a moment before finally agreeing.

"Fine," he said with a huff. "We'll check the food. But when we're counting out portions, make certain to exclude the Count of Mantra Krishna over here."

"Fine by me," Coop replied breezily. "I'm sure John will bring more with him."

Everyone now looked at the lone holdout in the group.

"I don't like this plan," Beverly said quietly, still rubbing her arms for comfort. "We need to go."

This time, Lamar decided to take the initiative. He reached out awkwardly to comfort Beverly as he'd seen Gaby do. Beverly pulled back instinctively as he extended his arm, which he hastily dropped it to his side.

"Beverly, we're all scared," he said. "But we can't let fear make the decisions for us. Do you understand?"

"No," she replied quietly, repeatedly shaking her head. "We need to go while we still can."

"Why don't you wait here with Coop, and we'll be back shortly," Gaby joined in. "We can decide then, okay? Can you wait for us that long?"

"Yes," she said softly, still shaking her head no.

Gaby and Lamar exchanged worried glances.

After giving Lamar a few minutes to change into warmer attire and make a stop at the outhouse, the trio set out for the creek, leaving behind an unconcerned Coop and a very concerned Beverly.

* * * * * *

Ken led the group west into the floodplain, past the archery range and down a gently sloping hill into an open field surrounded on all sides by small clusters of maple and ash trees. At the field's western edge he paused for a moment, as if trying to remember the way, before heading into a dense brake of huckleberry bushes.

"You sure this is the way?" Gaby asked, none too convinced.

"Positive," Ken said confidently. "On the other side we'll find the path to the water's edge."

The sound of rushing water was faint but audible, so the others followed him one by one into the foliage. On the other side they found a small mound with a single oak sapling growing out of its peak, flanked on either side by rows of painful-looking stinging nettles and thistle weeds. No trail.

Gaby sighed in frustration and tugged on the neckline of her turtleneck to let some more air in.

"It'll be on the other side of this hill," Ken said as he pointed westward, his confidence unflappable.

"We didn't cross a hill last time," Lamar noted.

"This is just a shortcut," Ken insisted. "Trust me."

Gaby and Lamar exchanged a dubious look but followed him up the slope.

Ken continued up the hill, taking steps so wide that one misstep would have permanently changed his vocal register. When he was halfway up, Ken suddenly paused and faced the pair, who were struggling to keep up.

"So, we need to talk about who's in charge," he told them out of the blue.

"In charge of what?" Lamar asked, almost afraid to hear the answer.

"The group," Ken replied with a small waggle of his head,

as though the answer were obvious. "We're in a crisis, and as dad would say: 'the greater the crisis, the greater the need for leadership.'"

"We did just fine letting majority rule decide," Gaby replied.

"Did we?" Ken asked, charging up the hill again. "We wasted an hour or more going round and round on things, and we're still divided; you two want to stay, Becky and I want to go."

"Beverly," Lamar gently corrected.

"Whatever," Ken said dismissively with a wave of his hand. "The point stands. A crisis can't be solved by committee. We need someone to steer us through this."

Gaby cocked an eyebrow.

"By which you mean you?" she asked.

"Who better to lead than the CEO of a multinational brokerage with over 75 employees?"

"We don't need your resume, thank you," Gaby replied curtly.

"But you do need my guidance," Ken answered before pausing to deliver a maxim. "'Some are born to lead, others are born to follow.'"

"More words of near-wisdom from dear old dad?" Gaby replied cuttingly.

"Don't take it personally," Ken said. "Only a select few are meant for it. And those of us who are have an obligation to seize the mantle."

"That doesn't sound like leadership to me," Lamar mumbled.

Ken reached the top of the hill. It offered a decent view of the surrounding plain, towering as it did two stories over everything else. It revealed that the floodplain had a gradual north-to-south slope as it fed into a valley dense with trees in the distance. While waist-high overgrowth on the other side of the tree obscured what was immediately in front of them, beyond it they could see a rocky path far below, meaning the drop-off just behind the overgrowth must have been fairly steep.

He proudly pointed to the path, which looked to be the same one they followed down to the creek.

"Like I told you: some are born to lead," Ken said smugly as he started toward the overgrowth with a newfound swell of confidence.

Gaby, who was just behind him, looked carefully at the overgrowth and rushed forward to stop him.

"Ken, wait!" she fairly shouted, holding her arm out in front of him before pointing it downward. Ken leaned forward and peered over the curtain of brush. He could see that this side of the hill wasn't a hill at all. It was an overlook, hiding a precipitous 20-foot drop to the rocky path below.

"You're about to lead us off the edge of a cliff," Gaby cautioned before motioning for the others to follow her to the right, where the hill offered a much safer path downward.

By the time they reached the rocky trail below, the sound of rushing water was significantly louder. They were close. They found their way into a clearing and were suddenly by the water's edge. This section of the creek looked different from the one they'd seen yesterday; it was narrower, with pebbled shoals that forced the water through a narrow channel that cut sharply to the right as it flowed downhill. There was minimal vegetation on the opposite bank.

"I think we're just south of where John took us," Lamar said, trying to get his bearings. "If we follow the creek north, we should find the spot."

Sure enough, 100 yards up they found what looked like the same section of the river that John had shown them. The creek was wider, the water clearer, and the eastern bank hosted a rocky path leading back to camp, the same one they'd spied from the top of the overlook.

"This is it," Lamar said, spotting the muddy indentation of their footprints on the eastern bank. "We were standing over there."

Gaby walked ahead of them and knelt beside the small collecting pool where John had deposited the cooler. She peered into the pool's murky depths.

"Well?" Ken asked impatiently.

"I don't see anything," Gaby said, confused. She got down on one knee and started fishing around in the icy water, in case silt had covered the coolers. "There's nothing in here."

"You sure this is the right spot?" Ken asked searchingly as Lamar examined a fallen tree branch on the eastern bank. "Maybe those aren't our footprints."

In answer, Lamar moved the branch to reveal part of a metal cleat embedded in the ground, in the same location that John had shown them yesterday.

"Where are the tethers?" Ken asked.

Lamar lifted the branch higher to reveal the nylon cords, still tied to the cleat. Each of them had been severed several inches below the knot, their frayed ends dangling loose.

"Oh, fuck me!" Ken said with a sharp intake of breath. "He took the food! That crazy old fuck stole all our food!"

Gaby held her hand to her mouth in dismay.

"It ... it can't be," she stammered, blinking back tears. "This has to be a mistake."

"The only mistake," Ken fumed, "was coming to this stupid fucking forest in the first goddamn place!"

Ken started swinging wildly in the air, screaming every invective he could think of and inventing a few new ones for good measure. He picked up the largest rocks he could find on the bank and started hurling them at the water in a blind rage.

"I hate this fucking place! Every rock and every ... God ... damn ... tree!" he shouted, picking up a heavy branch and smashing it against the side of a nearby walnut tree.

While Ken vented, Gaby fell to her knees, overcome by shock and despair. Only Lamar kept his composure; the shame of having lost it not an hour ago was still fresh in his mind.

"Let's just keep calm and focus," he said, though his quavering voice belied the reassuring message.

"Focus?" Ken screamed as he rounded on Lamar. "Focus on starvation, you blubbery beta-bitch! Focus on dying to the elements! Got any more brilliant suggestions?"

"This, uhmm, wasn't my fault," Lamar said, taken aback by Ken's misplaced fury. "I didn't take the food."

Ken wasn't listening, anyway. He'd already moved on to raging against their guide as he vented his fury on every inanimate object nearby. He seized on a branch the size of a switch — the only unthrown object nearby — and hurled it at a small maple tree by the water's edge, which sent it ricocheting into the back of Gaby's head.

All of Ken's rage immediately dissipated. He ran over to check on Gaby, who seemed more annoyed than injured.

"¡Pinche pendejo!" she exclaimed, rubbing her head. "What's wrong with you?"

"Oh, shit!" Ken exclaimed, crouching down beside her. "I didn't mean to! I was angry and I just lost it. Are you okay?"

"I'm fine," Gaby insisted, standing up and flashing Ken a dirty look.

She turned to walk back toward camp, pivoting on her right foot, only to feel it give way on a stone still slick with creek spray from Ken's earlier temper tantrum. Gaby lurched forward in free fall, watching helplessly as the rocky ground rushed to meet her.

Ken reached out and caught her by the waist, leaning forward and pulling Gaby toward him to help absorb some of the forward momentum. Gaby found herself leaning back, her feet barely touching the ground, while Ken held her in his arms, his face hovering six inches from hers. Had someone walked up at that moment, they would have thought the two were in a passionate embrace.

Gaby looked up at him, still in a daze. But as she got her bearings, instead of looking relieved, Gaby's eyes started to go wide with fright.

"Lucky I was here," Ken said, the relief evident in his voice. "If I hadn't caught you ..."

A piercing, almost inhuman wail escaped Gaby's lips.

"Let me go, let me go, let me go, LET ME GO!!!" Gaby shrieked, flailing like mad, her eyes wild with fear.

Ken immediately loosened his grip and pulled his hands

back to his chest, stunned at this irrational display.

Gaby pushed Ken away, scurrying back several feet into a defensive posture. Her eyes flitted back and forth between a slack-jawed Ken and an equally perplexed Lamar, watching the pair warily, like a cornered animal looking to escape.

"Don't touch me!" she shrieked at the pair. "Don't ever touch me again!"

She turned toward the path back to camp and ran off crying.

"What ... the ... fuck?" Lamar mouthed silently as he watched her flee.

Ken's shock faded faster and was rapidly replaced with raw indignation.

"Excuse me for saving your sorry butt, Taco Bella!" he called after her, cupping his hands to his mouth. "Next time, I'll let you fall right on your face!"

He looked at Lamar for affirmation.

"Is everyone here off their meds?" he asked. "First Wade, then Beverly and now her. You'd think there was something in the water."

"Did you do anything to set her off?" Lamar asked, trying to make sense of what they'd just witnessed.

"Yeah, I saved her from a face-plant!" Ken seethed. "What kind of question is that? You saw what happened."

"You didn't pinch her behind when you were holding her?" Lamar probed.

"Unbelievable," Ken fumed. "I save somebody, and as thanks, she screams at me and now you accuse me of copping a feel. Fuck this and fuck you all!"

Ken scanned the creek for the narrowest point and found

it two yards up. He walked over and started fording the water, wading thigh deep as he crossed.

"What are you doing?" Lamar asked.

"What I should have done at first light: leaving," Ken shouted back in reply without bothering to look over his shoulder.

"Are you coming back?"

Ken paused to shake out his pants legs as he reached the other bank.

"Not if I find a way out," Ken called out.

"I thought you wanted to be in charge. What kind of leader abandons his team?" Lamar shot back.

"In this case, a smart one," Ken responded, holding up his middle finger behind him for emphasis as he left the opposite bank and disappeared into the forest.

Lamar shook his head in disgust and started up the rocky trail back to camp.

As he walked he realized that for the first time since coming to Quehanna that he was completely alone. It was an eerie feeling. Coming from a large and noisy family, Lamar was accustomed to the peripheral din of people all around, even if he wasn't comfortable interacting with them. Now the only noises he heard belonged to the forest. It was unsettling, this sense of total isolation.

As he approached the thicket at the end of the rocky trail, he realized he heard a new sound: panting. The thicket started rustling and Coop burst out from the other side, out of breath with his glasses askew. He spotted Lamar and immediately rushed to his side. Up close, Coop was drenched in sweat and took lungfuls of air in heaping gulps as though he'd run all the way here.

"Gaby said I'd find you here," Coop said between ragged breaths. "We have a problem."

* * * * * *

The sun was directly overhead when Ken noticed the slopes of the valley starting to turn upward again, indicating he'd reached the western edge of the floodplain. The dark, earthy soil he'd seen for much of his trek over the past two hours had turned sandy and granulated. Much of the land around him was bare except for wild grasses and the occasional uprooted tree. He also noticed an uptick in wildlife. He took all of these as signs that he was nearing a major water source.

He followed a natural channel upward as it cut up and back a slope at the base of a double-humped hill leading out of the floodplain. He had stripped off his leather jacket over an hour ago as the temperature started to climb and spent the rest of the trip with it folded over his arm. But now that the path westward was growing steeper, he tied it around his waist to free his hands for climbing.

Ken made for the larger hump to the southwest, reasoning that it was still an easier climb than the lower, southern-facing portion with its punishing verticality. The larger hump was still a daunting climb, not least because it towered some 15 stories above him, but the angle wasn't nearly as steep, and there were plenty of trees and large rocks he could use as handholds on the way up. More importantly, he knew the surest way to get his bearings was to scout from the highest point in the region, and this was it.

As he climbed, Ken fantasized about what he'd see when he reached the peak. A highway, a campfire in the distance, some backpacking tourists. He'd settle for anything that would get him out of here. Ken debated whether he'd even report the others as missing when he got out of here. Just thinking about them triggered him; he still seethed at Gaby's meltdown earlier in the day. And to think that fat nerd had the nerve to blame him after Little Miss Green Card went Bitch Factor Five. Knowing her, it was probably something hormonal. Not that tubby would understand a lot about that.

And then there was that psychopath Wade. Ken flashed back to when Wade had choked him to the brink of unconsciousness. The memory scared him more than it angered him. On second thought, he would report the others as missing, if only to ensure that Wade wound up in leg irons like he deserved.

Ken was already starting to daydream about the trial — he'd point to Wade as the culprit, and Wade would go crazy, leaping up from his defense table and rampaging around the courtroom, forcing the bailiffs to use their tasers on him again, and again, and again, and again, until he was reduced to a quivering mass writhing on the floor in excruciating pain — when he paused to wipe the sweat from his brow and look up. He had been so preoccupied with his fantasies that he'd lost track of time. Some 30 minutes had passed, and he was nearly at the top. Ken paused to look back and saw the basin of the floodplain looming far below.

The last section of the climb was the steepest, and Ken had to take it on all fours, anchoring himself with his hands and pushing off with his feet to propel himself forward. He finally reached the summit, breathing heavily and dripping with sweat. He pushed past a grouping of waist-high ferns at the top and stared in wonder at the view before him.

To the south was an enormous lake; so large, in fact, that he couldn't see the opposite bank, even from his elevated position. It was situated on a large plateau that extended to the south and the west, roughly 50 feet above the floodplain, with the lake extending almost to the edge. That explained the sparse vegetation and the sandy soil on this side of the plain; the lake likely overflowed its banks every spring, sending tens of thousands of gallons of snowmelt and rain-water into the plain each year.

Much of the land to the west was covered by a dense canopy of trees, many of whose leaves had begun to turn seasonal shades of orange, red and brown. The tree coverage extended out of view to the north as well, although the tree density wasn't as great due to the more rugged terrain, with many steep hills and crags.

Ken sat down on the southern edge of the peak, whistling in admiration as he drank in the view. While he spent as much time as he could outdoors, he rarely stopped to appreciate nature. It was always about the activity, never the experience. But even he had to admit, the view of the lake from 12 stories up was breathtaking.

He watched as several ducks paddled across the pond's surface, then with a series of quacks launched themselves skyward to join a flying-V formation of ducks heading south for the winter. Their activity sent ripples pulsating across the lake, which caught the light overhead as they lapped against the shore. It was moment of pure serenity.

As he watched the shadows of clouds bounce up and down the rolling hills to the west, he spied a fox along the shoreline, approaching the lake cautiously as it searched for a meal. Ken stared, fascinated as the fox sniffed the rocky shore by the lake's edge and then followed its nose toward a thick clump of reeds. The fox studied the reeds intently for a few moments, wary of any predators hiding in them. After a few moments, it decided that whatever it smelled in there was worth the risk and start creeping toward the grasses. It hesitated again when it was within a couple of feet.

Ken was beginning to wonder what could be in there that would be so enticing when the densest grouping of reeds suddenly sprang to life, rising up and spouting arms that drove a crude wooden spear through the bewildered creature's neck before it could even react. The reeds stood up from their crouching strike, and Ken could see it was a man covered in dried mud with reeds sticking out of the front and back of his shirt.

Ken had just enough time to wonder whether Quehanna was large enough to hide wild aborigines, like those found in the Amazon, before he noticed the man's face was badly sunburned and peeling.

Ken hastily left his exposed perch on the edge of the peak and ducked behind the ferns, hoping he hadn't been spotted. He'd already seen how dangerous and unpredictable Wade could be in a group setting. Lord knows what he was capable of out here, with no one around. He kept his head down for several seconds before curiosity eventually overcame his sense of self-preservation and he bent back the ferns to watch.

Wade was dancing around his kill, whooping and hollering and thrusting his spear over his head like a savage. Ken noticed that Wade's cap was gone and he'd torn his shirt open at his chest, letting all the reeds lose. After a minute or two of celebration, Wade pulled out his hunting knife and carved a vertical line several inches long into his left breast. Ken winced at the sight. Even from his elevated perch, he could see the blood spilling out and mixing with the dried mud. He noticed two raised welts beside the cut, both vertical and about the same length. Ken surmised that each cut represented a different kill, like the duck from last night. As for the first cut, Ken preferred to remain in the dark. He didn't want to know what — or who — Wade's first kill was.

Wade knelt down by the fox's corpse and thrust his knife into it six inches below the spear wound. Ken raised his head up, straining to see from this angle.

Wade had removed the knife and his hand was now in the incision. He gave a small grunt of exertion and withdrew his hand — now caked in both mud and blood — with something in his palm. Ken raised up a little higher to get a better view. It was the creature's heart.

Wade held the fox's still dripping organ over his head, ceremonially, and slowly lowered it to his mouth. He took a couple of tentative bites before scarfing the remainder down, swallowing it nearly whole.

Ken grimaced in revulsion but couldn't bring himself to look away from the gruesome display. It was almost as if he was watching Wade devolve in real time. He thought back to John's words yesterday about this experience being transformative, and how Wade's transition was accelerated. Ken began to seriously question whether he would end up like Wade if he remained here.

Wade was now removing the animal's remaining organs, carelessly tossing them on the muddy banks of the lake. Ken figured this was as good a time as any to beat a stealthy retreat. He'd just made up his mind to head back east into the floodplain — north looked too rugged and he couldn't risk going south or west because Wade might see him — when he started to feel something crawling up his pant leg.

Ken immediately rolled onto his back and started tugging like mad at his left leg, which he raised in the air for easier access. He fished in the left pant leg and came out a moment later with a squashed millipede. He felt an immediate swell of relief that it wasn't anything worse, a feeling that was replaced a second later with dread when he realized how much noise he'd just made. Ken peeled back the ferns and saw Wade looking directly at him from 12 stories down. His expression was inscrutable underneath all that mud. Wade made his intentions plain a second later when he picked up his spear and started up the slope toward him.

That was all the motivation Ken needed to get moving. Naked fear enveloped him, took hold of his mind, and sent him hurtling down the slope at a dangerous, uncontrolled pace that straddled the line between fleeing and falling. Ken flailed blindly for tree limbs, nearby rocks, even tufts of grass, anything to control his descent as he skidded downhill, his feet scrambling to keep pace with gravity's pull.

* * * * * *

Two hours of searching and nothing to show for it.

Lamar, Gaby and Coop trekked through the forest east of camp, keeping a spread of 20-30 feet between them to cover more ground, while still maintaining line of sight. They'd already covered most of the eastern basin between the camp and the ring of high hills separating them from the rest of Quehanna, and were now heading southward as the terrain started getting muddier.

Coop, who was carrying one of the plastic archery targets, paused to tear a foot-long strip from the target and tie it to a low-hanging branch as a marker. He wiped his brow on his robes. It was shortly after noon, and the temperature had risen considerably.

Gaby, who was on Coop's left, called out, using the standard refrain the trio had employed for the past two hours now.

"Beverly? Are you out here?" she shouted.

The only reply came from a black squirrel in the tree canopy overhead, which chattered its displeasure before going back in its hole.

Lamar, who was on Coop's right, stopped to lean against a tree. He was unused to long walks and was struggling to keep up with the others. He opened the canteen and upended most of it over his head to cool off.

"That water's supposed to be for the three of us," Coop scolded, though it came off as merely whiny thanks to his high-tenor voice.

"Four, if we ever find Beverly," Gaby added. "You sure she went this way?"

"All I know is she was heading east when she ran out of camp," Coop replied. "Who knows where she went after that?"

"Guys, I don't think she wants to be found," Lamar said, shaking the water from his head like a dog. "We should head back."

"You said that an hour ago," Coop reminded him.

"I meant it then, toooo!" Lamar said, drawing out the last word as he took a wrong step and slid several inches in the mud before steadying himself. "This is not productive."

"Let's give it another 30 minutes," Gaby said. "Beverly would do the same for ..." She paused midsentence as she saw Lamar and Coop both shaking their heads no.

" ... okay, maybe not," she finished lamely.

"Make that definitely not," Coop insisted. "The whole reason we're out here is because she didn't think of anybody but herself."

"You know, you could have done something about it," Lamar intoned.

"Am I my stranger's keeper?" Coop asked rhetorically. "I'm not going to hold her against her will. I alerted you both; I figure that's plenty."

"Any idea what set her off?" Lamar asked.

"She got a lot worse after you all left," Coop said, grimacing at the memory. "She was hysterical; babbling incoherently. The only thing I could get out of her before she bolted was that she had to get out of here."

He paused again to tear another strip from the target and tie it to a nearby tree branch. There were tiny pools of brackish water all around. Evidently, it had rained shortly before they arrived in Quehanna, and some of these low-lying areas had yet to dry out. Coop gave silent thanks that mosquito season had come and gone.

"This is why we need to stick together," Gaby said. "To prop each other up when things get rough. We can't count on the others for that."

"You don't think Ken is a suitable outlet for emotional support?" Lamar teased.

"Only if schoolyard taunts and childish nicknames qualify," Gaby snickered. "And Wade ..."

A chill ran down her spine and she left the sentence unfinished. Judging from the others' reaction to his name, she didn't need to.

"So, we're the Three Musketeers, are we?" Coop joked, trying to restore levity to the conversation.

"Minus the fancy costumes and swords," Lamar quickly joined in.

Gaby chuckled and pumped her fist in the air.

"All for mice and mice for all!"

Dead silence. She turned and saw the others had stopped in their tracks, looking at her like she'd lost her mind. This only made her laugh harder.

"I think whatever Beverly has may be contagious," Coop intoned as Gaby doubled over with laughter, resting her hand on a nearby tree for support.

"It's ... an inside ... joke," she managed to spit out between laughing fits.

"Deep inside," Lamar answered, bewildered. "Mind clueing us in?"

"My parents emigrated from Cuba," Gaby started after

taking a few moments to compose herself. "They had trouble assimilating, so they moved to Little Havana where they wouldn't have to. Growing up, all I heard was Spanish in the home and Spanish in the streets. I learned English from watching television. And my favorite program growing up was the *Mickey Mouse Club*."

"Ahh!" Lamar said, making the connection.

"I thought that show was from the '50s," Coop said, confused.

"They revived it in the late '80s," Lamar explained as the group resumed their search. "That's where Britney Spears and Justin Timberlake got their start."

"Anyway, a lot of phrases from the show imprinted on me. When I was 14, I did a book report on Dumas' *The Three Musketeers*, and the teacher flunked me because I kept spelling it as 'The Three Mouseketeers.' It kind of became an inside joke. Even today, I have trouble reading it as anything other than 'Mouseketeer.'"

Lamar smiled and raised an pretend sword skyward.

"All for mice ..." he called out with mock seriousness.

"... And mice for all!" Gaby and Coop joined in, both chuckling as they walked.

The trio found themselves in a small clearing littered with table-sized rocks jutting out of the ground and a downed tree overlaying a dry creek bed.

"Okay, fellow Mouseketeers, I need to sit down before I fall down," Lamar said as he headed for the nearest moss-covered rock and collapsed onto it.

Coop chose a rock several feet away and removed his sandals, which were caked with mud.

"All right, but let's make it a short one," Gaby said. "Beverly's still out there somewhere."

"Have you considered that she may not want our help?" Lamar asked. "What if she's still hysterical? Are we going to drag her back to camp, kicking and screaming?"

"Look, she panicked, but she's had time to cool off," Gaby said, picking off some branches from the downed tree to make herself a seat. "I'm sure we can reason with her."

"Speaking of which," Coop said, "you seemed pretty shaken up yourself when I found you, Gaby."

Out of the corner of his eye, he saw Lamar gesturing for him to stop.

"Let's *not* talk about it," Gaby said in a tone that permitted no dissent.

She plopped down in a huff and immediately leapt up, screeching in pain.

"¡Dios mio!" she cried, clutching her backside and running several feet away.

"What? What's wrong?" Coop asked, concerned.

"Something bit me!" she cried, rubbing her left cheek.

Lamar stood up and investigated the tree. He noticed that two of the branches Gaby removed before sitting down were splintered near the base, with several jagged edges. One had blood on its tip.

"No creatures," Lamar called out. "I think you got a butt-full of wood."

"Splinters can be serious out here," Coop said, standing up. "I'd better take a look at it."

Gaby backed away from Coop, shielding her posterior with her hands.

"You'll do no such thing," she warned.

Coop rolled his eyes.

"Relax, you're not my type."

"Oh, thank you very much!" Gaby shot back, incensed.

Coop folded his arms defensively over his chest.

"That's not what I meant, and you know it."

"Coop, man, let it go," suggested Lamar, who could already see where this was going. "You're only digging yourself in deeper."

"But ..." Coop protested.

"Look, I'm fine, okay," Gaby insisted. "Nobody needs to examine any part of me, understand?"

"If you'll just let me take a look ..." Coop began, circling toward Gaby's rear as she spun away, resulting in a peculiar dance between them.

Coop grunted in frustration and grabbed her by the waist. Gaby's eyes shot open in panic and she shoved him as hard as she could, sending Coop sprawling. As the magnitude of what she'd done started to sink in, Gaby covered her mouth in dismay.

"I'm trying to help, not playing grab-ass!" Coop shouted, growing heated as he picked himself up and dusted off his robes.

"I'm sorry," Gaby said quietly, hanging her head. "I know you didn't mean anything by it, but ..." she paused, searching for the right words. "I don't like people touching me. It's nothing personal. Please don't do it."

Coop closed his eyes and let out a long sigh, trying to calm himself.

"You could have just told me," he intoned.

An awkward silence fell over the group. Gaby hobbled over to the nearest tree and braced herself against it as she craned her neck to see if she could locate the injury herself. She gave up after several attempts and started hobbling southward, walking with a peculiar shimmy to try and minimize the pressure on her glutes.

"Break's over," she said.

"Hang on," Lamar said. "Did you hear that?"

All of them paused and held their breath. An indistinct sound wafted across the breeze, so faint they couldn't be sure if it was even real, much less where it was coming from.

"Is someone there?"

"Hello?" Coop shouted at the top of his lungs. "Anybody there?"

They heard the noise again, a little louder and clearer.

"Who's out there? Identify yourselves."

"That's Beverly, all right," Coop said with a snort. Even in a dire situation like this, she still found a way to be imperious.

"I think it came from over here," Gaby said, pointing toward a grassy ridge about 100 yards east.

She and Lamar set off while Coop paused to leave a marker on the edge of the clearing.

At the top of the ridge they found a narrow, crescent-shaped ravine whose depth could only be guessed at, because all visibility ceased after 50 feet due to a mazelike hedge of thorny hawthorn shrubs that covered it.

"Beverly?" Gaby called from the top of the ridge.

"Down here," a voice replied weakly from the bottom of the ravine.

The incline into the ravine looked steep but manageable. Those thorned bushes, though, were a bigger problem. Lamar motioned to their left, where the ridge tapered off into a small meadow with a gentle backslope that fed into the northern end of the ravine, one without any such impediments.

"If we start at the head of the ravine, we should be able to reach Beverly without having to tear through all those bushes," Lamar said.

"Beverly, we're coming to get you," Coop shouted. "Are you hurt?"

"I twisted my ankle," came the reply.

"Just stay put," Coop advised as the group headed down the northern face of the ridge.

The meadow was overrun with wild grasses that came up to Lamar's thigh, alongside thimbleweed and asters. Its southern edge was also matted with small leaf piles, likely swept downhill by the wind.

Coop viewed the piles warily.

"Watch your feet," he warned. "I read that rattlesnakes often nest in leaf piles."

The group gave the piles a wide berth and stepped gingerly among the grasses as they headed toward the northern edge of the ravine. Gaby and Lamar were walking side by side, with Coop directly behind them, when Gaby put her arm out in front of Lamar, stopping him in his tracks.

"Hey ..." he started to complain until he looked down and saw a metallic glint among the high grasses where he was about to step. "What is that?"

In answer, Gaby grabbed a nearby tree branch and thrust

it into the grass. Three-foot-wide metal jaws sprang from either side and clamped down on the stick with a heavy clang, snapping it neatly in two.

Coop gave a low whistle of admiration.

"Meanest rattlesnake I've ever seen," he said.

"What's a bear trap doing out here?" Lamar asked quietly.

"John said there are bears in these woods," Gaby answered. "I guess bears bring poachers."

They stood around the trap, examining it. It was badly rusted along the hinges, with telltale flakes of red and brown coating both sides. Clearly, it had not been used in a very long time.

"There may be others," Gaby warned.

Silently, each of them picked up a stick and started forward again, holding the sticks out several feet in front of them and tapping the ground as they walked, as though they'd all spontaneously gone blind. This process set off another bear trap some 20 feet northward, making them all jump. The trio also spotted two more before arriving at the ravine's entrance.

"Anyone else thinking this ravine may have been a bear's den?" Lamar asked, giving voice to what they all were secretly dreading.

They all hesitated at the downward slope into the ravine, each looking to the others, waiting to see who would go down first. After several agonizing moments, Gaby shook her head in disgust and started down the slope, much to the relief of Coop and Lamar. She grimaced in pain with each step as the rough terrain forced her to put undue pressure on her barking glutes.

As she started winding her way down, Gaby kept her eyes peeled for any signs of bear activity, such as scat, bones or claw marks along the ravine walls. She saw nothing beyond earthen walls and a rocky base until they moved beneath the cover of the hawthorn bushes, which blotted out most of the light and made searching for signs futile. Fortunately, the ravine was sufficiently deep to afford adequate headroom so long as they kept their heads bowed.

"What took you so long?" came an irritated voice in the dark.

The group followed the voice, scanning for Beverly's outline in the dim light until they found her some 30 yards away, lying prone in the center of the ravine.

"Are you hurt?" Coop asked, kneeling beside her while the others searched the area for any signs of bear activity.

Beverly's face was smudged with dirt, and her right ankle looked swollen, but she appeared otherwise unharmed.

"I turned my ankle back there," Beverly said, pointing toward the opposite end of the ravine. "How'd you find me?"

"We just followed the complaining," Coop joked as he gingerly lifted her leg and tested her ankle's range of motion. Beverly grimaced when he rotated it too far right or left.

"It doesn't look like a sprain," he decided after a few seconds. "You should be able to put weight on it in a day or two."

Beverly extended her hand to Coop.

"Here, help me up."

As Coop did so, the others returned from scouring the far side of the ravine.

"There's nothing back there," Lamar informed them. "If there was a bear here, it would have mauled us already."

Beverly looked the others over with a mixture of relief and condescension.

"Well, I'm glad you all finally came to your senses," she said. "Now, if you take turns supporting me, we can finally get out of here."

"So, which Mouseketeer wants to help her back to camp?" Gaby asked, hoping one of the others would volunteer.

"To camp?" Beverly responded indignantly, as though she'd just been offered a social disease. "I'm not going back to that awful place! I thought you were here to rescue me!"

"We are," Gaby said reassuringly.

"Then get me out of this godforsaken forest!" Beverly shouted, flailing her arms as her emotions started to take over once more. Coop struggled to maintain his grip on her.

"I'm going home, where there are laws and food, and if someone abandons you, it's not an automatic death sentence," Beverly blathered. "If you three want to succumb to the elements, that's your own affair. Me, I'm getting out of here."

She shirked Coop's support and began hopping on her good leg to the far side of the ravine, holding onto the dirt walls for support.

"Beverly," Gaby said, throwing her hands up in exasperation. "You're going the wrong way. The north side of the ravine leads back to camp."

"I told you I'm not going back!" Beverly spat back.

"We're not leaving you!" Gaby insisted, running past Beverly and barring her path.

"Well, you're certainly not taking me back there, and that's final!" Beverly said, smacking the dirt wall for emphasis. "So, I guess we're at an impasse."

"Not hardly," Gaby replied, and motioned to Coop and Lamar, who took Beverly by either shoulder and raised her up.

"Hey, put me down!" Beverly shouted, kicking at the air like a little child. "This is undignified!"

Lamar clucked his tongue in irritation as he prepared for the long journey back to camp.

"This day just keeps getting better and better."

* * * * * *

Ken was well and truly lost. He stumbled through the forest, exhausted, not even sure what direction he was walking anymore.

It had been hours since his lakeside encounter with Wade. In his mad scramble to escape, Ken had sprinted from the floodplain into the southern edge of the forest, propelled forward by fear, without a plan and little to no awareness of his surroundings. Only a singular thought — survival — echoed in his mind as he pushed his oxygen-starved lungs and cramped legs to the limit. He had collapsed in an exhausted heap at some point — Ken wasn't certain when; time was relative in his endorphin-addled mind — and as he rested, he began to wonder where he was.

Some good had come from his headlong flight; he hadn't seen or heard Wade in some time. He kept staring skyward for a glimpse of the sun, hoping to orient himself by its position. Unfortunately, it had retreated behind a thick layer of low-lying clouds that darkened the sky and threatened rain.

Ken headed in what he guessed was a northern direction,

figuring that he could get his bearings if he found the flood-plains again. He felt inside his pants pockets for his smokes, figuring they might take the edge off. Empty. He cursed, realizing he must have left them back at camp.

Ken hopped over a dry creekbed and wended his way through a tightly packed birch grove before emerging into a football-field-sized dell surrounded on all sides by sturdy beech, oak and birch trees. The interior was large fields of knee-high grasses occasionally punctuated with wildflowers, all of which led to a small mound in the center marked by the largest ash tree Ken had ever seen. It was easily seven stories high, dwarfing all the surrounding trees. Ken marveled at it because it was totally bare; while all the other trees ringing the dell were just beginning to turn and discard their leaves as autumn slowly gave way to winter, the giant ash had apparently grown impatient for winter's arrival and shed all its foliage a month early.

As he walked toward the towering tree, Ken became acutely aware of the sound of his footfalls and the swoosh of the grasses as he passed. It wasn't because of how much noise he was making; it was how still everything around him had become. The forest always teemed with noise: birds chirping, wind rustling, streams ambling, squirrels chattering; a symphony of wildlife. But an eerie silence enveloped the dell, as though all the animals and the very elements themselves avoided it. And each unsettling step Ken took reminded him that he was disturbing this peace.

As he approached the tree, Ken saw it had a heavily knotted base of exposed roots that twisted into pretzel-like shapes before plunging into the ground. In the center, just in front of the trunk, was a dark hole large enough for a small child to squeeze through. It looked too small to be a wolves' den, so Ken concluded it was probably an abandoned badger's hole.

He had a much harder time explaining what he found all over the mound. Spread out from the base of the tree was a charcoal-gray, powdery substance that traced thick, spiral-like patterns across the mound, like a pinwheel of granules. All of these spirals, which extended in every direction around the twenty-foot-wide mound, converged at the same point: the hole in the ground.

Everything on the mound was dead. The grass — so tall and vibrant across the rest of the dell — was withered and brown on the mound, while the few wildflowers Ken could pinpoint in this granular maze had wilted. Even the patches of dirt that could be seen between the swirls had a sickly gray tone to them, as though the land itself was blighted.

Ken stopped just short of the mound, looking down at his feet to be certain he didn't step onto the powdery substance. Whatever this was, he didn't want any of it getting on him. He knelt down for a closer look, careful not to touch anything. He'd seen diseased plant life before and it looked nothing like this. There were no obvious signs of mold or rot, no visible cankers on the tree.

As for the powdery substance, Ken had no idea what to make of it. It was finely grained, like sand from a pristine beach, only this beach was gray and mottled. The pinwheel patterns it spread in were undisturbed; not even the wind had altered their course.

Whatever did this wasn't natural, Ken told himself as he

stood up and backed away. He made a beeline for the shortest route out of the dell, which was which was a cluster of
trees on the opposite side of the hole in the ground. As he
hastily walked around the tree, something caught his eye.

Dangling from a nail on the other side of the tree was
a feathered mandala. Ken squinted his eyes as he examined the trinket. It looked just like the one overhanging the
entrance to the wigwam; same crimson frame with eight
petals in the center. Same eight feathers hanging down.
Could there be a connection between the two? And why
would that Native American phony place another one way
out here?

Ken felt his skin start to crawl. Everything about this
dell seemed creepy and off. He walked faster, casting wary
glances over his shoulder every so often, as if the trees would
uproot themselves and charge at him.

He started to feel better almost as soon as he exited the
dell, and it was several minutes before he realized that the
forest sounded alive once more, with bird calls overhead
and the wind gently whistling through the trees once again,
sounds that blended with the crunch of fallen leaves underfoot. Ken found it comforting after his earlier experience,
and set off with an added spring in his step. He followed a
grove of maple trees up a gentle slope, walking alongside
them as the spaces in between the trees were lined with
fallen branches that formed a patchwork blockade.

Ken was so relieved to experience something familiar
again that he scarcely noticed where he was walking as he
reached the top of the rise and passed the last maple tree,
nearly setting foot on the road before he even registered it

was there.

A road! Never before had a simple dirt road looked so good to Ken. It was patchy in spots, with clumps of weeds and brush encroaching on it, and was little more than six feet wide, but it was the most inviting thing Ken had seen all day. He pumped his fist in the air with excitement, forgetting not only his odd experience from five minutes ago, but his exhaustion after hours of walking.

But which way to go? One direction led downward and disappeared behind a rock outcropping some 40 yards away, while on the opposite side it ended in a wide, rolling field some 100 yards in the distance. Ken hesitated for a moment before taking the field path, reasoning that if the road didn't resume on the opposite end of the field, he could always backtrack.

While the sun remained stubbornly hidden behind a thick layer of clouds, it was pleasantly warm, and a gentle breeze invigorated him as he walked. The grass on this side of the field — the upper slope — barely rose over his sneakers, suggesting that it was a popular grazing area. He noticed several honeybees foraging nearby, taking advantage of the temperature for a few precious hours before the night's chill forced them back to the hive.

Ken could already see the other side of the field; it was lined with trees, and between them he could see the road. Only it didn't pick up where the other one had ended. Instead, the road ran parallel to the field; that and the fact that it was made of gravel indicated it was a completely different road. Ken noticed that the gravel path ended shortly after crossing the field, but the road continued, a dirt path that forked left and wound its way up a small hill that vanished on the other side of the hill's crest.

As he drew closer, Ken couldn't shake off the oddest sense of déjà vu. There was something about this place that seemed familiar, but he couldn't put his finger on it. It was then that he heard the voices.

Two people, talking. So faintly that he thought he was imagining it. But as his feet moved from grass to gravel, the voices grew clearer. They were both adult male voices. They seemed to be coming from the other side of the hill.

Ken started charging toward the hill, his weariness after hours of walking forgotten. With each step he felt a surge of adrenaline coursing through his veins, making his limbs impossibly light as he ran across the gravel road and followed it to the dirt path uphill.

"Hey!" he shouted exuberantly. "Over here! Help!"

The voices on the other side of the hill ceased.

"Help me!" Ken called out again. "I'm lost out here!" he shouted, forgetting in his excitement that he wasn't the only one abandoned.

"Hello?" a man called out in the distance.

Ken crested the hill and felt his heart leap into his throat when he saw two figures downhill, maybe 200 yards further down the road. They were still too far away to make out clearly. He waved wildly in the air. After an agonizing second, one of them waved back.

Ken started laughing in excitement as he charged down the hill. A wave of relief washed over him as they drew closer and he realized this nightmare was about to end. He was saved! Saved!

He could barely contain himself as he bounded toward his rescuers. No doubt they were hunters or intrepid backpackers that could escort him to safety. Details about either of his rescuers were hard to make out because they were standing in the shadows of a shading tree on the side of the road, and because many of the intervening trees had low-lying branches that obscured the view downhill. The taller one looked to be white, and was wearing light-colored clothing. The other one was harder to make out through the foliage, but he appeared to be dark-skinned and shorter than his traveling companion.

As Ken drew closer, the pair left the comfort of the shading tree and stepped out into the road to greet him, giving him his first good look at them. The shorter of the two was stocky and black, while the taller one had shaggy red hair and was wearing light-colored robes.

Fuck.

All the enthusiasm drained out of Ken's body, and he quickly stopped jogging downhill.

"Fuck you two for getting my hopes up," Ken greeted them while pausing to catch his breath.

Lamar looked to Coop knowingly.

"I told you it was him," he said.

"We thought you were gone," Coop said. "Like, permanently."

"I'm not that lucky," Ken replied, drawing close enough to the pair to speak in a normal voice. Ken noticed the two of them were walking stiffly, with a side-to-side motion, like they'd just run a marathon and could barely stand. "Why are you two walking like that?"

"Long story," Coop intoned. "Just don't ask us to carry anything heavy for the next 24 hours."

"Or anyone heavy," Lamar chimed in.

Ken shook his head in confusion.

"Whatever, we can play catch-up some other time," he said. "What the hell are you two doing all the way out here?"

They looked at each other, confused, and then back at Ken.

"You do know where you are, right?"

"What's that supposed to mean?" Ken snapped.

"Uhmm ... you're a quarter-mile south of camp," Lamar said quietly.

"Get the fuck out of here."

"It's true," Coop chimed in. "This is the same road John used when he brought us here. We only got back 30 minutes ago, ourselves. Gaby and Beverly are down there right now."

Ken rolled his eyes in aggravation. All this time Ken thought he was heading north, he had actually been heading east. Now at least he understood that sense of déjà vu earlier. He'd stumbled on the same spot they had visited yesterday morning, when John showed them ...

A puzzled expression crossed Ken's face. He ran a few yards back up the hill, to the crest, and looked back the way he'd come. They weren't there.

"It's not the same road," he insisted, walking back to Lamar and Coop, who at this point were vacillating between annoyed and amused. "You two must have gotten turned around."

"See that ridge?" Coop asked sharply, his annoyance plain as he pointed the way they had come. "The camp's on the other side of it."

"It can't be," Ken insisted stubbornly.

"Why are you so certain?" Lamar asked.

"Because," Ken said with a dramatic pause, "there are no totem poles."

Ken walked the pair to the top of the hill, and they looked down at the gravel road and the open field.

"If this was the same road, the totem poles would be there, right?" Ken said, motioning to where the poles should have stood, the ones John had shown off yesterday.

"See, they're not there," Ken finished with a self-satisfied little smile.

"What are those marks there?" Lamar asked, pointing to two deep indentations on either side of the road at the bottom of the hill, right where the totems poles would have stood. Ken hadn't spotted them when he passed by earlier because of the difference in elevation. His grin quickly vanished.

Several minutes later, the trio was down by the fork in the road, investigating the imprints in the ground, which were nearly two feet deep. Lamar ran his fingers lightly along the outer edges of the clay that had once contained the left pole. The edges were completely smooth to the touch. If something as heavy as one of those eight-foot poles had been extricated, there would have been cracking along the outer rim, fissure marks showing where it had been torn out at an angle. There was nothing of the sort.

"Where are the drag marks?" Ken asked as he examined the hole on the right. "Something that heavy gets dragged away."

Lamar checked his side and noticed the same thing. The only tracks in the dirt around the poles were their own shoe imprints. It was like the poles had simply vanished.

"How'd he do it?" Ken asked. "Those things must have been 400 pounds each. You'd need a backhoe to cart one of those things off solo."

"That's a lot of work just to mess with us," Lamar responded. "And there'd be tread marks all around here."

"Maybe they were imitation, like fiberglass," Coop suggested. "John could lift that, right?"

"Then they wouldn't be able to stay upright. A light breeze could knock them over," Lamar pointed out.

A thought occurred to Coop.

"Remember what he said when we were here yesterday?" Coop asked. "He said that the next time we see them, we'll be different people."

Ken shrugged.

"So?"

"So maybe the vision quest hasn't changed us enough," Coop explained. "I don't feel any different from yesterday, do you?"

"I feel a lot more pissed off than I did yesterday," Ken replied dryly. "And what do you mean 'hasn't changed us enough?' Hasn't changed us enough to what?"

"To see them," Coop replied in earnest.

Lamar quickly turned away to mask his snickering. Ken wasn't as polite.

"Are you shittin' me, Fanny Farmer?" Ken said, laughing right in his face. "Maybe we should consult a Ouija board or say 'Bloody Mary' into a mirror three times!"

Coop stiffened.

"We ruled out reasonable explanations, so ..."

"So you decided to break out the most batshit crazy one ever?" Ken interrupted with a demeaning laugh. "You keep talking like this, and I'll put you in the loony bin with Wade."

Coop stormed back to camp in a huff, and an apologetic Lamar quickly followed him. Ken, on the other hand, continued to laugh long after the two were out of earshot.

"Enjoy your 'vision quest,' dipshit!" he called out in a cruel imitation of Coop's shrill voice. "The rest of us will concentrate on getting rescued!"

* * * * * *

Gaby helped Beverly lay back onto her sleeping blanket, holding her bad ankle stationary as the older woman slowly lowered herself. She winced as Gaby set it on her monogrammed carry-on bag.

It was late afternoon now, and the interior of the teepee was already darkening, even with the door ajar. The odor of last night's fire still lingered.

"Can I get you anything, Bev?" Gaby asked, kneeling down beside her with some difficulty.

"A stiff drink," Beverly muttered, still annoyed by her treatment earlier.

"All we have is water."

"I can't spend the rest of the day in here with nothing to do," Beverly insisted. "I'll go out of my mind with boredom."

"We're a little short on reading material here," Gaby responded patiently. "So try to imagine all the things you'll do when we get out of here."

Gaby put her hands on her knees and started to stand up. She immediately fell to one knee, her face contorted in pain as she bit her lip to keep from crying out.

Beverly leaned forward, concerned.

"Let me take a look at it," she said. "It's not getting any better."

Gaby held up her hand to ward Beverly away.

"I'm fine," she said through clenched teeth. "I just stood up too fast, that's all."

"You are *not* fine," Beverly said emphatically. "You can barely walk and you refuse to sit. Whatever you sat on is still in there. What happens when you have to use the outhouse? How long before it becomes infected?"

Beverly could see Gaby starting to waver. She reached out to take her hand in a compassionate gesture. Gaby tensed up and jerked her hand away. She looked at Beverly warily, as though the older woman was going to strike her.

An awkward silence hung in the air as the two looked at each other.

"Sorry," Beverly said, lowering her offered hand. "I forgot that you don't like to be touched."

Gaby relaxed slightly.

"I never thanked you for helping me today," Beverly started. "I know I was ... well, I was kind of a pill about it. But if you three hadn't helped me, I'd still be at the bottom of that ravine. I was stubborn and behaved badly. Now it's my turn to help," she said, drawing closer to Gaby. "Let me help you out of your ravine."

Gaby mulled this over. She opened her mouth to refuse

when Beverly held up her hand.

"I know you're hiding something," she said quietly. "The long-sleeved shirts, refusing to wear a swimsuit during the sweat. Whatever it is, you don't have to be afraid to show me."

Gaby started to protest, but Beverly cut her off again.

"There's nothing you could have done to yourself that I haven't seen a hundred times before," Beverly continued. "Self-cutting, injection marks, I've seen it all."

At this, she reached out her hands. Gaby instinctively reared back but saw that Beverly hands had stopped several inches shy of her, hovering in mid-air as a gesture of trust.

"Take a chance and trust me," Beverly said, gesturing with her fingertips for Gaby to clasp them. "Let me help you."

Gaby swallowed hard before reaching out and cautiously touching Beverly's outstretched hands. The older woman smiled warmly at her and interlocked her fingers with Gaby's, giving a light squeeze of encouragement.

"You can't tell anybody," Gaby said in a hushed voice. "Ever."

"Not a soul," Beverly promised.

Gaby stood up slowly with a grimace and unbuttoned her jeans. She closed her eyes, took a deep breath, and after a moment or two of deliberation, pulled down her jeans.

Ugly purple blotches decorated the front and sides of Gaby's thighs. There must have been half a dozen bruises, though it was hard to count because many of them blended together to form a patchwork of discolored skin tones ranging from a deep purple near the center of each to a sickly yellow on the outer fringes. At the epicenter of each was a raised welt in the shape of a belt buckle.

Beverly inhaled sharply and covered her mouth with her hands.

Gaby stood there mortified, willing herself not to weep.

"On your arms, too?" she asked in a hushed tone.

Gaby nodded silently.

"Oh, child," Beverly said, searching for the right words. She wanted to hug her, but now understood why that would never comfort her.

"Who's doing this to you?" she asked. "Is it your husband?"

Gaby shook her head.

"Boyfriend," she replied, her voice barely above a whisper. "He's my boyfriend and business manager."

"He'll be your end if this keeps up," Beverly said, trying to put on a brave face. "Now, turn around. Let's see if I can do something about that splinter of yours."

Gaby turned and placed her hands on the structure's lattice frame for support. Beverly, who remained on her knees to avoid reinjuring her ankle, waddled behind her.

"Left cheek, right?" Beverly asked.

"Yes," Gaby replied quietly.

She stiffened as a hand touched her bottom and peeled away the left edge of her underwear. She could feel Beverly's hot breath on her posterior as the older woman leaned in for a closer look. This was beyond mortifying.

"I see it," Beverly declared. "It looks flush with the skin."

Gaby heard her knee-walk a few steps away.

"Fortunately, I think I brought some eyebrow pluckers

with me," the older woman declared as she rummaged through her bags. "You never know when those little devils will try to merge."

Gaby closed her eyes and prayed for this to all be over soon.

"Here we go," Beverly declared, pulling a pair of tweezers from one of the bag's interior pockets. She shuffled back toward Gaby.

"Now hold still."

Gaby flinched as the cold metal came in contact with the splinter.

"Looks deep," Beverly declared. "So, how long has this been going on?"

"With Bill? Almost a year."

"A word of advice, my dear," Beverly said, pausing dramatically as she tried to pluck the splinter out. "Never try to reform the violent ones. It always ends in tears."

"He wasn't always that wa ... oww!" Gaby declared when Beverly missed, pinching sensitive skin near the splinter.

"Sorry," Beverly said.

"At first it was platonic. I hired him to help sell the workout videos, the ones your niece likes so much. After a year, we moved in together. Sales started to take off, so a year later, we bought a condo together. I was even thinking about marriage," Gaby said with a wistful shake of her head. "Then the endorsements started drying up. Sales leveled off. I was 30, and the producers were already telling me I was over the hill. Bill didn't know how to handle failure so ..."

"He started to hit you."

"Yes," Gaby sobbed. "He blamed me for everything. He

would get so mad. At first, it was open-handed. Before long, he started using his fists. Last month, he began using a belt."

Beverly shivered at the thought.

"Leave while you still can," Beverly advised. "I've walked out on two husbands, and believe me, neither would have dared to raise a hand to me. It's not worth it."

"I know," Gaby said tearfully. "That's why I came here. I told him this was a two-week retreat, so by the time he came to pick me up, I'd have a seven-day head start. Time enough to start ove … rrrowwww!" Gaby cried out, leaping in pain as Beverly yanked out the splinter.

"Got it," Beverly declared, holding up an evil-looking fragment coated in blood and nearly an inch long.

Gaby looked over her shoulder as she rubbed her sore bottom and saw Beverly again going through her bags.

"What are you doing?" she asked.

"Improvising," Beverly said as she fished out a pair of nude pantyhose. "We don't have any gauze, so I figure this is the next best thing. I never liked this pair, anyway."

With a resigned sigh she tore the pantyhose into strips. One of them she folded into a small square and handed to Gaby.

"Use this. Your underwear should hold it in place as long as you don't make any sudden movements."

"Thank you," Gaby said, wiping away a tear, touched by the older woman's compassion.

"You did the same for me," Beverly reminded her warmly. "Besides, we need to stick together. If we let those clowns out there call the shots, we're all doomed."

* * * * * *

"Fifteen … sixteen … seventeen," Coop counted to himself as he inspected the food rack behind the shed. He turned his head and called out to the rest of the group.

"We've got seventeen cans of food, he shouted. "And two bags of trail mix."

Gaby pulled on a fleece jacket to stave off the evening chill. The afternoon's rain-laden clouds had departed without making good on their threat, giving the group a clear view of the sun as it retreated behind the western edge of the floodplain, leaving behind an indigo sky flecked with countless stars. They looked so pristine compared to the ones dotting the hazy skies over her Los Angeles home. On hearing Coop's progress report, she reluctantly tore her eyes away from the night sky.

"That's not enough," she told the others huddled around the outside firepit. "We can't stretch that out over a week."

Ken, who was stoking the fire with a blackened tree branch, broke into his all-too-familiar condescending smirk.

"Who needs a week?" he asked. "We could go two days easily on that, three if we're careful. That should be plenty of time to escape."

Gaby sighed.

"We've already discussed this: walking in any old direction and hoping for the best is not a plan," she reminded him.

Ken thrust the stick into the guts of the fire, sending up a shower of sparks.

"I decide what's best for me," he insisted, jabbing a thumb

at his chest to drive home the point.

Gaby shrugged almost imperceptibly.

"You can go anytime you like, but the rest of us are staying put until help arrives. And the food's staying with us."

"Either way, I suppose we'll have to learn to hunt," Coop chimed in, cradling an armload of cans for the evening meal. He took a seat on one of the stools around the firepit and started stripping the labels from the cans so they could heat them on the grill.

"What happened to 'John works in mysterious ways' and all that other fruity crap you were spouting earlier?" Ken needled him, his smirk now reaching punchable proportions.

Coop smiled stiffly, his annoyance just as evident as his refusal to let Ken goad him twice in one day.

"John will come back for us," he said in a lilting voice as he peeled away can labels. "And yes, I still believe this is all a test. But if passing it means lounging around camp for a few days with a full belly, that doesn't sound like much of a test. We need to learn to hunt and trap, so when he does return, we'll have proved our mettle."

Ken chuckled to himself with a sad shake of the head. These two were clearly a lost cause, but there was one person he hadn't asked, one who might be more pliable.

"What say you, Sherman Plump?" he asked Lamar, who was standing on the southern edge of camp, tying plastic cording between two large trees to create a makeshift clothesline. "You still think we can rough it out here for another week?"

Lamar paused a moment to consider.

"Uhmm ... I think today was an object lesson for all of us," he answered after a moment, thoughtfully stroking his goatee. "You and Beverly both set off on your own, and look what happened: you got lost and she wound up injured in the bottom of a ravine."

Ken's smirk quickly turned upside down.

"If we try again, something worse could happen," Lamar continued, too busy with the clothesline to notice Ken's rapidly souring reaction. "We should wait for help to ..." Lamar paused midsentence as he finally looked up and saw his words were not having the intended effect.

"Not that there's anything wrong with a little exploration," he squeaked out under Ken's withering stare.

In the firelight, Ken's glare looked downright malevolent.

"Just remember, Porky," he intoned after several uncomfortable seconds, "if we run out of food before anyone comes, bacon goes on the menu. You read me?"

Lamar nodded nervously, too intimidated to respond verbally.

"Just ignore him," Gaby advised, giving Lamar a reassuring smile. "He's all bark and no brains." She sat down gingerly on one of the stools, leaning at an angle to avoid putting pressure on her injured left cheek.

Ken muttered under his breath for several seconds before suddenly turning to Coop and frog punching him in the bicep. Hard.

"Owww! What was that for?" Coop protested in wide-eyed surprise as he rubbed his sore arm.

"Well, I can't very well hit her, can I?"

"You could try not hitting anyone at all," Coop complained, eyeing Ken warily as he handed out utensils and cans of stew.

"So, you do have standards," Gaby said, pleased to see that Ken had some kind of moral compass. "I was beginning to wonder."

Ken snorted in irritation.

"I don't hit women. What kind of monster do you think I am?"

Coop hesitantly extended a can toward Ken, who yanked it out of his hand with such force that Coop nearly fell off his stool.

Lamar, meanwhile, stared dubiously at his tiny meal, unconvinced it would do much to quell the rumbling in his empty belly. He was so preoccupied that it took him several seconds to realize that someone else had joined the group.

He turned to the western edge of camp and there was Wade, silhouetted against the setting sun, carrying what looked like a small animal carcass slung over his shoulder. Ken immediately stood up and backed away, overturning his stool in the process. He remembered all too well his run-in with Wade earlier in the day and sought refuge in the Braves' outhouse.

The other three were more polite, but no less alarmed by Wade's presence. All of them quietly rotated their log stools to the opposite side of the fire.

As Wade drew closer to the firelight, they could see he was bare-chested, and barely visible amid all the caked-on mud was the self-inflicted scar he'd made earlier, marked by a trickle of dried blood. How he was able to withstand the evening's chill with no upper body protection was anyone's guess.

Wade dumped the carcass unceremoniously on the ground beside him. It was the fox Ken had watched him kill hours ago. He grabbed an empty pail, placed it between his legs, pulled out his hunting knife and started skinning the animal right in front of his startled companions.

They watched, mesmerized as Wade cut along the animal's flank, following the dividing line between its orange coat and the white fur of its underbelly, pausing at each haunch to cut along the joint before snapping the limb clean off. The cracking noise each made when it came off was truly unsettling. Wade casually tossed both limbs in the fire and continued with his work.

Gaby had just claimed her heated stew from the grill when Wade began peeling away the fox's fur, exposing the muscles and tendons below. She recoiled and quickly faced the other direction, trying to think about anything else as she ate. Coop quickly followed suit. Lamar had no such qualms and continued to watch Wade work as he ate, looking away only long enough to shovel more stew into his mouth.

"I hope you left some from me," came a voice from the wigwam. Out hobbled Beverly, using a long tree branch as a makeshift crutch.

"I do believe I'm getting the hang on this," she declared as she clambered toward the group, swaying from side to side with each step to preserve momentum. She landed, more than sat, on a stool beside Gaby.

"How's the ankle?" Coop asked as he handed the older woman a can of stew and a spoon.

"Better, now that I can … oh, dear God!" Beverly gasped when she finally saw what Wade was doing. She started dry heaving in revulsion and quickly turned away until the spasms subsided.

"I thought you ritzy folks were all about farm-to-table food," Coop said with a hint of a smile.

"Only when I'm on the 'table' side!" Beverly exclaimed, fanning herself to keep from fainting.

Beverly's outsized reaction, coupled with her surreal experiences over the course of this long, confusing day triggered a primal response deep within Gaby, one that was impossible to ignore. She turned her head and covered her mouth to conceal it, but it was too late. It had escaped.

Beverly grew indignant at the sound of Gaby snickering.

"Stop it," Beverly pouted. "It's not funny."

Gaby's laughter quickly proved contagious, and before long Coop and Lamar were both chuckling.

"Okay, maybe it was a little funny," Beverly relented, and the four shared a long and badly needed laugh together.

"A little too much reality for Sunday night?" Coop asked, still chuckling.

"This is too much for *any* night!" Beverly responded hammily, which was greeted with roars of appreciative laughter from the others, just when the mirth was starting to peter out.

Wade seemed impervious to the merriment, continuing to work as if no one else was around. He had skinned the fox past its hind legs and was now pulling on the folds of fur and skin, yanking them down to the carcass's midriff like he was peeling an banana. His arms were matted with blood, with the remainder spilling into the pail, which he was using as a makeshift drip pan.

"Is he still ... you know?" Beverly asked.

"Still skinning it?" Lamar responded, finishing his stew and wiping his hands on the front of his shirt. "Not exactly. More like unwrapping it."

"Ugh," Beverly responded while trying to control her gag reflex.

"Shall I describe it to you?" Lamar asked mischievously.

"Don't you dare!" Beverly intoned.

Lamar was impressed by the near surgical precision of Wade's movements. It was clear this was not his first time.

"You think he's a taxidermist?" Lamar asked, keeping his voice low.

"Wade? It would explain a lot," Coop replied. "And it's a lot more comforting to think of him stuffing pets than people."

"I think you're onto something," Gaby said, a little loudly for the others' tastes. "Maybe we've been reading this guy wrong all along. Sure, he's eccentric and not very friendly, but I think he could be a big help in our present situation. I'm going to invite him to join us."

Coop and Lamar exchanged worried glances, remembering all too well finding Ken choked to near unconsciousness yesterday.

"I don't think that's a good idea," Coop whispered to her. "Let rabid dogs lie."

Gaby ignored him and raised her voice so that Wade could hear her from across the fire.

"Hey, Wade, do you want to take a break from ... that, and

join us for dinner?" she asked. "We've got beef stew."

Wade looked up from his work, his reaction impossible to read in his sunburned facade. He appeared to be genuinely considering their offer when a shouting voice from the direction of the outhouse caught everyone's attention.

"What is wrong with you people?" Ken fairly screamed in outrage, gesturing wildly with his hands for emphasis. "You yuck it up like there isn't a care in the world, you lounge around waiting for rescuers that'll never come and now you decide to make friends with fucking Hannibal Lecter over there?" he exclaimed, pointing at Wade as his voice grew more shrill. "Are you people fucking insane?"

Coop shifted uncomfortably on his stool. Lamar looked down at his shoes. Gaby and Beverly both looked away in embarrassment. No one said a word until Wade suddenly stood up, the fox skin delicately folded over his arm.

"If you hate it here so much, then why not leave?" he drawled in a husky, menacing voice, raising his blood-spattered blade to drive home the point.

The two stared each other down for several agonizing moments before Ken broke eye contact and spat on the ground.

"Fine, I will!" he shouted and stormed off into the wigwam. Gaby and Beverly exchanged puzzled looks before he emerged with his sleeping blanket and metal suitcase.

"As long as Wade's here, I won't be!" he declared, and stomped off to sleep down by the archery range.

Without another word, Wade went back to work, making an incision in the skinless creature's skull and scooping out its brain bare handed. He deposited it in the same pail he'd used to collect the creature's blood and set the mixture on the grill to heat.

The others saw none of this. They were still trying to process Ken's outburst, looking at one another slack jawed. It was nearly a minute before anyone spoke again.

"Well," Beverly intoned, "thank goodness that wasn't awkward."

* * * * * *

The sun had set as the last of the stragglers — Lamar and Coop — entered the wigwam. Lamar was explaining the concept of botnets to a bewildered Coop, whose computer prowess was limited to navigating the OS and working in Excel.

Beverly was already nestled in her sleeping bag, her makeshift nightshade on top of her head, while Gaby was trying to find a comfortable position to lie in hers without inflaming her tender tush. Wade, on the other hand, was still hard at work on his pelt, having moved from skinning the hide to tanning it. He had spread the skin out over the cooking grill, with each end of it threaded through holes in the grill's perimeter to hold it in place as he worked. With the fur side facing the grill, Wade carefully scraped away the interior flesh and fat. Beside him was the pail holding the brains and blood, which he'd cooked and mixed together to form a grayish, viscous material with the consistency of toothpaste.

"That's why, up until last week, I always used an anonymizer," Lamar explained as he ducked through the low entrance. "Tor is great for surfing, but it's too slow to run a

DDOS on open resolvers. I'm partial to OnionShare, though I know guys who swear by GitHub."

Coop nodded, but it was clear he had no idea what Lamar was talking about.

"Fair warning," said Gaby, who was lying down to the right of the entrance.

"Warning about wh ... what is that?" Lamar cried, wrenching his head away in disgust as the smell of brain pâté reached his nostrils.

Coop, who was standing right behind him, had a similarly strong reaction, and began waving away the smell with his hand.

"That," Gaby said evenly.

Scraaape-scraaape-scraaape-scraaape

"Do you really need to do that in here?" Coop chided Wade.

Wade responded by dipping a finger into the nauseating concoction and rubbing it into one of the scraped sections of the skin.

"I think I'm going to be sick," Beverly declared, looking the other way.

"At least he's not eating it," Lamar whispered to her as he passed, a joke that elicited no laughter.

"Should we build a fire?" Coop asked as he tied the tee-pee's entrance closed.

"I don't think we need to," Gaby responded, still trying to find a comfortable sleeping position. "It's warmer than it was last night. If we keep the flue closed, our sleeping blankets should be enough."

She sat up and tugged on the pull chain hanging from the rafters, narrowing the opening into the wigwam.

"That's not what I'm talking about," Coop said as he located his sleeping blanket. "John told us to always keep a fire going from dusk until dawn. Plus, it might help with the ... odor."

"If you want to go out there and split some logs and collect the kindling, we won't stop you," Beverly declared with a yawn, pulling down her improvised eyeshade.

Scraaape-scraaape-scraaape-scraaape

"Lamar, what changed last week?" Gaby asked.

"Huh?"

"You said you used to do all that hacker stuff, but something happened last week," Gaby pressed. "What changed?"

Lamar reddened with embarrassment, and his voice dropped slightly.

"It's a bit complicated, but lets just say it ended with mom taking an axe to my rig and my phone," Lamar said.

Gaby and Coop both looked over at him wide-eyed, sparking a small smile from the young man.

"I'm not joking," he said quietly, miming several wild axe swings with him arms to drive home the point. "I'm not allowed any kind of tech now, not even an iPod. That's why I use this," he said, pulling the Walkman from his rucksack.

"Ugh," Gaby replied. "It's only been two days since I've used my Android and it already feels like two years. I can't imagine going a week with no phone or email."

Beverly chortled to herself.

"All any of you can think of is life before all this," she said sardonically. "Try imagining life after it. Just think about all the money you'll get when this is over."

Gaby looked at her quizzically.

"What money?"

Beverly raised her eyeshade slightly and propped herself up on one elbow.

"From the lawsuit, obviously," she said as though it were obvious to anyone. "We'll file a class-action suit and take that man to the cleaners. He'll wind up in debt to us for the rest of his miserable life."

Coop, who had pulled a photo from his wallet and was staring thoughtfully at it, rolled his eyes but said nothing. Gaby, however, wasted no time articulating her feelings.

"None of us are going to see a dime from this," she insisted. "Do you really think he has any money to his name? I mean, look at this place. Even his office is a rental."

"Besides, he's long gone by now," Lamar chimed in. "Face it: the only thing any of us are going to get out of this is fame. Six people abandoned in the woods escape with no training — that makes for one helluva story. We'll go viral overnight."

"Fame?" Gaby said slowly, contemplating the idea. "Not sure I like the sound of that, even if it is for only 15 minutes."

"Sure, we'll be just another meme within a couple of months," Lamar acknowledged. "But until then? Our faces will be plastered all over TV and the internet."

Scraaape-scraaape-scraaa...

Wade abruptly stopped scouring the skin and put down his knife.

"I don't want to be famous," he spontaneously declared. "And I'm not going back."

He picked the knife back up and continued his work, the scraping noise now more pronounced in the stunned silence of his pronouncement.

Gaby and Lamar looked at one another, confused not only by his words but by his sudden decision to join in the discussion. Even Beverly seemed taken aback, giving a small "Hmm," before pulling her eyeshade back down.

Only Coop seemed unflustered.

"To be honest, I'm with him on the fame," Coop said, returning the photo to his wallet and lying down with a huff. "I don't want any part in a media circus. If you all sell your stories to the tabloids, be sure to keep my name out!"

Coop rolled over on his side with a huff as Lamar and Gaby watched in confusion. One by one they lay down and closed their eyes.

Lamar slipped on his headphones, hoping the Eagles would drown out the noise Wade was making. It was a long time before he could get over the unsettling sound of serrated steel scouring flesh and once more embrace the world of dreams.

MONDAY

It was mid-morning and Coop, Gaby and Ken were all in line for the shower, waiting for Beverly to finish her turn. Ken made no mention of last night's events; he seemed like his old, smug self again, handing out demeaning nicknames and cutting remarks with such alacrity that the others could be forgiven for thinking that last night's meltdown had simply been a dream.

Perhaps it was the fact that Wade wasn't there; just like yesterday, he was gone at first light. His fox fur remained behind, air drying on Lamar's jerry-rigged clothesline.

Coop — who was at the front of the line — was quietly talking with Gaby behind him while Ken did his best to dominate the conversation from the back of the line.

"You still bothered by it?" Gaby asked Coop gently.

"A little," he admitted in a disheartened tone.

"That's what you get for putting your faith in a plastic shaman," Ken said derisively, earning him a glare from Gaby. She opened her mouth to upbraid him but Coop stopped her.

"It's okay. He's right. I really thought John would be back by now."

"He may still come back," Gaby said comfortingly.

"Now you're just deluding yourself," Ken said with a laugh. "Dances With Dickheads is long gone. The only way we're getting out of here is on our own two feet."

"For someone so pessimistic, you sure are cheery about it," Gaby observed.

"I came to a realization this morning," Ken replied with an anticipatory grin. "Waking up in that open field, watching the sun rise surrounded by dew-covered grasses, I remembered why I came out here in the first place. Yesterday, I was so angry, so confused about our situation that I wasn't thinking straight. I got so caught up in all the life and death stuff that I forgot that this is precisely why I'm here. I want the kind of challenge you can't find in a boardroom. I was never interested in any of that frou-frou mystic mumbo-jumbo you all signed up for. I came to be challenged. And this," he paused, lifting his arms and motioning to the wilderness surrounding them, "this is the greatest challenge we'll ever face."

Coop tried to process Ken's new outlook.

"So does that mean you're sticking things out with the rest of us?" he asked.

"Fuck no!" Ken scoffed. "Every one of you deserves a padded cell for thinking that anybody's coming for us. It just means that I'm not going to rush out again blindly. I want to do it smarter, get the lay of the land before I try again."

Gaby knocked on the cedar door of the cabana-style shower.

"Beverly?" she asked. "How're you doing?"

"It's freezing in here!" Beverly complained as icy river water cascaded down her body.

"Don't force yourself," Gaby replied. "The last thing you want is to catch a cold out here."

"Just a little longer," Beverly replied through chattering teeth. "I still need to clean ..."

"Don't say it," Ken muttered to himself, trying to block out any accompanying mental pictures.

"... my hair," Beverly finished, much to Ken's relief.

Coop rolled his eyes at Ken's theatrics.

"Just for that, you can prime the water pump for me and Gaby," Coop insisted. Much to Coop's surprise, Ken neither mocked nor challenged him. He simply shrugged his acquiescence.

Beverly shut off the water and grabbed her towel hanging over the shower door.

"I'll never take hot water for granted again!" Beverly exclaimed as she ran the towel vigorously over her body, focusing more on generating friction heat than drying off. She grabbed a black one-piece draped over the shower's rear wall and emerged 30 seconds later, shaking like a leaf. She had weaned herself off the makeshift crutch, but walked slowly and with a pronounced limp.

Instead of making a beeline for the comparative warmth of the teepee, she lingered for a moment, taking Gaby aside and speaking in a hushed voice as she shivered.

"When you're done in there, would you mind helping me put on my face?" she whispered to Gaby. "I seem to have left my compact at home and I don't want to look like the rest of these savages," she said, not registering that she'd managed to insult Gaby and ask her for help in the same breath.

Gaby took the unintended slight in stride and nodded her agreement. Beverly smiled in gratitude and limped toward the wigwam to change, rubbing her arms furiously as she went.

In front of her, Coop was laying his towel over the stall door, fussily smoothing out the creases as he waited for Ken to finish priming the hand pump at the rear of the showers.

"You just about finished there, Ken?" Coop called out.

"One more pump should ..."

Ken's voice trailed off and the pumping abruptly ceased.

Concerned, Coop leaned back to look past the stall wall. Ken was staring at something off to his left, out of Coop's sight line. His face was a study in slack-jawed wonderment.

"I ... I don't believe it," Ken managed to spit out after a few moments. "He's back!"

Ken turned to Gaby and Coop with the look of a small child on Christmas morning.

"He's back! John's back!"

He started waving his arms wildly in the air.

"John! Hey, over here!"

Gaby and Coop rushed over to look. They pushed past Ken and followed his gaze to the downward slope leading into the floodplain. They didn't see anything except for trees and grass swaying in the wind.

"Where is he?" Coop asked.

Ken said nothing.

Coop looked back over his shoulder to ask again, only to find that Ken was gone. That's when he heard the stall door open and the water start.

"You unbelievable bastard!" Coop shouted as Ken howled with laughter.

"Dammit, Ken!" Gaby exclaimed. "That's not funny!"

"You should have seen the looks on your faces!" Ken chortled as he pushed Coop's towel off the shower door to make room for his own.

"You better hope the water doesn't cut off before you're done, because if you step out to prime the pump, I'm taking your place," Coop warned.

In contrast to Beverly, who viewed the cold shower as an unfortunate necessity, Ken seemed to thrive under the icy creek water.

"This is soooo invigorating!" he exclaimed as he lathered up, mainly to annoy the others.

Lamar emerged from the Braves outhouse to find Ken gargling loudly, Gaby warning him not to drink the water and Coop kicking the stall in frustration. He decided to see what all the fuss was about.

"Morning. What's going on?" he asked as he drew closer. Ken had shifted from gargling to imitating a water fountain, spraying water overhead.

"Just Ken being himself," Gaby replied with a sad shake of her head as she plucked Coop's towel from the ground and dusted it off. "You joining us?"

"Ehh, maybe when the air's a little warmer," Lamar said.

"You could use one," Coop said tersely. He was standing downwind and still fuming over Ken's prank.

Lamar looked at him dumbstruck. Gaby quickly jumped in with a more diplomatic approach.

"Lamar, I didn't want to say anything, but you are getting a bit whiffy," she said, her tone almost apologetic.

Lamar lifted an arm and buried his face in the pit.

"I don't smell anything," Lamar said as he reemerged.

On the other side of the campsite, Beverly exited the wigwam in a cashmere pullover and champagne-colored slacks, carrying her damp towel and bathing suit as she hobbled over to the clothesline. Not 30 seconds later, Wade emerged from the forest with a dead hare in hand and a fourth bloody scar carved into his chest to commemorate the kill.

Lamar saw his approach and rapped on the shower door.

"Heads up," he said. "Your BFF is back."

Ken, who was just tall enough to peer over the shower walls if he stood on his toes, cursed when he spied Wade.

"Fucking peachy," Ken groaned as he turned off the water and started toweling off, hoping he could make a quick exit from the campsite before Wade spotted him.

Wade took no notice of the group congregating at the shower, instead making a beeline for the firepit just as Beverly was hobbling toward it, en route to the clothesline. Even though the two seemed to be on a collision course, Beverly continued limping forward, assuming Wade would stop out of courtesy, allowing her to pass. Instead he barreled right through the older woman like she wasn't even there, knocking her to the ground and sending her wet clothes flying.

Wade paused a moment to look over his shoulder at a dazed Beverly before continuing on as though nothing had happened.

Beverly rolled onto her hands and knees and tried to get up, but her arms were rubbery after the collision and struggled to support her weight.

Gaby and Coop rushed to Beverly's side and helped her to her feet.

"Are you hurt?" Gaby asked, concerned as she saw Beverly's knees begin to buckle.

Instead of answering, Beverly started shouting at Wade.

"Hey," she gasped. "What's the matter with you? Apologize!"

Wade kept on walking.

Beverly shrugged off the others and staggered toward Wade, struggling to keep her feet.

"I know you can hear me!" she shouted. "Don't you walk away from me!"

Wade didn't respond and continued walking to the fire-pit.

"Your mad-dog killer routine doesn't frighten me!"

Wade stopped suddenly, but Beverly was so livid she scarcely noticed as she lurched toward him.

"You have no idea who you're messing with!" she continued. "When we get back, I'll sue you ..."

Wade suddenly spun on his heels to face her.

The hatred in his sunburned face could not have been more palpable. His eyes had narrowed to dangerous slits as his jawline quivered with rage. He clenched his fists until his knuckles whitened. He looked for all the world like a bull about to charge.

Beverly stopped short, caught off guard by the pure aggression that Wade radiated. Her face, flush with anger at his rudeness, slowly drained of all color as she started to grasp the gravity of her situation.

Wade dropped his prize kill and strode forward.

Beverly began backtracking, afraid that if she turned to flee, it would only provoke the bull. Words continued trickling out of her mouth, but they no longer held the same power as her mind and body hastily divorced themselves from her voice.

"... for every ..." she continued.

The others stood on the periphery, uncertain what to do. Gaby and Lamar worried that intervening would only worsen the situation. Coop stood to one side, mouth agape as he tried to process what was happening. Even Ken, who had finally finished drying off and was now standing a few feet behind Gaby, had no idea what to do.

Beverly was so preoccupied with the murderous glint in Wade's eyes that she didn't even realize where she was walking until she felt stacks of logs against her heels. She'd backed herself into the log rack and now had nowhere to go. Wade pressed forward, unmoved by the pleading in Beverly's pallid face. He now stood three feet away.

"...dime..." she continued breathlessly.

Two feet away.

"...you ..." she said shakily.

One foot. If Beverly could have merged with the logs, she would have.

"...own," she whispered, pressing her back against the logs.

Wade stood toe to toe with her and leaned in menacingly. His hot breath reeked. Beverly couldn't look away, entranced by the malevolent glint in his eyes, like a deer caught in headlights. In this light, his brown irises appeared flecked with red, as though his hatred were so consuming that it literally shone forth from his eyes.

Wade thrust his forearm against Beverly's throat, choking her. She slapped at it with flailing, ineffectual hands as she struggled to breathe.

Ken decided to intervene and rushed forward. The others watched, wanting to help, but unable to coax their limbs to cooperate. Ken grabbed Wade by the shoulder, trying to pull him off. It was like trying to move a brick wall.

Wade, momentarily distracted, eased up on Beverly's windpipe just long enough to rear back and elbow Ken in the throat, dropping him instantly. Beverly took a long, tortured breath before Wade doubled the pressure, making her gag.

Unwilling to make the same mistake as Ken, who was now floundering in the dirt like a landed trout, Gaby kept her distance, pleading with Wade to listen to reason.

"Let her go!" Gaby begged. "Please!"

Wade ignored her, focusing all his hatred on Beverly.

"Don't threaten me, you high-tit bitch!" Wade bellowed at Beverly with such force that spittle flew from his mouth. "You may be hot shit back in the real world, but out here, you're useless. I wouldn't think nothing of carving you up. You fuck with me again, I'll hang you upside down and gut you like a pig. I've done it before, and so help me, I'll do it again."

Wade leaned in until they touched noses. Beverly's flailing grew weaker.

"And you'd better pray you bleed out fast, because if you don't, the coyotes will get you," he continued, his raspy voice exuding malice. "They can smell blood from miles away. And they're always hungry this time of year."

Beverly, who was starting to fade out, could see the absolute conviction in Wade's eyes. He meant every word that he said.

"Wade, she can't breathe!" Gaby shouted. "Dios mio, let her go!"

He held his forearm against Beverly's throat for another agonizingly long second before relaxing the pressure and slowly pulling away. Beverly collapsed to the ground, gasping for air.

Wade turned to face the others.

"And that goes for all of you," he roared, looking at each of them in turn. "You're in my world now. You want to stay? Then leave me alone. Anyone that gets in my way again … dies."

With that, Wade walked back to the center of camp to reclaim his hare carcass, pulled his fox fur from the clothesline and left without another word.

* * * * * *

It was late morning before Lamar managed to get a fire going. Coop placed two cans of beans on the grill to heat, while Gaby fetched water to boil. Ken sat by the fire, rubbing his swollen Adam's apple, which Wade's sharp elbow had turned an angry shade of purple. Beverly was in the teepee, convalescing. Nobody spoke.

All around them the forest teemed with activity as critters of all shapes and sizes took advantage of the warming weather to forage for more food. Every so often, a strong breeze would blow chestnuts from some of the nearby trees, which squirrels in neighboring trees would rush to collect. The distinctive noise the chestnuts made when they landed spooked Coop; it sounded too much like Wade's approaching footsteps for comfort.

Gaby came back from the water pump with a pail full of water. She lifted it onto the grill to boil with a grunt of exertion.

"He's only getting worse," Lamar said, breaking the silence.

"I told you all, but you wouldn't listen," Ken croaked, rubbing his injured throat to soothe it. "You were all, 'Oh, Wade? He's not so bad. He's just misunderstood.'"

Coop glared at him contemptuously.

"Are you done? Because we need to figure out something fast."

"When he threatened Beverly, it made my blood run cold," Gaby confessed, shivering at the memory.

"That was no idle threat," Lamar said. "He meant it. And he meant it for us, too."

"So what do we do?" Coop asked.

"I say we leave," Ken suggested in a gravelly voice. "What'd he say, that we're in his world now? Let him have it. Let's pack up everything and take our chances in the forest."

"If we leave here, our chance of rescue is basically nil," Gaby reminded him. "What we need is a united front. Can we all agree that Wade's not allowed in camp anymore?"

"That's not the issue," Ken warbled impatiently. "He won't go away just because you ask him nicely. We need to be able to enforce it."

"But we need everyone here to complete the truth circle, like John told us. Otherwise, it won't work," Coop protested, drawing a derisive laugh from Ken.

"Jesus Tapdancing Christ, are you for real?" Ken mocked.

"We're trying to keep everyone alive, and your priority is what Chief Sitting Bullshit wants, so you can fulfill his precious shamanistic fantasy."

"Actually, shamanism is practiced in Asia," Coop corrected him before seeing in Ken's face how trivial his point was. "You know what, just forget I said anything."

"Wade's out, and that's final," Ken said before turning to Lamar. "Where do you stand, Poppin' Fresh?"

Lamar, who normally squirmed in embarrassment whenever Ken referenced his weight, didn't react at all. He seemed lost in thought. Ken was about to repeat the question when Lamar finally weighed in.

"If we're not going and he can't stay, that leaves us just one option," Lamar said in a measured tone, scanning the faces of his companions as he spoke. "We arm ourselves."

A hush fell over the group as Lamar's words sunk in. In the distance, more chestnuts fell.

Ken whistled low, although with his bruised windpipe it sounded more like a death rattle.

"That's pretty ballsy."

"Do you know what you're saying?" Gaby asked.

Lamar nodded.

"And you're willing to die over a campsite?" Gaby pressed.

"It's five to one," Lamar replied. "Nobody has to die. All we need is a display of overwhelming force. If we show him how far we're willing to go, he'll back down."

"You don't know that for certain," Coop interjected, alarmed at the direction this conversation was going.

"No, I don't," Lamar admitted. "But if we leave, he could

just as easily stalk us and pick us off one by one. At least here we can prepare defenses."

"So, what do we arm ourselves with?" Gaby asked. "A few sharp sticks won't stop him."

Lamar thought for a moment.

"Black hats learn to probe systems before attacking them, so they know the countermeasures and activity log triggers beforehand," he said, tugging thoughtfully on his goatee.

"Meaning what?" Ken asked, growing exasperated.

"We need to take inventory before we decide on a battle plan," Lamar responded. "What do we have to work with?"

"We have the pocket knife John gave me," Gaby said. "We can make fire, too."

"So those things and all the rocks we can throw," Ken said dismissively, convinced that this conversation had outlived its usefulness. "There's nothing here. Short of weaponizing your B.O., that's everything."

"No," Lamar said quietly as an idea began to take root. "Not everything."

The others looked at him, baffled.

"We haven't looked in there yet," he said, motioning to the storage shed on the other side of the campsite.

* * * * * *

"Is it in?" Ken asked, his voice still hoarse as he strained against the shed door, trying to pry it away from its frame.

"Almost there," Gaby responded through clenched teeth as she struggled to wedge her arm through the narrow opening Ken was making.

It was just blind luck that John hadn't replaced the door lock — which the last set of visitors had somehow dismantled — with anything better than a knotted bungee cord. Without that chink, the supply shed might as well have been Fort Knox. Unlike the outhouses with their unevenly spaced plywood boards, the supply shed was solidly built, made of two-inch-thick teak boards with no gaps. The door was solid oak and at least an inch thicker.

Unfortunately, the group's only way in — the bungee cord — was knotted from the inside and looped so tightly that Ken couldn't open the door more than a few inches.

"I can't believe we didn't think of this yesterday," Coop lamented as he watched Ken pull and Gaby try to squeeze her forearm inside. Lamar was in the teepee, checking on Beverly after her earlier assault.

"And I ... can't believe that ... you aren't helping!" Ken rasped as he gave one final, desperate tug at the door.

"I'm in!" Gaby exclaimed just before Ken lost his grip. She winced as the door closed tight against her arm, pinning her in place.

"Thank God!" Ken exclaimed as he leaned against the shed wall, exhausted and breathing heavily.

Ken and Coop watched Gaby's face for any sign of hope. It only amplified the pressure she felt. She trained her eyes skyward to avoid their gazes and set to work.

"I can feel the knot," she declared.

For the next few minutes, her face was a study in concentration as she struggled to untie the knot with a single, immobilized hand.

"I can almost ... no, it slipped," she said.

After five minutes of this, Gaby gave a sigh of resignation and shook her head.

"I can't get a proper grip. My fingers keep slipping off."

Coop and Ken started debating the best way forward while Gaby stood there, waiting for someone to assist her.

"Forget the lock," Ken said. "Let's just break down the door."

Coop shook his head.

"It's solid oak," he declared. "You'd break every bone in your hand."

"I can use my shoulder."

"If you don't mind dislocating it," Coop replied.

"Excuse me!" Gaby suddenly shouted. "Is someone going to help me out of here or what?"

Just as Ken and Coop finished extricating an annoyed Gaby from the door, Beverly exited the teepee, still favoring her ankle and leaning on Lamar for support. Gaby shook the numbness out of her arm and gave Beverly a polite hug.

"How're you feeling?"

"Like I got attacked by a madman," Beverly replied with a small, but forced, smile.

Coop and Ken continued debating how to open the door.

"If we could just remove these somehow," Coop said, studying the three stainless steel hinges holding the door in place.

"I don't see the screwdriver fairy anywhere," Ken groused in frustration. "I just wish we'd thought to break in here yesterday, before Wade went rogue. We could use some of his psychopath strength right now."

"No," Gaby said softly as the gears in her mind whirred.

"We don't need him; we need his knife."

"Well, anytime you want to ask him for it, be my guest," Ken replied dismissively as he mulled over how to break into the shed.

Gaby pulled away from Beverly and ran into the teepee. When she emerged several minutes later, the others were trying to force the door open with a three-foot length of plywood they'd wedged through the crack, using it as a fulcrum as they pushed and pulled on the exposed side with all their might.

As Gaby drew closer, she noticed it was the "Braves" sign that normally hung over the men's outhouse.

"Put your back into it, twinkle toes!" Ken growled at Coop as he pushed against the sign, head down and dripping with sweat.

Coop's face was rapidly turning purple as he pushed beside Ken. He managed to grunt out a barely audible "fuck you" as he drove his shoulder into the board.

On the other side of the plank, Lamar had the wood pressed against his sizeable stomach and was pulling on it so hard that he was in danger of falling backward.

"See, that's what you should be doing," Ken said of Lamar's technique. "Biggie Not-Smalls is finally putting all that extra weight to good use."

Gaby sidled up to Ken.

"I have an idea," she said.

"That's great," Ken grunted as he continued pushing against the board. "Now, less thinking, more helping."

Instead of moving to the other side of the board, Gaby tried to push past Ken, whose large shoulder blocked access to the door. Ken didn't budge.

"I said 'help,' not 'tickle,'" Ken barked. "If you want some loving, at least wait until we've stopped the knife-wielding lunatic."

"Oh, for God's sakes, Ken!" she vented. "What I want is for you to get out of the way."

Ken gave one more push against the board before pausing to look Gaby in the eye.

"You can't weigh more than 120 soaking wet," he said, mopping sweat from his brow. "What makes you think you can do it?"

Gaby reached into her pocket and brandished the penknife John had given her.

"Because I'll use brains, not balls," she said.

When Ken didn't take the hint and move over, she lowered the knife until it was level with his crotch.

"Speaking of which ..."

Ken immediately scooted back.

Gaby grabbed a handful of bungee cables through the hole in the door and started cutting. The tiny knife was surprisingly sharp and made quick work of them.

Ken spat in disgust, though it wasn't clear whether it was from Gaby threatening his manhood or annoyance that she came up with the solution before he did. Lamar and Coop were more gracious, giving a polite golf clap as she threw the severed cables to the ground and grabbed the door handle.

* * * * * *

Gaby opened the door wide so everyone could see inside.

The shed was small — three feet wide and four feet long — but tightly packed with all sorts of odds and ends. A shelf along the back wall contained a dozen canned goods, a bag of dried apricots, an old flashlight approximately the length and width of Coop's forearm and a box whose contents were obscured by a tarp and layers of dust.

The walls on either side were lined with implements hanging from nails: a tiny hammer, a rake, a hand spade, a plastic bag of loose nails and the bow drill that Gaby had struggled to use earlier.

On the floor they found several plywood two-by-fours stacked in a corner, a few fold-up lawn chairs and an earthen-ware jug. They also found items from Saturday's sweat: the metal funnel used to cover the fire during the ceremony and the lava rocks that lined the cylinder.

A musty odor permeated the shed. Dust and cobwebs decorated most of its exposed surfaces.

Coop entered the shed first. He brushed away a few cobwebs with his robes and then knelt down beside the jug. He jiggled the container and heard the swish of a large volume of liquid inside.

"We've got something in here, maybe gasoline," he said. He uncorked the spout and took a sniff.

"Doesn't smell like gas," he declared, tipping it back and taking a tentative sip.

"Coop, don't!" Gaby warned.

Coop threw his head back and made a pained sound, shaking after drinking it. His reaction was strong enough that the others started to worry he'd drunk something poisonous.

"Ngggghhh!!!" he exclaimed, hastily recorking the jug.

"It's not gas, but you'd be hard pressed to tell from the taste."

"What is it?" Gaby asked, still concerned.

"Firewater," Coop declared, wiping his mouth on the back of his hand. "Just like mama used to make."

"Moonshine?" Lamar asked.

"Yeah, strong stuff, too."

Ken started to laugh.

"'Think warm thoughts' my ass!" he said mockingly, recalling John's words when introducing them to the cold-water shower. "Looks like geriatric Geronimo had his own method of keeping warm."

From the back of the group, Beverly stared at the jug and shivered before walking away from the group, muttering under her breath. Gaby, who was closest to her, was barely able to make it out. She was spelling out letters, over and over again.

"S … A … L … T … S … A … L … T," she repeated, pronouncing each letter separately, as though it stood for something else.

Ken, unaware of Beverly's odd behavior, scoured the shed for anything that could be weaponized. They might be able to file down the handle of the rake and fashion it into a spear, but there were plenty of branches in the forest that would work equally well. And the hammer could work as a close-range weapon in a pinch. Other than that, there was nothing.

He gave a disheartened groan.

"Well, this was a fucking waste of time," he said dejectedly.

"Not completely," Coop insisted as he examined the rows of canned food. He handed the cans back to Gaby for safe-keeping. "We have more food."

"Great," Ken deadpanned. "So when Wade strolls in with his big-ass knife to kill us all, we can throw ..."

He paused to pluck one of the cans from Coop's outstretched fingers and read from the label.

"... lima beans blended with natural sea salts at him," Ken said. "Splendid." He tossed the can haphazardly toward Gaby, who barely managed to catch it.

"This was precious time we could have spent preparing for Wade or packing up and leaving," Ken continued. "We need real solutions."

As Ken chided the others, Coop was still examining the shed's contents. He located a box on the top shelf, one covered by a blue tarp. He pulled it down and gently blew dust off the lid to reveal its contents. He stared at the box in confusion, trying to make sense of the picture on the cover. After several long moments, his expression changed from confusion to wonderment to elation.

"What about this?" he asked, walking out of the shed cradling the box with the lid upturned so the others could see the contents. "Would this work?"

* * * * * *

Coop knelt down and laid the box gently in the dirt as the rest of the group gathered around him to watch.

The faded and partially discolored picture on the lid declared that this was a "Genuine Sears Portable Citizens Band Two-Way Radio," with the letters 'C' and 'B' displayed with a zoom-in effect not seen in advertising since the early '80s. This impression was reinforced by a prominent picture of a young teen with a bowl cut dressed in earth-toned clothing eagerly operating the knobs on the C.B. His hands were partially obscured by a gold sticker announcing: "Great fun for kids, too!"

Coop removed the lid and found the same C.B. pictured on the front, though with a few more scuff marks and nicks in the laminate wood paneling decorating the unit's front. Coop lifted the device out of the box and set it on one of the log stools. It was surprisingly heavy.

The device had one input: a coiled cord walkie-talkie that ended in a fist-sized microphone with a transmission button on its side. The unit's front panel had three small control knobs, a transmission window in the center that used a needle to indicate signal strength, and a large dial with 40 numbers that took up the rest of the C.B.'s faceplate. At the back of the unit was a retractable antenna that was bent in the middle.

Coop tried the volume knob, which gave an audible click as he turned the dial. The needle didn't move.

"So, what do you think?" Coop asked. He seemed to be directing the question to Lamar.

"Uhhmm, I think it's worth trying to fix it," Lamar responded, uncertain why Coop and the others appeared to all be looking at him now.

Coop pushed the log stool holding the device toward Lamar.

"Then try fixing it."

"What? Why are you asking me?" Lamar asked, confused and irritated by all the attention.

"Lamar, you're the most tech-savvy person here," Gaby said.

"Translation: you're a nerd," Ken chimed in.

"Forget it," Lamar declared, growing indignant. "Let Coop do it."

"Coop would only break it," Gaby said, before quickly adding: "No offense."

Coop waved the remark off.

Lamar was starting to feel like the others were ganging up on him. They all seemed to be imploring him with their eyes.

"I know computers!" Lamar said in a raised voice as he grew resentful. "My knowledge begins and ends in the 21st century! Give it to Ken, he looks like the right age for it."

"First of all, I'm 33," Ken replied. "Second, fuck you!"

"We could ask Beverly," Coop hastily interjected to lower the tension.

Beverly shook her head no emphatically.

"I had to call the Geek Squad just to set up my TiVo," she said. "I don't know anything about electronics."

"Gaby can't do it, either," Ken said. "That just leaves you, Mr. Wizard."

"I don't care," Lamar shot back, crossing his hands over his chest defiantly. "I'm not touching it."

Coop put his hand on Lamar's shoulder.

"Lamar, please," he pleaded. "This could get us rescued."

"And it'll get me pinched by the Triad!" Lamar shouted in a surprisingly loud voice for such a meek individual.

The others just stood there, staring blankly at him, struggling to process both his outburst and his words. Faced with their bewildered expressions, all of Lamar's rage slowly filtered out of him. His hands, which had been balled into fists, relaxed and fell to his side.

"The Chinese mafia … wants you?" Ken asked, struggling to control his laughter.

"It's not funny," Lamar said.

"And here I thought the Army's enlistment standards were bad," Ken chortled.

Lamar barely even registered the barb. He sighed and decided to come clean.

"I told you all that my folks banned me from using tech," he said, hanging his head dejectedly. "But I didn't explain why. Does anyone here remember The Fappening?"

A look of recognition crossed Ken's face.

"That thing with naked celebrity pics getting distributed online?"

Lamar reddened and slowly nodded.

Ken noticed that Gaby and Coop were glowering at him contemptuously.

"What? I'm as red-blooded as the next guy."

"The Fappening was the brainchild of a hacker friend of mine," Lamar explained. "And I gave him the software to do it. He asked me if I could dummy up something that could break cloud security protocols. Just something for the lulz. So I came up with a simple exploit that could brute-force a password by tricking the host into thinking multiple entries were a single request. I didn't think anything of it. It was a toy for cracking off-the-shelf software. Six months later, he leaked the photos on 4chan. All of them captured with my program."

"What does any of this have to do with the Chinese mafia?" Gaby asked, still bewildered.

"I made the mistake of telling my brother," Lamar explained. "He told some people, who told some other people ... you know how it goes. Then one night, mom spots some Triads parked in front of the house. Asian gangbangers in a black neighborhood; it caused quite a stir. After a couple of nights of this, Grammy goes out to confront them with a broom. All they're willing to say is they want to talk 'business' with me. That shit freaked my folks out. Mom trashed my gear and Dad sent me up here, hoping my absence would cause them to give up on me."

"You think word of this will serve as some kind of underworld recruitment drive?" Coop asked.

"If we make it out of here ..." Lamar started.

"*When* we make it out of here," Beverly corrected.

"Fine, when we make it out, it'll be all over the news," Lamar continued. "And if we escape by jerry-rigging a 40-year-old C.B., you might as well drop me off in Chinatown, because once word gets out that I can code and MacGyver, it won't just be the local gangbangers hassling me; it'll be the whole damn organization. Every parking space for 10 blocks will be filled with Triad cars."

"You don't think that's a little paranoid?" Gaby asked.

Lamar snorted.

"I'm not sure it's paranoid enough. What if a rival gang gets wind? How's a turf war in the backyard sound?"

"Like you're being paranoid," Beverly deadpanned.

Lamar gave her a disgusted look, prompting Gaby to try another tack.

"Lamar, if we make it out of this, I'm sure any one of us would be happy to put you up until all that blows over,"

Gaby said, trying her best to comfort the young man.

Ken and Beverly exchanged amused glances.

"But unless we get rescued, all of that is speculation," she continued, seeing Lamar starting to waver. "The media coverage, the Triad, the turf wars, all of it." She paused and looked him square in the eye.

"What we're facing now is not speculation," she pressed. "Wade, the forest, starvation. These are all very real threats. And unless you help us, we'll never get past the real dangers to the potential ones."

"If it's a choice between the devil you know and the devil you don't, I know which one I'd pick," Coop added.

"Fine," Lamar said with a sigh of defeat. "Give me the stupid thing."

Coop scooted the log stool with the C.B. toward Lamar, who knelt down to examine it.

Despite its age, the C.B. looked to be in good condition, with no visible evidence of warping or damage apart from the bent antenna. Lamar noticed a red mark on the outer ring of the dial and leaned in closer to study it. Someone had painted a tiny but unmistakable "E" over the ninth position of the dial with what appeared to be nail polish. After a few moments of contemplation, he concluded that it stood for "Emergency," meaning setting 9 must be the emergency frequency.

Lamar tested all of the knobs. Nothing. He turned the unit on its side to inspect the battery case. He noticed congealed white foam around the edge of the battery compartment. Lamar started to pry the cover off when a cough over his shoulder distracted him. He looked up and saw Ken staring down at him, judging him with his eyes. The others were all watching him intently as well.

Lamar had been so engrossed in his work that he hadn't noticed the others were still there. His self-consciousness went into overdrive. He found himself sweating, unable to concentrate as he wilted under their collective gaze.

"Can you all just … just … " he sputtered.

Gaby recognized the problem immediately and started to corral the others toward the wigwam to give Lamar some privacy.

"C'mon," she insisted, as she tugged on the lapel of Ken's shirt. "We've got to plan our defenses."

* * * * * *

Ken, Gaby and Coop sat in a loose-knit circle around the teepee's dormant firepit, alternating between staring at their feet and staring at each other as they tried to formulate a plan.

"I say we dig a tunnel in the side of the cliff," Ken suggested. "The one going down to the floodplain. That way we can be close to camp if anyone ever does come to rescue us, but relatively protected if Wade comes back."

"We can't dig a tunnel that fits five people in half a day," Gaby pointed out. "And any tunnel that large needs support or it'll collapse."

"We could …" Coop started, but rejected the idea before he even vocalized it. "No, never mind," he finished, sighing in frustration.

"What about this?" Ken asked, taking a tree branch and sketching out two concentric circles in the dirt. "We dig a channel around the perimeter of camp. It wouldn't have to be deep. Then we fill it with wood and leaves and set it ablaze when Wade comes. That should make him think twice."

"That should make all of us think twice," Beverly said as she opened door to the wigwam and joined the others. "Because it's a terrible idea. We'd need truckloads of wood to keep the fire high enough to scare him off."

"Nice of you to join us, Mrs. Howell," Ken intoned. "Get lost on the way to the outhouse again?"

"The name's Sutton," Beverly replied as she sat down in between Gaby and Coop, seemingly oblivious to Ken's pop culture reference. "And where I go is my business."

Ken opened his mouth to make another cutting remark, but Gaby spoke first.

"Beverly's right. The only thing your plan will do is start a forest fire," she said, erasing Ken's etchings. "We need practical solutions."

"I'm not hearing any ideas from the rest of you," Ken pointed out.

"We can't defend the whole camp," Gaby said after a moment's reflection. "It's too big, and it's accessible from every side. So let's protect what matters: this," she said, touching the interior lattice wall of the wigwam. "All of us can fit in here, there's only one entrance and we can store supplies and weapons in here. This is the prize."

Beverly and Coop nodded their agreement.

"The problem is what to reinforce it with," Coop said. "We could apply Ken's idea to the wigwam."

"A ring of fire around the building?" Beverly asked contemptuously.

"No, not that part," Coop said with a laugh, drawing an ugly look from Ken. "The trench part. We could dig a deep trench around the whole structure, one that's too wide to jump across."

"That could be dicey," Gaby said. "If the water table is too high, all we'd wind up digging is a mud puddle."

She suddenly brightened as an idea occurred to her.

"Instead of digging down, what if we build up?" Gaby suggested. "We could erect a dirt mound around the building, one that's steep from the outside but with a gradual slope on the interior."

"You think a few feet of dirt is gonna stop him?" Ken chuckled.

"It doesn't need to stop him," Gaby replied. "All it needs to do is give us an advantage. If we do it right, it'll restrict his movement without seriously hampering ours."

"And how are we going to collect all this dirt in six hours with only a spade and our hands?" Ken asked, pointing out the weak point in Gaby's plan with obvious relish.

Gaby was struggling to come up with an answer when the door to the teepee opened and Lamar appeared in the doorway.

"Any luck?" Coop asked hopefully.

Lamar shook his head.

"Not really," he answered, holding up a 9-volt battery. Half of it looked normal, if a bit weathered, but the other side was partially melted and topped with a whitish substance that resembled mold.

"The battery leaked acid into the rear compartment,"

Lamar explained, "eating through the transmission wire. I was able to switch it out for the receiving wire. That's not a big deal; we're more concerned with people hearing us than us hearing them. But without a power source, it's moot."

Ken shrugged.

"Use the batteries from your Walkman," he said dismissively.

"They're As," Lamar responded. "Different voltage, different amperage, different shape; they won't work. Same with the batteries in the flashlight."

"So, there's no chance?" Gaby asked, crestfallen at the news.

Lamar thought for a moment before answering.

"I can clean the contacts and pry them loose so we can hook them up to another power source," he said, trying to give her some semblance of hope. "But barring us finding a 9-volt battery just lying around, our only chance would be to use …" Lamar trailed off again, but not out of embarrassment this time. His eyes turned glassy and he began stroking his goatee thoughtfully.

After several long seconds, Gaby spoke up.

"Lamar, you stopped midsentence," she prodded him.

"Rechargeables," Lamar said softly, speaking more to himself than the others.

"Rechargeable what?" Coop asked.

Lamar snapped out of his daze.

"A rechargeable battery cell is smart; they're designed to work with a wide range of amperages and voltages," he explained to the others, the words tumbling out his mouth as he grew more excited by the idea. "That's why one battery can work in so many different types of phones. If we had something like that, I just might get this puppy working."

"What are you getting all excited about?" Ken jeered. "You know perfectly well John confiscated all electronics at the start of the trip. Those battery cells won't do us any good from 75 miles away."

Lamar stole a glance at Coop.

"Not all of them," he said quietly. Lamar unfastened his binary watch and held it up.

"This has a battery cell," he said. "Now, this one's too low-power for the C.B., but maybe one of you brought something with a little more juice."

He scanned the faces of the others one by one, lingering on Coop just a little too long.

"You may have brought something here powered by a battery cell and not even realized it," Lamar continued with his appeal. "Something you've packed that you forgot about. It could be something simple, like a pedometer or a smart watch. Maybe a pair of Bluetooth earbuds, or ... uhmm ... a tracking device," he said, stealing another glance at Coop, who refused to meet Lamar's gaze.

Ken folded his hands over his chest.

"Do you know something you aren't telling us?" he asked.

"Yeah," Beverly added, her eyes narrowing with suspicion. "And why do you keep looking at Coop?"

"Wha .. what?" Lamar stammered, taken aback by their reaction. "No, no, it's nothing like that. I was just ... hoping someone would come forward," he finished lamely.

The others looked far from convinced. Ken and Beverly both studied his face intently, looking for any hint of deception. Even Gaby seemed to have her doubts. Lamar didn't want to know what Coop's reaction was, because looking at him again would only confirm that he'd just lied.

Coop stood up, flustered and irritated at the implication.

"I turned in my phone, the same as the rest of you!" he huffed. "I have no idea what he's talking about!" he added before plopping down into the dirt again.

"I'm sure that's true for all of us," Gaby said to be supportive, although she did so with a noticeable lack of conviction.

An awkward silence settled over the group for several long seconds as they looked one to the other, uncertain of who to trust. Coop finally spoke up.

"Can we get back to something actually productive?" Coop asked, the aggravation evident in his voice as he tried to steer the conversation back to safer ground.

"I agree," Ken said unexpectedly. "Even if we do find another battery, we have no idea if that thing'll even work. Wade is the problem du jour. Let's focus on that."

"Fine," Lamar said, making a mental note to confront Coop later, when the others weren't around. "What have you all come up with?"

"Coop wants to build a moat around the wigwam, and Gaby wants to erect a dirt barrier around it," Beverly said.

"That's all you have to show for …" Lamar paused to consult his watch. "Forty-five minutes of work? Seriously?"

"Well, Ken wanted to burn the forest down," Beverly responded drolly. "But we considered that impractical."

"I like the idea of focusing on the teepee," Lamar said. "That makes things more manageable. But why are you all fixated on dirt?"

He looked to Gaby and Coop. Coop merely glowered at him while Gaby shrugged.

"It's the only building material we have to work with," she said.

"We have wood," Lamar replied. "Lots and lots of wood."

Ken shook his head and chuckled.

"You can't chop down trees with just a hatchet," he explained. "You'd need an army of chainsaws to do that in the time we have left."

An enigmatic smile slowly spread across Lamar's face.

"I didn't say anything about trees. And the only tools we'll need are in the shed."

The others listened carefully as Lamar outlined his plan, which they immediately embraced, as it was far more practical than the other solutions. To speed things up, they agreed to split into three teams: Gaby and Beverly would use the spade to dig a trench around the perimeter of the wigwam; Coop and Lamar would use the hammer to gather the wood; while Ken would use Gaby's pocket knife to fashion weapons for the group.

"Why am I the only one without a partner?" Ken asked, somewhat miffed.

"Because you have the best chance of surviving a one-on-one fight with Wade," Gaby explained, handing over her knife. "And because nobody wants to work with you."

As the powwow broke, Lamar and Coop headed for the shed while Gaby and Beverly moved to the eastern end of the wigwam to map out the optimal route for the trench. Ken started scouring the perimeter of the campsite for branches that would make suitable spears, while humming "I'm All

Alone."

When Coop reached the shed, Lamar was already inside, gathering an armful of canned food from the back shelf.

"Hey, why don't we start by moving everything we can use into the wigwam?" Lamar suggested.

In response, Coop slammed the shed door behind him. Lamar started as the tiny space was instantly cloaked in darkness.

"What the hell was that all about?" Coop demanded in a fierce but hushed voice. "Now everyone thinks I'm holding out on them."

"Uhmm … you are," Lamar said, nervous but unbowed. "We both know what your 'jewelry' really is. What's on your ankle could literally mean the difference between life and death for us."

"If you know what this is, then you know what'll happen if I remove it," Coop retorted.

"I know it'll be a parole violation, but …"

"No, no buts!" Coop hissed. "I am not going back to prison on your hunch. You want to find us a way out, try one that doesn't get me shivved for refusing to swear allegiance to the Aryan Brotherhood!"

"You didn't have a problem with exposure when it was my butt on the line," Lamar muttered.

"Going to prison and getting harassed by gangsters are *not* comparable!" Coop spat back. "We're talking about my life here!"

Lamar set down an armload of supplies he'd gathered to transport to the wigwam.

"No, we're talking about everyone's lives," he retorted.

"The battery powering your ankle monitor could save all of us."

Silence. Through the closed shed door, they could hear Ken calling out from the other side of the camp.

"I'm going into the forest of death now ... alone," Ken shouted to no one in particular. "My tombstone will read: 'He gave his life for wooden spears.'"

Coop still didn't respond. In the darkness, Lamar couldn't tell if Coop was wavering or if he was trying to control his emotions. He took a chance and forged ahead.

"Coop, listen, I'm doing my part, despite the risk," Lamar pressed. "Now it's your turn."

Coop exhaled slowly. Lamar was secretly relieved it was so dark, as he didn't want to see the look on Coop's face right now. He felt Coop's breath on his face as the slight man leaned in.

"Screw ... you!" he hissed and shoved the door open, temporarily blinding Lamar as he stalked out.

"Hey, Ken!" Coop shouted as he walked across the compound. "Wait a sec. I'll join you. I'm getting sick of this place, anyway," he said loudly with a backward glance of disgust at Lamar.

Lamar watched him walk off with a pang of regret before picking up the supplies again to move them to the wigwam. He was so unsettled by the exchange that it took two more trips before he noticed that the jug of moonshine was missing.

* * * * * *

Coop was traversing a wide ravine about half a mile south

of camp, searching a fallen tree near the bottom for branches suitable to weaponize. Ken sat on the edge of the ravine, overseeing him. They'd been out here for barely 90 minutes, and Coop was already regretting his decision.

For starters, Ken was surprisingly fussy about branch selection. He was the Goldilocks of the forest; every branch Coop found was too thin or too thick, too long or too short. And all of them needed to be perfectly straight. Additionally, Coop's inability to locate the perfect branch was making Ken more dickish than usual.

"Hey, Butthole Buddha, you find anything?" Ken called from above.

Coop pulled a candidate branch from a pile of leaves, hoisting it over his head so Ken could see it.

"How about this one?"

"Looks flimsy," Ken responded. "Can you snap it in two?"

Coop gripped it firmly on either end and pressed his knee against it. After a few seconds of exertion, the branch cracked.

"That's what I thought," Ken crowed. "One hard thrust and it'll snap. It needs to be thicker."

After searching several more minutes in vain, Coop climbed out of the ravine and rejoined Ken at the top. Ken was busy whittling four branches he'd deemed satisfactory, all found by him, of course. He tested the sharpened tip of one with his palm and smiled.

"I think this one is just about ready for Wade's face," he said, setting it on the ground beside him. "One more good one should do it."

Coop smiled thinly.

"And how much longer will it take to find that last one?"

"If you were pulling your weight around here, we'd have found it a long time ago," Ken replied snidely. He pointed to a cluster of ash trees in the distance ringed by a chest-high thicket of brambles. "You haven't checked over there yet. Ash branches are usually sturdy."

He tossed the newly fashioned spear at Coop, who caught it with a grunt of surprise.

"For reference," Ken explained as he held another spear level with his eye to check its balance. "Since you don't seem to know what a decent spear looks like. And who knows? Maybe you'll find a bird or deer. Then you can take it for a test drive."

"I don't want to kill anything," Coop declared obstinately. "I just want to protect myself."

Ken stopped studying the spear point just long enough to roll his eyes.

"Have you always been a pantywaist?" he asked. "Or did it come with your decision to start dining on dick?"

Coop snorted in annoyance and looked away, trying to find the right words.

"Why are you so convinced I'm gay?" he finally asked.

Ken made a face like it was the most ridiculous question he'd ever heard.

"You mean, apart from the fact that you don't deny it? How about because I have working gaydar," he said, tapping his temple. "Hey, don't get me wrong: I don't have anything against homos. It doesn't mean shit to me if you take it up the ass."

"Then why do you keep bringing it up?" Coop insisted,

growing heated.

Ken stopped whittling and looked him in the eye.

"Because I want to know what kind of man is fighting beside me," he said. "Are you willing to kill to survive? Or will you drop to your knees at the first hint of trouble and blow Wade in exchange for your miserable life?"

Coop seethed with resentment. His grip on the spear tightened.

"I'm no coward," he said through gritted teeth.

"Then prove it!" Ken shouted. "Go out there and find us another spear or kill something with that one. Just don't come back empty handed."

Coop stalked off for the ash grove with his blood boiling at the affront to his pride. Questioning his sexuality was one thing; questioning his manhood was something altogether different.

As he approached the grove, Coop entertained visions of Ken prostrating himself, humbled by Coop's skill after single-handedly defeating Wade.

Even with his blood up, Coop still had enough presence of mind to make for the thinnest section of brambles, which formed a wide ring around the oak grove that extended at least 15 feet. He pushed through the hedge, ignoring the thorns tugging at his robes and skin. He held the spear in front of him to force a path through the brambles. On the other side, Coop found nine ash trees at various stages of development, clustered together in a space about half the size of a tennis court.

Coop wended his way among the trees, hunting for suitable low-hanging branches, occasionally stopping to compare candidates to the spear in his hand. As he searched, he noticed that the wild grass beneath his sandals was thinning out the further he walked. The trees themselves seemed to change, with the ones at the front of the grove vibrant and in full leafage, while the ones further back seemed wilted, with fewer leaves and smaller canopies, as though each step brought him closer to winter. The leaf count on the ground started to decrease, and eventually only a handful of shriveled leaves appeared on the ground, alongside blighted grasses that highlighted the discolored dirt, which had taken on a chalk-like coloration.

At the back of the grove Coop found a single dead ash sapling. At its base was a fine line of a grayish powder, whose snaking tendrils extended into the brambles at the back of the grove and out of sight. Near the edge of the thicket he saw two more of these spiraling "arms": one several feet to the right of the main one, which extended in a semicircular pattern several feet into the grove before disappearing back into the thicket. The other one started several feet to the left of the main one, and only reached a foot into the grove before ending in a fine point. The three tendrils collectively formed a swirling, pinwheel shape, one drawn with an unnatural level of precision.

Everything within the powder's radius was dead: plants, grasses and trees alike. In the center of the spiral pattern was a dead squirrel. Its forepaws extended skyward while its haunches were splayed out to either side.

Coop stopped at the edge of the powdery trail as though there were an invisible barrier preventing him from continuing. His machismo-fueled anger from earlier had dissipated, replaced initially by curiosity and now by concern. Whatever this substance was, Coop instinctively knew not to touch it.

He poked his spear at the furthest extension of the substance — right at the base of the dead sapling — to test it. The grayish powder smeared black against the pasty dirt, just like ash from a fire.

After wiping the tip of his spear clean, Coop plucked up his courage, stepped as close to the substance as he dared and leaned forward to peek over the thicket, hoping to locate the source.

A voice in the distance stopped him.

"Hey, rump ranger!" Ken shouted. "What's taking so long?"

The memory of Ken's earlier insults reignited Coop's anger, and he pulled back from the edge of the substance, determined to complete his mission and shut Ken's big mouth once and for all.

Looking around, he couldn't see any spear-worthy branches on the ground or hanging from the trees. He suddenly remembered the second part of Ken's challenge. He looked back at the dead squirrel. It must have died recently, as there were no flies or maggots on it; in fact, Coop had neither seen nor heard any animals since stepping into the grove. There was no visible damage to it, but its tiny body looked desiccated as though its squirrel buddies had mummified it. Coop leaned forward to jab it with his spear tip while still avoiding the powdery substance. The spear pierced its body easily, and Coop hoisted it aloft and started back the way he came. He felt strangely proud as if he'd killed the squirrel himself.

Ken chided Coop as he saw him reemerge from the thicket.

"What, did you stop to take a piss?"

"No," Coop said as he drew closer, holding the spear aloft. "I got us dinner."

"No shit?" Ken exclaimed, studying the tiny body dangling from the spear tip.

"Man, that's one butt-ugly squirrel!" he declared. "And you found it in there?"

"Yeah, it was just … gathering nuts and stuff. I snuck up on it and … BAM!" Coop lied. "It never knew what hit it."

"All right!" Ken said, clapping Coop on the back hard enough that he nearly knocked him over. "So you finally popped your cherry. Maybe you're not so useless, after all!"

Coop basked in Ken's armchair accolades, even as he recognized how hollow they were. It felt good, even for a moment, to be accepted into the world of real men.

By the time the two arrived back in camp, some 40 minutes' worth of Ken's increasingly vulgar and misogynistic stories had completely cured him of that feeling.

* * * * * *

Gaby and Beverly were making good progress. It had been slow going at first — given that they only had one single garden spade between them — but in the past two hours they'd managed to dig a two-foot-deep trench around the front and the left side of the teepee, and had moved on to the right. They figured out after some trial and error that the most efficient way to approach it was to have Beverly do a first pass with the garden spade, breaking up the soil and digging a crude trench, while Gaby would come in behind her to deepen and straighten it out with her bare hands.

They made a good team, too, although Beverly had some frustrating habits that grated on Gaby the longer they worked together.

As if on cue, Beverly suddenly stopped digging to examine her spade hand.

"Damn, another nail broke," she said with an exaggerated sigh of regret before eventually returning to work.

That was the first problem: complaining. Beverly complained about anything and everything, turning insignificant issues into cases for martyrdom. After the first few times, Gaby had reminded her exactly what was at stake for all of them. Now she didn't even bother. It wasn't that Beverly had forgotten; she simply needed to complain the same way others need oxygen.

As Gaby made her first pass on an untouched patch of dirt, Lamar came by with an armload of timber.

"Coming up behind you," he called out as he passed, before dumping the lumber in an unceremonious heap on the edge of the trench. He paused to catch his breath, resting one palm on the hammer hanging from his belt loop as he mopped his brow with a corner of his T-shirt. His actions exposed his sweaty belly — which overhung his pants — to Beverly, who looked away in disgust. After a few more gasps of air, Lamar staggered back to the shed to collect more wood.

"Ughh!" Beverly said when he was out of earshot. "Every time that Lamar passes by, I have to suppress my gag reflex."

Gaby paused her digging to look back at Beverly with a raised eyebrow, trying to decide if she should be offended or not.

Beverly registered the meaning of her stare and reciprocated with a look of mild annoyance.

"I didn't mean it *that* way," she said. "I'm talking about his odor. He smells like Pig-Pen looks."

Gaby took her meaning and covered her mouth to stifle a laugh.

"I don't think hygiene is Lamar's top priority," she said before returning to work.

"I doubt it's even in his top 10," Beverly deadpanned. She watched Gaby work for a moment before getting up and dusting herself off.

"Where are you going?" Gaby asked.

"I need a break," Beverly insisted.

And here was the second problem: Beverly was constantly taking breaks. If it weren't for those, they'd probably have finished the job already.

"But we took one 20 minutes ago," Gaby protested.

"I'm not as young as you," Beverly reminded her. "Besides, I need to take my ... medicine," she said cryptically, staring off into the floodplain.

Gaby noticed that the older woman was pale and fidgety.

"Can you at least wait until we finish this section?" Gaby asked, but Beverly was already walking away, muttering something under her breath.

"S ... A ... L ... T ... S ... A ... L ... T," she said quietly to herself as she walked. Gaby watched, confused, as Beverly walked past the shower down to the floodplain, rather than to the wigwam, which would be a more logical place to store pharmaceuticals, since it held everyone's luggage, including Beverly's.

As Gaby watched her leave, Lamar came by with another load of lumber.

"I haven't gotten this much exercise since middle school," he said with a laugh as he dropped the lumber on the ground. He noticed that Gaby didn't respond. "Is everything okay?"

"That's her third break in the last hour," Gaby replied.

Lamar misinterpreted her remark as a condemnation.

"Well, even with that, you two seem to be moving at a good clip," he said cheerily.

"That's not the point," Gaby insisted, the concern now evident in her voice. "She's acting strange."

Gaby stood up and stretched her back.

"I wonder if it's that salt thing," she said, still staring at the showers even though Beverly was long since out of view.

Lamar looked at her, puzzled.

"Salty?" he asked. "Like, she's pissed off?"

Gaby shook her head.

"She spelled it out — S-A-L-T — like it was some kind of acronym. She did it once when we were looking in the shed and again just now. Any clue what it means?"

Lamar stroked his goatee as he thought.

"Nothing that fits," he said after a few moments of reflection. "The only SALT I know is a list of triggers: Stress, Anger, Loneliness, Tiredness."

Gaby tried to absorb this.

"Triggers for what?" she asked.

"For relapsing," Lamar explained. "Alcohol, drugs and other addictions. They use it in 12-step programs as a reminder of what triggers to avoid when on the wagon. My father used it like a mantra on bad days."

"You think Beverly is an addict?" Gaby asked, slightly alarmed at the prospect.

"Addicts go to 28-day programs, not on wilderness retreats," Lamar said with a shake of his head. "I have no idea what it means to her."

Beverly returned several minutes later, looking more herself and appearing in better spirits.

"All right, let's finish this," she said, rolling up her sleeves as she strode past the central firepit. In contrast with her high-strung demeanor not five minutes ago, Beverly now seemed at ease and more confident. Gaby started to hope that the older woman — despite her obvious distaste for roughing it — was finally adapting to her circumstances. That's when she noticed that Beverly was about to walk right into one of the wooden stools surrounding the firepit.

Gaby called out to warn her, but didn't get further than "Beverly!" before the older woman caught the stool in the shins and fell flat on her face.

Gaby and Lamar ran over to check on her. Beverly raised her head, dazed.

"What in the hell was that?" she asked as they helped her to her feet. She seemed disoriented, and was unsteady on her feet. Lamar supported Beverly as Gaby looked the older woman over.

Fortunately, Beverly seemed to have come away from her tumble with nothing worse than a bruised shin and a skinned palm from when she landed. Beverly laughed it off, insisting that she was fine.

"There's no need to make a fuss over me," she said. "I just need to watch where I'm going next time."

Despite her protestations, Beverly still seemed dazed. When Gaby asked if she wanted to lie down again, Beverly gave her answer to Lamar. The two exchanged glances but said nothing.

Beverly insisted on returning to work and jumped back into her role with gusto, picking up the spade and quickly extending the trench. After a few moments of consideration, a worried Gaby joined her.

Lamar went back to the shed for more wood, puzzled by Beverly's behavior. It was only later that he remembered the missing moonshine and started to question his earlier assessment.

* * * * * *

It was late afternoon before Ken and Coop returned, only to find a camp that looked very different from the one they'd left. The trench was complete, most of the wood had been salvaged and the others were already working on the fortifications.

"Hollleeey shit!" Ken exclaimed, marveling at how much had changed in such a short span of time. "This place is almost unrecognizable."

Gaby, who was reinforcing the fortifications around the wigwam, stopped hammering and waved the two over.

"I see you all kept busy," Coop remarked, equally impressed by the others' work.

"We've been expecting you for a while now," Gaby said, pausing to rub her aching shoulders.

Ken walked over to help out when Beverly's head peeked out from behind the fortifications.

"Where have you all been?" she groused. "We'd be done now if it weren't for you!"

"Careful," Ken said with a smirk as he yanked Coop's spear right out of his hands and raised it so everyone could see the squirrel impaled on its tip. "Complainers don't get squirrel for their supper."

Gaby and Lamar — who was coming over with another armful of timber — oohed and aahed at the accomplishment. It wasn't that they needed the food; it just made the forest and its inhabitants seem a little less insurmountable. Perhaps they *could* overcome their perilous circumstances. Beverly, however, sniffed at the kill.

"Good, then I can go right on complaining," she replied, disgusted at the sight of a corpse dangling from the stick.

The others quickly crowded around Ken for a closer look at tonight's dinner.

"How'd you manage it?" Gaby asked him.

"Well, actually it was ..." Coop began before Ken cut him off.

"It was easy to find," Ken interrupted. "It was just sitting there in this mess of brambles. One thrust was all it took," he said, omitting who exactly did the finding and thrusting.

"We can cook it later," Gaby said. "For now, we could use your help building this thing," she said, motioning to their construction project. "Both of you," she said with a reassuring smile to Coop, who was beginning to feel marginalized.

"Sure thing," Ken said, dumping the squirrel in a pail on the grill to cook later.

"I'll help Lamar with the wood," Coop said, drawing an askance look from Lamar, who had been pointedly ignoring Coop since his return. Lamar walked off without waiting for Coop, who followed quickly behind.

"Hey," Coop said when the others were out of earshot. "Can we talk for a second?"

Lamar just kept walking.

"I'm sorry about earlier," Coop said, trying to keep pace. "I didn't mean to lash out at you like that."

"Uh-huh," Lamar intoned.

"You're pissed," Coop said. "I get it. But you put me in a real bind there."

"You don't say," Lamar responded coldly as he continued walking.

"Will you just talk to me already?" Coop asked, grabbing Lamar by the shoulder to stop him.

Lamar wheeled around to confront him. His eyes were hard and distant, his jaw clenched tight.

"This isn't about an apology!" Lamar whispered fiercely. "No amount of 'sorry' is going to get us out of here alive. You want to make things right? You know what you have to do."

Lamar turned his back to him and started quietly gathering timber as Coop considered his demands in silence.

Lamar had collected an armload of timber and was starting to walk away when Coop finally caved.

"All right," he said reluctantly. "I'll do it."

Lamar turned slowly around. His expression was warmer now, but cautious, like a drowning man being offered a life preserver filled with explosives.

"No fooling?" Lamar asked. "Because if you renege ..."

"You can have the battery," Coop said. "But on one condition: you can't tell the others where it came from."

Lamar nodded his acceptance.

"I have an idea on how to handle that," he said. "Just out of curiosity, what changed your mind?"

"Two hours alone with Ken," Coop deadpanned, eliciting a small chuckle from Lamar. "By the end of it, prison was starting to sound downright inviting by comparison."

"Hey, are you two on a break or what?" Ken shouted from the top of the fortification. "Quit sucking each others' dicks and help out already."

Lamar and Coop shared an eye roll before returning to work.

* * * * * *

Two hours of backbreaking labor later, the fortifications were complete. The end result wasn't pretty, but in the group's exhausted eyes, it was the greatest thing ever constructed. More importantly, it was functional.

The sun had dipped low in the sky and was casting its brightest rays near the edge of the horizon as the group prepared dinner. To Beverly, it looked like a final, defiant gasp before the sun expired; a fitting simile considering what they were about to face, but one that left her cold.

Ken had skinned and spitted the squirrel, which he was holding over the flames of the firepit with one of his newly fashioned spears.

Coop was passing out cans of beef Stroganoff and spaghetti to the hungry crew while Lamar raised his shirt to wipe his forehead, treating everyone to a view of his paunch. Beverly chose a log stool downwind of him and immediately changed seats after a faint breeze carried his scent over to her.

"So, you two just found it out in the woods?" Gaby marveled.

"Actually, just past the archery range," Lamar said, lowering his shirt. He motioned to Coop, who held up the battery cell for the others to see. "It was in a pedometer half-buried in the dirt."

"I would have stepped on it if Lamar hadn't spotted it," Coop chimed in before tucking the battery into a pocket in the folds of his robes.

"So then where's the pedometer?" Ken asked, his tone registering suspicion at this alleged stroke of luck.

"Well, uhmm ... it was busted, so we kinda just left it there," Lamar trailed off, finding the direction of the conversation uncomfortable.

"And you have no idea how it got there?" Ken pressed.

"I don't know, maybe one of the previous groups that came here left it," Coop responded, irritated by Ken's grilling.

"Maybe," Ken said, unconvinced.

"I'll work on it later," Lamar said as he polished off a can of unheated spaghetti with an appreciative belch. "Just remember that this might not work. Low-voltage batteries like this were never meant to power something as large as a C.B."

Lamar dropped the empty can at his feet and wiped his

hands on his shirt, smearing the front of it with spaghetti sauce.

"Ugh," Beverly exclaimed in disgust. "Do you really have to do that?"

"Do what?" Lamar asked, mystified.

"You have the table manners of a Viking," Beverly scolded him. "At least have the decency to wash your hands before wiping them on your shirt. You still have stains from last night's beef stew on there!"

Lamar looked down to discover a brownish smear over the left breast of his shirt, several inches away from the marinara stain, meaning he'd forgotten to change T-shirts this morning. He blushed and looked away in embarrassment.

"Cut him some slack," Gaby said with a yawn. "We have bigger concerns than getting Lamar into finishing school."

Ken, who wasn't listening to any of this, pulled his squirrel out of the fire and examined it closely, turning the spear over to ensure it was equally charred on all sides.

"Looks about right," he said. "So, who wants the honor of the first bite?"

He extended the spear to Coop, who quickly declined.

"All you, man," he said.

Ken looked to Beverly next, who emphatically shook her head no.

He then extended the spear toward Lamar.

"Big man," he said coaxingly. "I know you want a bite."

"No way!" Lamar said, turning his face away.

Ken turned to Gaby next. She considered it for a moment and then shrugged.

"What the hell," she said, taking the spear from Ken. She examined the crispy critter up close. Its skin was completely blackened, with cracks in the skin revealing the meat beneath. She sniffed it and had to admit it smelled tantalizing.

She took a cautious nibble from the back flank.

A blissful smile crossed her face as the charred skin touched her tongue. As she started to chew, that smile rapidly turned into one of shock and revulsion.

"Bllegghh!" Gaby exclaimed as she spit the food into her hand and started wiping her tongue on her sleeve, desperate to get the taste out of her mouth. "That thing is inedible!" she finally declared. "Where the hell did you find this thing, Ken?"

"What?" Ken asked, suddenly defensive. "Don't blame me! It was the Queen of Sheba who found it," he insisted, pointing an accusatory finger at Coop.

Remembering all too well Ken's eagerness to claim credit for the kill, Coop quickly rounded on him.

"Ken just overcooked it, is all," he said.

"It's fine and I'll prove it," Ken said, reclaiming the spear-kebab. "She's just being a prima donna."

Ken took a healthy bite from one of the rear legs to illustrate his point.

"See?" he said through a mouthful of squirrel meat. "It's perfectly ..."

He shuddered, made a face like he'd bitten into the sourest of lemons, and spat the remains into the fire.

"What the fuck?" he exclaimed as he reached for the pail of drinking water and upended it into his mouth. Coop couldn't help but smile as Ken swished the water around in his mouth to sweep up every last trace of the food before spitting it on the ground behind him.

"It tastes like ... soot!" he finally explained, and Gaby quickly nodded at the description.

Ken stood up and rushed into the wigwam. When he emerged a minute later, he had two cans of beef stew in his hands. He sat down, opened one, and immediately started chowing down.

"Hey, you already had the spaghetti for dinner!" Beverly complained.

"Palate cleanser," Ken said between mouthfuls of stew. "If you'd tasted that fucking squirrel, you'd be doing the same.

"Be that as it may, we don't have an infinite food supply," Coop pointed out. "We need to ration it."

"I agree," Gaby joined in, after washing the taste out of her own mouth with the last dregs of the drinking pail. "*People* can't just take food as they please," she said, looking squarely at Ken.

"Let's appoint someone to keep track of the food," Beverly joined in. "Someone to pass it out at mealtime and safeguard it the rest of the time, to make certain nobody steals it."

"Makes sense," Lamar said.

"Who should it be?" Coop asked.

"Someone trustworthy," Lamar replied.

Gaby smiled.

"I'm glad you think so, Lamar, because I'm nominating you," she said.

Lamar started at this.

"Wha ... what, me?" he stammered, genuinely surprised.

Coop quickly seconded Gaby's selection, followed a few moments later by an indifferent Beverly. Ken, however, merely chortled.

"You want *that* to guard the food?" he said, his voice dripping with disdain as he pointed toward Lamar's pronounced gut. "You people are a hoot! That's like giving O.J. the keys to the knife drawer."

"Says the guy who just ate two cans," Coop said.

Ken reared up in his seat to intimidate Coop, but Lamar spoke up before Ken could say anything truly cutting.

"Look, I don't really want this, but if you all trust me, I'll do it," Lamar said a tone of resignation. "And Ken, if you don't trust me ..."

"If?" Ken asked mockingly.

"...Then you'll know who to blame if any of the food goes missing," Lamar continued, speaking as though Ken hadn't interrupted.

Ken considered this for a moment.

"Fine," he said. "On your own head, be it."

When dinner was finished and the sun neared the horizon, the group started mapping out their battle plans. If Wade followed his usual pattern, he'd arrive from the southwest around sundown, which gave them precious little time to prepare.

Ken laid out the plan, which was simple enough: they'd wait until Wade entered the camp, at which point Gaby would give the signal and they'd all rush out with their spears from designated hiding spots and close ranks on Wade.

Gaby would be hiding in a maple tree on the southwestern edge of the site to block his retreat. Ken would be hiding in a slightly larger ash tree about 20 feet away to block off Wade's access to the southern edge of camp. Coop would be hiding behind the Squaws' outhouse to block off access to the eastern edge of the camp, while Lamar and Beverly would be hiding behind the fortifications around the wigwam. They would rush out to block off the northern and northwestern sections of camp.

Then they'd all close in, spears at the ready, and order Wade out of camp. Critically, the group would intentionally leave a gap in their circle to the west — leading down into the floodplains — to drive him out of camp.

"After all, the goal is to scare him away, not kill him," Ken explained.

The beauty of the plan, which Ken repeated often and loudly, was that it still worked even if Wade didn't come in from the southwest. The spacing of the hiding places enabled the group to adapt on the fly if he came in from the south or the west.

"Whaddya think?" Ken asked with a self-satisfied smile.

The others had to admit that, Ken's self-congratulations aside, it sounded like a solid plan. They agreed to conduct a few practice runs to get a feel for how things would go. Coop passed out spears to everyone, but since there were only four, he had to make do with the small hatchet. Lamar consoled him by pointing out that this wasn't a serious problem because he'd be the last to close in on Wade, owing to his far-flung location.

While Gaby kept an eye out for Wade from her perch in

the maple tree, Ken drilled the others, barking out instructions like a drill sergeant as they practiced charging at one of the log stools — a stand-in for Wade — placed at various points to the southern, western and southwestern sections of camp. While the others normally would have balked at Ken's militant drilling, they all recognized how high the stakes were; one mistake or miscommunication could cost them dearly. So for a rare change, they listened and followed instructions.

The trick, Ken assured them, was to let Wade walk 10 to 15 feet into camp before springing into action; that way, he be far enough in that Gaby would be able to prevent him from beating an immediate retreat, but still close enough to the edge that they could drive him westward with minimal effort.

After four run-throughs, Ken was satisfied that they had the pattern down. Everyone got into position to wait for Wade's arrival.

* * * * * *

Coop was getting anxious. It was now dusk, and the light was fading fast. He was already straining to see farther than 20 feet and worried that their carefully laid plans would be for naught if Wade waited until dark to return.

He also was less than pleased about hiding behind the Squaws' outhouse. It wasn't the smell so much — a rural upbringing had exposed him to plenty of unsavory odors — it was the three-foot drainage ditch behind it, which he had to straddle to remain hidden. Maintaining such an unnaturally wide stance had gone from amusing to uncomfortable as the minutes ticked away, and was now verging on painful.

Even though he wasn't supposed to, Coop occasionally snuck a peek around the right edge of the outhouse to see if anything was happening, if only to break up the tedium and take his mind off his barking quads. Still no sign of Wade.

Coop mulled his assignment. He'd been given the farthest post from the front lines: stationed on the eastern edge of camp while all the action would be on the southwestern end of camp. While this was an enormous relief, as Coop detested violence, some tiny, primal part of his brain railed at this perceived insult to his masculinity.

In preparation for the upcoming skirmish, he'd cut a foot of cloth from the bottom of his robes to make running to the other side of camp easier. It's not like he needed them to be that long anymore, now that his ankle monitor was lying in a gully a quarter of a mile away.

Coop tried to calm his mind by silently mouthing his mantra as he stared across the eastern expanse of the forest, watching a cluster of rhododendron bushes in the darkening distance swaying gently in the breeze. He noticed some of the leaves seemed to be reflecting the rays of the sun setting in the west. He squinted his eyes, wondering why dry leaves would cast such vibrant reflections from 30 feet away. The bushes suddenly began to shake, moving rapidly and erratically, as though the light breeze had suddenly turned into a squall. Except the wind hadn't shifted at all.

An arm bearing a long hunting knife emerged from the bushes, the blade catching and reflecting the light. A moment later, the rest of Wade emerged from the bushes.

He'd fashioned the fox fur into a Davey Crocket-style cap,

with the tail swaying to and fro as he walked. A dead beaver dangled from the belt loop of his jeans, which were in tatters below the knees, like he'd been hiking through a forest of thorns. He'd carved a fifth scar into his bare chest, one that crossed through the other four diagonally, making them bleed anew. And his eyes burned with a savage purposefulness that eclipsed the setting sun.

Coop felt his mouth go dry. His screaming quads were suddenly drowned out by a tidal wave of cold, irrational fear as Wade stalked toward the camp from the wrong direction.

"Whyisheherewhyisheherewhyishehere?" Coop's mind shrieked at a million miles an hour as his pulse skyrocketed. His hands started to tremble uncontrollably. "Howdidhegethereheshouldbeontheotherendofcamp!"

Wade stopped suddenly as he spied all the changes to the campsite.

The Braves' outhouse was gone; the only evidence it ever existed was the raised baseboard with its one hole cut out, which had been covered with a rock. Every other timber was gone. So too was the storage shed across from it. Aside from the concrete foundation, it had simply ceased to exist.

All of that lumber had gone into a new structure: a seven-foot fence that surrounded the teepee on three sides. Boards had been planted vertically in the ground, reinforced at the top and bottom with horizontal crossbeams to form a crude but effective barrier. The boards were not all uniform in length or grain, nor were they all perfectly placed, lending the structure a ramshackle look. There was a narrow gap at the front — one granting easy access to the teepee's door — that was just wide enough for one person to squeeze through. The tin roof that had once covered the shed now sat atop this makeshift entrance.

The only section of the wigwam not fenced off was the backside, which had a small shelf of land on either side before the ground plunged downhill a dozen feet. A row of foot-long wooden spikes had been planted at the rim of the shelf to discourage anyone from climbing up.

Wade stared at the setup for a few moments, his impressions clouded by his inscrutable expression and grimly clenched jaw. As he scanned the area, his eyes at last came to rest on Coop, who still hadn't moved from his hiding spot. Wade's eyes zeroed in on the hatchet in Coop's hands and narrowed menacingly as he strode forward, knife in hand.

Coop watched as Wade closed in. He couldn't move; no matter what his brain shouted to his legs, they stood stock still. He opened his mouth to scream but the words refused to come out. The hatchet he had been holding fell from his trembling fingers into the drainage ditch, narrowly missing his right foot. Coop didn't even notice.

Wade's stride widened and his pace quickened. When he was 15 feet away from Coop, he raised his blade menacingly and charged forward.

Seeing the knife pointed at him finally broke Coop's paralysis. He pressed his back up against the rear wall of the outhouse, and the words started tumbling out of his mouth.

"Helphe'shereWade'scominghelpsomebodyanybodyhelpme!"

* * * * * *

Lamar watched the sky slowly darken from his hiding

place behind the fence, a few feet to the left of the narrow entrance. He rocked back and forth on his heels, trying to stave off boredom. To the right of the entrance was Beverly, who was sitting with her back to the fence as she traced patterns in the dirt with her spear tip. Ken had demanded that nobody talk to avoid distraction, leaving the pair little to do except stare off into space, replaying his instructions in their minds as they waited.

At Gaby's signal, Lamar and Beverly would charge out from their hiding spots, spears pointed upward to avoid accidentally skewering each other. Ken had also insisted after a couple of dry runs that Beverly be the first out of the gate — which by design was too narrow to accommodate two people at once — because she was slower and needed more time to reach her mark than Lamar.

He was fine with that; it made sense, after all. But the lack of anything to do as the minutes slowly ticked by grated on him. He found himself checking his watch every few minutes, just to have something to do. If Wade was planning to show, he was certainly taking his sweet time with it.

Wailing.

Lamar heard a strange, high-pitched shriek from the eastern end of camp. He looked over at Beverly, who seemed just as confused as he was. He had just enough time to wonder if it was some kind of exotic animal call before the pitch went up and he realized two things: it was a human voice, and it belonged to Coop.

Panicking, Lamar charged blindly at the entrance, not even pausing long enough to look where he was going. In his haste, he'd forgotten Ken's instructions, and realized it too late as he raised his head and saw Beverly running to the gate at the same time. The look of shock and confusion on her face came too late for either of them to stop. The pair collided headfirst with a sickening thud.

* * * * * *

Gaby heard a strange noise in the distance. It was hard to pinpoint where it was coming from, and even harder to determine what it was. She looked all around from her perch in the boughs of an old maple tree near the southwestern outskirts of camp. Nothing. She looked to Ken, who had a better vantage point in a large ash tree just south of her. Judging by his expression, he'd heard the sound too. He scanned his sector of the camp and shook his head no at her.

Several seconds later there was a crashing noise by the fence line. Now Gaby was getting seriously worried. A moment later, Lamar stumbled out of the gap in the fence, holding his head. He appeared dazed and took a few moments to find his spear before charging toward the outhouse. Beverly was right behind him, clutching her shoulder and running in the same direction.

Gaby threw her spear to the ground and grabbed hold of a sturdy branch by her feet, using it to lower herself to a safe falling distance. Something must have gone wrong. Gaby just hoped she'd arrive in time to prevent a total catastrophe.

As she hit the ground and tucked into a crouch to absorb the impact, she saw Ken leap from his perch some 20 feet in the air. Gaby located her spear and bolted toward the outhouse. Behind her, Ken cried out as he landed. Gaby was so preoccupied with what was happening on the other side of camp that she scarcely registered it.

* * * * * *

"OhmyGodhe'sgoingtokillmepleasesomebodysto-phim!" Coop shrieked as Wade lunged at him with the hunting knife. He couldn't hear anything over the ringing in his ears, feel anything apart from the pressure expelled by his screaming lungs and see anything except for the glinting tip of the blade as it sped toward his midsection. Coop's entire world shrunk down to the edge of that knife. A single thought echoed in his mind as it rushed toward him, moving impossibly fast.

"I want to live."

Coop twisted to his left and the blade grazed him, snagging his robes before embedding itself in the rear wall of the outhouse. Coop tried to tear his clothing loose, but Wade pinned him to the wall with his free hand. Frighteningly strong fingers bit cruelly into Coop's shoulder. Rancid breath assaulted his nostrils.

Coop clawed ineffectually at the face of his much larger assailant, trying desperately to distract him as Wade struggled to work the knife free. Wade's free hand moved from Coop's shoulder to his throat. He located the windpipe and clamped down, like a lion suffocating its prey. Coop gasped for breath and started convulsing.

In a hazy vision he saw Lamar rush down Wade and thrust at him with a wooden spear. Wade pulled his knife free just in time to sidestep Lamar's thrust. Coop spasmed as he gasped for air, his lungs burning, his mind feverish. He fell to his knees and lay panting against the outhouse wall, only dimly aware of what was happening around him.

Lamar was shouting something as he stood between them. Coop couldn't make out what. He collapsed just as Beverly arrived.

* * * * * *

"Coop, are you okay?" Lamar shouted as he held Wade at bay, jabbing the spear repeatedly in his direction. "Coop?" He wanted to look back to see if Coop was still alive, but knew full well what would happen if he took his eyes off Wade for even a moment.

Wade stalked back and forth just outside of Lamar's range, his knife hand at the ready. In the fading light, Lamar could see that Wade's eyes seethed with rage, but his face betrayed a hint of confusion as well, like a wolf suddenly finding itself challenged by the sheep.

Out of the corner of his eye, Lamar saw something rush up from his left. He flinched reflexively, but it turned out to be Beverly, who stood shoulder to shoulder with him, leveling her spear at Wade's chest.

Lamar had never been more scared in his life. He struggled to keep his spear tip from shaking as he trained it on a man with both the means and the motive to murder all of them. Beverly, on the other hand, seemed to almost relish the chance at revenge, taunting Wade with her spear.

"Come on!" she challenged him, thrusting the spear at him. "Try choking me now, you son of a bitch!"

While Lamar's spear pokes had been hesitant, serving

only as a warning, Beverly meant business. She leaned into each thrust, trying to skewer Wade.

He didn't respond to her provocations. Instead he seemed to be watching her movements intensely. As she unleashed another thrust closer than ever, Wade lunged forward and grabbed the spear just below the tip. He yanked hard on it as Beverly tried to pull it back. A momentary tug-of-war broke out before Beverly lost her grip, falling on her butt as Wade wrenched it from her grasp. She watched it sail through the air behind him, landing against a tree some 20 feet away.

Deprived of her weapon and lying prone on the ground, Beverly's bloodlust quickly evaporated. The look on Wade's sunburned face was truly chilling. He looked at her like she was his next meal, and the tiniest hint of a sadistic smile emerged. She started scooting desperately back, using her feet to propel her as she struggled to escape.

Before Wade could make a move, however, Gaby joined their ranks, running in from the right side of the outhouse. She saw Wade and started momentarily but kept her composure. She lowered her spear until it was pointed at Wade's throat and then shuffled to her left to stand shoulder to shoulder with Lamar, forming a human wall around Coop's prone form.

Ken limped over a few seconds later, leaning on his spear like a walking stick and favoring his right leg. He stopped beside Gaby and quickly joined the wall formation.

Wade watched them with a primal fury, sizing them up as though he was about to pounce at any given moment. His jawline quivered not with fear, but barely contained, animalistic savagery.

The others kept their eyes locked on Wade, too scared to look at one another for direction. Nobody spoke. Wade continued pacing back and forth, just outside of range.

"Somebody say something," Gaby hissed.

That was when it struck them: they'd spent so much time practicing how to corner Wade, they'd never considered what to say once they did.

"W ... wade," Lamar fumbled, nervous and unprepared. "We order you ... uhm ..." he trailed off, uncertain where to take it from here.

"You're banned," Ken said, backing him up. "Don't come back again. Because if you do ..."

Ken swallowed hard and steeled himself.

"If you do ... we'll kill you."

Wade didn't respond. He continued staring at them, unmoving and unblinking, long enough for more than one of them to wonder if he even understood their words anymore. The fire shimmering in his eyes was mesmerizing, even as they narrowed to dangerous slits. He kept the point of his blade trained on the group.

Ken prepared to issue his ultimatum again when Wade's eyes suddenly went wide and his mouth opened. And out it came.

"GGGGRRAAAWWWWHHHHH!!!"

The veins in his neck bulged as the deafening roar burst forth from his wiry frame. Gaby and Lamar reflexively winced at the noise, but kept their spears aimed at him. The primal shout of the apex predator echoed through the trees, a warning to all within earshot.

Wade backed slowly away from them, his blade still raised. His eyes shifted rapidly from side to side, scanning them for any hint of a threatening motion. When he was 30 feet away, he turned around and stalked off into the forest.

Lamar tried to calm himself. His heart was pounding like a trip hammer, and his breath was coming in ragged gasps borne of pure fear. When Wade was out of sight he dropped his spear to check on Coop. Coop's glasses had slipped off his face in the melee. He was unconscious but breathing. He appeared unhurt except for some bruising around the throat and the tear in his robes.

Gaby and Ken continued staring in Wade's direction long after he was out of sight, still trying to process what they'd just experienced.

"What was that?" Gaby asked breathlessly.

Ken lowered his spear and inhaled sharply.

"A war cry."

The words hung in the air, looming over them like the rapidly expanding shadows. Gaby exhaled and realized it was cold enough to see her breath. She marveled at this, because she was sweating so profusely. That sweat quickly turned cold when Lamar asked a chilling question.

"Where's Beverly?"

They looked around and realized they hadn't seen her since she'd lost her spear. A quick check of the camp and a few shouted calls of her name yielded nothing. Beverly was gone.

* * * * * *

Ken nailed an empty can to the interior wall of the fence, just to the right of the entrance. He handed the hammer to a dubious Gaby, who tentatively rapped on the hollow can. It made a surprisingly loud clatter that could heard all the way across camp.

"Okay, if you're on sentry duty and you see Wade coming, don't challenge him," Ken said. "Hit this with the hammer to wake the rest of us up and then fall back to the teepee. That way, if he wants to fight us, he has to come in, where it'll be five on one."

"Couldn't he just set the wigwam on fire?" Gaby asked.

"No," Lamar answered. "Remember how John told us the plastic sheeting was fire resistant? The animal furs on the outside will burn, but the sheeting should hold up. If Wade wants us dead, he'll have to come in here to do it."

"How're you coming on those traps, Lamar?"

Lamar held up three empty cans connected by the plastic cording that they'd used earlier as a clothesline.

"I'll set these up between some trees," Lamar explained, pulling the cord tight to demonstrate. "If Wade tries to sneak into camp ..." Lamar flicked the cord and the cans immediately started jangling and clanking against one another, producing a terrific racket.

"We also have this," Lamar said, dropping the cans and holding up a leftover plank of wood. He'd embedded several nails in the underside that gleamed wickedly in the pale moonlight. Gaby shuddered to think what would happen if she stepped on one.

"I'll set a few of these up at the main access points to camp: the entrance, the path down to the floodplain and behind the woodpile. Then we can search for Beverly."

"Good," Ken said, appearing genuinely impressed by what Lamar had rigged together. "Just be certain everyone sees where you're placing them. The last thing any of us needs is tetanus."

"Now, before we go out looking for her, remember the rules," Ken instructed them. "From here on out, no one goes out unarmed, and no one goes out alone. You plan to use the outhouse? Take a friend. And above all, know where everyone else is at all times. Remember: we're on war footing."

They cautiously filed out of the fence line one at a time. Gaby and Ken formed a perimeter while waiting for Lamar and Coop to join them. Coop carried Lamar's spear for him, as he had his hands full with the traps. The moon was waxing full, which made seeing in the dark easier, although passing clouds would intermittently blot out the light.

Lamar headed over to the woodpile to lay the first trap, accompanied by Coop, while Gaby and Ken kept watch. Lamar noted how quiet and downcast Coop seemed, even when factoring in their present circumstances.

"Hey, you okay?" Lamar whispered to him.

Coop didn't even answer. He still seemed shaken by his experience from an hour earlier.

"It's not your fault, you know," Lamar said, trying to comfort him.

Coop shook his head.

"It is," he said quietly. "I just … froze, like a deer in headlights. I didn't even try to fight him. I just stood there like an idiot. I'm afraid the same thing will happen again."

Lamar hid the trap in some thigh-high grass between the woodpile and the outhouse. He motioned to Ken and Gaby so they saw where he'd placed it. They nodded in response. He then stood up and did his best to give Coop a reassuring smile.

"Now that you know what you did wrong, you can work to overcome it," he said. "So the next time you face him, you'll be prepared."

Coop looked skeptical and said nothing, but he was less mopey as they went around the rest of camp setting up traps. Lamar was tying off the cans on a string between two large poplar trees when they heard a noise in the darkness. Something large had crashed through nearby bushes, judging from the sound. Lamar hastily stepped back. Everyone held their spears at the ready.

"Who's there?" Ken shouted.

No response, but they continued to hear leaves shaking in the bushes. The sound was getting closer.

"Identify yourself!"

Still no response. The rustling noises grew louder, more frantic. A cloud passed overhead, blotting out the moonlight and preventing the group from seeing anything outside of the camp.

"Maybe it's Beverly," Coop said hesitantly, even as he took two steps backward.

"Maybe it's Wade," Ken replied, and stepped back himself.

Ken was about to bark his command again when the rustling suddenly stopped and a shape emerged from the forest. It staggered toward them. They could see tiny puffs of warm breath floating in front of it in the chill night air.

"Halt!" Ken barked, taking another step back. "Identify yourself!"

The moon peeked out from behind the clouds, and there in the ghostly moonlight was Beverly. She had branches and leaves sticking out of her hair. Her eyes looked glassy, as though she were in a daze. Her head bobbed unsteadily from side to side. Her eyes focused on Ken, and she held up her middle finger with a triumphant smile on her face.

"Identishfy this!" she said, slurring her words.

"Oh, thank God!" Gaby exclaimed, pressing her hand against her chest in relief.

Beverly staggered toward them, lurching from side to side as she drew closer.

"Beverly, are you OK?" Lamar asked, concerned about her behavior.

"Never better," she replied with a lazy wave of her hand.

As she staggered closer, the others could see a jug in her hand. The moonshine that had gone missing from the shed. Judging from the lack of sloshing noises it made as she swayed, it must have been nearly empty.

"She's drunk," Coop said contemptuously.

Beverly laughed, and the reek of her breath confirmed Coop's suspicions.

"Ash a skunk!" Beverly chimed in. "You would be too if you faced that maniac and his knife," she added, apparently forgetting that the others had been right there beside her.

"Beverly, we were worried sick about you!" Gaby scolded as she drew closer. "We were about to go out looking for you."

Beverly held Gaby at arm's length as she made an odd face.

"Don't mention sick," she said before doubling over and violently expelling her dinner at the others' feet.

"Charming," Ken intoned, stepping back in revulsion. "Madmen and winos at every turn. Let's clean her up and get her inside."

* * * * * *

Coop pried the jug out of Beverly's grasp as Lamar and Gaby tried to get her to lie still long enough to remove her shoes and jacket. She was squirming, resisting, like a little child at bedtime.

"Let's call it a night, Beverly," Gaby said as she tried to hold the older woman's legs still.

"Pfffhhtt!" Beverly said with a wave of her hand that clipped Lamar in the nose. "I don't need to sleep. I feel fiiiiine!"

Coop uncorked the jug and peered inside. As he'd feared, there were only dregs left.

"That thing was full this morning, wasn't it?" Lamar asked as he tried to work Beverly's right arm free from her down jacket.

Coop nodded.

"It was strong stuff, too," he said. "At least 100 proof, maybe more."

"How's she still conscious, then?" Gaby asked as she struggled to unlace Beverly's boots.

"No normal person can drink that much," Coop insisted as he tossed the near-empty jug in the corner and made his way to his own sleeping bag. "It takes years of alcohol abuse to build up that kind of tolerance. I lost a sister to it; toward the end, she was downing a fifth every night."

Ken snorted.

"So now we know what you really are," he chided Beverly. "Despite all your pretension, you're just a garden-variety lush."

"You know, it all shtarted with Graham, my second husband," Beverly said as Lamar pushed her head back onto the sleeping bag. "He wash an animal, always … pawing at me," she said, miming paws with her hands to illustrate the point. "Whenever he was in the mood, I'd insist on a glass of wine first, just to take the edge off."

"We do not want to hear about your sex life, granny!" Ken insisted, thoroughly nauseated. Beverly kept right on going.

"He was gone within a few yearsh, but the wine … Oh, that wine!" she said, rolling her head from side to side as she talked. "A drink before lunch, then two with dinner. I started going on tasting tours every weekend. The guides began to recognize me. Shooooo embarrassing!" she added with a pronounced roll of the "O's" that sent spittle everywhere.

"Then a friend introduced me to gin. All the fun of wine, but so … much … fashter. Wine tasting became trips to distilleries. Thingsh got really out of control with my third marriage. Preston, he was so uptight. Shave the whales, my ass! Sanctimonious little prick! It got to the point where I couldn't even look at him without being squiffed. Speaking of hish little prick …"

"Can someone please shut her up?" Ken asked loudly.

Lamar put his hand lightly over her mouth, careful not to cover her nose. Beverly kept right on talking under it.

"Brewh brer shusht vhbtot gwregh bwersh," came her muffled voice.

"Thank you," Ken said.

"She's spitting all over my hand," Lamar complained.

"Okay, who wants first shift for guard duty, now that Beverly's out of the picture?" Ken asked, eager to move on.

Nobody answered. Gaby was going through her bag for a change of clothes while Coop was sitting on his sleeping bag, staring wistfully at a wallet-sized photo.

"Coop, stop looking at your mini-issue of Playgirl," Ken said to get his attention. "Are you up for taking first shift?"

"No way," Coop said, stowing the photo in his wallet once more. "I'm not taking it on just because she got liquored up."

Lamar finally couldn't take it and removed his hand to wipe off all the spittle. Beverly's babbling suddenly filled the wigwam.

"So after the crash, I shee the judge," she said. "Biiiig stern look on his fat face. He says: 'Twenty-eight days at Life Rescue Rehab or one week of Mystic Tours.' And I couldn't do another stint with those Bible-thumping rehabbers. What would you do? I ashk you, what would you do?"

Ken immediately rounded on Lamar.

"What gives?" he asked. "I thought you were handling her."

"I have a low tolerance for drool," Lamar said as he wiped his hand on the outside of his sleeping bag.

Ken shook his head.

"Can you handle guard duty?"

"After everything today, I can barely keep my eyes open," Lamar said. "I'd fall asleep as soon as I stepped outside."

"Everybody hatesh me," Beverly bitterly declared. "My

daughter won't return my calls. My friends don't visit any-more. Even you all don't want me around. You all think I'm useless, don't you?"

"No argument here," Ken intoned.

"Hey!" Beverly exclaimed, pointing a finger skyward. "I'll remember that."

"I doubt you'll remember much of anything when you wake up," Gaby joked.

"She may not wake up at all," Coop cautioned quietly as he settled into his sleeping bag. "There's a real chance she has alcohol poisoning."

"Are you people talking about me?" Beverly asked, indig-nant in the way only a confused drunk can be. "Come shay that stuff to my face."

"Not without a bag of breath mints, first," Ken muttered. "How about you, Gaby? Think you're up for first shift?"

Before Gaby could reply, Beverly gave a cryptic chortle.

"You want *her* to protect us?" Beverly laughed, her eyes closed as she thrashed in her sleeping bag in the throes of exaggerated laughter. "Oh, that's richhhh! Looks like I know something you don't."

Ken rolled his eyes.

"Enlighten us, oh pickled one," Ken said sardonically.

"She can't even protect hershelf," Beverly said. "She lets her boyfriend beat her. Don't believe me? Her body ish one giant bruise! That's why she always covers up."

Beverly started cackling to herself as Ken, Lamar and Coop stared in silent disbelief. The older woman's laughter slowly faded away as she began to nod off. The others looked at Gaby, who turned scarlet with outrage and mortal embarrassment. She opened and closed her mouth several times, struggling to form the right words.

"You ... bitch!" she finally exploded, balling her fists and charging toward Beverly.

"No way, Jose-ella!" Ken said, jumping between them with his arms outstretched. "I don't have a lot of rules about violence, but hitting a sleeping drunk is *not* cool."

Gaby seethed for several seconds, her lower lip quivering as she struggled to maintain control, before turning on her heels and stalking wordlessly out of the wigwam.

Coop lay back in his sleeping bag.

"I guess Gaby's taking first watch."

Lamar slipped on his headphones and tuned out the world. For several minutes, the only sound in the wigwam was Beverly's light snoring. Coop finally broke the silence.

"Is it just me, or are the crickets getting louder?"

"What crickets? Ken asked, mildly irritated, as he'd just closed his eyes.

"Listen."

Ken strained to hear. He finally picked up a faint chirping sound in the distance.

"I hear something, but it's not crickets," Ken said.

"How do you know?" Coop challenged him.

"Because it's mid-October. Crickets die after the first freeze."

"Then what's that noise?"

"Dunno," Ken said with a shrug of indifference as he rolled onto his side and closed his eyes. "But it's not crickets."

* * * * * *

Pain-Pressure-Urgency-Awake

Beverly opened her eyes reluctantly. Every muscle in her body ached. Her head felt like it had been invaded by hordes of angry Black Friday shoppers, all of them shoving, pushing and screaming for attention.

The wigwam was pitch-black. It was still night. She could hear the rhythmic inhalations and exhalations of the others fast asleep in the teepee.

She woozily raised herself up to one arm and immediately felt herself overwhelmed by four sensations, each more acute than the last. Her hazy thought process told her she was still drunk, something she would have welcomed if not for the difficulty it presented in handling the other sensations. She also awoke to a nasty crick in her neck from passing out with her head at an angle and her neck unsupported. She reflexively reached up to massage her neck, a motion that alerted her to a more serious concern: the bile roiling her stomach urgently needed to be released. But the most pressing message came from her bladder, which was screaming at her for release.

Beverly couldn't sit up without immediately peeing her pants and vomiting all over herself, so she rolled out of her unzipped sleeping bag and pushed upward with unsteady hands and feet until she was in a crouching position. She rose cautiously, trying to find her balance, and then lurched toward the entrance, nearly tripping over Ken in the process. She found herself outside in the moonlight staring at the fencing surrounding the teepee.

While she welcomed the option for something to lean

on while staggering to the bathroom, she couldn't understand why someone had replaced the camp with a fence. She looked off to her right and saw Gaby curled up into a ball against the fence, a blanket wrapped around her to stave off the night's chill. Why on earth was she sleeping out here? Beverly felt a pang of regret as she looked at Gaby, though she didn't quite understand it.

Her other needs were more urgent, so Beverly shook the cobwebs out of her head and stumbled her way toward the gap in the fence.

The camp was still there, although it looked strange in the moonlight, like someone had strategically rearranged portions of it. She just hoped no one had moved the outhouses. She headed in what she guessed was the right direction and trusted to luck.

Beverly quickly found herself on the outskirts of the camp. Someone had replaced the outhouses with the shower. How rude! She was just about to complain when she saw something at her feet twinkle in the moonlight. She bent over to look but leaned forward too far, nearly falling over in the process. She struggled to make sense out of what she was seeing as her head swayed to and fro. After a moment's examination she concluded that it was a wooden board, with the twinkling coming from four exposed nails in it. How careless of her companions! That could hurt someone. She made a mental note to give the others a firm talking to when she returned.

Beverly woozily sidestepped the plank and blundered her way into the forest.

The air was cold on her face as she lurched forward in

search of the missing outhouse. The forest was filled with an incessant chirping sound all around. The crickets must certainly be busy tonight. Beverly stopped in front of an old oak tree and looked around, trying to get her bearings. She didn't recognize anything in the dark. She wasn't even certain which way the camp was. The fear that thought sparked tightened her gut, which was the final straw for her poor stomach. The pressure on it became overwhelming, and she leaned against the tree for support as she vomited up the last remnants of dinner.

She felt slightly better when she was done, although her throat burned and her stomach ached from the exertion. The relief only heightened her sense of bladder pressure. Looking desperately around, she didn't see the missing outhouse, but did find some waist-high bushes that would do. She staggered toward them, squirming with discomfort and holding her crotch as she did so. She found a suitable spot, lowered her jeans, crouched down and let nature do its work.

The feeling of release was overwhelming, causing her to sigh with relief. The pressure on her bladder slowly subsided and Beverly started to feel more herself again. After wiping with some nearby leaves and pulling her jeans back up, Beverly made her best guess at where the camp stood — assuming someone hadn't moved it along with the outhouses — and stumbled forward, leaning on the many trees lining the route as she went. She noted hazily that the chirping sound was growing louder the further she walked.

A cloud passed in front of the moon and the light vanished. Beverly blundered forward in the dark, worried she'd catch her foot on an exposed tree root or find another carelessly placed wooden board with nails in it. That would certainly be unpleasant. The ground felt strangely uneven beneath her feet.

The cloud passed and the moonlight slowly returned. Beverly saw she was walking along the edge of a 20-foot drop into the floodplains, with her left foot only partially on solid ground. No wonder the ground felt uneven! She leaned back and took a few cautious steps away from the precipice. Clearly she'd taken a wrong turn somewhere. Next time, she'd ask for better directions.

The floodplain looked magical in the moonlight. Instead of the usual trees, scrub plants and grasses, Beverly instead paused to marvel at something new that had swept the floodplain. A black, teeming mass that seemed to absorb rather than reflect the moonlight blanketed the floodplain in darkness, blotting out any signs of plant or animal life. The heaving blob of unlight extended as far as Beverly could see, seething and rolling like the sea in a storm. More unnervingly, the center of the giant mass expanded and contracted at regular intervals, almost like it was breathing. On the periphery, it undulated in a chaotic dance of conflict as it lashed the base of the overlook with its inky tendrils as though it were trying to topple the plateau. Beverly knelt down and saw the bands of darkness nearest the edge leaping in the air, dozens at a time, as though they were desperate to meet her.

Out of curiosity, Beverly snapped a branch from the tree she was leaning against and tossed it into the floodplain. It sailed through the air, spinning end over end. When the branch reached the black ooze, the substance immediately parted before it like the Red Sea, leaving the branch to land on a small rock outcropping with a ringing clank. The mass swirled around the stick, its tendrils testing the branch, prodding it cautiously. Each of them was small, no larger than a ferret, but they were closer in shape to a gerbil, rounded and blob-like, with no visible appendages. They seemed to move by wriggling, undulating their torsos to and fro. And they all seemed to move independently, even as they collectively surged and swelled. Confident that the branch posed no threat, the inky darkness once again consumed the rock outcropping and the branch with it.

That's when it dawned on Beverly that this black mass wasn't a single object. It was some kind of swarm, like an ant colony; one numbering in the billions. Beverly watched them undulate a little longer before staggering her way back to camp. Her final thought before passing out was that she had to locate the nearest payphone and call National Geographic to report her amazing discovery.

TUESDAY

Lamar tightened the last screw on the C.B.'s outer chassis with the pocket knife before setting it aside to admire his handiwork.

The C.B. looked more or less normal, except the side panel that would normally house the batteries had been removed and now dangled free, connected to the unit's base by a tangled mess of wires and coiled cable, giving it the appearance of a mutant appendage. Nestled within the center of the panel was the battery cell that he'd scavenged from Coop's ankle monitor, fastened to a cannibalized circuit board by plastic wrap and four multipronged transistors. The battery contacts for the C.B. had been removed from their housings, bent into more-or-less rounded shapes and mounted onto the top and bottom of the power cell.

The only part of the unit Lamar had left alone was the retractable antenna, which was bent so badly that he feared trying to straighten it would snap it clean off.

Lamar placed the device and its odd appendage on one of the log stools surrounding the firepit and nervously looked over at Coop and Ken, who were standing just to his right and watching intently. Lamar said a silent prayer and tried the volume knob.

After several excruciating seconds, a low-frequency hum

emanated from the box, and the transmission window on the faceplate flickered on. The needle measuring signal strength started to slowly climb.

"It's working!" Lamar exclaimed in an awed whisper. "It's really working!"

Ken and Coop both leaned in, eager to see the ancient device in action. Several yards behind them, Gaby was quietly washing yesterday's clothes in one of the pails. She stole occasional glances over at the others, curious about their success with the device, but said nothing. In fact, Gaby had been avoiding them all morning. Anytime her eyes met theirs, she would instantly look away. All of them understood, even Ken. After last night's humiliation at Beverly's hands, Gaby was deeply uncomfortable around anyone who knew her terrible secret. Lamar and Coop had agreed to give her as much time and space as she needed, an approach that Ken seemed to have picked up instinctively.

As the trio looked with wonder at the functional C.B., Ken leaned forward and rapped appreciatively on the top of the unit, as if congratulating it for working after all these years. The transmission window light suddenly flickered again and went dark. The humming noise disappeared, and the needle dropped down to 0. Coop gave him an ugly glance and was about to upbraid him when the device flickered back to life just as suddenly as it had died, only to peter out again after 20 seconds.

Lamar turned the device off with a huff and tested the power cell with the pad of his index finger. It was warm to the touch.

"Why's it keep cutting in and out?" Coop asked.

"I think the battery's overheating," Lamar replied. "The C.B. requires a lot more juice than this is designed to deliver, so it stresses the power cell."

"Can't you do anything to solve that?" Ken asked.

Lamar shook his head.

"We're fitting a round peg into a square hole, and no amount of MacGyvering will change that," Lamar explained. "Intermittent power is the best we can hope for."

"A C.B. that shuts off mid-transmission isn't very practical," Ken replied, the annoyance evident in his voice. "How was this anything other than a waste of time?"

Ken had been insufferable all morning, and his attitude was beginning to grate on the others, even more so than usual. His domineering attitude had made more sense last night, when their lives were on the line; indeed, his militant insistence on repeated drilling before confronting Wade had probably saved their lives. But now that the danger had passed, he showed no signs of letting up. If anything, his Patton routine had deepened.

"A slim chance is better than no chance," Lamar countered. "We'll just have to make every word count." He stood up and stretched, trying to work out a kink in his neck after spending the past hour hunched over a log stool while building his Frankenstein machine. He raised his arms over his head as he stretched, giving Ken and Coop a good whiff of body odor, causing both to involuntarily step back and turn their heads from the stench.

"Here's what I think we should do," he continued, not seeing Ken and Coop's pained responses as he finally lowered his arms. "Let's set it up on the highest peak around to give us better broadcasting range and just hope the battery holds out."

"Any idea how long that'll be?" Coop asked, his head still turned away from Lamar as the stench gradually faded.

"No clue," Lamar replied. "It depends on how much of a charge the battery has left. What I do know is the C.B. will drain it fast. We could get an hour of use or 10 minutes. I suppose it's really a blessing that it can only transmit now. If it was receiving, too, that would double the battery consumption."

"Say what?" Ken asked, too shocked by this revelation to bother insulting Lamar about his poor hygiene. "Are you telling me we won't hear any replies?"

"The leaking battery ate through the receiving wire," Lamar reminded him. "And I 'borrowed' the receiver's circuit board to hold the battery in place," Lamar explained. "So, yes, that means one-way communication only."

Ken chuckled and shook his head in disbelief.

"For fuck's sake! This just gets better and better," he exclaimed.

Lamar ignored his sarcasm.

"So, who wants to give it a go?" he asked, hoisting the C.B.

"I'll do it," a voice behind them said. The trio turned and saw Gaby wringing her wet clothes out after washing them. It was the first thing she'd said all day. She squirmed under the group's gaze but didn't break eye contact this time.

Lamar smiled warmly at the overture. Gaby slowly, hesitantly, responded in kind.

"I'll come with you," Ken said.

Gaby's small smile instantly disappeared.

"No," she replied, now beginning to regret volunteering.

"It wasn't a suggestion," Ken said.

"I could really use some alone time, Ken," Gaby intoned, making her displeasure clear.

"Nobody goes out alone, nobody goes out unarmed," Ken reminded her, motioning to the spear in his hand. "My strategy kept everyone alive yesterday, and it'll keep working so long as everyone abides by it."

"You're not Napoleon, and this isn't Waterloo," Gaby shot back, balking at the demand. "We scared away one guy."

"I think Napoleon lost at Waterloo," Lamar chimed in.

"That's not the point!" Gaby snapped. "Ken's strategy barely held together, and now he thinks he's some military genius. You trade stock!"

"I run a Fortune 500 company," Ken corrected her with an air of self-satisfaction. "I have day traders to do the buying and selling."

Gaby looked to Lamar and Coop for support, but could read in their faces that none would be forthcoming.

"Gaby, I can't believe I'm saying this, but Ken's right," Coop said, sounding almost embarrassed. "Safety comes first."

Lamar nodded his agreement.

"What if one of you comes with me, instead?" Gaby asked, now resorting to bargaining.

Ken scoffed at the idea.

"Coop's scared of his own shadow, and Lamar would collapse before making it halfway up the ridge," he said with a sneer. "Face it: it has to be me."

"Fine," Gaby said with a sigh of resignation. "I'll consider it."

"You do that," Ken said. "But before that, there's something else we need to address."

Lamar looked at Ken, confused. As far as he knew, everything was settled.

"What?" he queried.

"You," Ken replied, glaring at Lamar. "You're coming with us."

"Us?" Lamar responded, confused and quickly growing alarmed.

Ken nodded to someone behind Lamar. Two hands clamped onto his right arm from behind, immobilizing it. It was Coop, and his face was grim.

"What the ..." Lamar began to protest but stopped when Ken seized his other arm and locked it in place with powerful fingers that dug into his flesh.

Lamar started struggling, but the two held fast. He was now genuinely frightened.

"Guys, this isn't funny!" he insisted. "What are you doing? Let me go!" he shouted, flailing and kicking ineffectually as the two started dragging him toward the western side of camp.

Lamar felt the pit of his stomach drop as he saw Ken and Coop share a knowing look together. Had these two been plotting against him all this time?

Several yards away, Gaby stopped laying her clothes out to dry on the low-lying branches of a beech tree.

"What are you doing to him?" she asked, her voice rising in alarm.

"What needs to be done," Ken said coldly, his voice deadly

serious as they dragged Lamar to the shower and stopped.

Coop opened the shower's cabana door and reached in.

Lamar squeezed his eyes shut, unwilling to see what hellish torment Coop and Ken had secreted away in the shower as they plotted his demise.

"Coop, I don't know what you're thinking, but let's talk about it!" Lamar pleaded.

"You can't talk your way out of this," Coop replied severely.

Lamar gulped in anticipation. He opened one of his eyes a crack and could see Gaby in the distance, dropping her clothes back in the water pail and rushing over to stop Ken and Coop. But it was too late. Coop slowly withdrew his arm and revealed his instrument of torture.

A bar of Irish Spring.

Lamar stared, confused for a moment. Then Ken reached for the waistband of Lamar's sweatpants and yanked them down.

"Strip him!" Ken ordered, and Coop obliged by grabbing the collar of Lamar's T-shirt, trying to pull it over his head. Lamar finally realized what they were trying to do and struggled even harder.

"Get off me! Knock it off!" he demanded.

But it was two on one, and Lamar quickly found himself standing only in his underwear, shivering in the chill morning air and doing his best to cover himself. He snuck a glance over at Gaby, who was now standing a few feet away. She was covering her mouth to disguise her amusement, which only added to Lamar's mortification.

"Okay, He Who Shall Not Be Laid. Insy-winsy," Ken said.

Lamar shook his head no, so Ken shoved him inside and blocked the door while Coop ran to the back of the stall to prime the pump.

"Ready?" Ken called out after a few moments.

"Ready!" Coop replied from the other end of the stall.

Ken hit the button in the shower. Cold water immediately streamed out of the spout head, causing Lamar to scream like a little girl. Ken grabbed the bar of soap and started scrubbing Lamar's rolls of belly fat.

"I can do it myself!" Lamar insisted.

"You had three days to do it yourself," Coop countered as he joined Ken in blocking the door, a savage smile plastered on his face. "We've had enough of your B.O. to last several lifetimes!"

"Mouseketeers don't do this to one another!" Lamar lamented.

"Make sure to scrub his pits," Gaby instructed Ken. "It smells like something died up there."

Lamar stared at her in disbelief.

"Et tu, Gaby?"

"Mouseketeers bathe more than once a week!" she countered with a smile.

"This is unnecessary," Lamar wailed.

"This is *very* necessary," Ken said as he moved on to Lamar's pits, turning his head to the side to avoid the foul reek.

* * * * * *

About 30 minutes later, Coop was cutting thin strips of plastic from the remains of the archery target, while Ken hovered over him doing what he did best: micromanaging.

"No, I said 'thinner'! We want them to focus on the bait, not the line!" Ken chided him.

Coop closed his eyes and prayed for patience.

"I can't get it any thinner," he explained after a moment. "If I cut any deeper, I'll sever the cord."

Ken leaned in.

"You poncey types are supposed to be good with your fingers. If all those hairdressers named 'Dante' and 'Raoul' can do it, so can you. Now make it thinner!"

Just as Coop was about to unload on Ken, he noticed Lamar emerge from the wigwam, fully dressed but still shivering as he dried his hair.

"Feel any better?" Coop asked, grateful for the company of anyone other than Ken.

In answer, Lamar raised the left sleeve of his shirt to reveal a bluish bruise forming on the lower half of his bicep, where Ken had grasped him.

"Don't expect a Purple Heart," Ken said dismissively as he took a break from berating Coop to whittle a crude wooden hook. It was a six-inch spike, pointed at both ends and curved toward the center to hold whatever it came in contact with in place. It was primitive but functional.

"Are you all going fishing?" Lamar asked as he drew closer and saw what they were both working on.

"If we're stuck in these woods until Saturday, I'm going to make the most of it," Ken said, not looking up from his carving. "I'm taking Coop up to the lake to try our hand at fishing, and you're joining us."

He handed Lamar his spear, which had already been fashioned into a fishing pole, with a 15-foot line tied just below the tip and an even cruder wooden hook on the end.

"What's the 411 on Madam Margarita?" asked, pointing to the wigwam so there was no doubt who he meant.

"Still out like a light," Lamar replied, looking over his primitive fishing gear. Judging by the ragged cut of the plastic line and the double knotting on both ends, his was the prototype.

The trio had just finished converting the last of the spears into poles when Gaby exited the sole remaining outhouse. When she saw them jerry-rigging the spears, Gaby walked over for a closer look, vacillating between amusement and bemusement.

"Care to join us for a little fishing?" Coop offered.

"Not a chance," she said with a chuckle as Lamar fashioned dried apricots into bait, spearing two on each end of the primitive hooks. "Tell me you're not fishing with dried foods."

Lamar and Coop both looked again at the apricots dangling from hooks, trying to decide why Gaby was so down on them as bait. Ken, on the other hand, responded with characteristic bluster.

"Yeah, so?" he challenged. "What do you know about fishing?"

"I know dried foods won't attract any fish," Gaby replied, covering her mouth to hide her amusement. "They hunt by scent. Use the canned beef Stroganoff."

Coop liked the suggestion and started to fetch some when a barked command from Ken stopped him in his tracks.

"Hold it," Ken demanded. "Who's in charge here, her or me?"

"Nobody's in charge," Coop replied coolly, with only a hint of his irritation seeping through. "And she has a good point," he added before leaving to fetch the canned food.

Lamar noticed that Ken's face was turning a distinct shade of purple as he silently seethed at Coop's insubordination. He hurriedly steered the conversation in another direction.

"So, what are your plans this morning?" he asked Gaby.

Gaby, who also registered Ken's wrath but seemed altogether indifferent to it, shrugged.

"Figured I'd chop some wood, maybe work on the fortifications a little."

"Would you mind keeping an eye on Beverly while you're at it?" Lamar asked.

Gaby immediately stiffened.

"I'd say there's no chance of that."

"It's only to keep her from wandering off again," Lamar pleaded. "I'm not saying you need to make up with her, if you could just ..."

Lamar trailed off as he spied Coop exiting the teepee with a can of beef Stroganoff in one hand and Beverly in the other. Coop had his left arm around Beverly as he escorted her gingerly over to the others. Her head weaved unsteadily from side to side, and her feet shuffled as she struggled to keep pace with him. She looked pale and badly hungover as she squinted and turned her face away from the sun's rays.

"Well, speak of the devil," Ken intoned.

"Incarnate," Gaby muttered, her expression instantly darkening.

"Look who's awake," Coop said cheerily. "Thought I'd

bring her by to say 'hello.'"

"How long was I out?" Beverly croaked in a voice barely above a whisper. She attempted a feeble smile.

"You mean, 'How long was I drying out?'" Ken responded, crossing his arms defiantly.

Beverly did her best to glare at him, but between her squinting and her parched lips, the best she could manage was an Elvis-esque half-sneer.

"We don't know how long you were out because you wandered off in the middle of the night," Coop explained as he held her steady. "Ken found you passed out by the showers just after dawn. You're lucky you didn't get hypothermia."

Beverly didn't appear particularly surprised by this revelation.

"I had a dream about walking in the moonlight," she said hazily, wrinkling her nose as she struggled to remember what else was in the dream. It was something really important.

"The only thing you were dreaming about was pink elephants," Ken replied with a snort.

"So I tied one on last night," Beverly said with a dismissive wave.

"Beverly, you downed the entire jug. It's a wonder you didn't need your stomach pumped," Coop said emphatically and a little too loud for Beverly's comfort, causing her to wince in pain and pull away.

"Can you lower your voice, please? My head is killing me," she begged as she removed Coop's arm from her shoulder and took a step back, determined to stand on her own power. She wobbled unsteadily for a moment but soon found her balance.

"Well, if your head doesn't finish the job, I know someone who wants to," Ken offered, making no attempt to hide his amusement at her suffering.

Beverly finally noticed Gaby glaring daggers at her.

"What's the matter, Gaby?"

Instead of answering Beverly directly, Gaby turned on her heels and addressed the whole group. Loudly.

"I have work to do!" she yelled before storming off to the other side of the fortifications.

Beverly winced in pain, covering her ears with her hands and waiting several seconds before cautiously removing them.

"Was it something I said?" she asked earnestly.

"And how," Ken snickered.

"Don't you remember?" Lamar asked her, not even trying to hide his surprise.

"You all keep alluding to something, so out with it!" Beverly demanded, her confusion turning to irritation as it became increasingly clear that everyone knew something she didn't. "What did I do that was so terrible?"

"Oh, it's not what I did, darling, but what I said," Ken responded mockingly in an exaggerated version of Beverly's posh New York accent, fanning himself with his hand as though he were some genteel socialite. "I relayed the most awful gossip about Gabriella of the Muffington clan at last night's polo match! Can you believe a lady of her pedigree keeps running into her husband's fists, again and again? It's simply ghastly! Now, be a dear and pour me another mint julep."

Beverly's eyes shot open in horror.

"I didn't."

"You did," Coop assured her. Lamar nodded affirmatively as well.

"Oh, God," Beverly replied, covering her mouth in shock. "So much of the evening is a blur. I remember fragments. I talked about rehab, and … I didn't describe anything personal, did I?"

"That depends. Does your sex life count?" Ken replied with obvious relish.

Beverly's face turned several different shades of red and purple as she wrestled with warring emotions. She sputtered, trying to find the right words as humiliation slowly won out over anger.

"If … if you tell anybody about this, I'll … I'll …" she stammered, trying to regain her composure.

"I'm gonna stop you right there," Ken said, talking over her. "You're not in any position to dictate. You want to buy our silence? Then keep an eye on Little Miss Green Card while we're fishing. She seems to be doing a lone-wolf number this morning."

"It should only be for a few hours," Lamar chipped in, eager to lessen the blow.

"I don't think she wants to talk to me," Beverly said quietly.

"Who said anything about talking?" Ken replied. "She's your responsibility. And teaching these clowns how to fish is mine."

Ken stood up and nudged Coop to follow him as he headed

for the floodplain.

"You didn't have to be so hard on her," Coop chided him as they walked.

"Mind your own business, Dharma Chameleon," Ken snapped.

Lamar stood up and silently mouthed the word "sorry" to Beverly before running to join the others. Just as they were walking past the shower, Lamar stopped and turned, flashing her a hopeful thumbs up. She didn't respond.

Beverly stared off in the distance, feeling spent. Apart from the shock of last night's indiscretions, she was struggling with a 10-ton hangover and the realization that she'd done irreparable harm to her relationship with Gaby. And she expected to spend all afternoon trying — and failing — to make it up to her. Beverly closed her eyes and steeled herself for what must come next.

On the other side of the fortifications, she could hear chopping noises. Beverly peered around the fence line and found Gaby splitting logs by the woodpile. Her swings were wild and erratic. Beverly suspected it was her face Gaby projected onto each log as she swung the hatchet.

Gaby heard Beverly approaching and looked over her shoulder. Her already stormy demeanor visibly darkened. She turned away and resumed chopping logs with renewed ferocity.

"Mind if I join you?" Beverly asked timidly.

"It's a free country," Gaby replied coldly, her back still turned.

"Gaby, I understand that last night, I may have … said certain things," Beverly started awkwardly. "I just want you to know ..."

Gaby suddenly dropped the hatchet while it was still buried in a log.

"Excuse me," Gaby said as she spun on her heel and stalked off.

After a few moments of hesitation, Beverly followed her, walking along the edge of the fence line and to the beech tree on the other side of camp, where Gaby had hung her clothes to dry.

She found Gaby checking her clothes, feeling them to see which were damp, but it was clear she was agitated. Her touches became pokes before escalating into finger stabs.

Beverly felt the bottom of her stomach drop out. She hated confrontation. But she hated open wounds more. She clenched her fists in resolve and strode forward.

Gaby spied her approach and flashed a look of disgust.

"What do you want?" she asked coldly.

"I just want to talk," Beverly pleaded.

"You did plenty of that last night," Gaby spat at her as she selected a green turtleneck and a pair of acid-washed jeans.

Gaby ripped the clothes from the low-hanging tree limb, sending a cream-colored blouse and a pair of socks flying. She charged toward the wigwam but hesitated a moment, not wanting to leave the rest of her clothes on the ground. Seizing the opportunity, Beverly started collecting them for her. Gaby threw up her hands in disgust and stalked off to the wigwam.

Beverly refused to give up, and after gathering the scattered clothes, took a deep breath before entering the wigwam. She found Gaby haphazardly stuffing the clothes and a couple of cans of food into her backpack.

Gaby's eyes flashed a warning to Beverly as she entered.

"Why are you following me?" she demanded.

Beverly held up the clothes in front of her as both an explanation and a peace offering. She laid the clothes down on Gaby's suitcase and slowly backed away.

"I know you're angry at me," Beverly tried again. "I wish I could take it back. I don't know what to say to make things right."

"Then don't say anything," she replied.

Gaby pulled a canteen from her pack and dipped it in the drinking bucket. She stowed it in her backpack and zipped the bag closed.

Beverly was growing concerned. Not only was Gaby acting out, she appeared to be packing for a journey.

"Where are you going?" Beverly asked hesitantly.

Instead of responding, Gaby slung the backpack over her shoulders, stood up and pushed past the older woman.

Beverly grabbed her by the wrist.

"If we could just talk for a moment. I want to ..."

Gaby tensed up like a live wire at Beverly's touch and pulled her arm free as if it had been dipped in boiling acid. Beverly remembered Gaby's phobia about human contact and instantly regretted her decision.

"How dare you, you bitch!" Gaby exploded, finally unleashing all of her pent-up hostility. "I trusted you! But you just had to open your big mouth and tell everyone about it! Do you have any idea how small that made me feel?"

"Gaby, I'm ..." Beverly started, hanging her head in contrition, when Gaby cut her off with a hard slap to the face. Beverly saw stars momentarily and caressed her wounded cheek as she stared at Gaby in shock.

"Don't you ever speak to me again!" Gaby shouted as tears welled up in the corner of her eyes. "I don't want to see you, I don't want to know you! Just stay the hell away from me!"

Gaby charged out of the wigwam in such a fury that she nearly fell out the door.

Beverly followed and saw her picking up Lamar's Frankenstein C.B. from one of the log stools beside the firepit and heading east without so much as a sidelong look at Beverly.

"Where are you taking that?" Beverly tried, knowing it was futile. "We're not supposed to go out by ourselves!"

"Drop dead!" came the shouted reply as Gaby stalked off into the forest, leaving Beverly feeling very much alone.

* * * * * *

The men all stood on the edge of the cliff overlooking the floodplain, gawking in wide-eyed amazement at a view unlike any they'd ever imagined.

As far as the eye could see, the floodplain was covered in 30-foot-wide swirling spirals of some steaming, grayish substance. These swirls looped in and around each other, creating a kaleidoscope effect of endlessly converging and diverging circles, like an extreme close-up of a thumbprint that extended out of view.

Everything the substance had come in contact with was dead. The sparse vegetation and abundant grasses of the floodplain had all withered and browned. The handful of trees that it sustained had lost all their leaves as though fall had turned into the dead of winter overnight. Those leaves lay strewn across the landscape, blackened and shriveled.

Watching the steam slowly rising from the remains of a devastated ecosystem, while standing on an untouched plateau not 20 feet away, was indescribably eerie. They felt like they were staring at an alien landscape, not a familiar stomping ground that had been radically remade in the course of a single night.

In a panorama of inexplicable sights, perhaps the strangest was the mysterious gray substance. It was hard to tell from the haze of steam coming off it, but it appeared to be some kind of powder, set in swirls that were impossibly precise and completely undisturbed. Not a grain was out of place, as if they'd all been inked into the dirt by Paul Bunyan wielding the world's largest tattoo needle. The substance also seemed to have infected the soil itself, as the landscape had taken on a sickly, grayish pallor, even in places untouched by the swirls of powder.

The three of them were dumbstruck as they looked out over the blasted landscape, struggling merely to process the surreal scene before them, let alone articulate it. Lamar was almost afraid to speak, as if commenting on what he saw would somehow crystallize it.

Beside him, Coop's quivering fingers lost their grip on his spear/fishing pole. It clattered loudly to the ground, startling all of them out of their stupor.

"What ... the ... fuck ... happened ... here?" Ken asked in a hushed whisper.

"It looks like the aftermath of a forest fire," Coop said, the awe in his voice unmistakable.

"One that incinerated the most barren section of the forest while sparing everything else?" Ken replied with a snort.

"If this was a fire, where's the smoke?" Lamar pointed out. "All I see is steam."

"Nothing about this makes any sense," Coop agreed.

After a few more moments of silent contemplation, Coop voiced what all of them were thinking.

"One of us should go down there. You know, to investigate."

Ken crossed his arms defiantly.

"Well, I'm not doing it."

The two turned to Lamar.

"Don't look at me," he insisted. "It was your idea."

"I was suggesting, not volunteering," Coop clarified.

Ken threw up his hands.

"We'll all go, okay? Will that shut you two up?"

Lamar cautiously made his way down the slope leading to the floodplain, with the other two following behind in single file. As he descended, the haze from the rising steam made everything look increasingly translucent, as though he were viewing the world through a shower curtain. He paused at the bottom, where the green of the slope ended and the gray of the floodplain began, trying to work up enough courage to step onto this otherworldly landscape.

"Quit being a pussy," Ken said after waiting several seconds.

Lamar extended his right foot onto the edge of the plain, testing the ground for a moment.

"Jesus Christ," Ken intoned, face-palming as he watched Lamar pull his foot back, unwilling to take the next step onto the floodplain.

"You know what? If you're so gung ho, you can go first," Lamar replied in irritation.

Ken brushed past him with characteristic bravado.

"This isn't scary," he assured the others. "Pumping and dumping while under SEC review; that's scary. This is just fucking weird."

After a long moment, he took a cautious first step onto the plain, and then another.

"See? It's fine," he crowed.

Lamar and Coop exchanged nervous glances before following him onto the floodplain, making certain to follow in one another's footsteps.

Through the haze they spotted a dappled goldfinch lying on its back on the outer edge of one of the gray, powdery swirls, its tiny legs pointing skyward. It looked shriveled and desiccated, like a tiny mummy. It must have died recently, too, because it hadn't been touched by predators. Its blank eyes staring into nothingness reflected the confusion in the faces of the trio staring at it. It reminded Coop of the dead squirrel that he'd tried to pass off as a clean kill.

Ken watched his feet as he walked, mindful not to step on any of the powdery swirls, which looked like big brothers to those pinwheel shapes he had found days earlier by the dead tree with the mandala nailed to it.

Lamar, who was walking behind the others, strayed from their footsteps slightly and accidentally stepped on a downed tree branch that snapped loudly underfoot, making all of them jump a little. Ken looked back in disapproval as Lamar mouthed a silent apology. The episode gave Coop pause, and he suddenly stopped in his tracks.

"Why don't we hear more noises down here?" he asked.

"I hear your stupid questions and the Badyear Blimp's heavy breathing just fine," Ken replied dismissively.

"Forest sounds," Coop elaborated. "Where are all the birds chirping, or the insects? All I hear down here is us and the things we touch."

Lamar closed his eyes and listened for any external sounds. In the heart of a wilderness teeming with life, he heard nothing, not even the wind whistling through the trees. He'd heard and felt its bracing caress up on the plateau. But down here, there was no wind. There was nothing living or moving except for them. The sense of isolation was unreal; it reminded him of a recording booth, where all exterior noises are cut off.

It wasn't just sound, either. They all slowly started to register a knot in the pit of their stomachs that felt like equal parts dread and nausea. It made them feel unsteady on their feet, like a sailor struggling to find his land legs after weeks at sea.

Through the haze of steam, Ken nearly walked into one of the hay bales on the archery range. One of the gray swirls actually went vertical along the side of the leftmost bale, the steaming particulate matter clinging to the edges through some unknown power.

Curious, Lamar leaned forward and extended a finger toward it.

"No, don't touch it!" Coop cautioned.

Lamar touched the hay bale with the pad of his index finger. Despite the steam, it was only lukewarm. It felt like it was made from fine granules of sand. He pulled his finger back and saw it was smudged with a blackish film.

"Ash," he declared as he wiped his finger on his shirt, smearing the soot over the "Zero Day Dude" logo on the front.

"Ash?" Coop asked, puzzled by Lamar's assessment. "Could some coal company be using this area as a dumping ground?"

Ken rolled his eyes in frustration.

"Sure, Coop. They rolled dozens of dump trucks up here without our noticing, and instead of unloading it in giant piles, they spread it out in intricate patterns just to fuck with us."

Coop was too unnerved to respond to Ken's taunt.

"What leaves ash but isn't a fire or illegal dumping?" Lamar asked, like he was posing some philosophical riddle on the meaning of life.

"I dunno, something underground, like maybe lava?" Ken posited.

Now it was Coop's turn to roll his eyes.

"An active volcano in Pennsylvania? Try again."

"He's right," Lamar concurred. "If there were, this whole place would reek of sulfur. And that shower you gave me earlier would have boiled me alive."

"Then maybe it's some kind of bacteria," Ken guessed.

"That kills everything in sight in less than 24 hours?" Lamar asked skeptically.

"Then you explain it," Ken challenged.

"I can't," he admitted after a few moments of consideration. "And that's what scares me."

"We should go," Coop said. "We may be ... infected if we

stay here."

As they turned to leave, something off in the distance disrupted the cone of silence enshrouding them. Footsteps, though they were too faint to determine the direction.

Ken clutched his spear tightly as a human shape came shimmering into view through the steam haze, approaching from the direction of the plateau. Just as he was about to bark out a warning, the hazy image grew more distinct, and they recognized the feminine features and bundled clothing of Beverly as she slowly came into view. Ken relaxed his grip on the spear.

"Tell me you're seeing the same shit we are," he called out to her.

Beverly nodded slowly.

"I remember my dream now," she responded in a serene voice that clashed so wildly with their circumstances that the others wondered if she was still dreaming. "I was walking in the moonlight up there," she said sedately, pointing in the direction of the overlook, "and saw writhing, black shapes swarming the floodplain. Untold millions of them."

"Maybe it wasn't a dream," Coop offered.

"Maybe you're both being stupid," Ken countered. "There's no creature on Earth that could do this in one night, even if there were millions of them."

"Beverly, is it possible that you mistook all this ash for creatures?" Lamar probed gently. "The moonlight can play tricks on your eyes, and owing to your ... condition ..." Lamar said, trying to be tactful.

"Fifty sheets to the wind," Ken chimed in, not giving a damn about diplomacy.

"...You might have had some fanciful interpretations of what you saw," Lamar continued, ignoring Ken. "Is that possible?"

Beverly shook her head no.

"I threw something at them. A branch, I think. They dodged it," Beverly said simply.

Ken ground his teeth in frustration.

"What you saw came out of a bottle. Period. End of story."

Beverly was about to respond when Coop suddenly cut in.

"Hang on. Why aren't you with Gaby?"

Beverly's face darkened and her dreamlike calm faded.

"She's still angry," Beverly explained.

"You were supposed to watch her!" Ken said with a scowl. "Where is she now?"

"I tried talking to her but she picked up that C.B. thing and took off."

Coop balked at this explanation.

"And you just let her go?"

"She needed some personal space," Beverly replied weakly.

"You let her leave unarmed and alone?" Lamar exclaimed, growing more concerned with each syllable. "With Wade on the loose? What's wrong with you?"

Without waiting for a response, Lamar rushed back to camp. Coop flashed Beverly a look of disgust before following.

Beverly hung her head in shame as Ken eyed her coldly. He leaned in and paused there until she reluctantly raised her eyes to meet his gaze.

"You really are useless, you know that?" he said before

hurrying to rejoin the others.

Beverly looked out over the blasted, desolate landscape, knowing with the surety of despair that she would never be whole again. And as she looked, she replayed Ken's parting words in her mind, over and over again.

* * * * * *

The sun was riding high in the sky when Gaby finally stopped for a break. She set the C.B. down gingerly on a bed of moss-covered stones near the edge of a 30-foot-wide draw that separated her from the eastern edge of the forest. It didn't look especially deep; maybe a 15-foot drop before returning to the same elevation on the other side, but the edges were steep. It was filled with trees canted at dangerous angles and scrub plants masking numerous foot-snagging crannies, all of which she would have to navigate while safe-guarding her precious cargo. A short break would give her time to plot out her course through the depression.

Gaby slung her pack from her shoulders and sat beside the C.B. It was surprisingly heavy, and her arms ached after carrying it for nearly an hour, though not nearly as much as her shoulder muscles, which she had kept tensed this whole time to prevent the pack from slipping off. She idly rubbed one of her throbbing shoulders with one hand while the other dug around in her pack for the canteen.

She unscrewed the top and tilted her head upward to re-ceive the restorative liquid. Despite her exhaustion and the dire circumstances, Gaby was starting to enjoy herself. This was the sort of thing she had envisioned when signing up for this trip: long and peaceful walks through the forest with nothing to distract or detract from the splendor of nature.

Sunlight trickled through the trees overhead. Gaby kept her face pointed skyward, a small smile starting to develop as she basked in the light's warm caress. Maybe what she was doing wasn't the smartest thing when they were effectively at war, and she knew the others would be furious with her, but after three days of high tension and zero privacy, she needed the kind of perspective that only solitude could afford. And if she could get them all saved in the bargain, that would be the icing on the cake. She imagined the others thanking her: Lamar, Coop, Ken and ...

A low-lying cloud blotted out the sun, and the warm glow slowly faded, along with Gaby's smile. Gaby lowered her gaze until it came to rest on her ultimate destination: the high hills marking the eastern edge of the three-mile-wide crater that sheltered the campsite from the worst of the region's inclement weather. The peaks were among the highest in the region, perfect for sending a transmission.

After studying the depression for several minutes, Gaby settled on a route that should avoid the worst of the hidden crannies. She'd just take it nice and easy. One misstep and the C.B. could be damaged beyond repair. One serious misstep and she'd be dealing with a broken ankle. Gaby stood up and reclaimed her burdens, the pack and C.B., the latter of which she hoisted with a small "oomph!" of exertion. She took a deep breath and started down the slope. As she wended her way downward, Gaby went over the plan once more in her head.

She'd been out here for an hour or more and appeared to be making good time; the terrain was already getting rougher. It looked like she had another mile to go before she reached the lower slopes of the eastern ridge, where hiking would turn to climbing. She figured the best way to handle it would be to dump all the nonessentials from her backpack at the foot of the slopes, placing some sort of marker to locate them again, and then stuff the C.B. in the bag to free her hands for the daunting climb ahead. The first leg of the climb looked especially steep, 45 degrees or more, as the ridge rose precipitously from the forest floor before tapering off to a more gentle incline at a fork between the two lowest-lying peaks, which coincidentally were also the closest.

Gaby reached the other side of the draw and lifted her arms to set the C.B. on the other side, standing on her tiptoes to reach. After it was secure, she used a toppled tree as a foothold to push off and hoist herself up on the other side. That wasn't so bad, Gaby assured herself as she brushed the dirt off the front of her jacket. She knew that far more perilous climbing lay ahead.

Gaby calculated that reaching the highest peak of the eastern ridge would take at least another three hours, which if she factored in an hour or so of C.B. time — a prospect she did not relish — that would put her return to camp somewhere around 5:00 p.m. if she made good time on her descent. That wouldn't give her much time to recuperate once she reached the top, but she knew that if she dawdled in any fashion, it would put her return trip perilously close to twilight. She did not relish the idea of trying to find her way back to camp in the dark.

Before long, Gaby found herself in a muddy, low-lying region comprised mainly of smaller, spindly trees and heavy grasses that reached halfway to her thigh. Something about it seemed oddly familiar, sparking a sense of déjà vu that Gaby couldn't place.

Up ahead she noticed tracks in the mud. She leaned down to study them. Shoeprints. Someone had traveled southward here rather recently. That put her on edge. Wade could be in the area. The chances of running into him in a region this large seemed astronomical, but Gaby didn't want to take any chances. She started looking around for a sharp stick or some heavy rocks, anything she could use as a weapon, when she noticed another set of tracks. And another.

Gaby was trying to process this information when she spotted something from the corner of her eye that looked out of place. She turned to find something white tied in a knot around the base of a denuded sapling not 15 feet away. After a few moments of examination, Gaby recognized it as a strip of plastic torn from one of the archery targets. That could only mean …

Gaby looked around once more and that sense of recognition grew stronger. She had been here before. She had crossed this area, coming via a different route, with Lamar and Coop on their second day here. The white strips of plastic were route markers Coop had laid down so they could find their way back to camp as they searched for Beverly. Now that she had reoriented herself, Gaby spotted the tree she'd leaned on 48 hours earlier while doubled over with laughter, trying to explain the concept of the Three Mouseketeers to a mystified Lamar and Coop.

She beamed at the happy memory. It had only been two

days, and yet she found herself pining for it as though it were years ago. It seemed mildly absurd to wax nostalgic for a period when they'd just been abandoned and were all petrified, and yet, compared to what they'd gone through since then, the memory seemed positively innocent. Gaby didn't linger too long and pressed on eastward, outside the boundaries of her previous journey.

After another few minutes of walking Gaby encountered the first real sign that she was near the base of the ridge: a 15-foot-high earthen wall running north to south that was sheer in both directions as far as the eye could see. Above the wall was a steep, rocky outcropping that shot upward at an acrophobia-inducing angle for 20 stories or more. A narrow foot trail peeked out between the scrub bushes lining the slopes, one that cut up and back as it wound its way out of sight. She'd reached the base of the ridge.

Gaby loosened the straps on her backpack and let it slip from her shoulders as she mentally steeled herself for the climb ahead. The noise prompted a small raccoon nesting along the ledge to poke its head over the lip of the wall, and seeing Gaby, skitter its way southward, scattering pebbles as it went.

Just as Gaby had selected the perfect hiding spot for the supplies she would leave at the base — a waist-high clump of snowberry bushes at the foot of the earthen wall —she heard a tree branch snap in the distance. The noise came from the northwest, and it was too large to be another raccoon.

She hastily stowed her backpack in one cluster of bushes with most of its leaves intact and then ducked behind a larger clump, clutching the C.B. in her unnerved fingers. Before long, she could hear leaves crunching underfoot. Whatever it was was drawing closer. Gaby ducked her head and tried to will herself invisible, praying that it was nothing more than a passing elk.

Something broke through the undergrowth 20 yards away. Curiosity finally overcame Gaby's survival instincts, and she raised her head just enough to peek between the branches. Through her leafy peephole, Gaby caught fleeting glimpses of mottled brown fur and a creature that looked to be the size of a large wolf, although it was difficult to discern much of anything through her narrow aperture. The creature moved strangely as it shambled in and out of view, as though it were favoring its hindquarters. It also appeared to have some tuft of skin dangling from its head. The creature suddenly paused and raised its head, giving Gaby her first decent look at it.

Gaby recognized the tuft on its head as a mud-encrusted fox tail. But before she could even ask what it was doing on the fox's head, she noticed that this was no fox, as the side of its face was pinkish. The creature suddenly turned its face toward her, and Gaby saw it was no creature at all. It was Wade.

Gaby inhaled sharply and covered her mouth to stifle the sound.

Wade had replaced his tattered pants from last night with a tanned beaver hide, that he had fashioned into a kilt, which, along with his fox-fur cap, was all he was wearing. He was hunched forward, low to the ground, as though he were ready to strike at any moment. His movements were sharp and quick, like a predator stalking its prey. Gaby leaned in slightly and saw that his bare chest contained two fresh scars, signifying two new kills. But it was his expression that she couldn't get over. One of the things that had scared the group about Wade was how he always seemed to be a man on the edge; his rage bubbled just below the surface, kept in check by the twin veneers of humanity and self-control. The creature crouched in front of Gaby showed none of these traits. She saw no signs of rage, uncertainty, or reasoning; no spark of humanity at all. This was a purely instinctual being, hunting not for sport or the thrill of the chase but for sustenance. The sadistic hunter was gone, replaced with a pure predator.

His eyes flitted back and forth, scanning the area for something. He leaned back on his rear legs, raised his head and started sniffing the air. Had she not seen him walking and talking yesterday morning, Gaby would have sworn he was feral.

Gaby tried to breathe as shallowly and quietly as possible, but her elevated heart rate and racing pulse conspired against her. A nearby bush branch pressing up against Gaby's head had managed to worm its way into her ear after she'd leaned in for a closer look. The sensation was unbearable, but she didn't dare move a muscle.

Wade stopped sniffing the air and lowered his head until he was at eye level with Gaby, staring in her general direction for so long that she started to fear he'd spotted her. He moved a few steps closer. Gaby squeezed her eyes shut and waited for the inevitable discovery.

The sound of pebbles falling from the rock wall behind Gaby distracted Wade, sending his gaze upward. Gaby craned her neck as far upward as she could without moving the rest of her body. Looking out from over the ledge was the raccoon from earlier, probably trying to return to its nest only to be confronted with two intruders this time. It sounded a cautious complaint to its new neighbors in a high-pitched trill. Wade responded with a guttural growl that sent the raccoon packing, fleeing south down the wall before leaping into a poplar sapling and scampering out of sight.

Wade's growl slowly subsided. He looked around, as if trying to remember why he'd stopped here in the first place. He padded a few steps to the right — out of Gaby's sight-line — and sat there for a minute or more, doing who knows what. Gaby said a silent prayer for it to all be over soon.

After an agonizingly long time, she heard footsteps again. From the sound of it, Wade was retreating northward. He padded out of view and Gaby listened with bated breath as his footsteps slowly faded off into the distance. She held her pose, too scared to move, until she was certain he was gone. It seemed like an eternity.

Gaby rose cautiously, scanning the area for any sign of Wade. All was still. She heaved a sigh of relief, trying to lower her heart rate and calm her frayed nerves. That had been close. Gaby took it as a sign. She had wrestled with the wisdom of coming out here alone and unarmed all morning, and this near miss with Wade had clinched it.

She stood to her full height and retrieved her bag from the neighboring snowberry bush. Gaby hated admitting defeat, but she liked the idea of dying at some lunatic's hands even less. She tried to work out what she would tell the others. Grimacing at the prospect of their disappointed reactions,

Gaby knew she would never be taken seriously — or trusted — again.

As she put her arms through the knapsack's straps, Gaby heard more pebbles falling from the rock ledge behind her. She shook her head with a mixture of annoyance and amusement. That was one persistent raccoon. Maybe it was a mother protecting her young. Then she remembered watching it flee to the south, having abandoned the ledge in favor of the forest floor. So if it wasn't the raccoon up there, what was it?

Gaby whirled around. Standing on the ledge, towering over her, was Wade, with his buck knife drawn and a hungry look in his eye.

Wade tensed and pounced. Time stood still. Gaby's eye focused on small details as she watched him leap toward her. The dull glint of his downturned blade, which was aimed right at her head. The dried smears of blood on his arms, presumably from the last unfortunate animal Wade had caught. The dried and cracked mud on his stomach, which obscured several of Wade's self-inflicted trophy scars. Gaby realized that if she didn't do something, she'd be the next one.

She hoisted the C.B. It had always been heavy, but now it felt like it was made of lead. Time resumed, but Wade seemed to move at half-speed, gliding lazily through the air toward her as though he were suspended by wires. But if he was moving at half-speed, Gaby felt like she was moving at quarter-speed. It took an impossibly long time for her arms to raise the C.B., moving so sluggishly that she might as well have been swimming in molasses.

Just as Wade was upon her, his knife barely a foot from

her face, she summoned the strength to raise the C.B. up the last few inches to absorb the strike. Time suddenly resumed its normal flow. The C.B. turned Wade's blade in a shower of sparks. The edge of the contraption clipped him in the jaw, sending his head rocketing backward as he fell with his full weight on Gaby, knocking the wind out of her and sending the C.B. flying several feet behind her, where it shattered into countless pieces. Gaby's head smacked the ground and she blacked out momentarily.

When she came to, Gaby felt a searing pain in her scalp. She raised her head and blood started oozing into her left eye. Gaby blinked it away to get her bearings. She was flat on her back. There was something heavy on her legs. She looked up and saw Wade, unresponsive and face down, laying across them. She tried to wriggle away, desperate to extricate herself from this lunatic. Wade gave a low moan in response. Gaby's fear turned to panic, and her flailing grew wilder.

Wade turned his head and raised his arm just as Gaby managed to squirm out from under him. Still only semi-conscious, he feebly pawed at the hem of her jeans, trying to restrain his prey.

Gaby kicked his hand away, grabbed her backpack and bolted. Her legs felt like rubber and her head was still throbbing, but she knew she didn't have long until ...

"Rraawwwrrrr!"

She hadn't made it 30 paces before a deafening roar sounded in the distance. Guttural and unintelligible as it was, Gaby had no doubts about the intent behind it. She pushed herself harder, unsteady legs be damned, knowing that Wade would soon be in pursuit. The hunt was on.

Gaby ran for her life. Panic reasserted itself and slowly took over. It deprived her lungs of badly needed oxygen, cramped her legs and robbed her brain of any rational response to the threat. She had no idea where she was running and scarcely noticed her surroundings. In her mind, all she saw was Wade's knife, and her only thought was to get as far away from it as possible.

She was sprinting now and avoiding ankle-snagging rocks and tree roots more by luck than any skill. Off in the distance, Gaby could hear crashing noises as Wade barreled through the forest toward her, desperate to claim his kill. In the back of her fear-addled mind, she knew she didn't have long until he caught up and put that big-ass knife to use. She had to think of something — anything — and fast.

As she ran, desperate and scared, a glimmer of white in the forest up ahead caught her eye. She struggled to focus her eyes on it as she ran. When she was within 10 yards, she recognized it as one of Coop's markers tied to a tree. And farther south, some 40 yards in the distance, she saw another one. Gaby changed direction and followed the trail of white markers. Within moments, she emerged through the brush in a small clearing. She recognized it immediately: it was the same clearing she had visited days ago with Lamar and Coop when they'd been searching for Beverly. That fallen tree on the other side of the clearing was where she'd gotten a splinter in the backside. The memory was so strong it overshadowed her panic and forced her to pause in her tracks, even as her ears warned of Wade's impending arrival. Gaby reflected back to that day, replaying the rest of the trip in her mind, and lying in wait there was the answer to her plight.

She now knew what to do.

Gaby hopped over the downed tree and the dried creek bed it straddled and ran eastward, where the clearing fed into a grassy ridge that ended 100 feet away. Just as she reached the base of the ridge, Wade broke through the brush of the clearing on the other side, his eyes scanning the region for his prey. Gaby saw he had a nasty laceration to his cheek from where the C.B. had clipped him, with the skin around it hanging down in a flap as blood poured from the wound. He spotted her by the ridge and his eyes narrowed.

Gaby charged up the hill. Another guttural roar sounded behind her as the chase resumed. Gaby pushed herself harder as the slope of the ridge grew steeper. Heavy breathing and crashing footfalls rang in her ears. As she neared the top of the ridge, the ravine where they found Beverly came into view. The slope leveled out and Gaby's footfalls came faster. She veered north, heading for the leafy meadow she and the others had crossed two days earlier to reach the entrance to the ravine.

She could hear Wade closing in behind her, but she didn't dare to turn around. Gaby barreled down the slope to the meadow, running so fast that she nearly lost her balance. Her heart was jackhammering in her chest, while her oxygen-starved lungs burned. Her backpack felt like it weighed a million pounds.

Behind her, Wade was so close that she could feel his breath on the back of her neck, causing the small hairs there to stand up in revulsion. His hand grabbed hold of her backpack and tugged, trying to hold her back. Gaby shrugged it off her shoulders and kept running.

Her panicked eyes scanned the high grasses and leaf piles of the meadow as she closed in, desperately searching for a sign. She saw a small metallic glint in the tall grass between two trees in front of her and knew she'd found what she was looking for. She tried her best to gauge its location while fending off the gnawing panic that threatened to consume her. Gaby knew that if she miscalculated, she was as good as dead.

Gaby reached the trees and dove between them, rolling as she landed some five feet behind them into the meadow. She came up with a mouthful of grass and dead leaves. Now came the tricky part. She knew she couldn't outrun Wade, so she had to outsmart him.

Gaby braced herself with her hands and rose up into a runner's stance. She tensed up as though she was about to break into a sprint and then let her left leg buckle, sending her back to the ground. She rolled over to see if her ruse was having the desired effect.

Standing in front of the two trees was Wade, sizing up his fallen prey. He allowed himself a small, grim smile. Now that his hunt was at an end, it was time to feast. Gaby's eyes darted back to the gap between the trees, where she saw that glint again. She turned her head and closed her eyes, feigning surrender. It was all the encouragement Wade required.

He raised his knife and charged toward her, running right between the two trees. A swooshing noise sounded as two ends of a bear trap shot up from their grassy hiding place, clamping their steel jaws around Wade's right leg. He dropped his knife in shock and pain, bellowing with rage as the rusty trap bit into either side of his calf muscle, locking him in place.

Gaby stood up for real this time and sprinted past Wade as he struggled to free himself, praying she didn't stumble on any of the other illegal bear traps lying in wait.

Her heart pounding, her muscles aching and her ears ringing, Gaby ran.

* * * * * *

Ken and Coop sat on opposite sides of the unlit firepit in the center of camp, both of them lost in their own little worlds, trying to process what they had just witnessed. Coop cleaned his glasses with the frayed hem of his robes while Ken poked the ground with his spear.

"Have you ever seen anything like that before?" Coop asked, breaking the silence.

Ken shook his head.

"Never. And I've been backpacking on four continents."

Ken continued stabbing the dirt. After a long pause, Coop spoke up again.

"I still say we should have gone after her."

Ken shrugged.

"We have no idea where she went."

"She took the C.B.; that means she's looking for a peak to broadcast from," Coop explained, growing annoyed with Ken's indifference.

Ken gestured to the ring of high hills on three sides of them, capped with dozens of peaks to choose from.

"And which one did she pick? As Dad would say: 'Choice

is man's greatest curse.' We could easily wind up lost while searching for her."

Coop blinked several times before answering.

"But we're already lost."

Ken rolled his eyes. He was pondering what cutting barb to respond with when Lamar returned from a quick trip to the overlook.

"Is Beverly still down there?" Coop asked.

Lamar nodded as he sat beside Coop.

"She's just sitting there, rocking back and forth."

"Hang on, how can you see Mama Crass through all the steam?" Ken asked.

"Most of its dissipated by now," Lamar explained. "It's just ash and Beverly down there, now." Lamar paused a beat before quickly adding, "And if you want someone to collect her, forget it. I'm not going down there again."

Ken waved his hand dismissively at the prospect, as though Beverly's safety was the least of his priorities.

Coop held his glasses up to the sun, checking them for streaks.

"Did anyone else feel sick to their stomach down there?" he asked as he seated his glasses on the bridge of his nose.

Lamar raised his hand.

"That was weird, but not hearing any other sounds was plain creepy," he said quietly. "It was like we were trapped in some kind of soundproof bubble."

"That can't be natural," Coop agreed. "I felt like an intruder in the land of the dead."

Ken shook his head in annoyance.

"Can you two drama queens give it a rest?" he growled.

"Let's stick to what we know. What could explain all this ... weird shit?" Ken said, struggling to find the right words.

"Nothing," Coop replied with a dejected sigh.

"One thing might," Lamar said slowly, staring off into space as he stroked his goatee thoughtfully. "Radiation."

Ken, who was still poking the ground, paused mid-spear thrust. Coop covered his mouth and looked at Lamar quizzically.

"We know there's an abandoned research base nearby, and we know they were working with nuclear reactors," Lamar said. "Maybe they buried all that nuclear waste in the floodplains, and now it's leaking to the surface. You hear stories like that from a lot of nuclear dumping sites."

"That might explain the nausea, but not what happened with the sound," Coop insisted.

"Neurological symptoms," Lamar replied. "The floodplain was probably full of noise, but we couldn't tell because the radiation was trashing our nervous systems. My mom's an oncology tech, so I hear stories all the time about chemo patients with these symptoms."

Ken snorted in disgust. While the shock of what they'd seen down in the floodplain had knocked the wind out of his sails, it was starting to pass, and he was fast becoming insufferable once more.

"So we'll all die of radiation sickness or turn into the Toxic Avenger," he said. "Fucking peachy."

"But John said ..." Coop started to protest.

"No one gives a damn what that Nava-hobag said," Ken replied sharply, cutting him off. "He's gone. And you know what? So are we."

Ken stood up purposefully.

"Where are you going?" Lamar asked, suspicious.

"*We're* leaving," Ken responded emphatically. "Crazy-town express leaves in 10 minutes. I'm not waiting to see which kills us first, that psycho Wade or some toxic sludge."

"You have no idea where to go!" Coop protested.

"I run a top-flight brokerage with 75 employees," Ken said dismissively, as though that was somehow relevant. "I think I can lead a bunch of pansies out of the forest."

"Hang on," Lamar insisted, standing up to make his point. "Let's think this through: there's no dead animals or plants up here. If it stays contained to the floodplain, then we should be fine just avoiding it."

Ken glared at him in disgust.

"Where do you think our drinking water comes from?"

That gave Lamar pause. He and Coop both glanced at the drinking pail beside the shower, viewing it with a new degree of suspicion.

"But Gaby's still out there," Coop protested.

"So we'll leave her a note," Ken replied vaguely with a dismissive wave of his hand.

"Saying what?" Lamar insisted. "Dear Gaby, thanks for trying to get us rescued. Enjoy fending for yourself. Sincerely, the gang."

Ken glowered at him for several long seconds before responding.

"If you have time for melodrama, you have to collect your shit," he insisted. There was an edge to his voice that made it clear no further insubordination would be tolerated. "We leave in 10 minutes."

Lamar crossed his arms defiantly and sat back down, practically daring Ken to respond.

Coop observed this behavior and quickly followed suit.

"We're not going without Gaby," Lamar said emphatically, his ultimatum lingering in the space between them. "That's final."

"If it weren't for me, Wade would have dumped both of your sorry asses in a shallow grave last night," Ken browbeat them. "Now ... move it!"

Lamar and Coop exchanged an uneasy glance but held firm.

"I could make you, you know," Ken continued, leaning forward menacingly toward the pair, causing Coop to lean back. "It would be easy."

Out of the corner of his eye, Lamar spotted his spear, resting on the edge of the firepit. He was trying to gauge whether he could reach it in time if Ken attacked.

Fortunately, a disturbance in the rhododendron bushes clustered on the western edge of camp ensured he'd never have to find out. Everyone instantly forgot about their feud and focused on the new threat. Coop picked up his spear while Ken cracked his knuckles.

Out of the underbrush came Gaby, looking spent and disheveled, with coagulated blood crusting on her forehead.

Coop was so surprised to see her that he dropped his spear. Ken and Lamar stood there watching, dumbfounded.

Gaby dropped to her knees, either out of gratitude or exhaustion. She clutched her hand to her chest, trying to catch her breath. She took a deep, panicky breath and spoke her first words all afternoon.

"He's back!" she gasped. "Wade's back!"

* * * * * *

Ninety minutes later, the motley crew stalked through the forest with a grim purpose: either capture or kill Wade Rollins. Ken led the party, refusing to lower his spear even as they negotiated increasingly rugged terrain, convinced that Wade was hiding around every large tree or rock formation. Coop, who was bringing up the rear, looked nervous, starting at every robin's call and wind gust that disrupted a leaf pile. Lamar, who was center-left, seemed the most composed, using his spear as a walking stick and speaking words of comfort to Gaby, who stood center-right. Her head wound had been cleaned, but she was still visibly shaken by her ordeal.

Ken stopped at a cluster of oak trees that formed a loose semicircle.

"Alright. Where do we go from here?" he asked Gaby.

Gaby studied the terrain, looking for anything familiar. She seemed slightly dazed, as though she were walking through a thick mental fog.

"Left ... I think," she replied fuzzily after a few moments.

Ken threw up his hands in exasperation.

"How could you not remember the way? You were literally here two hours ago!"

Gaby said nothing in response, seeming to barely register Ken's gripe, so Lamar spoke up for her.

"Will you ease off the throttle? She's had a helluva scare," Lamar reminded him. "Try facing down Wade alone and unarmed and then tell us how perfect your recollection is."

"Well, whose fault is that?" Ken shot back.

An awkward silence fell over the group for several seconds before Gaby spoke up.

"That wasn't Wade," she said, quietly but firmly. "Whatever that thing is, it's no longer him. I'm not even sure it's human anymore."

Ken rolled his eyes but held his tongue.

Within a few minutes they arrived at the base of the ridge and quickly located the shattered remains of the C.B. The rest of the scene also bore out Gaby's story. Ken and Coop searched the perimeter for any weapons or tools Wade may have abandoned in the chase, while Lamar stood over the remains of his pride and joy, surveying its shattered and split chassis, snapped antenna and transistors scattered in every direction. It was beyond any hope of repair.

"I'm sorry, Lamar," Gaby apologized. "I know how hard you worked on that. For what it's worth, it saved my life."

Lamar managed a thin smile.

"Better that it gave its life for you than vice versa."

"Hey, can we get back on track here?" Ken snapped. "We've got maybe two more hours of daylight left. Let's find this bastard and gut him, already."

Gaby nodded.

"I think I've got my bearings now," she said. "I should be able to find my way back to the meadow from here."

"Well, halle-fucking-lujah."

Gaby was true to her word, and after 10 minutes of scouring the low-lying region to the southeast they located one of Coop's white markers. The group followed the markers to the now-familiar clearing, which Lamar and Coop instantly recognized, and headed east up the grassy ridge before stopping near the edge of the ravine, where they found the backpack Wade had ripped off of Gaby's shoulders. The zipper on it had busted in the scramble, and her belongings were strewn all over.

"He's down there?" Ken asked, pointing his spear toward the meadow 100 yards north.

Gaby nodded nervously as she collected up her belongings.

"Okay everyone, form up like we discussed," Ken ordered. "Lamar, watch our six; Gaby, you take left flank; Coop, you and me have point."

"Sir, yes sir!" Lamar said mockingly, giving a snappy salute.

Ken glowered at him.

"I'd like to remind you that we're only in this situation because a certain someone didn't follow orders," he intoned, motioning toward Gaby. "One more wisecrack and you all can handle Wade by yourselves."

"What's to handle?" Coop asked. "He's stuck in a damn bear trap. He's probably bleeding to death while we argue."

Ken shook his head no.

"Wade is stronger than he looks, and a helluva lot more dangerous. Beverly would tell you that, too, if she weren't busy sulking in the floodplain. We have to be prepared for anything."

"If he's such a threat, then why'd you leave Beverly alone?" Lamar chimed in.

"Let's see: one, she's a useless pain in the ass; two, he can't hobble to the camp that fast," Ken retorted, counting the answers out on his fingers for effect. "If he's loose, he'll be somewhere nearby. Oh, and three, shut the fuck up!"

The group cautiously made its way downhill, aiming for the two trees on the edge of the glade where Wade had been snared. There was no sign of Wade. They looked down and saw the trap had been reset.

"Holy shit!" Lamar exclaimed.

"Told you," Ken said. "That's crazy strength for you."

Tall grass on three sides of the bear trap bore blood droplets, suggesting that it took Wade more than one attempt to open the trap. A quick search of the immediate perimeter revealed a faint blood trail leading south past the ravine.

"He couldn't have gone far. Fan out and search," Ken instructed the others.

"Woah, hold the phone," Lamar jumped in. "This place is littered with bear traps. We're not risking life and limb on a stupid plan like that."

Coop and Gaby both nodded their agreement.

"Are you trying to tell me what to do?" Ken intoned, bristling at the challenge to his authority.

"No, I'm telling you what the rest of us won't do," Lamar retorted, holding up the blood-speckled chain of the trap so Ken could see. "Do you want this to happen to us?"

Ken looked to Coop and Gaby and read the same resistance in their body language. His face grew flush with anger.

"It was my plan that saw us through last night, my leadership that drove Wade away!" Ken raged, as though he were the hero of Quehanna. "And it was my rules that kept everyone safe; that is, until Naturalized Nancy here decided to play hooky, and you see how that went! If it weren't for me, you would all be dead right now! And all you people do is complain! Fine, if that's what you want!"

Ken stripped off his leather bomber jacket and seated it on Lamar's shoulders with a flourish as though he were ceding the mantle of leadership. It looked comically oversized on him.

"If you fucktards would rather listen to a basement-dwelling loser who thinks Nutella is one of the four basic food groups instead of the CEO of a company with 70 employees, knock yourselves the fuck out!" Ken fumed. "Have fun playing scoutmaster!"

"But I don't want command," Lamar trailed off, embarrassed at all the attention.

"Hang on," Coop interjected. "I thought you said you had 75 employees."

"Zip it, pillow-biter!" Ken fairly screamed, pointing an accusatory finger at Coop before turning on his heels and stomping his way north.

"Ken, the camp's west," Gaby called after him.

"I'm taking a leak first," Ken declared. "Anybody got a problem with that?"

"I thought we were supposed to stick together," Coop offered timidly.

"I don't do performance art, ya fucking pervert!" Ken shot back, eliciting an eye roll from Coop as he stormed off into the forest.

Gaby let out a deep sigh of relief once Ken was out of earshot.

"I don't know how much more of his 'leadership' I can stomach," Gaby groaned, her disgust nearly palpable.

"He's getting worse by the minute," Coop said, nodding

his agreement. "I'm starting to think Wade is a better option."

Gaby rounded on Coop.

"Joking! I'm just joking," he insisted, putting up his hands defensively and taking a step back.

The only one who didn't weigh in was Lamar, who hadn't said a word since Ken's meltdown. He was staring intently at the leather jacket Ken had draped over his shoulders, seemingly deep in thought.

"Lamar, you're unusually quiet," Gaby offered. "What do you think?"

Lamar stroked his goatee several seconds before replying.

"Maybe I should go talk to him."

"No, that's a bad idea," Coop insisted, shaking his head emphatically. "Ken isn't exactly in a talking-things-out frame of mind at the moment."

"I agree," Gaby chimed in. "We need to wait until he's calmed down. And when we do confront him, it should be as a group. Strength in numbers."

"Yeah, I think a little one-on-one chat would help," Lamar said to himself, as if he hadn't heard a word the others said. The far away look in his eyes vanished and serenity filled the void, as though he'd just made some pivotal decision and was at peace with it.

"Whoa, danger, Will Robinson!" Coop said, the alarm in his voice beginning to show. "This will not end well."

"Trust me," Lamar said, exuding a level of confidence that seemed wildly disproportionate to the task, given Ken's increasingly volatile behavior. "I can reason with him."

Gaby and Coop exchanged worried glances that silently communicated a single message: Lamar's gone bonkers.

"You sure you don't want us to come with you?" Gaby offered. "Just in case?"

Lamar shook his head and, improbably, smiled.

"Naw. I got this."

"If you say so," Coop replied none too confidently as Lamar followed Ken's path north into the forest.

"Did we miss something there?" Gaby asked him.

"It kinda feels that way, doesn't it?"

* * * * * *

Lamar found Ken some 100 yards north of the meadow, facing the opposite direction as he whizzed into a pile of leaves at the foot of a gnarled maple tree. He'd set his spear and backpack against a rock jutting out of the ground and seemed to be muttering to himself.

"Buncha fucking ingrates," he mumbled bitterly. "When they come crawling back ..."

Ken let his sentence linger, as though he were still contemplating what he'd do if that ever happened.

Lamar looked for some way to announce his presence. He spotted an egg-shaped rock at his feet and kicked it a few feet. Ken started and looked over his shoulder at Lamar, sending his spray veering wildly to the right. He saw who it was and turned back to face the tree as he did his business.

"What do you want?" Ken's back asked. "You here to shake the dew off it?"

Lamar removed Ken's bomber jacket from his shoulders as he approached and draped it over the branch of a nearby tree.

"I'm returning your jacket."

Ken snorted.

"The mantle of leadership proved too much, huh? Well, if you're looking to apologize, you can forget about it. All three of you are now on my permanent shit list."

Lamar shook his head.

"Actually, I'm returning it because it doesn't fit."

"You could have done that back at camp," Ken said. "Why are you really here?"

"I thought we should discuss something."

"Yeah?" Ken intoned, clearly unconvinced of Lamar's intentions. "Like what?"

"The Series 7," Lamar replied.

Ken chuckled lightly to himself as his stream started to peter out.

"Sooo, you want to learn about trading securities from the master, huh?"

"No," Lamar responded evenly. "I'm wondering why the CEO of a brokerage has a how-to book on passing the Series 7."

Ken cocked his head to the side quizzically as though he were still trying to process what he'd heard.

"Come again?"

"The book in your suitcase," Lamar continued, his tone rapidly turning accusatory. "It's a test for a broker's trading license. How is it you don't have one already?"

Ken didn't reply immediately. He shook his hips as he finished and zipped himself up.

"You went through my personal belongings?" Ken finally

responded, his voice turning guttural in anger. "I've drop-kicked people for less."

Lamar seemed unfazed by the threat.

"I may have peeked."

Ken growled menacingly, his back still turned to Lamar.

"Give me one good reason I shouldn't rearrange your face."

Lamar smiled grimly, sensing Ken's unease.

"You don't run a brokerage at all, do you?" he pressed. "That's why you couldn't keep the number of employees straight. Did you really think ..."

Lamar was cut off as Ken suddenly whirled around and pinned him against the same tree his jacket was hanging from. His hands dug painfully into Lamar's shoulders, and his eyes burned with the same explosive rage that Wade exuded. His rank breath came out in steaming puffs of animus.

"You just don't know when to shut your mouth, do you, you little jackoff?" Ken roared between heaving breaths of barely controlled wrath. Despite the danger, Lamar knew he still held the trump card, and decided now was the time to lay it down.

"Careful, Ken," he warned. "One word from me and your whole charade goes up in smoke."

Ken seethed, and for a moment Lamar worried that he'd overplayed his hand.

"You tell anyone and I'll ...

"You'll what?" Lamar interrupted. "Beat me so bad I can't speak?"

"Fucking A!" Ken fairly screamed in that guttural voice again, spittle flying from his lips onto Lamar's cheeks.

"And how will you explain my injuries to the others? You think they'll just accept your version of events?" Lamar replied icily. "You'll be brought up on assault charges the minute we make it out of here. Good luck getting your precious Series 7 license with a conviction on your record."

Ken's face turned scarlet with rage. The vein on his forehead bulged in rhythm to his sputtering as he struggled to form coherent words, swept up in a maelstrom of impotent fury. Lamar just stared at him coldly, refusing to be intimidated.

Ken dropped his right hand from Lamar's shoulder only to ball it up into a fist and rear back. Lamar continued to stare him down, even as the cocked fist on the periphery of his vision suddenly shot forward at frightening speed. Half a second later his head snapped to one side as Ken's fist connected cleanly with his jawline. Hundreds of flashing lights danced before his eyes as he tasted his own blood. But Lamar never broke eye contact, even as Ken reared back again.

"You can't punch your way out of this one."

Lamar's voice rang out with such clarity and conviction that it broke through Ken's mania, startling him just as he was about to lash out again. Ken stood there, his fist primed to strike, shaking like a leaf as dueling emotions overwhelmed him. After several seconds the murderous hate in his eyes vanished, replaced in a blink by fear and self-doubt.

The color started to seep out of Ken's face as he lowered his eyes and his fist. His other hand, which had maintained a white-knuckle grip on Lamar's shoulder this whole time, slowly relaxed its hold before falling limply to his side. He was beaten and he knew it.

"What do you want?" Ken asked in a voice that was no longer guttural, but quavered instead with uncertainty.

Lamar smoothed out the lapels of his bubble jacket and smiled.

"Simple," he replied confidently. "An end to your reign of dickishness."

* * * * * *

It was nearly 6 p.m. before the pair made it back to camp. Their journey had passed in near-perfect silence — neither one had anything to say that hadn't already come out during their confrontation — and Lamar was looking forward to seeing the others. He was tired, he was sweaty, he had a blister forming on his left heel and he was desperately hungry. Ken, his unwilling companion, was so sullen that he'd spoken only two words, and that was just to give directions.

The pair came in from the south as the shadows started to lengthen, following the dirt road leading into camp. Lamar flashed back to the first time he'd taken this road: bouncing around in John's van, staring out the window at a primitive and hopelessly dilapidated campsite. Lamar smiled at the memory. After spending most of the day in the wilderness, this place now looked like Shangri-La to his weary eyes.

As they drew closer, Lamar could see Gaby and Coop in the distance, talking animatedly as they ate by the central firepit. Every so often, one of them would glance pensively eastward, presumably waiting for them to show. As Lamar drew closer, he started to pick up snippets of their conversation.

... you said what it was like but ... You didn't
believe me? More like I didn't want to believe.
It sounded so absurd. But there it sits, looking
like some post-apocalyptic nightmare. You
should have seen it when the ashes were still
steaming. It was indescribably eerie. It's plenty
creepy without it. What I want to know is: do
we have any plans in case this blight stuff
spreads? You worried it'll come up here? I'd
worry about anyone who wasn't worried
about it! But I can't imagine ... Hey, there they
are! I told you there was nothing to worry about.

Coop waved to Ken and Lamar as they approached the outskirts of the campgrounds. Gaby turned and motioned for the two to join them.

"Glad you could make it," Coop said, handing Lamar a can of chicken corn chowder and Ken a can of lima beans. "Hope you don't mind if we started without you."

"Sorry, we strayed nearly a quarter-mile south," Lamar explained. "It's tough to navigate with the sun in your eyes."

"What happened there?" Gaby inquired, pointing to Lamar's blood-encrusted split lip.

"Nothing," Lamar said as he glanced over at Ken, who was too busy wolfing down his dinner to notice. "I tripped, is all."

Lamar stared glumly at his unheated dinner for a long moment. Coop saw his reaction and anticipated his next words.

"We'll build a fire in the teepee tonight," he promised. "We've already gathered the kindling and wood for it, though I doubt you'll want to wait that long to eat."

Lamar nodded and started spooning food into his mouth.

"So, who takes first shift tonight?" Gaby asked as she rubbed her arms and shivered against the rapidly encroaching evening chill.

"Do we need to?" Coop asked. "I mean, Wade's badly hurt. He wouldn't try anything now, right?"

Lamar shook his head slowly.

"Logically, no," he responded between mouthfuls. "But crazy people aren't logical. We need to assume he's still a threat."

"If you had seen him today, you wouldn't even ask," Gaby said. "He didn't try to kill me out of anger, or even for sport. All I was to him was prey."

She paused, shivering at the memory this time instead of the cold.

Lamar polished off his meager dinner and started running his finger around the inside of the can, desperate to scoop up every last morsel. When he was finished, he wiped the finger down the front of his T-shirt.

"You keep that up and you're shirt's going to be another color before we get out of here," Coop joked.

Lamar looked down and saw he'd stained the left breast of his Pwn U shirt with sauce, partially obscuring the troll face meme in the center. On the right breast were grease stains from the fish they'd eaten the first night.

"I'll be sure to match the stains next time," Lamar responded blandly. "Is Beverly still down in the floodplain, with all of the ... dead stuff?"

Coop nodded solemnly.

"Just sitting on a rock and staring off into space," he replied. "I don't think she's left that spot this whole time."

"Even for Beverly, that's not normal behavior," Lamar opined, slightly worried. "Someone should talk to her, in case she's depressed or suicidal."

"Don't look at me," Coop said. "I'm not going down there again. That place gave off seriously bad vibes."

"You better believe I won't do it," Gaby unvolunteered. "Not after the things she said last night. Drunk or not, she can stew alone all she wants."

Coop looked over at Ken.

"Ken, you're being unusually quiet."

"Is that a crime?" he muttered sullenly, staring at his feet.

"Why don't you talk to her?" Lamar suggested.

Ken flashed him a dirty look. Coop closed his eyes, expecting an endless torrent of profanity and blustery threats, topped off with a vaguely racist nickname for good measure. To his astonishment, Ken said nothing. He merely made a guttural noise of general disgust, stood up and headed west toward the floodplains. Coop and Gaby watched him depart, wide-eyed.

"You just became my personal hero," Coop gushed once Ken was safely out of earshot. "How'd you do that without a chair and a bullwhip?"

"St ... stop it," Lamar stammered. "I don't like people making fun of me."

"He wasn't," Gaby reassured him. "You don't realize just how much you've grown since coming here. Three days ago, you could barely look Ken in the face. Now you're giving him orders. We're both impressed."

Lamar realized they were both serious and reddened in

embarrassment.

"So, how'd you do it?" Coop pressed. "What's your secret?"

Lamar bit his lip pensively as though he were trying to come up with a diplomatic answer.

"It wasn't my secret that was at issue," Lamar finally replied. "Ken and I talked, and I think we have an understanding."

"But are we good?" Coop asked. "Have we heard the last from General Disarray?"

"I think so," Lamar replied, nursing his split lip. "If I'm right, he won't be giving us any more trouble."

* * * * * *

Ken ventured down into the floodplain just as the sun started to kiss the horizon, painting the western sky in fiery hues of yellow and orange, while the colors overhead slowly bled away, replacing the brilliant blue of day with twilight's more subdued shades of blue and pink.

He found Beverly sitting on a broad and flat rock just past the archery range in this strange no man's land, ignoring her alien surroundings in favor of watching the sunset. As before, the minute he set foot on the contaminated soil all external sounds ceased, as if he were stepping into a containment bubble. Before long he also felt that sense of nausea that threw off his equilibrium and made it seem like he was walking with two left feet. He did his best to shrug off the sensations as he joined Beverly on the rock.

She made no effort to acknowledge him as he sat beside her; she just continued staring blankly at the sunset.

"Here," he said, plunking a can of lima beans down between them.

He leaned forward slightly to stare into her face for any sign of a response. He saw nothing.

"You still beating yourself up over last night?" he asked. "And today?"

No response.

"We've all done stupid shit we regret the next day," Ken continued, as if nothing was amiss. "The stories I could tell you from my college years would have you ..."

Beverly turned to face Ken, and his next words died in his throat. Bathed in the harsh light of the setting sun, Beverly's age lines and crow's feet were magnified, making her appear far older than she really was. But it was her eyes that shocked Ken into silence. They looked sunken and haunted, as if she were one unkind word away from slitting her wrists.

"Did the others send you to find out if I'm crazy?" she asked after several uncomfortable seconds. In Ken's ears, the question almost sounded like a plea for affirmation that she truly was sane.

"First off, nobody sends me anywhere. I come and go as I please," Ken insisted. "Second, I don't think you're crazy. Useless, maybe, but not crazy."

Beverly didn't respond. She just kept staring at him with her pained eyes.

"I don't know how you can stand it down here," Ken volunteered, growing uncomfortable. "The lack of other noises and the weird sensation in the pit of your stomach. Just ... ugh."

"Those things I told you about in the dream, those ... creatures," Beverly said softly, as though she were speaking to herself. "That was no dream. They did all this," she said, motioning to the radically altered landscape. "And when they return, they'll do the same thing to us. And thinking I'm crazy doesn't change that."

"If you're so convinced that these imaginary bogeymen are coming back, then why aren't you running?"

Beverly didn't answer. She just lowered her head to her chest and started slowly rocking back and forth as if she were trying to comfort herself.

"Look, I honestly don't give two shits what you're going through or whether you're stark raving mad," Ken finally admitted, dropping any pretense of small talk. "What I do care about is that you have the same problem as me: we're both on the outs with the group."

Beverly raised her head, revealing a new emotion to Ken besides the desperation and fear painted on her face: a tiny flicker of curiosity that shone through her passive acceptance of some terrible imagined fate.

"Since when did that matter to you?" she asked.

"Since the fat one started calling the shots. Let me show you something."

Ken reached into his pocket and fished out his wallet. He opened it and pulled a business card from the right billfold that he held out for Beverly.

The curiosity in Beverly's face quickly ebbed.

"Are you giving me your shrink's number?"

"Just read it," Ken instructed.

Beverly took the card and studied it.

Ken R. Berman
President and CEO
Berman Investment Solutions

"Okay," Beverly said, handing the card back. "So what?"

"It's a fake. I had it printed at Kinkos. Something I give to the ladies and the occasional scrub investor," Ken confided as he reached into the left billfold for another business card. "This is the real one."

Beverly examined it, her curiosity piqued once more.

Ken R. Berman
Junior Sales Associate
Shales & Wilder

"You're a glorified salesman?" she asked, puzzled both by the subterfuge and his inexplicable admission. "Why the façade?"

"My father is a ... difficult man," Ken explained. "You probably guessed that already from hearing all his maxims, but they don't fully convey just how demanding he is. As and Bs weren't enough in school. I had to have straight As. If the neighbor's boy ran the mile in seven minutes, I had to do it in six. Anything less than perfection was met with rejection. When I didn't make first cut for varsity football, he changed the locks and refused to let me in the house for two weeks."

Beverly gawked at the story, her depression and anxiety momentarily submerged by this tale of casual child abandonment.

"So senior year, I get an acceptance letter from his alma

mater," Ken continued. "Full scholarship. I'd never seen him so proud. It was the first time he ever treated me like an equal. That feeling … it was like mainlining heroin. I had to have more. By my junior year, I was struggling to make dean's list so I joined a test-sharing ring. I was caught and expelled. I couldn't tell him so I … kept pretending to go. When I 'graduated,' I naturally told him I'd gotten a plum assignment at a top brokerage. Things kinda snowballed from there. The lies kept getting bigger … and more expensive. Successful brokers don't drive 12-year-old Audis, so I started leasing a Lamborghini. A loft in the East Village. Expensive restaurants. Sales associates don't make much, so I went underwater pretty fast. I took out multiple bank loans, half a dozen credit cards, anything to keep the party going."

"The simple fact is, I didn't come here for a nature retreat," Ken admitted. "In two weeks, I have to file for bankruptcy. I'm going to lose everything. And I'm here because I don't know how to face my old man."

Beverly's expression was midway between pity and confusion. After a few moments of struggle, she finally raised the question that had been nagging her ever since he'd started his sudden, unprompted confession.

"Why are you telling me all this?"

"Because Lamar figured it out and now he's holding it over my head. As long as he's in charge, my days are numbered. And after last night's drunken escapades, I'm guessing yours are as well."

Beverly looked away. The shame of her conduct was still fresh in her mind, if not the details.

"Alone, neither of us can do much against a unified group,"

Ken said. "But together, we just might upend the status quo. Interested?"

Beverly paused to consider the offer.

"What do I have to do?" she finally asked.

Ken smiled wickedly, his eyes narrowing to fine points. In the light of the setting sun, he looked truly malicious.

"You're going to help me stage a coup. Listen closely."

Beverly listened.

* * * * * *

Gaby exited the outhouse with a sigh of relief. She hated using the outhouse after dusk. It was so dark and cramped that she imagined herself as a fetus waiting to be born. Plus, after four days of regular usage, it was beginning to stink, no matter how much sawdust she threw down the hole. She breathed deeply after closing the door, reveling in the crisp night air.

Things were only slightly brighter outside, even though it had scarcely been 20 minutes since sunset. A blanket of low-lying clouds blotted out the moon and most of the stars, rendering anything further than 15 feet away shadowy and indistinct. She could make out the wigwam's dim outline between the slats of the surrounding fence, along with the branches of nearby trees and bushes surrounding the campsite swaying in the breeze. Everything else was buried in a fog of darkness.

The din of chirping crickets was all around. She had heard them in the outhouse but didn't register how loud they were until she was back outside, either because the interior muffled the sound or because they were growing more active now that it was dark. Either way, it sounded like hundreds of them serenading the forest, transmitting their shrill song in every direction.

Gaby's breath came out in tiny puffs of heated air. She marveled at the temperature differential between the outhouse and the outdoors. It hadn't been this cold when she went in. Part of it was the strong breeze, which stabbed her cheeks and cut right through her multiple layers of clothing. She dimly wondered how so many crickets were able to tolerate this temperature.

Over the din of crickets, she heard the sound of the teepee's door opening.

"Gaby?" Coop's voice called out uncertainly in the darkness. "We're closing up for the night. You coming?"

"Be right there," Gaby called back.

From inside the wigwam, she heard Ken complaining about having to take first shift on such a cold night before the door's closure muffled his voice.

As she started toward the wigwam, a flash of light in the distance caught her eyes. A beam of brilliant light penetrated the darkness about half a mile south of camp, on the far side of the surrounding hills.

The searing shaft of white shot upward, like the floodlights used at movie premieres, only there was no diffusion; a solid, column of illumination. As tiny as it looked to Gaby, it had to be four stories high to be visible from so far away. She held her breath, fixated by the sight. After a few seconds, the pillar of light slowly dissipated, and darkness once more blanketed the region.

Gaby shivered, trying to decide what she'd just seen. No

flashlight was capable of projecting a beam so strong and concentrated from that distance. She kept staring off into the darkness, hoping to see the light again. As she strained her eyes, she could see the trees and bushes nearby swaying to and fro in the blustery breeze. She shielded her face against the wind with her hand as she continued staring, hoping for another sign. But none came.

Gaby had just made up her mind to inform the others when she noticed that the undulating plant life surrounding the camp was no longer confined to its edges. Shapes writhed and swayed in impossible patterns beside the central firepit, in front of the showers, and around the former location of the second outhouse. It looked like the forest had sprung to life and begun reclaiming the campground as its own. The shrill sound of crickets was overpowering.

Gaby slowly backed away, making for the fence line and the wigwam.

The moon briefly poked out from behind the clouds and bathed the campsite in an eerie glow, revealing hundreds of squirming, inky shapes swarming from all sides. They looked like softballs coated in tar, only these softballs could twist and bend in unnatural ways, like they were made of silly putty. They had no visible eyes or mouth; no sign of life to them at all. Gaby would have thought they were clumps of ash from the floodplain, except for their aggressive, jerking movements, which were too volatile for the wind to engineer.

The moon retreated behind the clouds once more, leaving Gaby alone in the darkness with these things.

She screamed and bolted for the fence line. Behind

her, Gaby could hear frantic chirping drawing closer. She stopped only long enough to throw open the door to the wigwam and dive through before spinning around and slamming it closed behind her. She looked around at her startled companions, who she could just make out in the dim glow of John's upturned flashlight, which was seated on a stack of firewood beside the central firepit. Beverly, who looked to have been asleep when the commotion started, groggily raised her head in confusion.

"Gaby, what's going on?" Coop asked, confused.

"¡Los ikus! ¡Están aquí para nosotros!" she shouted hysterically as she tried with fumbling fingers to tie the upper and lower enclosures to the door and then scooted backward. She was talking a mile a minute, barely making sense in her native Spanish.

"¡Nos matarán a todos! ¡Ikus! Ikus!" she continued ranting, her panicked eyes darting every which way as she kept scooting back until her rear pressed against the pile of wood, upsetting the flashlight. It landed in the dirt with the beam aimed squarely at Gaby's face, revealing to the others just how frightened she was.

"What are you going on about?" Ken asked as he bundled up, preparing to take the first watch.

"There's so ... something out th ... there," she finally managed to get out in English as she shook uncontrollably.

Lamar stood up and grabbed his spear, fearing the worst.

"Is it Wade?" he asked.

Gaby shook her head.

"It's these little bl... black things," she said between panicked breaths. "Thousands of them, all around the campsite.

They're all wriggling and ... we can't stay here! If we stay, they'll ... they'll surround us!"

Instead of rushing to reinforce the door, Coop and Lamar exchanged worried glances as Ken rolled his eyes and silently mouthed: "Here we go again." The only one who seemed appropriately alarmed was Beverly, who pressed her hand to her chest in worry.

"What's wrong with you all?" Gaby asked, vacillating between desperation and exasperation as her words started to run together. "We have to go now! They're right outside! Weneedtogetoutofhererightnowtheikuarecoming!"

Lamar set his spear back down and kneeled beside Gaby with a pained expression on his face, as though he were steeling himself for a difficult conversation. That's when it suddenly dawned on Gaby.

"You don't believe me," she said in astonishment.

Lamar tried to be tactful.

"Beverly described seeing something similar after drinking the moonshine," Lamar started. "Maybe she planted the idea of those things in your head, so when you saw the bushes rustling in the darkness, it looked like what she described. But it's just your mind playing tricks on you."

Gaby shook her head insistently.

"Nonononono!" You don't understand!" she insisted as tears welled up in the corner of her eyes. "She didn't tell me anything! I swear, they're out there right now!"

Lamar bit his lower lip as he struggled to convince Gaby that it was all in her head. He opened his mouth to speak but was interrupted by Beverly, who was now wide awake.

"If they're already here, it's too late to escape," she

warned ominously.

"Goddammit!" Ken intoned as he picked up the flashlight and trained its beam on the entrance. "Do I have to go out there and prove there's nothing there but a bunch of noisy crickets?"

"Well, you did draw first shift," Coop reminded him. "So you might as well get it over with."

"What?" Gaby shrieked. "Are you crazy? You can't go out there!"

Ken shook his head sadly as he loosened the door straps.

"Am I gonna have to check for monsters under your bed next?" he chuckled as he grabbed one of the door's struts and prepared to push it open. Gaby rushed forward, desperate to stop him, but Ken used his large frame to block her.

"If you open that door, they'll kill us all!" she shouted, giving in to hysteria as she futilely struggled with him. "Theikuwon'tspareanyonestopitnoworwe'llalldie!"

"Will someone get this crazy bitch off me?" Ken intoned as he pushed the door open and peered outside.

"See? Absolutely nothing to fea ..." he stopped mid-sentence as the flashlight's beam landed on a wriggling, black mass oozing its way through the gap in the fence. The gelatinous blob started smoking and writhing as soon as the light touched it, and split apart like the globules in a lava lamp, scattering in all directions to avoid the light. A small section at the center of the mass didn't move fast enough and quickly dissipated into a steaming, inky pool under the flashlight's glaring beam.

That's when Ken noticed movement on the beam's periphery. Hundreds of these things were scaling the fence or squeezing through the slats, wriggling their way toward him. It was like all the world's black Play-Doh had suddenly turned hostile.

"...rrrrrholy fuck! What the shit is that?" Ken shouted as he reared back and slammed the door closed behind him.

"She's not crazy! There's thousands of those things out there! It's some kind of invasion!" Ken screamed as he dropped the flashlight in favor of the one of the door struts and braced his feet against either end of the frame to keep it closed.

"Tie it down! Tie the door closed now!" he demanded as he held the door fast.

Lamar rushed over and reached between Ken's feet to tie the upper and lower clasps to the door. On the other side of the wigwam, Gaby had retreated to her sleeping bag, clutching it like a security blanket as she mouthed the word "iku" over and over. Beverly wasn't far behind in the panic department. Only Coop remained skeptical.

"Ken, if this is another one of your dumb pranks, like when you said John was back ..."

"I am dead fucking serious!" Ken shouted to cut him off. "There's really something out there!"

"Let me see," Coop said, sounding unconvinced as he tried to gently move one of Ken's hands out of the way so he could take a look.

Ken responded by violently shoving him away, sending Coop flying one way and his glasses the other.

"Anyone tries to open this door and I'll wring their neck!" Ken hollered.

In the awkward silence that followed, they could all hear

the high-pitched chirping noises growing in intensity. They were now coming from every direction.

Coop dusted himself off and hunted for his glasses as Lamar grabbed the flashlight and panned it from side to side. One sweep of the beam illuminated Beverly, who was curled up in a ball on her sleeping bag, slowly rocking back and forth as she cradled her arms for comfort. A second pass of the beam revealed Gaby on the other side of the teepee, still in shock after her ordeal, her eyes glued to the entrance for any sign of movement. A third caught the reflection from Coop's glasses in the firepit.

"Just great," Coop muttered as he dusted the soot off to find the left lens badly scratched from the fall. He placed them back on the bridge of his nose and squinted, trying to see past the damaged lens. He couldn't tell if it was from Lamar's unsteady grip on the flashlight or from the scratched lens, but it almost looked like the walls near the base of the teepee were … moving. He closed his left eye and focused on one section of the wall near the entrance to the teepee. After a few seconds, there could be no doubt.

"Look at the walls," Coop warned, his voice quavering.

Lamar followed Coop's finger and trained the flashlight on a spot to the left of Ken.

The fabric near the base of the wigwam was bulging inward against the lattice frame, as if someone or something was repeatedly pressing against it, trying to force its way in. The pressure on the fabric immediately ceased where the center of the beam was aimed, but in the dim light of the beam's outer edges, they could see the material still pressing inward from the base up to about a foot above the ground.

"Whatthefuckwhatthefuckwhatthefuck!" Ken started wailing in an unnaturally high voice.

Before long, the base of the walls began to bulge on all sides. The feathered mandala overhanging the entrance began to vibrate as the chirping grew more insistent.

"We're trapped!" Gaby shrieked.

Ken kept his feet firmly planted against the door, forgetting in his panic that it only opened outward. He noticed that some of the shadows to the left of the entrance appeared to be swaying.

"They're coming in!" he shouted, pointing toward the swirling mass in the shadows.

Lamar trained the beam in the direction Ken pointed, where it illuminated an inky mass trying to force its way through narrow gaps between the bottom of the canvas and the dirt. The black tendrils started smoking and quickly retreated. Ken scooted away until his back was against the stones surrounding the central firepit, his eyes frantically searching the shadows for any further signs of movement.

From the relative safety of her bedroll, Beverly comforted herself by huddling into a ball and slowly rocking back and forth, trying to convince herself that none of this was real. Out of the corner of her eye, she noticed movement in the gloom just over her right shoulder. She slowly turned, dreading what she might find. Something long and sinewy leapt out of the shadows at her.

Beverly's shriek pierced the din of incessant chirping. Lamar turned to see Beverly leap backward, landing in a heap several feet away from her bedroll. He aimed the flashlight at her bedroll and found a heaving mass of darkness swarming beside it. The creatures writhed in agony as the light seared them. Those caught in the light's central cone started smoking and quickly evaporated, while those on the periphery retreated to the shadows.

Coop and Gaby knelt beside Beverly to examine her. With her eyes still squeezed shut in terror, Beverly swung her arms wildly at them, convinced that it was the creatures. It took a lot of convincing before Beverly opened her eyes.

"They touched me!" she shrieked hysterically. "One of those things grabbed me!"

She motioned to her left arm, which was shaking like a leaf. Coop gently examined it and saw some grayish-black powder on the outer edge of her palm. Her palm felt cold and clammy to the touch. Coop studied the powder for a moment then broke into a smile.

"Beverly, it's just soot," he explained. "You probably got it from the floodplain."

Beverly looked at him in disbelief.

"It's not a bite?"

Coop shook his head.

"But it touched me. It felt so cold."

"You probably ran your finger along the zipper of your sleeping bag while running from those things," Coop gently suggested.

"I'm not going to die, then?" Beverly asked pitifully.

"Not from ash," Gaby said, suppressing the urge to laugh. "Priests use more soot than that on Ash Wednesday."

As the others let her be, Beverly cautiously examined her left hand. It appeared unharmed, and her fingers still worked. She wiped the soot off the palm. It smeared and gradually faded as she rubbed, except for one small black dot in the center. No matter how hard she rubbed, this pimple-sized black spot stubbornly remained.

After seeing what the flashlight had done to the creatures menacing Beverly, Lamar had a thought. He pointed the flashlight at a spot a few feet to the left of the entrance. The fabric stopped bulging. He spun and trained it on a section near the rear of the wigwam. Small inky tendrils were worming their way under the fabric and into the teepee. They started smoking the moment the light hit them and quickly retreated. He spotted another point a few feet away where the material at the base was bulging so far inward it looked ready to split open. He trained the beam on it and the pressure quickly relented. Everywhere the light focused the creatures retreated.

A look of understanding slowly spread across Lamar's face.

"They're afraid of the light," he said softly, almost to himself.

'We need to build a fire," he told the others. "Now."

"What if fire doesn't work?" Coop asked.

As if on cue, the flashlight momentarily dimmed. Lamar smacked it and the light came back.

"If you have a better idea, now would be the time," he replied.

* * * * * *

Lamar stood near the center of the wigwam and slowly rotated, like he was practicing the waltz, only with the flashlight as his partner. Its roving beam fended off whatever was outside, one section of the wigwam at a time. Behind him, Gaby and Coop were struggling to get a fire going.

Coop had raided his duffel bag and was tearing an undershirt into small strips that he laid over a pile of wood stacked in the firepit, while Gaby coated the strips in flakes of magnesium hastily scraped from the magnesium stick. Her hands were shaking so badly as she worked with John's penknife that it was a wonder she didn't nick herself. Once she had produced a small pile of magnesium flakes, Gaby flipped the stick over and ran the blade along the stick's flint backing, trying to generate a spark with unsteady hands.

After several attempts, the magnesium flakes ignited. The group watched as crackling flames greedily consumed Coop's undershirt and several twigs he'd thrown on the pile. Coop kept feeding the fire from his wardrobe, coaxing the flames to the firewood underneath.

Their eyes all quickly turned from the fire to the teepee walls. Sure enough, as the flames rose higher and the aura of light spread further, the pressure on the walls slowly eased.

Lamar turned off the flashlight with a sigh of relief. Coop fell to his knees in exhaustion. Gaby hung her head in silent gratitude. Whatever these things wanted, fire clearly wasn't on the menu, but the creatures' high-pitched chirps made it clear that they hadn't gone far.

As the minutes slowly ticked by, each of them struggled to deal with their new reality in different ways. Beverly seemed to be in complete denial, muttering to herself as she rubbed her right palm incessantly. Gaby sat several feet from the entrance with her spear at the ready, watching the door like a hawk for any sign of movement. Coop seemed to withdraw into himself, staring silently at a photo with a look of deep regret as he blinked back tears.

Lamar, who was the only one to keep his composure, albeit just barely, looked over the eight remaining pieces of firewood, trying to calculate how long they would last.

Ken openly panicked.

"What the fuck are they?" he said in a fierce whisper, as if he were afraid of offending the things outside. "No creature looks or acts like that. None. What the hell are they?"

Strangely enough, he seemed to be directing his questions toward Lamar.

"I don't know," Lamar replied. "Some undiscovered species, maybe."

"This isn't the wilds of Madagascar! It's fucking Pennsylvania!" Ken hissed. "Brand new creatures do not just appear out of nowhere several thousand strong! We're not talking about some solitary Bigfoot! And with the way they moved … those things are not natural!"

"Then you can sell your story to *The X-Files* when we make it out of here," Lamar replied, growing tired of Ken's rants.

"You really think we're going to make it out of here?" Beverly spoke up, surprising the others. "When the fire dies, those things are going to come in here … and then we'll die," she said in a matter-of-fact, oddly detached manner as she picked at her right palm.

"What if none of this is real?" Coop chimed in, briefly looking up from the picture in his hand. "Maybe we're all experiencing some mass hallucination."

Ken scoffed at the idea.

"Is this what they taught you at the ashram?" he sneered. "Some metaphysical what-if bullshit you say right after your mantra, like we're all a figment of someone else's dream? Fuck that!"

Lamar coughed politely. Ken caught his subtle warning to ease off the throttle and reluctantly backed down, knowing full well what would happen if he didn't.

"Fine, forget I said anything," Ken muttered in lieu of an apology, like a sulking child.

"I think Coop means that we're all stoned out of our minds on peyote or something," Lamar explained.

Coop nodded in agreement.

"Those things John did with the fire didn't make sense," Coop said, remembering how the flames danced in rhythm to John's voice. "He could have sprayed those lava rocks with a mind-altering chemical. We inhale it and start tripping. It could still be the first night and all of us are high."

Lamar considered this for a few moments before dismissing the idea.

"If we were all hallucinating, you wouldn't be asking these kinds of questions. And I think things would be more dreamlike, more surreal."

"This shit isn't surreal enough for you?" Ken asked.

Coop's idea seemed to register with Beverly, who stared dreamily off into space, muttering to herself that it was "all just a dream."

Lamar ignored Ken's smart-ass remark and turned to Gaby, who was still watching the door.

"Gaby, before, you gave those things a name: 'igloo,' or something. What was that?"

Gaby sighed as if she'd been anticipating the question.

"It's a long story," she said, setting her spear on the ground and turning partially toward the others; enough to see them, but not so far that should couldn't keep an eye on the door.

"You got somewhere else to be?" Coop asked grimly.

"It'll sound stupid," she warned.

"Gaby, stupid is better than nothing," Lamar pleaded. "And right now, we know nothing about these things."

"I saw something like those things once. In a book on Santeria."

Ken made a face.

"You mean voodoo with shrunken heads and shit like that?"

"It's a mishmash of African rituals and Catholicism," Coop answered for her, surprising everyone. "What? I read up on all religions."

"Voodoo is more a Creole thing," Gaby explained. "Santeria is Caribbean. Anyway, my parents practiced it in their native Cuba, and they tried to teach me when I turned 12. I think it was more about heritage than spirituality to them. But heritage or not, I didn't take to it; by that time, I was more interested in Jonathan Taylor Thomas than some creepy old religion."

"Can we skip the *Tiger Beat* recap and get to the point?" Ken asked impatiently.

Lamar looked at them both blankly.

"I understood literally nothing in that exchange."

"Count yourself fortunate," Coop intoned.

"One of the books dealt with the orisha, the gods of Santeria, and their minions, dark spirits called ajogun," Gaby continued. "They act kind of like divine enforcers, imposing the orisha's will on people. The book had illustrations of all the ajogun, and those things out there look just like the illustrations of the iku."

"So, I take it these iku are bad?" Lamar asked.

Gaby nodded.

"How bad?"

"The iku are the worst of the ajogun; they purify wayward souls, guiding them to Orun."

"That doesn't sound so bad," Coop sniffed.

"Orun means 'heaven,' because the purification process is always fatal," Gaby explained quietly. "They're the embodiment of death."

Coop went wide-eyed.

"Okay, on second thought, not so good."

"I don't know what those things out there are, but if they are the iku, then it's only matter of time," Gaby warned.

"You said you didn't believe in that mumbo jumbo," Ken reminded her.

"I don't. I didn't … I don't know," Gaby finally admitted. "Until those things appeared, I was an atheist. I thought I had a pretty good handle on life. But after seeing them, I don't know what to believe."

"Did the book say anything about how to stop or appease them?" Lamar asked.

"Once the iku have selected their targets, they never stop," Gaby explained. "It doesn't matter where we run. They can't be appeased, beaten or bargained with."

"Then why haven't they killed us already?" Lamar pressed.

Gaby thought a few moments before answering.

"I'm not really sure. Some ajogun telegraph their intentions in advance, giving their targets time to make amends and get their affairs in order, sort of like a boss giving you 30 days' notice instead of just summarily firing you. This could be a warning before they actually come to claim us. Or, it could have nothing to do with the iku at all. This could be something else entirely."

Ken snorted as he added a log to the fire.

"This is a waste of time."

"If we want to survive, our only chance is to learn about … whatever those things are," Lamar replied. "I can't explain what's out there, so I'll take all the answers I can get."

"You really think some bad juju spirits hitched a ride from Cuba to kill us because we aren't smoking their cigars or eating enough pulled pork sandwiches?" Ken said with a barking laugh. "We don't need her bull …" Ken stopped short, catching himself before Lamar had to signal that he was taking things too far again. "Look, all I'm saying is that I'll stick with real answers," he started again, slightly more diplomatically. "They fear fire and flashlights hurt them. That's enough for me."

Behind them, Beverly squirmed in discomfort as she picked at the black spot on her palm. No matter what she did, it wouldn't go away. In fact, it appeared to be growing, and was now the size of a small mole. And her mind, already awash in silent panic, started to produce horrible, destructive visions and fantasies that no amount of self-control could will away.

"All just a dream," she tried to assure herself. "All just a dream."

* * * * * *

Lamar checked his binary watch: it was just after six, but you wouldn't know it from looking through the ventilation hole in the roof of the wigwam. The sky overhead looked just as dark now as it had at midnight. Lamar hoped it was just from the cloud cover. He looked over at his companions, most of whom were sitting glumly around the fire.

Nobody had slept a wink; none had even tried, given the noisy chirping of the iku all around. Besides, dozing seemed like a lousy way to spend one's final hours on Earth. Coop, who was sitting on the last unburnt log, shifted uncomfortably from side to side; he hadn't been able to pee all night, and his bladder was making its displeasure known.

Gaby, who was constantly scanning the edges of the wigwam for any hint of movement, noticed the canvas begin to bulge several feet to the right of the entrance as the fire burned low.

"Lamar!" she called out.

Lamar stoked the embers with his spear and the fire briefly shot back up. The pressure on their fabric fortress immediately let up. Coop stood up and tossed his seat onto the fire.

"So, that's it," Coop said with an air of finality as he pulled the photo from his wallet once more to study it. "We're going to die."

Lamar nodded glumly.

"It was only a matter of time."

"I somehow envisioned death being a lot scarier," Gaby

said reflectively. "Sitting around a fire, waiting for it to fizzle out; it's a pretty boring way to go."

"Nobody's dying," Ken insisted, staring into the flames. "We'll fight our way out, if we have to."

"Fight how?" Lamar asked. "What good are spears against … whatever those things are?"

"We'll use them as torches then," Ken declared. "These iku things fear fire, so they should fear portable fire just as much."

Coop shook his head sadly.

"Even if that did work, the torches would burn out before we make it halfway across the floodplain. Face it: we're stuck here."

"There were so many other things I wanted to do with my life," Gaby said.

"All of us did," Coop agreed. "I wanted to learn another language. Maybe Japanese."

"I wanted to see the world," Gaby admitted. "Be an explorer."

Ken laughed savagely.

"We all know what Lamar wanted: to kiss something other than his blow-up doll."

Lamar flashed him a dirty look before responding.

"I'd be happy to tell the others what you wanted, Ken," he intoned, sending a not-so-subtle reminder that he'd leak Ken's dirty little secret unless he simmered down.

But instead of cowing Ken, Lamar's warning seemed to spark something primal in him. Ken's eyes flashed in anger as he issued his own warning. "Get off my back already!" he growled in the same guttural voice he'd used to threaten

Lamar in the woods before sundown. As before, it reminded Lamar eerily of Wade's threats against the group. But as menacing as Ken was, Lamar refused to back down.

"You get off everyone else's!" Lamar demanded, standing up for emphasis. Ken rose to his full height, and the two stared each other down for several awkward moments. Coop watched this war of wills anxiously, worried that a fight was about to break out. Fortunately, whatever bloodlust had overcome Ken departed just as quickly. He lowered his eyes and sat down with a huff.

In the awkward silence that followed, Beverly spoke up. She was the only one not beside the fire. Sitting on her sleeping bag, facing away from the others, she appeared to be deep in thought.

"You're all so preoccupied with death. Nobody here's going to die," she said in an odd, singsong fashion. It was the first time she'd spoken in hours. "None of us are really here. This is a dream. And you can't die in a dream."

"Sure, Bev," Ken said, humoring her.

That's when Coop noticed a glint of steel in her hands. He looked closer, favoring his right eye since looking past the scratches on his left lens was awkward. She appeared to be holding Gaby's penknife in her left hand, staring at it intently. She must have grabbed it in the earlier confusion.

"Beverly? What's the knife for?" he asked, trying to disguise his rising sense of alarm.

His question caught the attention of others, too, who were now actively paying attention to the older woman for the first time that evening.

"What? This?" she asked dreamily, still staring hypnotically at the blade.

Coop extended his hand cautiously.

"Why don't you give it over here?" he urged.

"This can't hurt anyone," she said distantly, as though her voice were coming from deep underground. "All it does is wake you up."

She turned the blade upward and reared back to plunge the blade into her neck. Ken was on her in a moment, grabbing her knife hand and slamming it to the ground, taking her down with it. Coop dropped his photo and leapt at Beverly, immobilizing her left shoulder. Gaby suddenly appeared from the other side to hold down the right shoulder, all while Ken tried to disarm her.

"Let me go! Let me go!" Beverly ranted as she thrashed wildly. "This isn't real!"

As Beverly flailed, Coop's eye fixated on something seemingly insignificant amid the chaos: a small black spot on the edge of Beverly's hand, about the size of a penny. Had it always been there?

"This can't be real! I want to wake up now! I want to wake up!!!"

"Lady, you're going about it the wrong way!" Ken said as he cranked Beverly's wrist until she gave a cry of pain and the small knife left her grasp. Ken kicked it away toward Lamar, who quickly scooped it up and put it back in Gaby's bag.

The others slowly loosened their grips on Beverly. She jerked away and threw herself face-first on her sleeping bag, wailing "It's not real!" over and over again into the fabric, muffling the sound.

As Coop was composing himself after the ordeal, Gaby found the photo he was staring at before Beverly's meltdown. He'd dropped it in the mad scramble to stop her. It was a wallet-sized photo of a blond boy on the cusp of puberty, smiling to the camera with a gap-toothed grin from what looked like a suburban backyard. It was faded and heavily creased as though it had seen a lot of exposure over the years.

"You dropped this," she said to Coop, handing it over.

"Thanks," he replied with a relieved smile.

"Handsome boy. What's his name?"

"Dylan," Coop answered as he smoothed out his robes.

"Does he live with his mom?"

Coop's smile faded.

"It doesn't matter," he declared as he stuffed it back into his wallet. "I'll never see him again."

"Whoa, Twinkle Toes is a father?" Ken asked, seemingly impressed. "You're messing with my worldview!"

"Can we please talk about something else?" Coop asked in embarrassment.

In the awkward silence that followed, Ken was the first to register just how quiet things had become.

"Is it just me, or are those iku thingies getting quieter?" he asked.

Everyone listened intently. Now that Beverly had finished wailing into her sleeping bag and was content to merely sob into it, they noticed the chirping outside was starting to abate. The distinction was subtle enough that more than one of them questioned whether it was real or merely wishful thinking.

After about 10 minutes, there could be no doubt; the chirps were decreasing in intensity and number. It was nearly dawn. The low-lying clouds overhead had dissipated, revealing an indigo sky overhead flecked with streaks of light.

"I think they're leaving," Lamar said optimistically, vocalizing what the others would not for fear of jinxing it.

By the time the stars were fading and the high-flying cirrus clouds were distinguishable from the rapidly brightening sky, the chirping had ceased. Dawn had come.

Everyone huddled near the entrance. Gaby and Ken wrapped thin strips of cloth around the tips of their spears. If anything went awry, they would stick them in the fire to set them alight.

"So, who goes first?" Coop asked.

No one spoke up.

"I nominate Ken," Lamar finally said.

"That sounds good to me," Gaby chimed in.

"God, you all are pussies!" Ken intoned with a roll of his eyes.

He handed his spear to Lamar and steeled himself in front of the door. He pressed his ear against it cautiously but heard nothing. He slowly undid the upper and lower enclosures, took a deep breath and pushed it open.

WEDNESDAY

As Ken pushed the wigwam's creaking door outward, he looked out on a campsite that was unrecognizable. Twilight's gray dimness revealed a desolate wasteland. The bushes lining the campsite were all withered and naked, their shriveled leaves littering the ground. So too were the trees, which only yesterday had been at peak bloom. Ash was everywhere, spread out across most of the campsite in the now familiar spiral patterns. The only exception was the fenced-in area, where the creatures appeared to have foregone artistry, coating every inch of ground in a thick layer of soot.

The wigwam had been largely spared the ash treatment, although the bottom foot was caked in the stuff all the way around. The smell — like the aftermath of Burning Man — was overpowering. Billows of steam rising from the ashes helped complete the otherworldly impression.

"What ... in ... the ... fuck?" Ken intoned.

The others, who couldn't see past Ken's large frame, grew anxious.

"What do you see?"

"Are they still out there? Is it safe?"

Ken answered by stepping out to explore this new, alien landscape. One by one, the others slowly funneled out to examine their new surroundings. Only Coop ignored the bizarre spectacle before him, focusing instead on more basic needs as he made a beeline for the outhouse, clutching his crotch as he ran.

Beverly was the last to exit the structure, still dabbing her reddened eyes and nursing her left wrist, which bore an ugly bruise from where Ken had yanked it. She looked more confused than shaken by what she saw, as though she had stepped out of one dream and into another one.

As they looked around, each of them started to register the same odd sensations they'd experienced yesterday in the floodplain: a loss of equilibrium that made every step feel off balance; a tightening in the pit of their stomachs that spawned waves of nausea; and auditory dampening, making all noises muted and voices sound fuzzy, like they were coming from deep underground. Coping with these symptoms only heightened their anxiety and bewilderment.

"All this in one night," Gaby said, her voice raised to counter the sound-dampening effects. "That doesn't make sense."

Lamar watched, transfixed, as steam rose from the largest of the ash piles at the entrance to the fence line. It took him several moments to realize there wasn't anything mystical about it; it was simply condensed water in the ash evaporating.

"Well, at least now we can rule out radiation," he said, shivering in the chill morning air.

Ken surveyed the blighted landscape, vacillating between awe and revulsion.

"So, anyone still think staying put is a good idea?" he asked.

Ken's question was greeted with the dead silence he'd expected.

"Wade was last seen fleeing southeast, and going by their trail, those ... things came from the south and the west," Ken continued. "I say we head north."

Gaby and Beverly looked skeptical, remembering how the northern hills ringing this region were some of the steepest in Quehanna. They both looked to Lamar, who had become the unofficial overriding vote anytime Ken pushed them to do something stupid. But for once Lamar was in complete agreement with him.

"Pack light," Lamar recommended as a much-relieved Coop exited the outhouse. "We've got a long hike ahead of us, so take only the bare essentials; a change of clothes, toiletries and a weapon. And be sure to pack some firewood, too, in case we have to spend another night in the forest."

"What if we take shelter in that military base John mentioned?" Gaby suggested. "It's gotta be better than trusting to luck. We might even find weapons there."

"He said a military contractor, not the military," Ken reminded her curtly. "And even if that place is still standing, you really think they're gonna have a pile of AKs out front with a sign saying: 'Take one, they're free'?"

"This isn't an enemy we can fight," Lamar said, siding with Ken. "Our best bet — our only bet — is to flee. Since these things are afraid of the light, we need to clear their territory before dark. And every minute we waste arguing makes it that much harder."

The others saw the wisdom in this and acquiesced with varying degrees of reluctance as they prepared for the long journey ahead.

Five minutes later, Ken spotted Beverly kneeling by the showers, trying to fit three suitcases worth of belongings into an oversized tote bag. She was alone, as usual. Her face was expressionless as she moved items from one bag to another with a numb detachment, as though she were resigned to living following last night's failed suicide attempt.

"Need a hand?" he asked as he knelt beside her, making certain to ask loudly enough that the others over by the fire-pit could hear him.

Beverly gave him a dark look.

"I need a new wrist," she replied with only the tiniest trace of emotion.

"Sorry about that," Ken said under his breath. "But I can't have you offing yourself just yet. Once that fat shit is dethroned, you can stab yourself as many times as you like."

"Your concern is touching," Beverly replied dryly, her voice almost drone-like in its indifference.

Ken stole a glance at the others to ensure none of them were coming over.

"You still remember what to do?" he asked.

Beverly nodded sullenly.

"Get the food now, while they're busy," he instructed, motioning toward the other three, who were busy preparing for the journey. "It's in Lamar's pack in the teepee. Two cans only. Just enough to arouse suspicion."

"And the other ... tactics we discussed?" she asked.

"Phase 2 comes later, probably during lunch. Fake a sprain or something. Just buy me 30 seconds alone with the luggage. Make it convincing, but don't oversell it."

"And what about your grand finale?"

"We won't hit Phase 3 until tonight at the earliest," Ken said as he stood up. "The others should be plenty suspicious of Lamar by that point. Just stick to the story I told you and follow my lead."

He started to walk away but paused mid-step and looked back over his shoulder.

"And make certain to eat something today. You look like shit."

Beverly's eyebrows knitted in frustration. It wasn't so much Ken's offhand slight — she was used to those by now — but her own reaction to it. Ever since the iku had touched her, she'd struggled with strange visions of death and destruction. Limbs hacked off, bullets raking children, pregnant women impaled on pikes. And always in the background was fire: glorious, crackling flames consuming entire buildings, roasting steel and flesh alike.

Now a voice had joined them, like the voice of reason or conscience, only this voice preached a very different sort of gospel. It cried for retribution, over and over again, gnawing at her mind, demanding that the others pay for last night's confrontation. And it got louder every time Ken or the others spoke.

As she finished packing up her tote bag, Beverly noticed that the black spot on her palm had grown again; it was now the size of a nickel.

Over by the firepit, Lamar was making certain the group wasn't leaving anything important behind as they prepared to journey into the unknown.

"Who has the magnesium stick?" he asked.

Gaby patted her pants pocket.

"Right here, along with the knife," she said.

Coop, who was sitting beside her, noticed movement from the corner of his eye. He turned his head and saw Beverly enter the wigwam with her tote bag slung over one shoulder. That struck him as odd. The only things left in the wigwam were spare clothes, unused luggage and the food. Why would she ...

"Coop?"

Lamar's question broke Coop's train of thought. He looked around and saw the others were staring at him.

"Do you have the hatchet?" Lamar asked again. "For chopping firewood?"

"Yeah, it's right here. Sorry. I spaced out for a second there."

"What about water?" Ken asked.

"We've got only the one canteen for five of us, so keep your eyes open for creeks and streams as we go," Lamar said.

"What about the risk of pathogens?" Coop asked. From the corner of his eye, he saw Beverly emerge from the wigwam and walk toward them.

"We can boil the water. We have fire-making tools, wood, and spare soup cans to heat them, so don't throw away your cans when you're finished with them," Lamar cautioned.

"Speaking of which, who's taking the food?" Ken asked.

"I am," Lamar replied. "It's in the wigwam. Between that and the wood, I won't have room for much else, so can someone carry a spare set of clothes for me?"

"I'll do it," Coop volunteered.

Two minutes later, they were ready.

"Is that everything?" Gaby asked as she fit the last of the firewood into her backpack.

"It should be," Lamar replied, tightening the shoulder straps on his rucksack in anticipation of a long journey.

Ken crossed his arms and looked northward toward the imposing hills in the distance.

"Let's get a move on, then."

* * * * * *

The group huddled together in small clusters as they trekked silently through this alien world, with Ken and Lamar out front, Gaby and Coop in the middle, and Beverly bringing up the rear. After 90 minutes of walking, the northern hills appeared no closer, although that may have had something to do with the fog-like haze of steam rising from the endless swirls of ash decorating the landscape. The haze obscured anything more than 50 yards away, making distant landmarks indistinct and inscrutable.

It was probably just as well, as everything they could see was dead: plants, trees, even the occasional animal. Through the curtain of steam Gaby saw the carcass of a fawn lying in a ditch 30 feet away. It stared at her with lifeless eyes that almost seemed to follow her as she walked. She was so haunted by the sight that she very nearly walked into Coop's back when he paused to wipe the condensation from his glasses.

What they could see of the landscape wasn't any better: stagnant pools of brackish water and ash everywhere. The air was almost as foul and stank of death. Not even the soil had been spared the ikus' dark touch; dirt that had once been a rich brown texture was now chalky and produced tiny dust clouds with each step. The blight, as the group had taken to calling the contaminated landscape, seemed to stretch on for miles. It was as though they'd stepped out of a vibrant forest and into the badlands of Montana.

Only the sun seemed oblivious to all of this death and decay, shining just as brilliantly as before as it climbed the eastern sky.

Ken, who was a few steps ahead of Lamar, cast a backward glance at the rest of the party and suddenly paused at the foot of a rocky mound.

"The others are lagging behind," he said with a nod behind. "Let's give them a chance to catch up."

"Not again, dammit," Lamar grumbled.

Lamar leaned against the lower-lying rocks for support as he waited. Keeping pace with Ken's long strides was exhausting, but the thought of spending another night in the forest with those iku things was proving a powerful motivator to keep up. He exhaled deeply and lifted the bottom half of his shirt to mop his sweaty brow, exposing his gut. There was a time not so long ago when he would have been too insecure to show the others his rotund belly. Now he was tired, achy and just didn't care.

The adrenaline that fueled last night's experiences had faded, and everyone was fighting back waves of exhaustion. And with that exhaustion came irritability.

"Let's pick up the pace, people," Lamar shouted so the others could hear him.

Gaby and Coop, who were lagging a good 30 yards behind, shook their heads in annoyance and quickened their steps. Gaby made no attempt to hide her irritation, glaring at Lamar as she strode forward. He'd kept the group moving at this punishing pace for an hour and a half with no respite, and for him to complain about their progress — while taking a breather, no less! — was maddening. Coop's face also betrayed annoyance, but it was subsumed, as though other issues weighed on his mind.

They no longer stumbled and weaved like drunken sailors on shore leave as they had at the start of the trip; their bodies were slowly adjusting to the equilibrium-disrupting effects of the blight, and the bile threatening to force its way out of their stomachs had begun to settle. They'd also overcome their irrational fear of stepping in the steaming waves of ash patterns. Earlier they'd tiptoed around them, as though they were afraid their touch was somehow corrupting. Now they trudged through them without a thought, leaving a smeared trail of soot behind.

"Why are you riding us?" Gaby asked as she and Coop drew closer. "We're not the problem." She turned and pointed to Beverly some 50 yards back, who at this distance was cloaked in the haze of steam. All they could make out was her silhouette — which the steam clouds distorted into something large and menacing — as she lurched toward them haltingly.

Lamar was already irritated at having to stop every so often for the others to catch up, but Gaby's pushback was galling enough to warrant a response.

"She's keeping pace with you two," Lamar retorted hotly. "If you both move faster, so will she."

Gaby and Coop looked at one another and exchanged eye

rolls as they brushed past Lamar without another word.

"Now you see what I had to deal with," Ken whispered to Lamar, leaning in to avoid being heard by the others. "They demand leadership, but the minute you give them direction, they act like you're slapping chains on them."

Impossibly, Lamar found himself nodding in agreement.

Ken knelt down on the rocky mound as they waited for Beverly, idly poking at the rocks with his spear, which produced a clinking sound like ice cubes landing in a glass. The imagery alone made Lamar reflexively long for such creature comforts.

"How far do you think we've gone?" he asked.

"A mile and a half, two miles, tops," Ken replied as he continued abusing his spear tip.

"That's it?" Lamar asked incredulously. "We'll never get out at this rate."

"No one's breaking any land-speed records walking in this soup," Ken said with a shrug.

"I honestly don't know if we're even heading north anymore," Lamar confided. "It seems way too easy to lose yourself in this stuff."

"There's a way to tell," Ken said. "But we need someplace elevated. Above this haze."

He pointed to the indistinct, shadowy outline of a ridge in the distance, in the same general direction Coop and Gaby were walking, whose peak just barely poked through the towering clouds of steam.

"Make for that point," he said. "We should be able to get our bearings from up there."

Ken put his pinkies in either side of his mouth and gave a

loud, shrill whistle that made Lamar wince. Gaby and Coop, who were about 40 yards ahead and already on the edge of visibility, stopped and turned to see what the ruckus was about.

"Make for the ridge!" Ken shouted to them, cupping his hands to his mouth as Lamar covered his ears with his hands.

A few moments later, Beverly emerged from the curtain of steam behind them, lurching forward as she dragged her overstuffed tote bag behind her. Lamar had been prepared to upbraid Beverly for slowing the group down, but it was clear there was something wrong with her. She staggered unsteadily, swaying as she stumbled from one foot to the next. Her upper torso seemed to lean into each step as though she were relying on gravity as much as her leg muscles to propel her forward. Lamar also noticed her lips were tightly pursed and her cheeks inflated as if she were struggling to keep from vomiting.

Whatever this was, it wasn't blight sickness; Lamar barely even noticed its effects anymore, and none of them had been this acutely affected by it, including Beverly. He made a mental note to sniff her breath when she drew closer, just in case she had found another stash of John's moonshine.

"You OK there, Bev?" Lamar asked hesitantly as she staggered toward them.

She continued walking as though she hadn't heard him, her glazed eyes fixed on some distant point on the horizon.

Lamar detected no hint of alcohol on her breath, but her complexion was pasty, and her eyes appeared sunken and vacant. She looked seriously ill.

"Beverly?" he said again, a little louder, causing her to

jump slightly.

"What?" she asked, irritated.

"You zoned out for a bit there," he replied.

"I'm fine," she said with a dismissive wave of her left hand. "I just … struggle without my beauty rest."

She noticed that Lamar was eyeing the black spot on the side of her hand, so she quickly dropped it to her side. The mark had grown to the size of a quarter and was now spreading up the side of her hand.

"Tell you what, why don't we take a short breather up ahead?" Lamar offered, pointing toward the ridge in the distance.

Beverly nodded. Rest was all she needed. Just a few minutes of shut eye to stifle the conflagration raging in her mind. The graphic images bombarding her brain were growing more extreme. The voice that had been whispering for retribution was now screaming for it, and it was no longer alone. New voices joined the chorus of hate, while others called out new instructions: torture, self-mutilation and other perversities she refused to entertain. And in the background, the flames grew higher and higher.

* * * * * *

Ken and Lamar slowly made their way up the ridgeline, using their spear tips like canes to help navigate through the haze. Lamar looked over apprehensively at his traveling companion. He would have preferred if at least one of the others had tagged along; Ken was always at his most overbearing in one-on-one exchanges.

About 30 feet below, Gaby, Coop and Beverly recuperated

at the base of the ridge, their faces already difficult to pick out in the foggy steam. Lamar had invited them to come along, but all of them had demurred; it was still bracingly cold this morning, and the steam's residual heat took some of the sting out of the chill.

Ken said nothing during their trip up the ridge; if he registered any of Lamar's trepidation, he didn't exhibit it. His face was a mask of concentration as he worked his way up the ridge, weaving between dozens of pointed stones jutting out of the earth.

The steam clouds slowly dissipated as they climbed the ridge, which narrowed the higher they went until they reached the peak: a 30-foot-wide rock face with a few patches of blighted soil and the remains of a toppled ash tree. Judging from the scorch marks on its side, it must have been struck by lightning. While the now-ubiquitous ash patterns also decorated the peak, Lamar noted that they were thinner and emitted only trace amounts of steam, the rising sun having already burned most of it off the ridgetop, giving the two their first unimpeded view of the path ahead.

Lamar tentatively approached the peak's edge and looked out over a field of steam clouds. They stretched as far as he could see, which was nearly three miles at that elevation. The shimmering sea of misty white was so thick in parts that it looked like a layer of cumulus clouds had dropped from the heavens. In the distance, he saw a series of dauntingly steep hills that loomed ominously above the steam cloud, taunting him with their seeming impassibility. They gradually tapered out the farther right he looked, until they ended in a series of smaller rolling hills that looked far more manageable.

Lamar closed his eyes for a moment, enjoying the sun on his face again after spending so long trapped beneath the steam curtain. The only part of this that felt wrong was the lack of wind on his face, a stark reminder that they were still deep within the ikus' territory.

When Lamar opened his eyes again, Ken was standing beside him, pointing to his right. Lamar followed his finger until he spied a concave area in the distance where the steam clouds hovered noticeably lower than the neighboring clouds as though they were the lip of an enormous bowl.

"That must be the edge of the floodplain," Ken said, tracing the contours of the bowl shape in the air with his finger.

"But it's so far away. We couldn't have drifted that far east," Lamar insisted.

"In this soup, I believe it," Ken replied. "But there's only one way to be sure."

He picked up a downed branch from the fallen ash tree and snapped off a foot-long twig before stripping the branch of its leaves.

"Uhmm, what are you doing?" Lamar asked.

"Putting the fruits of an Outback vacation to use," Ken responded cryptically as he knelt down to sweep away loose pebbles and ash swirls from a four-foot patch of chalk-colored dirt. He then planted the stick in the center of this dirt patch, gently twisting it back and forth, drilling it deep enough into the dirt that it could stand on its own.

Once that was done, he started tracing the contours of the shadow cast by the stick, which was pointing to their left. His finger stopped about two feet away from the stick, where the shadow finally ended. He picked up a palm-sized rock nearby and placed it at the shadow's tip.

"Time?" he asked.

"Uhhh, 8:42," Lamar replied, glancing at his binary watch.

"Okay," Ken said as he stood up and dusted himself off. "Now we wait."

"For what?"

"For the shadow to move."

"Solar navigation?" Lamar asked.

Ken nodded.

"My gift to the group," Ken said.

Lamar titled his head and looked at Ken askance.

"Since when are you interested in helping us?" Lamar asked, suspicious.

"Since the others anointed you God-King," Ken said derisively. "All I care about is getting out of here. And if that means teaching you my tricks, so be it."

"That's not what I mean. You don't need me for this. Why are you going to all this trouble teaching me this stuff?"

Ken smiled ruefully.

"Because you and your pals don't trust me. If I said 'go right,' you lot would go left out of pure spite. So, I'm teaching someone the group does trust: you."

As Lamar mulled this over, Ken added a new wrinkle to the conversation.

"And for that same reason, I recommend you not tell the others where you learned this. They're liable to have the same reaction."

Lamar raised an eyebrow at this.

"I don't like keeping secrets from the others."

"Hey, it's your funeral," Ken said with a shrug. "Just remember that it'll burn up any currency you have with them. They don't trust me, and by extension, they don't trust my ideas. Better to pass them off as your own so only one of us is a pariah."

"They trust me because I'm honest with them," Lamar insisted, but Ken could tell from his tone that Lamar was torn and had begun seriously considering Ken's advice.

Five stories below, Gaby was watching the pair talk and gesticulate through the haze of steam while Coop stared off into the distance beside her. Lamar and Ken were too high up for Gaby to hear anything, but they appeared to be passionately discussing something on the ground in front of them.

"What do you think they're talking about?" Gaby asked.

"Mmm," Coop mumbled in response, not paying attention.

"They sure seem chatty, dontcha think?" Gaby said, continuing to ply him.

"Hmm?" Coop replied, resting his hand on his chin and appearing lost in thought.

Gaby grinned mischievously and leaned in closer.

"I said, 'I'm having your baby!'"

Coop's serene detachment quickly turned to a look of confusion and then one of utter revulsion.

"WTF, Gaby?" Coop exclaimed, finally turning to face her.

"Sorry," she said, though her impish expression suggested otherwise. "It's just you seem so ... preoccupied."

Coop rolled his eyes.

"Want to talk about it?"

Coop hemmed and hawed for a second or two, running his fingers through his curly red hair before finally acquiescing.

"I've had something on my mind, a question, ever since we escaped those things last night: Why are we still alive?"

"That's a funny question. The iku fear the light," she replied, wrinkling her nose at the seeming obviousness of the answer.

"That's not what I mean. Last night, all of us thought it was the end. I did a lot of soul searching, trying to make peace with that."

"We all did," Gaby said with a nod.

"And when the sun came out and those things retreated, it felt like we'd been given a gift — another chance at life," Coop continued. "But why? Is it just to wander around the forest? What's my purpose?"

"The same as every other living thing," Gaby shrugged. "To keep on living."

Coop shook his head forcefully from side to side.

"No! We were spared for a reason."

Gaby drew closer and put her hand within a few inches of Coop's, which was about as close as she could come to someone else without triggering her deep-seated fear of physical contact.

"Coop, it's perfectly natural to look for deeper meaning in the chaos, but it just isn't there. We're alive because we are."

Coop clenched his fists as they rested on his knees.

"I can't accept that," he insisted. "Won't accept it. That's ... messy."

"That's life," Gaby said with a sad smile.

High above, Ken was idly spinning a stone between his

fingers, watching as his primitive sundial slowly moved.

"What time you got, big man?" he asked.

"8:56."

"Okay, that'll have to do," Ken said, slapping his knee for emphasis as he rose.

Ken placed the stone in his hand at the tip of the shadow's new location, roughly two inches to the right of the first marker. He then yanked the stick out of the ground and used its tip to draw a straight line between the two stone markers.

"This line shows us north and south," Ken explained, taking a step back from his handiwork so Lamar could see it easier. "South must be back that way," he said, pointing in the direction of the floodplain. "Which means that this direction is north," he finished, pointing toward the smaller and more manageable grouping of hills to their right, as opposed to the dangerous-looking ones straight ahead.

"Hang on, how can that be south?" Lamar asked. "That's the floodplain. The floodplain has always been to our west."

"We strayed east, remember?" Ken reminded him. "And land masses aren't fixed points. The floodplain probably widens as it moves north. I'll bet you if we walk straight toward it, we'd wind up right back in camp."

"Maybe," Lamar responded, clearly skeptical.

Ken steeled himself. This was it. One final push should do it. He tried to put out of his mind that all of his plans hinged on this one moment, and adopted the most earnest expression he could muster.

"I get it; you still don't trust me," Ken said as empathetically as he could manage. "You don't have to. All I'm asking is for you to trust the stick. It doesn't have an agenda; it doesn't get lost or confused. It's completely objective. Give it 15 minutes and it won't steer you wrong."

He held the twig out toward Lamar, inviting him to take it.

Lamar hesitated, trying to ascertain Ken's candor from his expression. If he was being duplicitous, he was hiding it very well. After a few moments, Lamar decided he was being sincere.

"You better be right," he said, taking the branch from Ken's outstretched hand.

Ken nodded appreciatively, his expression registering how hard it must have been for Lamar to take that first step. But beneath the surface, he was dancing a merry jig and cackling like a maniac in celebration. Lamar's expression told him everything he needed to know: the young man was wary enough not to fully trust him but still naïve enough not to consider that Ken might have taught him wrong on purpose.

He'd set the trap, and Lamar had taken the bait.

* * * * * *

It was now after 11 a.m., and the sun overhead had burned away most of the steam, revealing the full breadth of the blight's devastation. It was one thing to catch glimpses of it through the curtain of fog and mentally piece together the extent of the desolation but quite another to see it in all its terrible majesty, spread out across the landscape in every direction.

The ground had been steadily rising for the last 30

minutes, and in the distance they could see that the gentle rolling hills they'd spotted from the ridge fed into much larger, much more daunting slopes. Those to their left and right looked equally foreboding. They were surrounded on three sides by seemingly impassible obstacles, and everyone in the group steeled themselves for the challenge of scaling any one of those hills.

The air had warmed considerably to the point that they had shed their winter jackets, opting to either tie them around their waists or carry them draped over an arm.

Lamar called the group to a halt beside a grouping of tree stumps in the shade. The ragged gash marks on the trunks suggested they'd been cut with a chainsaw, but as there were no visible drag marks or tracks, it must have been long ago.

"Let's break for lunch," he said, sweeping ash from the top of the largest stump before plopping down on it. "It'll give Ken time to catch up."

"Oh, yes, let's do a favor for our 'good friend' Ken," Gaby said, making air quotes to drive home the sarcasm.

"What? You're faulting him for needing to plant a brown tree?"

Gaby winced at Lamar's euphemism and the accompanying mental image.

"She can't understand why you're defending him," Coop spoke up, taking a seat next to Lamar. "And frankly, neither can I. You act like he's your consigliore now."

"Look, I know he can be crass and overbearing, but …"

"No! No buts about it," Gaby interrupted him as she sat down, taking care to examine the stump for any jagged edges before trusting her posterior to it. "He's crass and overbearing, period."

"I'd only add that he's also a four-alarm asshole," Coop chimed in.

"Granted, Ken is all of those things," Lamar conceded. "But in case you haven't noticed, he's contributing now. The man has more wilderness experience than all of us combined, so we should at least listen to him."

"I'd say there's no chance of that," Gaby intoned.

"Is that what he was doing on the ridge?" Coop asked pointedly. "Teaching you survival stuff?"

"Yeah," Gaby added. "You two were up there a long time. What were you talking about?"

Lamar flashed back to Ken's warning. Judging by their distrustful tones, he reluctantly concluded that Ken's assumption was right on the money.

"Nothing, really. Just the best route to go and things like that," he lied, looking away in shame.

"I don't trust him," Coop said. "He's working an angle."

Lamar rolled his eyes as he unstrapped his pack from his shoulders and let it fall to the ground.

"You guys are too suspicious," he said. "Ken wants to get out of here as badly as any of us. What could he possibly gain from deceiving us?"

"Revenge," Coop answered without a moment's hesitation.

Gaby nodded in agreement.

Lamar threw up his hands.

"I'm not getting drawn into this," he insisted. "Whether you believe it or not, he's working to get us home. Get on board with that."

Their stony gazes and silent judgment suggested that Lamar's argument was less than persuasive.

Beverly, who had been lagging 20 yards behind the others, finally reached the grove of stumps and promptly collapsed on one just a few feet from the others. She had managed to keep pace with the group for most of the trip, even while dragging her overstuffed tote bag, but the exertion had clearly taken its toll on her.

She sat with her shoulders slumped, taking in heaving lungfuls of air with each ragged breath. Beverly looked up and her face was haunting; her eyes glazed over and her complexion sallow as she shivered, despite the rising temperatures. She suddenly flinched and wheeled her head sharply to the right as though she'd been struck by some invisible assailant.

"What's wrong with her?" Coop asked quietly.

"Beverly, are you OK?" Lamar inquired.

No response. She stared off into the distance, her eyes still glazed over.

"Beverly? Beverly?"

Gaby leaned in and clapped as loudly as possible. Beverly sat bolt upright and angrily rounded on Gaby.

"Don't do that!" she demanded.

"The guys were asking after you," Gaby explained. "They're worried."

"I told you all not to fuss over me," Beverly grumbled. "I'm fine."

"Maybe you should have some water ..." Coop tried suggesting before being sharply cut off.

"Maybe you should listen to your elders!" she snapped.

Lamar and Coop looked at one another but said nothing.

Gaby noticed a black smudge the size of a shot glass on Beverly's left hand, covering part of her palm and the side of her hand. It looked like soot, only it was pitch black. She must have tripped and put her hand in one of the ash swirls decorating the landscape, Gaby mused.

A disquieting silence descended on the group for several long moments before they heard a familiar call in the distance.

"Ohhh, Lucy, I'm hooome!"

It was Ken, waving from afar as he jogged toward them. He seemed weirdly upbeat, considering their circumstances.

"Well, now that you're here, let's eat," Lamar said, opening his bag.

"Maybe you should also do a food count," Gaby gently reminded him.

"Good idea, I haven't done one in a while."

Lamar pointed to each can while silently counting. He paused after a moment, got a perplexed look on his face and recounted.

"What's the problem?" Coop asked, reading trouble in the young man's expression.

"We should have 12 cans, half a bag of trail mix and a handful of dried apricots. I count 10."

"Maybe you miscounted," Coop said blithely.

"Maybe," Lamar replied doubtfully.

"Well, don't sit there all day brooding over it!" Ken declared. "I'm starving."

"Fine," Lamar said as he passed around the food. "But we need to think seriously about hunting or scavenging. Even with rationing, this will only last us another day."

Lamar handed out five cans. Ken put his back in the bag and grabbed the trail mix instead, while the others made do with cold soup and lima beans. All except for Beverly, whose can sat unopened in front of her as the others heartily chowed down.

"I'm not hungry," she protested.

"Eat up. You'll feel better," Lamar assured her as he ripped the lid off his and eagerly upended the contents into his mouth.

Gaby made a face at the sight.

"You could at least use a spoon."

"There are no spoons," Lamar replied between mouthfuls of canned clam chowder. "Didn't pack them."

"That seems a little … arbitrary," she replied, more confused than annoyed.

"I told you we were only packing the essentials."

"Yeah, but it's not like spoons take up a lot of room," Gaby argued.

"Or weigh all that much," Coop chimed in.

"Pipe down, you two," Ken said, coming to Lamar's defense. "Using our fingers for a day or two won't kill us."

"It's not that, it's just …" Gaby started to explain before Beverly exploded out of nowhere.

"Oh, God, will you shut up? Can everyone please shut up?"

Beverly slammed her food down on a rock beside her. The group instantly fell silent, dumbstruck by her explosive outburst. She was shaking with fury.

"Can't you people go five minutes without chattering?" she vented as she scanned the others' faces, glowering. "I can't take all the voices! Yackety-yak-yakking constantly! I want to have one meal in peace. One meal where I can close my eyes and pretend I'm not stranded in the middle of nowhere, under attack and stuck with the likes of you people! Is that too much to ask?"

Instead of waiting for a reply, Beverly threw her soup at a nearby tree, spraying beef barley stew everywhere. She then stood up with a huff and stormed off.

"And stop with all the threats!" she screeched as she stomped off, beating her fist against her head as if to drive out the voices. "I'm not killing anyone!"

The others sat in silence for several seconds, stupefied by Beverly's behavior.

"Did she say something about killing people?" Coop asked in a hushed whisper.

"Someone finally flipped her bitch switch," Ken said.

"There's definitely something wrong with her," Lamar confided in the others as he wiped his hands on the front of his shirt. "Did you see that weird black mark on her hand? It may be an infection."

Gaby nodded.

"Maybe it has something to do with the iku touching her last night," Gaby opined. "It was the same hand, and she's been acting squirrelly ever since."

"What if it's the change?" Cooped asked. "That thing John was talking about, the one that came over Wade and drove him insane? He said we'd all change out here."

"You certainly haven't changed," Ken said between

mouthfuls of trail mix. "You're just as gullible as ever."

"I think John was talking about spiritual development, not some physical transformation," Lamar said, trying not to laugh at Coop.

Just then, Beverly stopped some 30 yards away and dropped to her knees, retching uncontrollably. A blackish liquid came spurting out as she doubled over in pain.

"She may need a hand," Ken said indifferently.

Lamar stood up to help her when Beverly suddenly keeled over and started convulsing.

"Oh, shit!" Coop exclaimed, dropping his food in alarm. "She's seizing!"

Lamar, Coop and Gaby all raced over to check on her.

This was it, Ken decided. While Beverly wasn't exactly following the script — she was supposed to fake a simple ankle injury — this was the agreed-upon time, and her sudden collapse had certainly drawn the others' attention. There wouldn't be a better opportunity, Ken concluded, as he reached for the nearest bag.

In the distance, the others were completely focused on helping Beverly.

"Her pulse is racing!" Gaby informed the others.

Ken hurriedly rummaged through Gaby's bag until he found a lacy red bra, which he stuffed under all the cans in Lamar's bag. He stole another glance at the group, who now appeared to be arguing over a stick.

"What are you doing?" Coop asked Lamar as he moved to put a stick in Beverly's mouth.

"You're supposed to put something in their mouth to keep them from swallowing their tongue."

"That's an old wives' tale."

Ken chanced one more misdeed. He grabbed the group's only canteen from Beverly's pack, upended the contents into his mouth and then stuffed it in Lamar's rucksack.

"Turn her over on her side!" Coop directed. "It'll keep her from gagging."

"And don't touch her left hand!" Gaby warned. "We don't know how that black stuff spreads."

Ken had just finished snapping the container shut when the others noticed that he wasn't with them.

"Hey, Ken! Mind lending a hand here?" Lamar said, motioning him over.

Beverly had stopped seizing but appeared to be delirious, ranting over and over about voices and flames as the others raised her to a sitting position. Her eyes were open but unresponsive. Coop waved his hand in front of her face and got no reaction.

"Fuck me!" Ken said as he started to register that Beverly's illness might not be as fake as he'd thought. "Can she walk?"

Gaby looked at him like he was an idiot.

"She can barely even drool," Gaby intoned. "Of course she can't walk!"

"Now what do we do?" Coop asked, looking hopelessly down at her prone form.

* * * * * *

The group came out of a deep grove into a narrow clearing surrounded on three sides by withered trees and thickets, but in this blighted landscape, one could barely distinguish between a coppice of denuded trees and a wide-open field. The thicket to the right quickly petered out as the land before it dipped precipitously while the clearing ahead remained level. The two ran perpendicular for the next 100 yards before the clearing ended in a cliff overlooking the lower plane some 30 feet below.

Lamar and Gaby were in the lead, while Coop trailed behind as he dragged Ken's metal suitcase through the forest, leaving telltale drag marks in the grayish dirt behind him. He never should have volunteered to carry it along with his own pack. It was surprisingly heavy; Coop had no idea how Ken carried it around one-handed so effortlessly.

Of course, Ken now had a much heavier burden: Beverly. After her fit during lunch, it took 30 minutes for Beverly to come to her senses and another 30 minutes before she was well enough to stand on her own. It was now after 2 p.m., and her condition had only worsened. She struggled to walk even with Ken propping her up, forcing the others to constantly stop and wait for them to catch up. As a precaution, the others had insisted on bundling Beverly in her jacket and gloves — despite the warming weather — to minimize skin-to-skin contact while carrying her. It also kept the growing black spot on her hand out of sight, if not entirely out of mind.

Coop looked back over her shoulder and saw that Ken and Beverly had fallen behind again, some 200 yards back and barely visible.

"Let's wait over there for them," he said, pointing toward the furthest edge of the cliff, a 15-foot-wide crag that overhung the low-lying field, capped with an old elm tree that clung tenuously to the edge. It leaned over the precipice at a 45-degree angle, as though it were contemplating suicide. "It'll give us a good look at the rest of the terrain."

Lamar nodded his consent reluctantly.

"All right, but no more breaks for at least another hour," he said. "We have to pick up the pace if we're going to make it out of here before nightfall."

"There is one way," Gaby said as they reached the bluff.

Lamar looked at her, waiting for her explanation. Instead of responding verbally, Gaby crossed her arms and stared at Lamar probingly until he got the message.

"Nuh-uh. No way!" Lamar insisted as he placed his rucksack on the ground before him. "Don't even think it."

"I'm not saying we feed her to the wolves," Gaby protested.

"Just that we abandon her to those iku creatures," Lamar replied coldly.

"I hate to say it, but Gaby may be right," Coop said, dropping Ken's suitcase in front of him and plopping down on it. "She's not just slowing us down; her very presence is a threat."

"We've taken the proper precautions," Lamar insisted.

"I'm not just talking about the black mark," Coop said. "You heard what she said about killing us. That stuff has driven her crazy."

"Maybe that's the catalyst," Gaby chimed in. "The ikus' touch could be what triggers the change."

Lamar looked at them askance.

"That doesn't make any sense. Wade went crazy, and he was never touched," he pointed out.

"As far as we know," Gaby responded. "He did spend an

awful lot of time away from us."

Lamar shook his head as he located a decent-sized stick and started scouring the region for a flat patch of dirt.

"Look, I get that you're scared. We all are," Lamar said as he found a suitable patch and buried the stick vertically in the center of it. He noted where its shadow fell and marked its tip with an X drawn in the dirt. "But if we start writing one another off, we're no better than the animals. Beverly stays."

"You did that same thing with the stick right after lunch," Coop observed. "Is that some supposed to tell us which direction to go?"

"Solar navigation," Lamar said with a nod.

"Where'd you learn that?" Coop asked.

"Long story," Lamar deflected as he stood up and dusted off his hands on the front of his shirt. In the distance, he saw Ken stumble while carrying Beverly, falling to one knee.

"C'mon, let's help them," Lamar said, breaking into a light jog. He stopped after a few paces when he saw the others weren't joining him.

"Aren't you all coming?" he asked, the concern etched into his face.

Coop openly scoffed.

"I'm not lifting a finger for anyone who calls me 'Fairy Poppins,'" he answered, setting his bag behind him and defiantly nestling into it like a backrest.

"Seriously, Lamar, don't get invested," Gaby warned him. "That's what he wants."

Lamar shook his head sadly.

"Lack of sleep is making you paranoid," he said before

running over to Ken and Beverly.

Gaby watched him running away for a long moment, contemplating his words.

"Is he right?" she asked when she was sure Lamar was out of earshot. It was clear from her tone that his accusation had stung her.

Coop, who was lying on his back staring at the clouds, turned his head to look at her.

"I thought you trusted Lamar."

Gaby stood up and stretched her back.

"I trust his integrity, sure, and he's obviously intelligent, but you have to remember: he's used to interacting with people through a monitor, not face to face."

She paused to watch Lamar run toward Ken and Beverly, who were some 140 yards in the distance.

"He doesn't know enough to realize when he's getting played," she intoned.

Coop waved it off.

"I'm sure he's just pretending to cozy up to Ken to ply him for knowledge. Like he said, the man can teach us a lot about roughing it."

Gaby shook her head no.

"Lamar doesn't have a duplicitous bone in his body," she said.

In the silence that followed, Gaby decided to scour the terrain. She headed toward the crag overlooking the field below, but Coop stuck out his leg in front of her, barring her path.

"What gives?" she complained.

Instead of answering, Coop rolled onto his side and

picked up a clod of dirt by his head. He balanced it in his hand, feeling its weight, before flinging it with an overhead motion toward the edge of the crag. It landed on the bough of the elm tree overhanging the edge. The impact made the tree shudder, and Gaby felt the vibrations through the ground some 15 feet away, causing her to rear back in fright.

"Keep away from the edge," Coop warned. "See how deep the tree's roots are embedded in the soil? If that thing goes, the whole cliff face goes. And you along with it."

Gaby slowly backed away from the overlook and chose another, less dangerous spot to sightsee. Judging from what she could see, Coop was correct. Exposed roots as thick as her legs clung tenuously to the underside of the crag, which ended in a near-sheer drop-off as the land below plunged 30 feet before ending in a football-field-sized valley. The valley's basin was crescent shaped, with the top and bottom both narrowing the closer they came to the crescent's center. Everything past that was hidden by the cliff face. At the basin's outer edge, just below the crag, she saw a pile of debris with large chunks of soil and rocks the size of her head, suggesting that part of the crag had collapsed fairly recently.

On the other side of the clearing, Lamar caught up to Ken and Beverly. Ken had risen to his feet by this time and was continuing their slow, plodding journey as Beverly clung to him, her right arm draped over his shoulder as he pushed against the small of her back to propel her forward. Ken was sweating profusely from the exertion, and Lamar could see that Beverly's "steps" were really just her shuffling her feet in the dirt. Ken was doing the walking for both of them.

Up close, Beverly looked far worse than she had at lunch. She was still deathly pale, and she leaned with her full weight on Ken's shoulder, causing them to both lean at a precipitous angle. Her eyes were no longer glazed over, but instead appeared manic, darting every which direction as though unseen forces were closing in on her.

Lamar checked her left arm from any sign of exposed skin. Seeing none, he cautiously draped it around his neck and hefted her left side with a grunt of exertion.

"Thanks," Ken said, pausing to wipe the sweat from his brow. "You sure you should be doing this, though?"

"It's the right thing to do," Lamar insisted as they prepared to walk her together. "Ready?"

Ken nodded.

"On the left in 3 ... 2 ... 1 ... go!"

He and Ken stepped forward with the left leg at the same time, causing the balance of Beverly's weight to shift toward Lamar. He had just enough time to marvel at how heavy her dead weight was before Ken stepped to the right, shifting the burden to him as Lamar struggled to keep up with his brisk pace and long gait.

"So, which one gave you the most flak about helping me?"

Lamar was so startled by the question that he broke stride and had to hop forward to keep Beverly from falling over when Ken shifted her weight to his side.

"You heard that all the way from over here?" Lamar asked him in astonishment.

Ken barked laughter, but it did little to mask his pained expression.

"I don't need to hear them to know what they're thinking," he said. "They don't trust me, and I'll bet they've spent the last few hours trying to convince you."

"I've tried telling them that you're helping out," Lamar replied, realizing only after the fact that he had essentially confirmed Ken's suspicions. "But they won't listen."

"You're wasting your breath," Ken said grimly. "You won't change their minds. If you want them to take you seriously as a leader, the best thing you can do is keep your distance."

"That's not my idea of leadership," Lamar insisted as he put extra effort into his step, as if he was trying to reinforce his message with action. "And if the others can't accept it ... to hell with them!"

"Don't say I didn't warn you," Ken warned grimly. But beneath his dark façade, Ken was secretly yukking it up. This kid was waaaay too easy to manipulate.

As they drew closer to the others, another voice suddenly sprang up, hissing in their ears.

"Shhhhh!" Beverly warned, her eyes darting to and fro. "They'll hear us!"

Lamar stared at her, confused.

"I don't hear anything," he insisted.

"That's good," Beverly said thoughtfully. "Maybe the flames will spare us."

"W ... T ... F?" Lamar quietly intoned.

"She's been babbling like that on and off for the last 20 minutes," Ken said dismissively. "Just ignore her. That's what I do."

Coop waved lazily as the trio approached.

"Glad you could join us. Pull up some dirt," he said with a grin.

Lamar extricated himself from Beverly's grip and made a beeline for his impromptu sundial. It had moved about two inches, enough for a decent reading. He marked the shadow's current position and pulled the stick from the dirt to draw a line between that and the first reading.

"Huh, I'm off again," he said with more than a touch of confusion.

"You said that after lunch, too," Coop observed. "You sure you're doing it right?"

Lamar just glared at him in response until Coop backed down.

"Okaaay, forget I asked anything," Coop said, wilting.

Ken set Beverly's limp body beside Coop, who promptly scooted away while Ken headed for the edge of the crag, apparently having decided it made a suitable resting spot.

Gaby saw where he was walking and stood up to intervene.

"Ken, be careful where you ..." she started before Ken cut her off.

"I don't care if an entire horde of those blob-things is on our trail, I need 10 uninterrupted minutes of rest," he insisted, rubbing his shoulder as he sat down heavily right beside the leaning tree.

"Ken, don't do that!" Gaby exclaimed and took two steps toward him just as he lay back against the leaning tree's exposed roots, putting all his weight against it.

Just as Gaby reached him, a terrible shearing sound filled the air as the tree lost its grip on the crag, its roots popping loose from the soil one after another in rapid succession. Ken sat up too late, as the ground began to shake violently.

The tree fell over the edge of the cliff in slow motion, taking basketball-sized chunks of rock and dirt with it.

"What the ..." he exclaimed as the vibrations intensified and cracks started to appear on either end of the crag, five feet from the edge. He had just enough time to register his mistake before the ground seemed to swallow him up, crumbling beneath his weight as it obeyed gravity's call.

Gaby saw Ken disappear and tried to take a step back as the ground lurched sickeningly beneath her feet. A moment later she was airborne, her feet losing their purchase as she tumbled headfirst downhill, screaming the whole way. She saw the hulking remains of the toppled tree hit the bottom of the basin and realized she was about to join them as she tumbled downhill at a frightening speed. She put her hands up to shield her face just before impact and everything went black.

Coop and Lamar rushed toward what remained of the crag, which now had a five-foot-diameter crater where the tip used to be. They got on their hands and knees as close to the rim as they dared and peered over the edge.

"Gaby? **Kennn!!!**" Lamar shouted in a panic.

All they could see was a swirling cloud of dust, dirt and ash at the bottom of the basin. As it slowly dissipated and settled, Gaby and Ken came into view. Gaby was facedown near the bottom of the basin and about four feet from the overturned tree. Ken was lying flat on his back several feet to her right, his left arm covering his face. Because of all the dust still in the air, it was impossible to tell whether either of them was seriously injured.

"You guys alive down there?" Coop asked.

No response.

"If either of you can hear me, say something," Coop urged. "If you can't speak, signal us."

Through the cloud of settling dust, they saw Ken slowly extend his left arm in the air, followed swiftly by his middle finger.

Lamar and Coop looked at one another and grinned.

"Sit tight. We'll be right down," Lamar promised as the two slowly backed away from the edge and looked for a safer route into the valley below.

Gaby's head was swimming. She tried to get a sense of where she was. She was lying down, but her bed was bumpy. And coarse. Her arms and ribs ached. She slowly opened her eyes and found herself staring at the trunk of the fallen tree. She wiped the dirt and ash off her face and moaned, stretching to see if anything was broken or sprained. A quick check showed that she had cut her elbow, probably when she face-planted, and her arms and legs were bruised and battered, but she'd managed to avoid serious injury. Behind her, she could hear Ken spitting dirt out of his mouth.

"Did anyone get the license plate of that truck?" he intoned.

Gaby ignored him and raised herself up to one knee, feeling the strain of a pulled back muscle. Looks like she would be carrying her belongings one-handed for the rest of the trip. As she tried to get a sense of her surroundings, Gaby's eyes fixated on an anomaly just past the fallen tree trunk. She blinked and refocused her eyes, convinced she was hallucinating.

She stood up painfully and staggered around the periphery of the tree trunk, stopping just shy of a violet in bloom surrounded by a few blades of unblemished grass.

The flower was tiny, no more than a few inches tall, and its blossom had wilted from the cold, but it was still alive. This one little patch of land was an oasis of life in a sea of blighted, ashen death.

"Dios mio," she whispered to herself. She turned her head slightly and called out to Ken while keeping her eyes on the flower, afraid that if she looked away the spell would be broken.

"Ken? Ken!"

"If you want me to apologize, sister, you can forget it!" Ken's irate voice came from a few yards behind her. "Nobody said nothing about it being unstable."

"Will you forget the rock slide?" Gaby replied. "Just get over here."

"All right, all right," he muttered. "Dammit, my neck hurts."

In a few moments he was standing beside her, his face streaked in blood from a gash above his right ear.

"What's so important that ... holleeey shit!" he exclaimed, kneeling down in front of the violet in awe.

The two stared at it for several seconds, transfixed, before Coop's voice snapped them out of their stupor.

"How badly are you hurt?"

Gaby looked up and saw Coop rushing toward them from the left side of the valley, where the downward slope was gentler, while Lamar was still a ways behind, navigating the path with Beverly on his arm.

Instead of answering, Gaby motioned for Coop to come over and look.

"Wha … what is that?" Coop stammered as he joined them.

"We're still trying to figure that …" Gaby started to say when she looked up and saw that Coop wasn't looking down at the flower at all. He was staring off into the distance, pointing toward the other side of the crescent-shaped valley. She followed his finger and saw in the distance a 15-foot-wide patch of preserved grassland with a small sapling in the center. There were no flowers there, but as with this tiny scrap of land, it was somehow blight-free. The trio immediately forgot about the flower and wandered over to the grassland, not hearing Lamar as he shouted questions to them from the other side of the glen.

As they traversed the basin, they saw that the patch of unblighted land stretched further out of view as the valley narrowed, encompassing at least 30 feet: a tiny Eden that was nearly impossible to spot from above. As they drew nearer, Gaby saw that the delicate, budding branches of the sapling were swaying in a slight breeze only present within this space.

She stepped out of the wasteland and into this private sanctuary, looking around in wonderment. She reveled in the sight of healthy soil, marveled at the taste of clean air again; even the colors seemed brighter after traveling the gray wastelands for much of the day. Behind her, Coop was laughing with joy as he stepped into this hidden world. Ken held his hands up in wonderment as he entered. The three of them silently reveled in all the sensations that had been so dulled during their time in the blight. They simply had no words to express their delight at seeing green again after going so long without.

"What's it mean?" Ken asked as he ran his fingers over individual blades of grass in wonderment.

"I think it means we've reached the outer boundaries of those things' territory," Lamar said from behind as he entered the space with Beverly leaning heavily on his shoulder. They didn't realize how long they'd been standing there until he suddenly showed up. Lamar looked perplexed and overjoyed at the sight of all this greenery, while Beverly still seemed oblivious, looking around hazily.

"If I'm right, we should see a lot more green up top," he added.

They started for the end of the glen, about 70 yards away. They exited the unblighted lands as swiftly as they'd entered, excited at the prospect of more greenery. Their exhaustion after walking so many miles suddenly melted away. New strength surged through their aching limbs. Just the knowledge that safety might be on the other side of the valley gave all of them a second wind, except for Beverly, who still clung to Lamar for support.

Fortunately, the path upward was even and the slope gentle, and they soon discovered Lamar was correct. On the opposite end of the glen were two hills side by side with a narrow passage between them. The group walked between them and came across a wide plain, stretching as far as the eye could see, filled with nothing but luscious greenery and fecund foliage. They were finally clear of the ikus' territory.

Ken gave a low whistle of appreciation.

The looping, swirling ash patterns that had decorated the featureless wastelands tapered out right at the edge of the valley, with the blight only extending a few feet beyond. Everything else was pristine. It felt like they'd stepped into a different world. They could feel the wind on their faces again and hear the sounds of wildlife once more.

"This is incredible," Gaby marveled.

"I guess this is as far as they came last night," Ken responded.

"Does this mean we're safe now?" Coop asked.

Lamar stroked his goatee thoughtfully for a few moments before answering.

"I wouldn't count on it," he said. "Think of how much ground the iku covered just last night. Two nights ago, the blight petered out at the floodplain. Now it stretches for miles. I think we've got a ways to go before we can rest easy."

* * * * * *

The sun had crested the sky and was beginning its slow and inevitable descent before the group paused for another breather. Nearly two hours had passed since they had escaped the blight, and all of them were still grateful to be in a living, breathing forest once again.

They delighted in the little things — seeing squirrels stocking up for winter, hearing birds chirping again, the quality of the air, feeling the wind on their faces — all the things the blight had denied them.

Even Beverly was showing improvement. She was now walking unassisted, albeit slowly, and her delirium had abated, leaving her weak but alert. She said little and seemed to only half-believe the others' stories about their misadventures since leaving the campsite, which was the last thing she could recall. Despite her improvement, the black mark on Beverly's hand continued to spread, and now covered the front and back of her hand up to her knuckles.

The group's collective joy at seeing such abundance of life helped them to cope with some of the more challenging aspects of this leg of the trip. For one, it had taken some time for them to adapt to life outside the blight's equilibrium-disrupting influence; for the first 30 minutes, all of them walked like bow-legged sailors on shore leave trying to adjust to solid ground. Another issue was the steadily rising landscape, which made the going painfully slow as they fought against gravity as well as their own weariness.

But for Gaby and Coop, the worst change was the formation of a new power center in the group. Lamar and Ken, who had been spending increasing amounts of time together throughout the day, had been inseparable ever since they'd escaped the blight. They finished each other's sentences and took turns calling out instructions to the others, leaving them feeling increasingly like bit players in their own stories.

Even now, on a break, the two were still carrying on together. Lamar was performing another directional check while Ken regaled him with some ridiculous tale from his misspent youth.

"So, there we were, middle of nowhere in my dad's prize Mercedes," Ken said, speaking animatedly with lots of hand gestures. "I've got my pants around my ankles, she starts going down, and all of a sudden there's this flashlight in my eyes, and a cop starts rapping on the window. 'You two love-birds lost?' I roll down the window. 'Why no, officer, we found the back seat just fine!'"

Lamar looked at him, jaw agape for several seconds be-fore bursting out in laughter.

"You did not," he said with a shake of his head, still chuck-ling.

"Hand to God," Ken assured him. "Her father took a swing at me the next morning. That was our first and last date."

"Wow. Just ... wow."

Gaby and Coop watched the exchange from a small, grassy knoll some 15 yards away. Gaby was decidedly more downbeat, harrumphing at Ken's bawdy tale as she tried to pull her wavy black hair back into a ponytail with the help of a scrunchie, but Coop was more unsettled by the pair's easy rapport.

"Well, those two seem to be having a good time," he in-toned, making it clear that he was not.

"I'm glad someone is," Gaby muttered. "Meanwhile, we're on crazy-sitting duty."

She cast a backward glance at Beverly, who sat on her own several yards away, studying a leaf in her hand as though she were trying to remember what it was. Her complexion was still deathly white, and she appeared to be silently mouth-ing the same phrase over and over again.

"But that's not the frustrating part. See those hills in the distance?" Gaby said, pointing to the range of high hills in the distance. "I'd swear they haven't moved this whole time."

"Oh, they're moving, just not closer," Coop said with a

snort. "When we started, the hills were to our north, south and east. Now they're to our east, south and west. We're not going north anymore. I don't think we have been for some time."

"Then say something," Gaby encouraged him, nodding toward Lamar and Ken. Just then Ken gave a wave to Lamar as he disappeared behind a grove of pine trees, saying something about answering nature's call.

"No way," Coop said, folding his arms defensively. "The last time I questioned Lamar's navigation, he bit my head off."

Gaby stood up assertively.

"If you won't, then I will."

She stepped down from the mound and walked purposefully toward Lamar, who was just finishing up his reading by placing a stone where the stick's shadow had moved. Hearing her approach, Lamar looked up and smiled.

"Hey, Gaby. What's up?"

Before answering, Gaby craned her neck to look between the rows of pine trees that Ken had disappeared into. She saw no sign of him.

"I had a question, now that the human hair shirt is gone," she said.

Lamar clicked his tongue disapprovingly at her characterization of Ken.

"Lamar, why did we stop going north? Coop and I are worried you're getting us lost."

"We never stopped going north. That's what this is all about," Lamar said flatly as he gestured to his primitive sundial. "According to this …"

Lamar paused midsentence as he drew a line between the two shadow readings he'd taken and oriented himself accordingly.

"Huh," he said, seemingly surprised.

"Are we off again?" Gaby asked.

"Not much. Maybe 10 degrees from true north."

Gaby rubbed her temples in frustration.

"*That* is not the same north we followed this morning," she said, gesturing in the direction Lamar was facing. "There were giant hills there this morning. Where'd they go? We certainly didn't scale them."

"We went between them," Lamar said patiently, as though he were talking to an emotional child.

"Look at the sun!" Gaby insisted. "It's going down in the same direction we're walking. We're heading west!"

Lamar looked to the sky, shielding his eyes.

"It's too high in the sky to tell where it'll set. Now stop overreacting."

"I am *not* **overreacting**!" Gaby fairly shouted before covering her mouth in embarrassment, realizing she'd just proven him correct.

Lamar didn't even try to hide his disdain.

"You can disrespect me all you want," he said slowly, choosing his words carefully, "but don't question my decisions again. We're leaving ... with or without you."

Gaby stood there in stunned silence, trying to process the ultimatum she'd just been given, and positively aghast at who had issued it.

Lamar walked around her and cupped his hands together

as he called out to the others.

"Break's over, folks," he shouted. "We move out now."

Coop sidled up to her just as Lamar walked off, flashing her one more contemptuous look as he departed.

"So, how did it go?" Coop asked.

Gaby stared at Lamar walking away for several seconds.

"I ... I think I was just put in my place," Gaby said quietly.

"What?" Coop exclaimed. "By Lamar? Our Lamar?"

Gaby shook her head slowly.

"I think he's Ken's Lamar now," she said bitterly.

"If only we could get through to Lamar somehow," Coop lamented. "Make him realize that he doesn't have Ken on a leash at all; it's the other way around."

"Ahem!"

Someone to their left had just noisily cleared his throat. They looked over and saw Ken emerge from the grove of pine trees, zipping up his fly. His smirk made it clear he'd heard everything they said. Gaby and Coop looked away awkwardly and went to fetch their bags for the journey ahead.

Ken beamed with satisfaction. This was going better than he could have imagined. Now all he had to do was light the fuse at the other end. He scooped up his suitcase and hurried uphill to join Lamar.

He found the younger man muttering to himself, still fuming about his interaction with Gaby.

"The natives are restless," Ken warned him.

"So am I," Lamar groused. "I'm getting tired of them questioning my decisions. I feel like I'm walking on eggshells."

"Then stop walking and start stomping," Ken encouraged.

"I don't thrive on confrontation the way you do," Lamar replied, waving off the idea. "Gaby and I already had it out. I think one pissing match a day is my limit."

"Suit yourself," Ken said. "But they'll never respect you if you're afraid to lay down the law. Personally, if I heard them talking smack about me, I'd have lit them both up like fucking Christmas trees!"

"That's fear, not respect," Lamar said. "And I can't do that. I'm not like you."

In the distance they heard Coop calling out his name.

"LAMAR!" he shouted, waving him over, where he was standing with Gaby and Beverly.

Ken snickered.

"Then you better get used to hearing that."

The pair carefully made their way downhill to where the others were waiting.

"Is this about before?" Lamar asked Gaby pointedly. Her eyes shot open in anger, but she held her tongue.

"It's about the water," Coop said.

"What about it?"

"There isn't any," he said plainly. "I was thirsty, so I asked Beverly for the canteen, and she said …" He paused to point at Beverly, who finished his sentence.

"I don't have it," the older woman told them.

"So, who does?" Lamar asked.

"That's the point. None of us do," Coop explained. "We thought one of you two might have taken it while Beverly was … incommunicado."

Lamar looked to Ken, who shook his head no.

"I didn't take it, either," Lamar said, undoing the straps on his rucksack. "Let's everyone do a bag check. Someone here has to have it."

One by one, the others set down their backpacks and suitcases and began rummaging through them.

"Not here," Coop said after a quick search of his.

"Or here," Gaby said a few seconds later, zipping her knapsack back up.

"Nada," Ken said as he snapped his suitcase closed.

"Still nothing," Beverly said weakly after rooting around in her tote bag.

Lamar was getting worried. Even the thought of having no potable water the rest of the day made his mouth run dry. He opened up his rucksack and peeked inside. All he saw were cans of food, unopened ones for dinner tonight and empty ones, which he'd saved as a receptacle for boiling water on their journey. He saw a metallic glint underneath them and shifted the cans to the side. Staring him right in the face was the canteen, and even more improbably, a rose-colored brassiere, both buried at the bottom of his bag.

Lamar just stared at them for several seconds, trying to work out how they got there, and more importantly, how he would explain it to the others.

"Well?" Gaby asked impatiently.

"I ... uhm ..." he stammered, trying to figure out what he should say or do. His heart was pounding so hard in his chest it was a wonder the others didn't hear it.

As he stood there, paralyzed by indecision, Ken walked up behind him and grabbed the bag, lifting it to chest level so he could see inside.

"Just give it here," he said as he snatched it out of Lamar's numb fingers. The younger man was about to protest when Ken pulled the canteen from the bag and held it aloft like a hunting trophy.

"Here's the canteen," he said, tossing it in Coop's direction as he took another look inside the bag. "Is there anything else in ... oh-ho!"

Lamar winced. He could tell from Ken's tone that he had found the bra.

"Hey, anyone here missing a knocker locker?" Ken asked as he hoisted the bra in the air and spun it idly on one finger.

Gaby's eyes went wide with alarm.

"That's mine!" she shouted as she ripped it from Ken's grasp and clutched it close.

"Well, looks like Lamar's got a little crush," Ken said, smirking. "Either that or one strange-ass hobby!"

"That's not funny, Ken!" Lamar said, finally mustering the courage to defend himself. "Gaby, I swear to you, I didn't take it. I don't know how that got in there. You have to believe me."

"I don't *have to* do anything," Gaby replied coldly, glowering at Lamar as she stowed the bra in her bag. "Not 10 minutes ago you were lecturing me about respect and now I find that you've ... violated my belongings!"

"Gaby, I promise you this is some sort of misunderstanding," Lamar pleaded. "I would never go through your possessions."

"I better not find any ... stains on it," Gaby said, shivering in disgust.

"I'm telling you, it's some kind of mistake," Lamar said, trailing off into an embarrassed mumble at Gaby's insinuation.

"What the hell?" Coop suddenly shouted, startling the others with his uncharacteristic outburst. He was shaking the canteen. After a moment or two, the others realized that they weren't hearing any water sloshing around inside.

"Who cares about her stupid underwear?" Coop shouted, his face rapidly turning red with rage. "What did you do with the water, Lamar?"

"I didn't do anything with it!" Lamar protested.

"It's all gone?" Ken asked.

"All of it!" Coop said emphatically, upending the canteen for emphasis.

"Folks, I know how this looks, but I didn't take Gaby's underwear and I didn't drink the water. I promise you."

Coop rolled his eyes.

"Uh-huh," Coop intoned in disbelief. "So, how'd they wind up in your bag?"

"Maybe somebody else put them in there?" Lamar managed feebly, trying to avoid the accusatory stares of the others.

"Oh, for fuck's sake!" Coop vented, throwing up his hands and kicking at the dirt in his sandals. "Just 'fess up, already! The lies are now worse than the crime!"

"But I didn't do anything," Lamar pleaded.

Gaby shook her head in disgust. Lamar could tell that their trust in him had been irreparably damaged.

"As amusing as all this is, there's no use crying over stolen water," Ken interjected, trying to salvage the situation. "The sooner we get going, the sooner we find some."

"So, we just go thirsty until then?" Coop asked, disgusted.

"Afraid so," Ken said as he turned and headed back up the

rise. He could scarcely contain his glee. The tide had finally turned. If everything went as planned, he'd have the others eating out of his hand by tomorrow. As he strode forward through a thicket of thigh-high ferns, he noticed a small patch of grass was badly wilted, with two nearby ferns shriveled and brown. The smile on his face quickly sank. This was the third patch of blight he'd seen in the last 10 minutes. They weren't as far removed from iku country as he'd hoped.

One by one, the others followed Ken, with Gaby casting a final backward glance of disgust at Lamar, who stood alone, his head bowed as he tried to piece together how everything had managed to go so wrong for him so quickly.

* * * * * *

It was after 5 p.m., and the setting sun's position on the horizon made it clear that they were, in fact, heading north. But Lamar was in no mood to gloat about it, nor would he have found many sympathetic ears after his earlier fiasco. At this stage, the group cared about only two things: finding water and escaping the blight.

No one spoke as they scoured the landscape for any form of potable water, listening keenly for any hint of running water. Their salivary glands tingled at the mere thought of slaking their increasingly acute thirst. But no relief was forthcoming. To make matters worse, the occasional patches of blight they'd spotted earlier in the forest had rapidly overtaken it, and now they yearned for the sight of green again as they traversed the dusty and barren landscape.

It hadn't taken their bodies nearly as long to adapt to life in the blight as it had this morning. The nausea and disorientation passed within 15 minutes. But the psychological toll it took on them — knowing what was waiting for them in the blight as night came on — was devastating.

All of them had quietly resigned themselves to another night in the forest. But none of them were willing to accept another night spent beating back hordes of those creatures, so — even as exhausted as everyone was — they pushed themselves onward in the hope that the blight would clear up once more before the sun set.

Compounding their problems was Beverly. Within 20 minutes of crossing over into the blight, she'd collapsed and begun raving nonstop. Most of what she spouted was gibberish, but disturbing phrases like "burn it down" and "kill them all" kept cropping up in various forms.

Because she was no longer ambulatory, the group had fashioned a makeshift stretcher, using two spears as the handles and their jackets as the undercarriage, with the jacket arms knotted to the spears. Each was tied off at a different point to support Beverly's frame, and a fourth was tied over Beverly's midriff to hold her in place like a safety harness. The ends of the spears served as effective handles, while the sharpened tips dragged in the dirt behind them like some primitive plow tilling the soil.

But their brainstorm was proving better in concept than in execution, as it was too rickety to withstand the rigors of forest travel. Beverly was constantly sliding around on it, even with the jacket holding her to the frame lashed tightly. And any time the spear tips hit a rock or a small ditch, the whole thing fell apart, forcing them to waste precious minutes rebuilding it.

Right now, Gaby and Coop were on stretcher duty. It was hard work, as Beverly was deceptively heavy for someone so old and frail, and the pair were sweating profusely, which only further dehydrated them. Gaby looked over her shoulder to check on Beverly and saw she was still raving, only it was now a whisper due to a combination of dehydration and exhaustion. Perhaps more alarming, despite Beverly's constant fidgeting beneath the straps, Gaby noticed she wasn't perspiring anymore.

"She's not sweating," Gaby said, struggling to annunciate the words clearly through her swelled tongue.

"That's good news, isn't it?" Coop replied.

Gaby shook her head.

"Look closely," Gaby implored him. "Her pores are wide open. If she's not sweating, it's because she's seriously dehydrated. She needs water fast."

"She'll have to wait in line behind me," Coop said through gritted teeth.

It was then that Gaby noticed Coop was walking bow-legged, his flowing robes swaying wildly from side to side with each step. His face was contorted as well, as though he were desperately trying to mask his discomfort.

"Coop, are you in indescribable pain?" Gaby probed.

"I'm chafing," Coop admitted. "Every time my thighs touch, it feels like they're lined with razor blades."

"When we take another break, you should put on thicker shorts."

"We're not taking any more breaks until sundown," said Ken, who was walking 15 feet ahead of them. "Unless you two want to spend another evening with those ... creatures."

That was answer enough for Gaby and Coop, as the thought of encountering those creatures again convinced them both to quicken their strides. Well behind them was Lamar, who walked with his head bowed and his eyes glued to his feet, as though lost in deep contemplation as he walked.

The group emerged from a grove of denuded pine trees and found themselves standing on the threshold of a yawning valley whose shape could only be guessed at because it stretched out of view in every direction. Its rocky basin lay approximately three stories below them, connected to the higher ground by a slope with sides so smooth they could pass for manmade.

Every inch of the valley was covered in blight and the swirling ash trails the iku left in their wake. While the sight of the ash swirls at ground level was by now pedestrian to them all, seeing the exquisite, alien patterns stretching across the horizon from 30 feet up was disquieting. It seemed to affirm the unspoken fear echoing through all their brains: there was no escaping the iku tonight.

"Should we turn back?" Coop asked. "We could be back in the forest — the real forest — inside an hour."

"There's no going back," came Lamar's voice behind them, thick with exhaustion. They were the first words he'd spoken since the incident more than an hour ago. He looked at them pensively. "What we need is ahead of us, not behind us."

"Are you making that decision for the rest of us?" Ken asked, annoyed that Lamar was trying to take charge again.

"Going back won't help," Lamar asserted. "This blight stuff is some kind of trail they leave, not a boundary line." He paused to check his watch. "We've got maybe 90 minutes of daylight remaining, so let's prioritize what we need: water and shelter. I think the valley is our best bet for both."

"Water's our priority, not yours," Gaby replied cuttingly. "You had your fill earlier."

Lamar rolled his eyes in annoyance.

"I already told you I ..." he started and then suddenly stopped himself. "You know what? Forget it. It doesn't matter what I say because you've already made your mind up."

"If we don't find either one down there, then we head back to the forest. Agreed?" Coop asked, pressuring Lamar.

Lamar looked evenly at Coop.

"If we don't find either one down there, then we die tonight," Lamar said grimly.

Gaby and Coop exchanged a pained look before reluctantly starting down into the valley. With Ken's help, they carried Beverly down the slope into the valley, Gaby and Coop lifting by the handles while Ken hoisted her stretcher from the back. Lamar waited for them at the top of the slope, his brow furrowed.

The dusty air slowly turned rank as the group descended. The basin of the valley was rocky, with few trees interspersed among the multitude of desiccated grasses and scrub bushes, all of them coated with a fine layer of ash. There was something about the valley that unsettled all of them — Gaby in particular — some vague spark of familiarity amid a sea of horrible newness.

Ken dropped his end of the stretcher as soon as they

reached the bottom. The sudden jolt unbalanced the delicate structure, yanking the poles out of Gaby and Coop's hands and sending Beverly careening as the poles went one way and she and the jackets went another. She came to a stop about five feet away, wrapped up in so many jackets that she looked like a human sushi roll.

"What the hell?" Coop exclaimed.

Ken shrugged.

"Sorry, I thought we were going to take a break when we got down here."

Gaby shook her head in annoyance as she retrieved the spears and prepared to rebuild the litter. Coop and Ken checked on Beverly. She seemed unharmed by the spill; all the jackets had cushioned the impact. The pair started to extricate Beverly's upper torso from the knotted tangle of jackets when her left arm popped loose and flopped to the ground.

Her hand was almost entirely black now, with only some coloration above the second knuckle on two of her fingers. Worse still, the blackness had begun creeping down her wrist.

"It's still spreading," Coop said breathlessly.

"Then put on gloves and help me move Typhoid Mary here," Ken said, impatiently.

Coop hesitated.

"What if gloves don't protect against it?" he asked. "Gaby, what does Santeria say about touching people who've been marked by the iku if you're wearing gloves?"

"I don't know," Gaby replied as she lined the spears up. "They're religious texts, not owner's manuals. The iku purify wayward souls, guiding them to Heaven and killing their bodies in the process. You now know everything I do."

After another moment's hesitation, Coop helped Ken extricate Beverly from the jackets and set up the litter once more, careful to avoid her left hand. Lamar joined them down in the basin as they were putting the finishing touches on the litter.

Just as the group had finished strapping Beverly in, Gaby held up her hand for silence.

"What, did the spirits of Santeria just fax you new instructions?" Ken asked mockingly, eliciting a furious "Shush!" from Gaby.

"Can't you hear it?" she asked.

The others listened intently for any sound.

"I don't hear anything," Ken said, giving up after a few seconds.

"I do!" Coop exclaimed, his red curls bouncing in excitement. "It sounds like water!"

Gaby nodded excitedly in agreement.

The group struggled to pinpoint the faint noise and eventually made their best guess, setting out northwest. The sweet siren call of flowing water soon grew strong enough for Ken to hear, validating their decision and setting their salivary glands ablaze as they trekked across the largely featureless valley. All of them unconsciously quickened their pace, desperate to taste the life-giving fluid.

Within a few minutes the sound of rushing water reverberated in their ears. The land started to rise on either side of them as they closed in on the source, gentle and sloping straight ahead and to their left, while climbing steeply to their right, with 20-foot cliffs overhanging them. The group broke through withered underbrush that came up to their waists and stumbled upon a rocky, winding path leading northward.

That flickering sense of recognition Gaby had wrestled with earlier returned, stronger. It was like she had come home, only to find it filled with someone else's furnishings.

The sound of rushing water was now quite loud.

The group followed the rocky path around a large earthen mound decorated with a fallen tree and found themselves not 15 feet from the banks of a narrow, fast-moving creek. Ken fell to his knees in gratitude and started knee-walking through the mud to the shoal's edge, where he knelt down and dipped his hand into the icy waters. The stream was shallow, but moved quickly enough that the water never became silty.

"Shouldn't we boil it first?" Gaby asked, though she licked her lips as she did so, and it was clear she was struggling to keep from diving headfirst into the narrow stream herself.

"I can't wait that long," Ken said as he leaned forward and dipped his head toward the creek. "And neither can she," he added, motioning toward Beverly, who they had laid near the edge of the bank.

Ken leaned over and took a cautious sip. He swirled the liquid around tentatively in his mouth, like he was sampling the wine at a fancy restaurant. He took a cautious swallow. His eyes lit up and he immediately dipped his head back in. Seeing his reaction, the others threw caution to the wind and excitedly clustered around the creek like hogs rushing the trough at feeding time.

Lamar leaned in until his mouth was at water level and opened it, desperate to force as much of the life-giving fluid down his throat as he could stand. Coop struggled to get direct access, so he started splashing water into his open mouth, lapping it up and laughing the entire time. Gaby was only slightly more dainty, cupping her hands in the water and raising them to her lips so she could slurp as much of the precious liquid as she could. She could feel new strength surging through her, an electric tingle that coursed through her body like a passing storm, leaving her stronger than she'd felt all day.

After a couple of minutes of gulping water, Lamar raised his head and gave a satisfied belch. Ken gave a sigh of contentment as he drank another draught, while Coop stopped splashing long enough to fill the canteen so he could give some to Beverly.

As Gaby leaned back, her thirst momentarily slaked, her eyes fixated on the overhanging ridge some two stories above. That sense of déjà vu she'd been struggling with ever since they entered the valley doubled, and then trebled when her gaze fell upon the rocky path they'd just taken. Why did this seem so familiar? She had a sudden thought and stood up.

As Coop knelt beside Beverly and lowered the canteen to her parched lips, he noticed Gaby was walking north along the creek's muddy right bank. Ken and Lamar were too busy returning to the stream for a second helping to notice.

"Gaby, where are you going?"

No reply. She kept walking, as if in a daze, continuing northward some 50 feet before disappearing around a bend in the creek.

At the water's edge, Ken raised his head and started looking for Gaby.

"Hey, where did Miss Banana Boat go?" he asked.

"She headed north," Coop said, shaking his head in disgust at Ken's characterization as he gave Beverly a few more cautious sips of water.

An ear-splitting shriek pierced the late afternoon sky, making everyone jump. Lamar, who was on his hands and knees by the creek, nearly fell in.

"¡No se puede!" the voice shrieked. "¡Es un truco! ¡Truco! Truco!"

Lamar and Ken exchanged a brief glance before grabbing their spears, which they'd set on the bank. Lamar felt the pit of his stomach drop out as he stood up and bolted northward, already several paces behind Ken, their ears still ringing with Gaby's scream. Out of the corner of his eye, Lamar saw Coop pick up his hatchet and rush to join them.

Over the din of the current, they heard splashing and crashing noises as they stumbled through the forest, their spears at the ready. It sounded like some sort of struggle. Lamar silently prayed that Wade hadn't returned. All sorts of horrible images flitted through his mind as he sprinted, all the gruesome things Wade could do to Gaby ... or to the rest of them. Ken was in the lead and rounded the bend, disappearing from view around a man-sized rock formation. Lamar pushed himself to run faster, tightening his grip on the spear, steeling himself for whatever might be waiting for him around the corner. Lamar lowered his spear to waist level and shot across the bend with a visceral roar.

On the other side of the bend he saw Ken standing stock still, facing the opposite direction. Lamar looked over Ken's broad shoulders and saw, to his astonishment, Gaby kneeling in the ice-cold creek water, sobbing uncontrollably. He scanned the perimeter for any assailants or other threats. Nothing on either bank or in the distance.

Gaby shrieked again and started splashing the water with her fists, like a two-year-old throwing a tantrum. Lamar lowered his spear. Behind him, Coop rounded the rock outcropping with such speed and intensity that he slid two feet in the mud and nearly wound up in the creek. Lamar caught him by the robes, giving Coop time to regain his balance and composure.

"What happened? Are we under attack?" he asked, wide-eyed, as he tried to orient himself. Lamar simply pointed at Gaby, who wailed in anguish once more.

"We can't be here!" she screamed at the heavens as she continued rage-splashing. "We can't possibly be here!!!"

Lamar scratched his stubbly chin in confusion as the others looked around, trying to make sense of Gaby's outburst. Coop noticed that the creek was wider here and slower moving, forming a couple of small pools on its edges that ate into the muddy right bank. The same kind of pool their guide had used to store the food on their first night. He looked closer at that bank and noticed footprints in the mud. Realization slapped him in the face as the hatchet fell from his numb fingers, burying itself blade-first in the mud.

"Ohhh, no," he whispered in shock. "Guys, I think I know where we are."

"That's not possible," Ken said dismissively. "None of us have been this far north before."

"We aren't north of the camp," Coop said slowly, measuring his words carefully. "We're west. We're in the floodplain. This is Deer Creek."

"We never left! We never even left!" Gaby screamed, and the reason for her fit suddenly became apparent to all.

Lamar looked around wildly. On the right bank he saw the switch that Ken had accidentally beaned her with on Sunday, right beside the maple tree it had ricocheted off of.

"Nooo," he intoned, shaking his head in disbelief.

Ken knelt down a few paces from the right bank and lifted a fallen tree branch near the water, revealing the T-shaped metal cleat John had used to anchor the cooler in the water. The frayed nylon cords that had once held their food were still visible.

"This can't be real," Lamar exclaimed, taking a step back, scarcely believing his own eyes.

Ken whirled around to face Lamar, his face flush with rage.

"You stupid motherfucker," he hissed.

Lamar shook his head vehemently.

"Every time we veered off course, I kept us going north," he insisted, though his voice was cracking with despair. "I steered perfectly. There has to be some other explanation!"

"There is," Ken roared, standing up. "You're a fucking idiot!

"We spent all day walking around in a giant circle because you don't know which way north is!" Gaby screamed, hurling a stone at Lamar, who reflexively ducked even though the stone landed five feet to his left.

"This is all your fault, you stupid, underwear-stealing son of a bitch!!!" Gaby screeched as she leapt to her feet and charged Lamar. Coop put himself between them, throwing up his arms to block her path but careful not to lay hands on her, remembering how sensitive she was to contact with others.

"All of that walking for nothing!" she kept shouting, jabbing a finger at Lamar over Coop's shoulder. "All because of you!"

"It's not possible," Lamar insisted, feeling tears of shame and confusion well up in the corners of both eyes. "I followed the directions perfectly. *Your* directions!" he shouted at Ken. "Two shadows, 15 minutes apart. Straight line pointing north."

Ken stiffened momentarily, not expecting to be called out. Despite all his methodical preparations for this moment, he hadn't expected Lamar to blab about their shared secret. Ken saw the others' irate eyes shift toward him. He had to think fast.

"The line points ... EAST!!!" he fake seethed, clenching and unclenching his fists as he fed off the manufactured rage. "I told you east, with a 15-degree shift every goddamn hour! You've been doing it wrong this whole fucking time!"

Lamar gawked at the blatant lie, opening and closing his mouth silently like a fish trying to breathe out of water.

"You ... you didn't say any of that!" Lamar finally managed to stammer out, dumbfounded as much by Ken's seething rage as his deceit. Was he trying to cover up his own mistake, or was there something else going on here?

"You dumb motherfucker," Ken intoned, the vein on his forehead bulging in anger as he strode forward. "Don't blame me because you couldn't follow my directions," he lied. "You navigate like old people fuck: badly!"

"You're a liar!" Lamar spat back, slowly coming to recognize that he was being set up. He looked to the faces of the others, desperate for any sign of validation. Coop stared at him piteously, while Gaby was still in a rage.

"You stupid, simpering little shit!" Ken raged, his voice turning guttural for the first time today as he started toward Lamar. The young man flashed back to Ken's uncontrollable anger yesterday, when he'd used the same voice. It was like a brutal switch had been flipped in Ken's mind, one stripping him of all self-control.

Lamar raised his spear and pointed it at Ken.

"Stay away," he warned, taking a step back defensively.

Ken paused for half a second, just outside the range of Lamar's spear. His eyes narrowed to flint points at the provocation, and he stepped forward again.

"I mean it," Lamar insisted in a cracking voice, realizing how empty his threat sounded. He gave a tentative thrust. Ken batted away the feeble strike, knocking the spear out of Lamar's hands. He grabbed the younger man by the throat.

"Buckle up, babyfat!" he intoned as he made a fist with his right hand and reared back. Something caught on the sleeve of his right arm. He tugged against it and it didn't budge. He pulled harder and Coop lost his grip and was sent sprawling. Ken dropped Lamar and whirled around on Coop.

"What the hell do you think you're doing, Prancing Queen?" he raged gutturally. As Coop picked himself up from the mud, Ken noticed that Gaby was beside him, and she didn't look angry anymore, she looked concerned. It took Ken's rage-addled mind a moment to register that he was the source of her anxiety; that his fit of uncontrollable anger had burned all the hatred out of her and replaced it with naked fear.

"He's not worth it, Ken," Gaby implored him.

Ken looked over at Coop and saw that same fear in his eyes as he nodded his agreement with Gaby.

Ken bit at his lower lips, struggling to control the hate welling up inside him. He shook in anger for a moment, and then his eyes cleared. He turned back to Lamar and shoved him into the creek. Lamar came up sputtering a moment later.

"Some leader you turned out to be," Ken said, his voice no longer guttural as he slowly regained control of his emotions. He turned and started walking east, toward the camp. "If we die tonight, it's on you."

Lamar sat up in the freezing water, looking piteously at Coop and Gaby as he blinked back tears.

"He's lying," Lamar insisted. "You have to believe me. It's all some kind of setup."

Gaby shook her head in disgust and followed Ken.

Lamar turned to Coop, who stared at him with a mixture of pity and disgust.

"Coop, buddy? You believe me, right?" Lamar pleaded.

Coop turned away, shaking his head sadly as he went to collect Beverly.

"Fine! I don't need any of you!" Lamar shouted after him. "If you all don't believe me … then to hell with you! It's not my fault! I was set up! I was set up!!!" he screamed into the wilderness as hot tears of shame and bitterness streamed down his cheeks.

* * * * * *

Lamar kept his head down to avoid the burning stares of his former friends as they all worked feverishly to prepare for another night in the wigwam. Gaby chopped wood by the log pile, while Coop gathered twigs and leaves for kindling. Ken was in the wigwam, keeping an eye on Beverly, who was still delirious. And Lamar was busy raking away the mounds of ash scattered across the campsite following last night's ordeal.

No one spoke, though Lamar suspected the others had more than a few choice words for him. The campsite was exactly as they'd left it, right down to the baggage and clothing they'd abandoned when they set out this morning. This morning; it seemed strange to think that less than eleven hours ago, Lamar had been in charge and was best friends with Coop and Gaby. Fate could be cruel sometimes.

"Another glorious night in purgatory!" Ken exclaimed sarcastically as he emerged from the wigwam with the drinking pail in hand.

Coop rolled his eyes.

"For the last time, we're lost, not on *Lost*."

Ken sneered as he made a beeline for the water pump.

"You're right," Ken replied with a grunt of exertion as he

primed the pump. "If we're stuck in any show, it's *St. Else-where*. We're all trapped in that retard's snow globe!"

Lamar paused to stretch his aching lower back after raking out the entrance to the fence. That ache, along with the ire of his comrades, were all he had to commemorate the day's myriad misadventures. But he was taking at least some measures to avoid repeating the experience. After seeing how his bag had magically shed cans of food and gained unexpected things — like brassieres and empty canteens — he would made certain not to let it out of his sight again. That's why when the others dumped their bags in the wigwam like they normally did, Lamar went against the grain, setting his on a stool beside the central firepit in the middle of camp, where he could see if anyone approached it.

Ken gave Lamar the evil eye as he shoved past him with the water, sending some sloshing over the sides.

Lamar heard a "thunk" as Gaby dropped the hatchet and gathered an armload of wood. As he kept his eyes trained on the ground in front of him, Gaby's shoes suddenly appeared in his field of vision, followed rapidly by her jeans. He looked up, and there she was standing in front of him, cradling half a dozen split logs in her arms as he stood in front of the entrance. They locked eyes silently. Lamar waited half a second before deciding that he should be the first to speak.

"Thanks for doing that, Gaby," he said as he set the rake down beside the entrance, reflexively relapsing into his former role as group leader. "A few more armfuls should get us through the night. Now if you could just put those in the ..."

"If you're not going to move, then haul them yourself!" Gaby spat at him as she dumped the logs at his feet before turning on her heels and walking away.

"Or, you could just leave them here," he said under his breath, mentally chastising himself for his mistake. She hadn't approached him for advice; she had been waiting for him to move out of the way. The bitter recrimination in her eyes and voice stung deeply.

As he bent down to pick up the firewood, Coop knelt beside him to help.

"She's still mad at me," Lamar said, stating the obvious in hopes of breaking through the icy wall of silence Coop and Gaby had built around him.

Coop snorted his annoyance.

"She's not the only one," he muttered.

"I appreciate you helping with this," Lamar tried again, more tentatively this time.

"I'm not doing this for you," Coop insisted. The sooner we get the wood in there, the sooner we get a fire going. That's it."

"Nevertheless, I appreciate it."

Coop shook his head in disgust.

"I can't believe we trusted you," Coop continued after a moment, seemingly eager to unleash his venom after so long a wait. On the other side of the fence, they could hear Gaby chopping more wood. Judging by the forceful sound of each chop, she had found a viable outlet for her aggression.

"Look, I get it. I screwed up," Lamar admitted.

Coop made a noise that was halfway between a grunt and a forced laugh.

"That's putting it mildly."

"Okay, I acted like an asshole," Lamar said.

Coop simply stared at him, his pained expression reflecting the rift that had grown between them.

After enduring Coop's glare for several uncomfortable seconds, Lamar finally caved.

"Fine, I acted like a colossal asshole!" he conceded in exasperation. "Future generations will build monuments to my douchiness! There, does that get me out of the doghouse?"

Coop's narrowed eyes and piercing stare was all the answer needed.

"If it weren't for your string of fuck ups toward the end, you'd probably still be lording it over us as we speak," Coop whispered fiercely at him. "I still can't believe you threatened to abandon Gaby just because she questioned your decision."

Lamar winced at the memory.

"I admit it: I got a swelled head for a while there."

"Along with bad advice from a worse person," Coop said. "Your mistake was listening."

Lamar nodded penitently.

"I know," he said quietly. "And for what it's worth, I'm sorry. Friends?"

Coop scooped up the last of the firewood and stood up.

"Just don't do it again," he said resignedly. It wasn't a commitment, but it was the best Lamar was likely to get.

"I promise," Lamar vowed solemnly.

Coop's flinty expression softened a bit at Lamar's.

"As for Gaby, give her time," he advised.

"You really think she'll come around?"

"Eventually. I mean, you did steal her underwear."

Lamar rolled his eyes in exasperation.

"I already told you ..."

"Allegedly," Coop teased.

Lamar paused to watch the sun kiss the western edge of the horizon. The shadows around them were lengthening, but not yet deepening, because the sun had reserved its harshest light for the end of the day, as if it was signaling that it wouldn't go down without a fight. Lamar sympathized.

"Do you think those things from last night will come back?" he asked quietly.

"Those iku?" Coop responded. "Probably. I don't believe they're some mystical spirits coming for our souls, like Gaby, but they clearly want something from us. And since they didn't get it last night ..."

"What could those things possibly want with us?"

Coop shrugged.

"I imagine the same thing that most predators want: to eat us. I wouldn't ascribe any deep motivation to animals."

Lamar shook his head.

"Those aren't like any animals we've ever seen. Part of me thinks they want something else."

"Like what?" Coop asked as he gingerly deposited the rest of the firewood into Lamar's outstretched arms.

"Dunno," Lamar said, looking around the pile of wood in his arms to maintain eye contact with Coop. "But I'm pretty sure they're not here to sell us time-shares."

From over the fence they heard Gaby's voice.

"Coop, you're supposed to be gathering kindling," she called out testily, like a schoolmarm who'd caught her prize pupil passing notes in class. "How about getting back to work?"

"Duty calls," Coop said as he walked toward the northern boundary of camp in search of more dried leaves and twigs.

Lamar entered the fenced region and walked toward the teepee, his arms laden with wood, craning his neck around the pile to see where he was walking. He lifted his foot to kick at the wooden entrance when he paused at the sound of raised voices inside the structure. He recognized them — Ken and Beverly — but the heavy layer of animal skins decorating the teepee's exterior muffled their words. He leaned in closer. It sounded like they were arguing over something.

We have to get this right, or else everything we've done today will be for nothing. Hey, are you listening? Stop acting crazy for five fucking seconds...They're coming for us! They're coming and I can't..

A loud slapping noise pierced the din, suddenly cutting Beverly off. Lamar's eyes widened in alarm, but he made no move to intercede.

I'll do it again if you don't stop babbling and listen! We need just one more push, but I can't get to the bag with everyone else around. You need to distract the others, like I told you about yesterday. Will you stop messing with Gaby's stuff? They're coming, we have to stop them...Yeah, yeah, take it if it shuts you up. Sure, go ahead and take that, too. Why not? Just get out there and do your crazy routine for the others.

Lamar strained to understand the conversation, trying to piece together the occasional deciphered word like a jigsaw puzzle. It was clear that Ken was plotting something, but he couldn't discern what, and it didn't sound like Beverly was being very cooperative. If anything, it sounded like she was ranting again, but about what was anyone's guess.

And whatever you do, make sure that...Hey! I'm not finished yet!

The wigwam door pushed outward, and out stumbled

Beverly, shaking and drooling, her manic eyes darting every which way as she lurched drunkenly forward. It was quite a contrast from how frail and helpless she had seemed less than an hour ago. While she was ambulatory once more, Lamar wouldn't classify her condition as an improvement, as she appeared completely insane.

Beverly brushed past Lamar like he wasn't even there, bobbing and weaving awkwardly as she staggered toward the fence line, suffused with frenzied energy. Lamar spied Gaby's magnesium stick in her blackened left hand. She had something in her right hand as well, but Lamar couldn't tell what; he caught only a brief glimpse of something reflective between her fingers before she stumbled out of the fenced area and disappeared around the corner.

Lamar dropped the wood and bolted for the fence line, where he ran into Coop.

"Hey, any idea why Beverly just ran off into the woods?" Coop asked him, pointing north of camp. "She was acting weird, even by her standards."

"She has the magnesium stick," Lamar replied breathlessly. "I don't know what she's planning, but unless we find her, there won't be any fire tonight."

Coop's eyes went wide. No fire meant no protection from the iku, and they were getting perilously close to sunset.

Before he could respond, Gaby came over, resting the hatchet on her shoulder.

"Who took my magnesium stick?" she inquired, having overheard part of the conversation.

"Beverly, she swiped it from your bag," Lamar explained.

"Why the hell didn't you stop her?" Gaby exclaimed, incredulous. "She could set this whole place on fire, and she's crazy enough to do it!"

"She needs the knife for that, and you put it in your pocket this morning," Coop gently reminded her.

Gaby shook her head.

"I moved it to the pack after lunch because it was digging into my hip."

Lamar suddenly flashed back to the moment when Beverly pushed past him, with the magnesium stick in one hand and something small and reflective in the other. He had a sickening feeling he now knew what it was.

"She took both!" he shouted as he made a mad dash for the woods north of camp. Gaby dropped the hatchet and ran after him, with Coop following closely behind. In his panic, Lamar completely forgot about the food bag he'd been keeping such a close eye on.

Ken peeked out from the wigwam with a self-satisfied smirk. Once again, Beverly had delivered. He found her methods unorthodox and borderline obnoxious — who fakes crazy as a distraction? — but he couldn't deny the results.

He sidled up to Lamar's unattended food bag and rolled up his sleeves. While the others were away, he would play.

* * * * * *

Gaby took point, with Lamar on her left and Coop to her right, both of them several steps behind and a few feet to either side, as they stalked through the desiccated forest north of camp. Lamar couldn't help but remember walking this same path through billowing clouds of steam earlier this morning.

Everyone kept an anxious eye on the sun, which was rapidly merging with the horizon, losing its potency as it did so. In another 30 to 40 minutes, it would be completely dark.

"So, the Three Mouseketeers go hunting for Beverly … again," Coop said to make conversation.

Lamar smiled warmly at the memory. It was hard to imagine that was only three days ago. So much had happened since then that it seemed like a lifetime ago.

"Too bad one of us turned out to be Cardinal Richelieu," Gaby said through pursed lips as she stalked forward, her eyes scanning the region for any sign of Beverly.

Coop stopped in his tracks.

"Who?"

"She's implying I'm a traitor," Lamar explained.

"You're here because we need able bodies, that's it," Gaby intoned. "You're no Mouseketeer."

"Can we just focus on the task at hand, please?" Coop implored, striving to keep the peace.

"Does anybody know why she suddenly took off?" Gaby asked.

Lamar and Coop both shook their heads.

"No idea," Coop said, "But she looked sick, like she was hallucinating again."

"Keep your eyes peeled," Gaby told the others. "I don't know what she's planning, but if she starts a fire out here, this whole forest will go up like a Roman candle."

Suddenly, the crunch of the shriveled leaves and blighted plants beneath their feet took on added resonance. It was unnerving to think that everything they trod on was kindling just waiting for a spark to burst into a massive conflagration.

They spotted their quarry in a 30-foot-wide depression whose boundaries were defined by a rising hill on the left and a rock formation to the right. She was kneeling at the feet of a large ash tree with her back to them, shivering. From this distance, all they could clearly see of her was her white coat, which they nearly mistook for a shiny rock in the fading light.

Coop prepared to charge down into the depression, but Gaby held her arm up to stop him.

"That'll only set her off. Just keep calm and follow my lead," she asserted. "Beverly may still think of me as a friend, so let me do the talking. And make certain to keep your gloves on at all times. We can't have her touch us."

Gaby signaled for the trio to fan out as they slowly descended into the depression.

"Beverly?" she called out cautiously, taking slow, deliberate steps so as not to alarm her. From the corners of her eye, Gaby saw Lamar circling to the left and Coop flanking Beverly on the right. If Beverly heard them, she gave no indication, continuing to shiver as she kneeled at the base of the tree.

As Gaby drew closer, she noticed that Beverly had collected a large pile of debris — mostly twigs and dried leaves — at the base of the tree. It also became apparent that she was feverishly working on something between her knees, but from this angle, it was impossible to discern what.

"Beverly, what are you doing?" Gaby asked.

No reply. Gaby's ears picked out the sound of scraping, like something metallic being dragged across a rough surface.

"Beverly, do you have the fire-starting kit?" she tried again as she drew closer. "We need it to light a fire."

Still no reply. More scraping.

The trio slowly closed in on Beverly. Gaby shot an inquisitive look at Coop, who simply shook his head; the tree blocked his view of Beverly's work. Gaby turned to Lamar, who made a quick slashing motion against his palm to indicate a knife was being used, and then raised both hands to signal a massive conflagration. She was preparing a fire.

"Beverly, I don't know what you're thinking, but this isn't safe," Gaby cautioned, walking slowly toward her. "If you light a spark here, you could burn the whole forest down. You don't want to do that, right?"

Beverly said nothing but paused to shiver violently for a second before continuing to scrape magnesium stick shavings with the knife.

Gaby leaned forward and placed her gloved hand on Beverly's shoulder. The scraping stopped instantly. Gaby took a deep breath before turning Beverly around to face her.

Beverly's face was deathly white. She was sweating profusely, and her right eye was twitching like mad. But Gaby was most struck by the haunted, pained look in her eyes. During previous bouts, they had been glazed or sunken. Now her eyes danced wildly, screaming in mad agony of the nightmarish visions that threatened to consume her. Beverly's symptoms had returned with a vengeance.

In her right hand she had the knife; her left hand — which

was completely black and barely visible in the dim light — held the remnants of the magnesium stick, which she had shaved down to nothing. All that was left was the iron core and the flint backing. That must mean there were hundreds of magnesium shavings in Beverly's pile of tinder. A single spark could ignite them all.

"Gaby?" Beverly asked hesitantly, her voice quavering. "Are you … real?"

Gaby looked to the others, who appeared as confused as she felt, before answering.

"Yes," Gaby answered, nodding slowly. "Why don't you give me the knife?"

Beverly shuddered and struck the back of the knife to the flint. A spark shot into the air and fizzled out before it hit the ground.

"No!" Gaby cried and lunged for the knife.

Beverly reared back suddenly and swung wildly with the blade, which slashed Gaby's outstretched palm through the glove. Gaby reflexively yanked back her hand in pain, giving Beverly another opportunity to strike the back of the blade against the flint. More sparks flew before petering out in mid-air.

Lamar and Coop leapt into action, each grabbing one of Beverly's arms and dragging her down to the ground as she kicked and screamed.

"Let me go, demon!" Beverly shrieked, flailing wildly. "Let me goooo!!!"

While the pair struggled to pin Beverly down, Gaby clutched at her knife hand, desperate to pry it loose. The old woman was wiry, making it impossible for Gaby to safely claim the knife as Beverly twisted and writhed beneath her. With a violent thrust forward, Beverly yanked her knife hand free, punching Gaby in the nose in the process, and reached around to her immobilized left hand, which still held the remnants of the magnesium stick.

Coop saw what she was doing and tried to bat the knife away with his free hand, but Beverly's mania had made her strong. She swatted his hand away and stabbed the flint so hard that the blade tip snapped clean off, embedding itself in the base of the ash tree.

A shower of sparks shot into the air, and Gaby and Lamar gasped at the sight, watching them fall gently to the earth like the remnants of a climactic firework burst on the Fourth of July. Most of the sparks burned out mid-air, but one kept burning as it slowly sank onto the pile of tinder and magnesium shavings.

Everyone held their breath. Gaby and Lamar stood stock-still, like deer caught in headlights.

In the deafening silence, they heard a tiny "pop!" and saw the faintest whiff of smoke.

"Oh, God!" Coop cried, releasing his gloved grip on Beverly's wrist and rolling on top of the pile of leaves and twigs, frantically sweeping away magnesium shavings from the now smoldering pile, not realizing in his panic that his violent hand motions were also fanning air across the pile. A tiny orange ember appeared on the outskirts.

"No, you're feeding it," Lamar shouted to Coop. "Smother it! Smother it!"

Coop leapt onto the glowing ember like it was a live grenade and hugged it close, praying his robes wouldn't catch fire.

They heard a popping noise, and Coop writhed in pain. Then another, and another, as the magnesium shavings ignited like a row of firecrackers. Smoke and popping sounds filled the air, but no flames appeared.

"Aggghhhh!" Coop cried as dozens of magnesium flakes ignited against his robes, piercing them to strike the tender flesh beneath. It wasn't a scream of agony but rather a sharp cry of pain, like he was being jabbed with dozens of tiny needles at the same time.

"Dammit, that stings!" he cried out between coughs from the smoke as magnesium flakes kept going off under him.

Six feet away, Lamar and Gaby winced sympathetically, though neither could help him as they struggled to bring Beverly under control.

"They're coming for us, they're coming for us! We have to stop them! We have to burn it all down!" Beverly raved, spittle flying from her lips as she flailed like a woman possessed. Lamar grabbed hold of her knife hand and smashed it repeatedly against a flat rock until Beverly finally relinquished the blade.

Gaby struggled to immobilize Beverly's left hand, still afraid to touch the contaminated limb. The black spot had spread halfway down her wrist.

"She's as crazy as Wade!" Gaby exclaimed, finally bringing Beverly's left arm under control by kneeling on it, while pressing down on her shoulder to immobilize it.

"Burn it all! We have to burn it all!" Beverly screeched as she gave one final, especially violent thrust before her eyes rolled back in her head and she started convulsing.

"She's seizing again!" Lamar said, releasing his death grip on her arm so he could raise her head out of the dirt.

Gaby didn't move, however, fearing some kind of ruse. After a full minute of writhing, Beverly's whole body suddenly went limp.

The popping of magnesium flakes under Coop gradually petered out, like the final kernels in a bag of microwave popcorn. Neither Gaby nor Lamar made a move to help him, knowing full well that taking his place or merely moving Coop over to join him on the pile could give the oxygen-starved embers all they needed to burst into flames.

"I ... I think it's just about over," Coop said as the smoke started to clear, and right on cue, one final flake popped, eliciting a yelp of pain.

"What set her off?" Coop asked as he climbed off the pile stiffly.

In response, Lamar ran up and hugged him.

"That was the bravest thing I've ever seen!" Lamar exclaimed, clutching the confused Coop so tightly that he winced in pain.

"Okay, thanks," he replied awkwardly, clapping Lamar on the back.

Gaby joined them, but, as always, maintained a few feet of personal space.

"I'm not much for hugging, but everyone in camp owes you their lives," she told Coop as she offered up her gloved right hand for a fist bump, which Coop obliged awkwardly. He appeared deeply embarrassed by the sudden swell of attention.

As Lamar let go of Coop, they could see dozens of tiny holes and scorch marks had turned his robes into Swiss cheese.

"Are you hurt?"

Coop shook his head no, but immediately started scratching as soon as Lamar let go of him.

"No, but it stings like a sonofabitch."

"How about you, Gaby? Beverly tagged you pretty good, there," Lamar said, pointing to the blood oozing out of the gash in Gaby's gloved palm. Amid all the chaos of the last few minutes, she had completely forgotten about it. She removed the glove and held her hand up so Lamar could examine it.

After several seconds of grim observation in the fading light, Lamar's face brightened.

"It doesn't look too deep," he declared. "I think your glove got the worst of it. You may need a couple of stitches when we get back to civilization, but bandaging it should be fine until then."

Gaby looked at him askance.

"I don't see any first aid stations around here."

"We can tear up a T-shirt for a bandage. You can have mine," Lamar said as he grabbed the pocket knife and started sawing at the lower half of his shirt.

"No!" Gaby exclaimed, startling Lamar with the vehemence of her response. He paused, mid-slice, waiting for an explanation.

"Your shirts aren't exactly ... sanitary," she explained, quieter this time.

Coop, who was checking on Beverly, covered his mouth

to stifle the laughter.

"You do wipe your hands on your shirt a lot," he added.

Lamar looked away in embarrassment.

"Okay, you don't have to make a big production of it," he protested, trailing off.

"I'll use something of Beverly's when we get back to camp," Gaby said, feeling a little sorry for Lamar, despite everything he'd put them through today. "It only seems fair, since it's her fault."

"So, what do we do with her now?" Coop asked as he incessantly scratched at the scorch marks, desperate for relief.

"Well, we can't leave her out here," came a voice from behind the group, startling them. It was Ken, who must have followed the shouting to find them. "Let's get her inside and then figure out what to do."

Ken cocked an eyebrow when he got a better look at Coop, whose pockmarked robes were so riddled with holes that in parts they looked like a fishnet pullover.

"What happened? Kicked out of the gay rave for bogarting all the XTC?"

Coop blushed and moved to cover himself. Lamar stood beside him and put his arm around Coop's shoulder in a show of support.

"I'll have you know that he saved all our lives, including yours."

Ken gave a mock bow of gratitude.

"Well, thank you, Mr. Johnny on the Spot!" he said with a flourish and a sneer.

Coop visibly stiffened. His eyes narrowed, and an uncharacteristic scowl furrowed his brow.

"What did you say?" he intoned.

"I said, 'Thank you, Mr. Johnny on the Spot,'" Ken repeated, not picking up on the edge in Coop's voice.

Coop stared at him for five seconds before exploding with such ferocity that Lamar dropped his arm from Coop's shoulder in disbelief.

"Don't you ever use that name again, you alpha douche blowhard shithead!" Coop shouted before suddenly running off into the woods.

Ken did a double take, too puzzled by Coop's behavior and hasty departure to be angered.

"Who peed in her Cheerios?" he asked.

Lamar stood agog for several seconds, trying to process Coop's inexplicable Jekyll-and-Hyde routine before running after him.

"I'll bring him back," he called out as he ran, throwing Ken an accusatory glare. He may not have understood the reason behind Coop's outburst, but he felt certain that Ken was somehow responsible.

"Why do you insist on teasing him?" Gaby asked, shaking her head in disbelief. "If you want to lead this group, you need to learn to play nice."

"Why do you insist on being a stick in the mud?" Ken retorted. "And if you have a problem with how I run things, we can put Lamar back in charge."

"No!" Gaby said, recoiling at the thought.

"Fine," Ken said, putting on his gloves and grabbing Beverly by the shoulders. "Then help me get her back to camp."

Instead of assisting, Gaby bent over the tinder pile Beverly had erected at the base of the ash tree and reached into it.

The sound of distant chirping, faint but unmistakable, wafted past their ears. As muffled as the noise was, there were hundreds, maybe even thousands of different pitches contributing to the din. The iku were stirring once again.

Ken's ears pricked up at the sound, and he looked at the setting sun, which was more than halfway below the horizon.

"We gotta get moving," Ken warned. "C'mon, grab her legs."

Gaby wheeled around. In her bloody left hand she held the remains of the magnesium stick.

Even in the dimness of twilight, Ken could see that Beverly had shaved the stick clean of all magnesium, and the flint backing had shattered in the struggle, leaving only the iron core in the center. With no magnesium and no flint to start a fire, the device was now useless.

"She used it all," Gaby said softly, tears welling up in the corner of her eyes as she stared at the denuded stick in disbelief. "There's nothing left."

"If we can't use that to start a fire ..." Ken said aloud, but abruptly stopped himself when he came to the same realization as Gaby.

Unless they found another way to start a fire, they'd all be dead in an hour's time.

* * * * * *

Lamar scoured the woods in search of Coop, straining his eyes for any sign of the slight man in the dimming light.

The temperature was dropping rapidly, and Lamar shivered against the cold as he zipped up his bubble jacket.

Coop's outburst, his running off; Lamar struggled to understand any of it. Even his words had mystified the group. Ken had mocked him with a stupid expression — Johnny on the Spot — and Coop had lashed out over the use of the name, of all things.

The only thing Lamar knew for certain was that Coop was suffering, and he couldn't leave him out here alone, certainly not with those things all around.

As he was passing a clump of denuded trees, Lamar noticed from the corner of his eye tiny puffs of air some 30 feet in the distance. He zeroed in on the location and moved forward, keeping an eye on his path to avoid any foot-snagging rocks or gopher holes.

As he drew closer, he could hear sobbing, but struggled to distinguish Coop from the background. Coop's peach-colored robes and bright red hair were impossible to miss during the day, but blended perfectly with the surroundings as dusk started to drain the colors from the world.

When he was 15 feet away, Lamar could see that Coop was sitting on a rotted log covered in moss, his back turned, staring at something intently in his outstretched hands. Another exhalation from Coop provided just enough contrast for Lamar to identify it. It was a photo. Lamar surmised that it was the one of the little blond boy with the gap-toothed grin that Coop stared at so intently night after night.

Lamar coughed politely to alert Coop to his presence.

Coop immediately tucked the photo into his robes and dabbed his eyes with the flowing sleeves.

"You didn't see that."

"Of course not," Lamar said as he drew closer. "You seemed a little agitated when you left, so I wanted to make certain you were okay. Mind if I sit?"

Coop gestured beside, and Lamar joined him on the log, which creaked under the combined weight of the two.

"How are the burns?" Lamar asked after a moment of awkward silence.

"They still itch like crazy," Coop said with a sniffle. "They don't hurt that much."

"But something else does," Lamar surmised. "Want to talk about it?"

Coop gave no sign of either approval or opposition, so Lamar continued.

"The boy in that picture isn't your son, is he?"

After a moment's consideration, Coop shook his head no.

"He was your boyhood crush, right?" Lamar gently probed.

"No, not exactly," Coop said, fumbling for the right words. "It's ... complicated."

Lamar put his arm on Coop's shoulder in what was meant to be a comforting gesture but one that came off as merely clumsy.

"Dude, you don't have to suppress it," Lamar coaxed. "It's okay to be 'out' nowadays."

"No," Coop replied quietly, pulling away.

"It is," Lamar insisted. "In many circles, it's considered a plus. Like, 'Look at how progressive I am, I've got gay friends!'"

"Stop."

Lamar pressed onward, refusing to heed Coop's warning.

"I mean, you can't control who you love," he insisted with a chuckle to reinforce how obvious it was.

"Yes, you can!" Coop practically screamed, his face contorted in anguish as he leapt to his feet and confronted Lamar. "Some of us have no choice!"

Lamar sat there in stunned silence, shocked by Coop's outburst. Faint chirping noises could be heard in the distance.

Coop sighed and sat down again, struggling to regain his composure.

"His name was Johnny," he said after a few moments of awkward silence. "He was the boy next door ... literally. He used to come over and play all the time."

"A childhood friend," Lamar mused, nodding empathetically.

"He was curious about, well, everything," Coop continued. "One day, I showed him some videos. He didn't understand so I ... I ..."

"So you demonstrated?" Lamar offered.

Coop nodded.

"I convinced myself that it was love," he said, putting his hand over his mouth as he tried to rein in his emotions. "Even when he asked me to stop, I just couldn't. I thought I could win him over."

Coop took a deep breath and then continued.

"After a while, he stopped coming over. Then he began acting out at school and home. Three guesses why that was. His parents shipped him off to juvie."

Lamar nodded for him to continue.

"I heard the older boys there abused him," Coop said, his voice wavering in emotion. "He was victimized all over again. He couldn't take it, so one night he slit his wrists. That perfect, beautiful angel would still be alive today if it weren't for me!" Coop sobbed, his condensed breath coming out in short, ragged bursts.

"You can't blame yourself," Lamar said, trying to sound comforting as he put his arm around Coop. "You were just a kid."

"No, no, no! You don't understand!" Coop insisted, pulling away. "He was 12. I was 25!"

Lamar froze as he tried to process this. His eyes suddenly went wide with realization.

"You mean, you're ... one of ..."

"Just say it," Coop said with a sigh of resignation.

"A pedophile," Lamar said in a hushed whisper.

"I'm a convicted sex offender," Coop replied bitterly, fairly spitting out the words.

Lamar found himself unconsciously inching away from Coop, and had to will himself to remain in place.

"That picture isn't a memento of first love," Coop explained. "I look at it every night to remind me of the life I destroyed. Of the childhood I stole. He was so innocent, and I robbed him of that innocence!" he wailed, pounding the rotted log with his fist.

Beside him, Lamar struggled with his own emotions, trying to reconcile this new, disturbing side of Coop with the steadfast companion he'd come to know and rely on over the past five days. While this revelation explained many of the small mysteries surrounding Coop, it didn't make the knowledge any easier.

"So that's why you wore the ankle monitor."

"A thousand feet," Coop replied. "That's as close as I can come to any school without setting it off. I had to get special permission from my P.O. for this trip."

As they talked, Lamar felt as if he'd reached a spiritual crossroads of sorts. One was the path of moral outrage, and the other the road to compassion. He had no idea which one to take.

"Is that why you came here?" he asked, buying time while he tried to decide. "To control those urges?"

Coop sniffled and looked up at the night sky wistfully.

"This, and every ashram with decent online reviews," he said. "I keep hoping that if I find the right path, if I settle on the correct mantra, I can ... stop being what I am. That's what I do day and night: pray the pedo away."

That settled it for Lamar. Societal expectations be damned, he'd made his choice.

Lamar slowly put his hand on Coop's back, patting it comfortingly.

"And I take it nothing's worked."

Coop shook his head.

"So why is all this coming up now?"

"Last night, when everyone was trapped in the teepee and we were all convinced we'd die, all I could think of was Johnny," Coop explained, between sniffles. "The thought of seeing him again ... it scared me. Not just the dying part, but having to own up to what I did. How do you atone for something like that?"

Coop hid his watering eyes in embarrassment.

"It happened again when I leapt on the fire, only this time … after everything we've been through today …"

Coop paused a beat to compose himself before continuing.

"I felt like … part of me welcomed death, even felt grateful, like I was looking forward to it."

Coop fell forward, sobbing on Lamar's pudgy shoulder.

"I wanted to die! I really wanted to die!" he burst out crying as the floodgates on his emotions opened wide.

Lamar put his arms around him, unsure what to say as Coop sobbed in his arms, his breath coming in heaving, wrenching gasps between the tears.

"I want to die!" Coop screamed in anguish. "I want to die!"

Lamar held him fast, rocking his crying friend back and forth as he watched the sun's last rays disappear beneath the horizon.

* * * * * *

"No, I told, you to lock the spindle in place!"

"I can't see anything. Bring the light closer."

"You're only rotating it in one direction. Spin it back and forth."

Gaby hovered over Ken as he furiously worked John's bow drill in the wigwam's central firepit, shining the flashlight on his work and instructing him as he struggled to get a friction fire started.

Ken gritted his teeth as he sawed the bow back and forth on a rotating spindle that was slowly boring a small groove into a fireboard. As Ken's hand movements sped up, the friction between the spindle and the board produced friction heat and small wisps of smoke, but not the spark they needed so desperately to ignite the tinder in a small notch of the fireboard.

In the distance, the chirping of the iku was growing stronger and sharper, a cacophony of tens of thousands of voices as night gradually enveloped the forest. It was already pitch black within the wigwam, save for the flashlight trained on Ken's hands. The outer bands of light revealed Beverly, passed out on her bedroll, oblivious to their increasingly desperate circumstances.

"Pull it closer," Gaby instructed. "You're making more work for yourself by keeping it at arm's length."

Ken stopped working the bow and glared at Gaby.

"If you're such an expert, why don't you do it?" he groused, the agitation evident in his voice.

In reply, Gaby held up her injured left hand, which she'd bandaged with one of Beverly's scarves. Ken rolled his eyes and got back to work.

But lingering in the air between them was the unspoken fear that neither of them could make it work. Until now, Gaby had been the only one to even try using the bow drill, and that was four days ago. And despite operating it in the middle of the afternoon, with no pressure and under John's expert tutelage, her efforts had ended in abject failure. Now they had to do it on their own, in the dark, with legions of otherworldly creatures barreling down on them, ready to do God knows what to them.

The door to the wigwam creaked open behind them. Gaby whirled around in panic, shining the light on the intruders. In the flashlight's glow, Coop's red curls bounced into view as he ducked to fit in the narrow entrance, his hand shielding his eyes from the sudden assault of bright light. Behind him came Lamar, who closed the door tightly behind him.

Gaby relaxed and lowered the light. The pair both looked out of breath, as though they'd been running.

"Where the hell have you two been?" Ken greeted the pair in his characteristically caustic fashion before either could say a word. "We're busting our butts to get a fire going, while you two pop off to give each other tea and sympathy hand-jobs!"

"Those things are on our heels!" Lamar warned, ignoring Ken's jibe. "We've got maybe two minutes."

Everyone paused to listen. It sounded like the iku were right on top of them. Ken cursed under his breath and re-doubled his efforts.

Coop fretted as Lamar started to tie off the upper and lower enclosures to the door. In the peripheral glow of the flashlight, Gaby could see that Coop's eyes were red and puffy, like he'd been crying.

"No, don't tie it off," Gaby said.

Lamar stopped mid-knot and looked at her like she was mental.

"Someone needs to stall them until we have a fire going."

"I know you're not talking about me!" Lamar exclaimed, horrified by Gaby's suggestion.

"I'm not saying you have to sacrifice yourself," Gaby insisted. "Just distract them!"

"But we have the flashlight for that," Lamar pointed out.

"We'll just do what we did last night."

Gaby opened her mouth to answer, but Ken interjected.

"Will you bring that light over here? I can't see a damn thing!" he barked.

Gaby shrugged.

"The light's spoken for," she said simply as she turned the beam toward Ken.

"So what am I supposed to use if there's no light?" Lamar protested.

"How about your B.O.?" Ken sneered between gritted teeth as he furiously sawed with the fire bow. "One whiff of your pits should insta-kill those little fuckers!"

Lamar shook his head in disgust rather than engage with Ken.

"Hang on," Coop said as he headed for the rummage pile on the opposite end of the wigwam, where they'd discarded all the knickknacks salvaged from the former storage shed. After a few seconds of digging through the pile, he came up with lava rocks, the ones John had used during the purification ceremony on their first night.

"Throw these," he said, handing him six rocks.

Lamar took a deep breath before grabbing hold of the door handle.

"I can't believe I'm doing this," he muttered to himself before pushing the small door outward and poking his head out cautiously.

A gust of wind blew through the opening in the fence line, hitting Lamar with a blast of shockingly cold air that made him wince. He squinted, trying to see in the dark as he nervously clutched one of the lava rocks.

The moon was high in the sky but largely obscured by overhead clouds. And the night was filled with shrill chirping, like they were about to be invaded by millions of mutant crickets. Lamar forced himself to breathe slowly and steadily.

Inside, he could hear Gaby and Ken squabbling over their progress.

"Here's the problem," Gaby said. "Your jerking motion pulled the fireboard away from the leaves. There has to be something to catch the spark."

"I would have gotten it working ages ago if you'd stop butting in," Ken protested.

"Just give it here," Gaby insisted.

Lamar shivered in the cold, his exhalations rising into the night sky in a slow, uniform fashion. As his eyes slowly adjusted to the darkness, he could just make out the shriveled hedges on the opposite side of camp.

"See?" he heard Gaby saying with a note of self-satisfaction in her voice. "Now we're getting some real smoke."

"Just hurry up and get the fire started," Ken replied sourly. "You can pat yourself on the back if we survive this."

Lamar concentrated on the hedges. It looked like they were starting to sway ever so slightly. His puffs of heated breath began coming faster now as his pulse quickened.

"Why aren't we seeing a spark?" Ken complained from inside.

"Move the light closer," Gaby instructed him. "No, that's in my eyes!"

The hedges were clearly moving now, undulating wildly, even though the wind had died down. The moon came out from behind a cloud momentarily, bathing the campsite in an eerie glow that revealed the iku swarming the perimeter in piles of heaving masses three feet high. It looked like millions of them.

Lamar's breaths were now coming in short, panicked bursts.

"Uhhh, guys," he called out. "They're here."

"You hear that?" Ken asked Gaby. "Hurry up!"

"Stow it!" she shot back. "You couldn't do this even with two good hands!"

Lamar watched as the creatures spilled over into the campsite, crashing down upon the central firepit in a wave of inky, writhing bodies. The chirping was getting louder and more incessant. Lamar clutched the lava rock in his palm so tightly that he started to lose feeling in his fingers. He retreated a couple of steps into the wigwam, until only his head and his hands were peeking out of the entrance. The moon went behind another cloud, and darkness consumed the landscape.

Lamar looked to and fro, struggling to see anything. His heart was pounding so hard he thought it would leap out of his chest. He struggled to catch his breath, and some part of him dimly realized he was hyperventilating. He saw motion just in front of the fence line, not 10 feet away. He steeled himself, reared back and threw the lava rock in the general direction of the invaders.

The moon came out of hiding just in time for Lamar to watch the igneous stone sailing end over end toward the gap in the fence. The mass of creatures swarming just outside the entrance suddenly stopped chirping. They split ranks clear down the middle, moving as if they were one, leaving a gaping hole of ash-covered dirt where the lava rock landed with a muffled thud, kicking up a small cloud of dust that shone eerily in the moonlight.

The silence was suffocating. It was so quiet Lamar could hear Gaby furiously sawing back and forth on the fire bow.

The iku re-formed ranks and inspected the rock, probing it for a moment or two, as if trying to decide whether it was a threat. Lamar heard a single chirp. Then another, and another.

Suddenly the night was filled with their cries, and the iku pressed forward.

Lamar shrieked and leapt back inside, slamming the door behind him. He struggled to fasten the ties, his fingers shaking too much to obey him. All he could hear was the sound of his own heartbeat jackhammering in his ears as panic seized him in its icy grip.

"They're right outside!" Lamar said, his voice cracking in anxiety. "How's the fire coming?"

"It's not fast food! It'll be done when it's done!" Gaby snapped, grimacing in pain as she used her injured left hand to hold the spindle in place while her right feverishly worked the bow.

Through the haze of smoke Gaby was generating, Lamar could see blood oozing from beneath her makeshift bandage, staining the top of the spindle a dull red. Ken kept the flashlight trained on Gaby's work, but his eyes repeatedly flitted toward the canvas walls, which were beginning to bulge inward against the lattice frame near the door.

Coop grabbed the small wood hatchet and held it at the

ready, as though that would do anything to deter the creatures if they made it in.

The bulging at the base of the teepee started to spread as the creatures surrounded the structure and began trying to force their way inside, chirping incessantly. The siege had begun.

"C'mon, you almost got it," Ken coached Gaby, even though his eyes were glued to the swelling sides of their canvas cocoon.

"Watch the shadows," Lamar cautioned the others, though it was hardly necessary, as all eyes except for Gaby's were scanning the dark outer ring of the wigwam for any signs of movement. "If they squirm under the flaps like last time, we're going to need that flashlight."

"Nearly there, just a little more," Ken coaxed Gaby, who was grunting in pain. Sweat was starting to roll down her face, and her right hand felt like it was about to fall off.

Lamar scrunched his eyes as he stared into the shadows. He could have sworn he saw … there it was again. Movement.

"They're inside," he warned the others.

"Keep going, keeping going," Ken coached.

Inky tendrils swayed to and fro in a darkened section to the left of the door. They grew and massed until they eclipsed the shadows. Lamar held his breath. The black mass started to move inward.

Lamar snatched the flashlight from Ken's nerveless fingers and trained its beam on the moving mass, which started smoking and juddering uncontrollably, as though it were in its death throes, before vanishing. He spun the beam around, aiming it at another shadowy mass several feet from Coop, which met the same fate. The iku outside chirped furiously. He started to slowly spin in a circle near the center of the wigwam, training the moving light on the base of the wigwam.

As before, everywhere the light touched, the bulging ceased. Lamar spun faster, trying to keep pace with the relentless iku.

"That wasn't so bad," Coop said unconvincingly. He lowered the hatchet and exhaled slowly.

"How're we doing, Gaby?" Ken asked.

"I think I've got something," Gaby said, redoubling her efforts as smoke started to pour from the leaves beside the fireboard.

As Ken started to relax, he noticed movement along the canvas walls several feet above the base, much higher than the creatures had ventured the night before.

"Lamarrrr," he intoned.

"I see it, I see it," Lamar insisted, noticing movement out of the corner of his eyes at varying heights along their canvas border. The iku were climbing. He suddenly found he had a lot more surface area to cover as the iku wormed their way up the exterior of the wigwam.

Shuffling noises could be heard above the chirping din as the iku slithered against the fake animal skins on the wigwam's exterior. Anywhere the light wasn't touching, they kept climbing. Knee level, waist level, eye level.

Lamar shined his light to and fro wildly as his pulse quickened, not sure where to point the beam, as the canvas seemed to be bulging inward from all sides and heights. Everywhere he aimed the beam the iku quickly pulled back, but resumed climbing as soon as the beam moved. The others could see that despite Lamar's best efforts, he couldn't keep up. It was simply a matter of time.

The bulging appeared higher and higher up the fabric on all sides, no matter which way Lamar trained his light, until Coop looked up and saw movement around the wigwam's venting hole overhead.

"Lamar!" he shouted.

"I'm a little busy!" Lamar replied, gritting his teeth as he tried desperately to keep the iku from going any higher than eye level. He's already given up on stopping them at any point below, where the canvas walls were bursting at the seams with pressure as the iku tried to force their way inside.

Coop grabbed Lamar's flashlight arm and aimed it skyward.

Blackish squirming shapes clustered around the hole in the ceiling vanished in a puff of smoke, as did several in the lower-lying branches of the denuded pine tree overhead. The iku had climbed the tree as well and were now diving onto the wigwam's roof.

Ken lunged for the pull chain that controlled the central flue and yanked it tight, constricting the opening to less than a foot in diameter.

Out of the corner of his eye, Lamar could see movement in the rafters above. He aimed the light in that direction and caught several iku that had snuck in and were somehow clinging to the ceiling. They were instantly extinguished. He and Coop shared a nervous glance. These things could hang upside down, too.

"Gaby, give us good news," Ken begged.

"This would be so much easier if I could see properly!" she replied snappishly in the dim afterglow of Lamar's beam. "Ken, get down and blow on the leaves."

Ken dropped to his knees and started blowing furiously on the leaves.

"Gently!" Gaby instructed him. "Don't spit."

The iku were swarming on all possible surfaces now. Lamar's flashlight barely slowed them down. The bulging of the fabric on all sides was now almost uniform, so it looked like the whole wigwam was one organism breathing, and they were inside it. It was an unsettling thought.

The flashlight flickered and went out momentarily. Lamar smacked the handle and the flashlight blazed to life once more although it was slightly dimmer.

"We are going to die," Coop said urgently.

"I see an ember!" Ken said excitedly at the base of the firepit. "It's glowing!"

The others watched as the ember produced a tiny flame, which flickered and threatened to fade. Everyone held their breath. The flame leapt back up as it started to feast on a dead leaf. Its fiery tendrils reached for another. And then another. Slowly but surely, the flames spread, and the light in the wigwam began to grow.

Gaby dropped the bow drill and leaned back on her knees, exhausted, as Ken and Coop started feeding the flames more leaves and dried twigs.

Ken pushed the flaming mass onto the pile of waiting logs in the fireplace before adding more kindling to fuel it. As the flames grew, the pressure on the walls of the wigwam lessened.

After several agonizing minutes, the flames grew high enough and hot enough for the logs underneath to catch. They now had a proper, sustaining fire.

"We did it! We really did it!" Ken shouted triumphantly, as the iku began retreating and the canvas walls resumed their former shape.

Lamar and Coop hugged in celebration as Gaby removed the blood-soaked bandage from her left hand to see how much damage she'd done to it. It was hard to tell in the glow of the firelight, but the laceration appeared to have re-opened at either end, with blood trickling out. It didn't look too bad, all things considered.

She started rooting through Beverly's suitcase for garments that could be fashioned into a fresh bandage. She stole an envious glance at Beverly, who was still sleeping peacefully, with no idea how close the group had come to dying. As she picked through the clothing, she winced at the thick, black smoke pouring from the fire.

Coop and Ken tried to wave the smoke away from their faces as it started to fill the wigwam. The narrow opening in the ceiling wasn't enough to properly vent the smoke. Lamar's eyes started to sting and tear up. Beside him, he could hear Coop coughing.

Gaby dropped Beverly's suitcase and reached for the pull chain to vent the teepee.

Ken put his hand up to block her.

"We have to open the flue," she insisted between coughs.

"We can't risk it," he insisted, his voice muffled as he pulled his shirt collar over the lower half of his face to keep the smoke at bay. "We don't know if the fire will stop them from coming in through the hole."

"But we'll suffocate!" Coop shouted hoarsely as the smoke started invading his lungs. He was having trouble seeing through the billowing black cloud.

"Just keep low to the ground," Ken instructed as he lay flat on the dirt. "Smoke rises."

The others looked dubious but followed suit. However, it quickly became apparent that Ken's solution was anything but, as the smoke cloud sunk lower and lower to the ground. Lamar dry heaved, desperate to expel the smoke from his lungs. All of them were struggling to breathe. Coop had tucked his head into his robes like a turtle. Gaby had wrapped one of Beverly's Donna Karan sweaters around the lower half of her face like she was the world's most fashionable bank robber. But nothing worked.

The wigwam was swimming in front of Gaby's eyes. She got up on one knee and staggered toward the pull chain.

"Don't!" Ken shouted through the haze of smoke. "You'll kill us all!"

"We're already dead if I don't," she answered and tugged on the pull chain.

With a "Whoosh!" the smoke rushed upward and outward as the venting hole opened wide, expelling it into the night sky and replacing it with clean, breathable air. Gaby lowered the sweater and took a deep breath, her throat still burning from consuming so much smoke. Air had never tasted so good.

Lamar stood up, looking hesitantly toward the rapidly clearing rafters for any signs of the iku. Outside, the iku chirped their disapproval, but did not renew their assault. It appeared the fire was keeping the creatures at bay. Lamar allowed himself to relax a little.

"Thank ... God!" Coop exclaimed, rolling onto his sleeping bag and allowing himself to relax for the first time in what felt like hours, but in reality had been less than 20 minutes. They were safe for now.

Ken took a drink from the water bucket by his bedroll, sputtering as the lukewarm water triggered a coughing fit in his smoke-ravaged throat.

He looked disdainfully at Beverly, who was soundly sleeping several feet away, blissfully ignorant of everything that had transpired this evening.

"Look at her, sleeping peacefully while the rest of us suffer," he groused.

"More importantly, why does she look so peaceful?" Lamar remarked. "If not for her arm, you'd never know she was sick. She looked a lot worse earlier."

"I noticed that, too," Gaby added. "When we left the blight this afternoon, she improved. And when we went back on it, she took a turn for the worse."

"FYI, we're in the blight right now," Ken said with a sad shake of his head.

"Are we?" Coop posited. "I know it's all around us, but look at the dirt in here," he said, scooping up a handful and holding it up to the firelight. It looked richer and darker than the pasty soil outside, though that may have just been the light. "Maybe this truth circle thingy is protected," he said, his eyes drifting toward the crimson mandala over the entrance.

He caught a glimpse of Ken's incredulous expression and quickly wilted.

"Or something," he finished weakly.

"Let's put a pin in it and get some rest," Gaby said with a yawn. "I don't know about the rest of you, but I'm so tired I can't think straight."

Everyone nodded appreciatively. They'd been up for nearly 40 hours straight, and as their fear of imminent death started to recede, a wave of exhaustion consumed all of them. Lamar closed his eyes and started to drift when an unexpected voice called out.

"Did the signal fire work?"

Lamar opened his eyes and sat up.

It was Beverly, groggy and confused, but awake and seemingly recovered from her earlier fit of madness. Her eyes looked more lucid than they had all day, suggesting that she was on the mend. But a quick look at her blackened left arm quashed that idea. It had spread all the way to her elbow.

"She's back!" Coop exclaimed, rolling off of his sleeping bag for a closer look. The others similarly crowded around Beverly, eyeballing her like she was some freak specimen in a jar.

"Did it work? Have we been rescued?" Beverly pressed, raising her head slightly.

"Did what work?" Gaby inquired.

"My signal fire," Beverly said, as though the answer were plain. But before the others could answer, she spied the younger woman's bandaged left hand. "What happened to your hand, Gaby?" Beverly paused to sniff the air. "And why does it smell so smoky in here?"

Lamar cradled his head in his hands while Ken sat down and started laughing at the question. Neither wanted to recount the craziness of the past 20 minutes.

"Beverly, we're back in the teepee," Gaby said slowly.

"We are?" Beverly asked, dejected. "So that means that noise outside ..."

"Is the iku, yes," Gaby said, finishing Beverly's sentence for her.

"What's the last thing you remember?" Coop asked.

Beverly sat up slowly and rubbed her aching temples as though that would improve her recollection.

"Late afternoon. We were in the woods — the real woods, not this blight — when the canteen went missing," Beverly said, frowning in concentration. "I started to feel sick, and then the next thing I remember, it was dark and I was alone in the woods, building a signal fire. Those little black creatures were there, whispering all these crazy ideas. They tried to stop me, so I fought them off."

She shook her head, trying to remember.

"It all seems so ... fragmented," Beverly continued after a moment. "Almost like a dream. Why did we come back here?"

Gaby cast a dark look toward Lamar at the mention of being back in camp. Clearly, it was still a sore subject for her.

"It's ... complicated," Coop said as delicately as he could. "Who exactly were you trying to signal with that fire?"

Beverly scrunched her face up like this was the world's stupidest question.

"The outside world, obviously! Fires bring firemen, park rangers, state troopers. I was trying to get us rescued!"

"So your idea of placing a 911 call is burning down the forest with all of us in it?" Ken sneered. "Brilliant plan!"

"Don't talk to me like I'm stupid!" Beverly snapped. "We could have taken shelter in an open field or the floodplain."

"We would have died of smoke inhalation long before the fire ever reached us," Lamar said. "Trust us on this one."

Beverly considered things quietly.

"That wasn't the iku that fought me while I built the signal fire, was it?"

Gaby shook her head no.

Realization slowly crept across Beverly's face.

"Oh, God," she exclaimed, tears welling up in the corner of her eyes. "What have I done?"

"Spare us your self-pity," Ken said dismissively, looking down his nose at her. "It's bad enough we had to save your sorry butt, now we have to listen to you whine about it?"

While his words were cruel, the others had trouble disputing them. Everyone had suffered greatly that day at Beverly's hands.

"Look, let's just get some sleep," Gaby said, too exhausted to continue the conversation further.

"Amen to that," Ken said. "We should all try for some shut-eye, if we can. Who wants first shift?"

No one spoke up.

"I nominate Beverly," Lamar said. "Seeing how she nearly got us all killed."

"I nominate you," Ken replied snidely. "If it weren't for Lamar, we'd be back home right now."

Lamar glared at Ken.

"You lying sack of ..."

"Let's put it to a vote," Coop hastily suggested, anxious to avoid another conflict. "All in favor of Beverly, raise your hands."

Lamar and Coop both put their hands up.

"All in favor of Lamar?"

Ken's hand shot up like an express elevator. Beverly raised her hand after a moment. Everyone looked at Gaby. Slowly, reluctantly, she raised her hand.

"There we have it," Ken said as he lay back down on his bedroll. "Democracy in action."

"Beverly, why don't you take second shift?" Coop gently suggested. "Lamar, she can relieve you at 3 a.m."

"Don't forget to feed the fire," Gaby said through a yawn as she lay down.

"And don't fall asleep!" Ken sternly warned as he closed his eyes.

Despite the chattering of the iku and the crackling of the fire, exhaustion quickly sent the other four into dreamland, leaving Lamar alone.

He sat up on his bedroll and checked his watch: 7:50 p.m. There was no way he'd last another six hours. Already he could feel his eyelids drooping.

He sat beside the fire, his legs pressed against his stomach, and stared into the flames, hoping the kinetic imagery would keep him awake. And for a while, it did. But little by little, the rhythmic ebb and flow of the dancing flames proved more stimulating than soothing. This effect was compounded by the slow and steady breathing of his sleeping comrades. Lamar gradually found himself nodding off, his head drooping as the siren song of sleep beckoned, whispering tranquil words in his ear. Lamar felt himself slowly succumbing. His eyelids were heavy, so heavy. If only he could close them for a few seconds . . .

The pop of heated tree sap exploding inside the fire jolted Lamar awake. Several feet away, he could hear Beverly snoring. He rubbed his eyes and glanced at his watch: 8:22 p.m. He tossed another log on the fire and pulled the Walkman from his jacket pocket, hoping that some tunes would keep him awake.

He slipped on the earphones, cranked the volume and pressed play.

"Don't stand! Don't stand so! Don't stand so close to me!"

Even on maximum volume, the music couldn't drown out the sounds of the iku. But it blunted their noise and served as a pleasant distraction, which was all Lamar needed at the moment. He focused on the music and tried desperately to think of anything that didn't involve monsters or sleep.

"Please don't stand ... bzzptt! ... sooooo ... cloooooooooooo ... bzzptt!"

He looked at the tape through the clear plastic door of the Walkman and saw the spools had stopped turning. He smacked the battery case a couple of times, but nothing happened. He slipped the headphones off and tossed the unit on his sleeping bag.

Damn. He wasn't the only one running on empty tonight.

* * * * * *

Gaby came to groggily. The incessant chirping of the iku was louder than ever; their calls were so pervasive, they had invaded her dream.

Unlike most of her dreams, she recalled this one vividly. Iku-like creatures were chasing her and half a dozen friends through an empty office complex, the group running from room to room as the creatures swarmed under the doors and through the vents to get them. Only, they didn't look like the inky, mutant slugs she had seen. Instead, they looked like the soot sprites in *Spirited Away*, with expressive eyes and spindly, spiderlike limbs. But unlike those gentle creatures, these ones had enormous mouths lined with rows of serrated teeth, which they gnashed as they searched for the group. Gaby and the others were making their last stand in a corner office, first barricading the doors and then the ventilation shaft. But the creatures forced their way in en masse and began swarming. However, instead of devouring them with their horrible teeth, the creatures surrounded and enveloped them one at a time. And each time they did, an unearthly glow emanated from the swarming mass before the creatures disappeared, leaving her companions behind. Gaby was a bit fuzzy on what happened next, but at least it wasn't the gruesome fate they had feared.

She slowly opened her eyes. The fire had burned low; the only light came from the faint glow of the embers at the base of the fire. The interior of the wigwam was almost completely dark. She could see Lamar beside her, hunched over with his head resting on his knees and his arms curled around his legs. He was fast asleep. Gaby could just make out the glowing LED readout of his watch: 5:46 a.m.

She rolled over and prepared to go back to sleep when she heard a clattering in the rafters, just barely audible over the furious chirping of the iku. It must be the iku trying to get in. She didn't blame them. It was so nice and warm in here, with ...

The iku were in the wigwam!

Gaby sat bolt upright. She grabbed her spear and thrust it into the fire, stabbing repeatedly to stoke the embers.

"Wake up!" she shouted. "Everyone up now!"

Her stoking produced momentary flames that revealed squirming shapes in the shadows all around. On the periphery, the wigwam's canvas walls were starting to buckle under the weight of all the iku trying to force their way inside. Gaby grabbed some spare twigs and dead leaves from the pile and tossed them on the fire, which gained new life. The shadows slowly retreated but did not stop squirming.

The others were roused but did not yet understand the danger they were in. Gaby grabbed the metal canteen from

Beverly's pack and started banging on it with a stick, producing an awful clanging racket that quickly roused the others.

"What the fuck is your ... oh, shit!" Ken cried as he realized what was happening. He grabbed the flashlight and started shining it wildly in every direction. Every shadow it came across revealed hidden iku, which quickly evaporated in the light.

Lamar awoke to screaming. He uncurled from his ball and fuzzily tried to process what was happening. Everyone was running around. Beverly was screaming something about feeding the fire. He looked up and saw a black, squirming mass of iku hanging from the rafters. In a panic he overturned the pile of firewood, knocking several split logs into the firepit. The firewood rolled on top of the kindling Gaby was using to feed the fire and briefly blotted out the light.

The creatures in the shadows took advantage of the momentary darkness, closing ranks and pressing inward.

Gaby shoved one of the logs smothering the fire aside with her spear, creating some space to give the fire the oxygen it so desperately craved. The flames roared back to life, sending the iku retreating to the darkest corners of the teepee.

Coop, who had taken off his glasses to sleep, put them on to find a pack of iku charging him from the wigwam's outer ring. He shrieked and ducked his head into his sleeping bag to avoid their touch. His scream alerted Ken, who reflexively pointed the light in his direction. A cluster of iku hovering over Coop's sleeping bag disappeared in a puff of smoke.

After several more passes of the flashlight's beam along the outer ring of the structure and the rafters, Ken lowered the light, satisfied that they'd driven back the iku.

"I think that's the last of them," he said wearily.

"Coop, are you hurt?" Gaby asked.

He poked his head out from the inner folds of his sleeping bag.

"Are they gone?"

"Coop? Did they touch you?" Gaby demanded, louder this time.

"No, no," he replied as he slowly climbed out of his bag. "Just startled me, is all." He held up his hands as proof. Neither one showed any signs of the ikus' touch.

"What happened?" Lamar asked, still a bit disoriented.

Ken looked from Lamar to Beverly and back again.

"Whose shift was it?" he demanded.

Beverly jabbed an accusatory finger at Lamar.

Lamar checked his watch before pointing at Beverly.

Gaby quickly rounded on the young man as well.

"Did you fall asleep on us, Lamar?" she asked, her voice thick with suspicion.

"Maybe just for a moment, but ..." Lamar started to explain, before Ken cut him off.

"Then you know damn well what happened," Ken shot back, turning livid at a truly frightening speed.

"But, but ..." Lamar stammered, unable to come up with a suitable explanation.

"We all could have died!" Gaby scolded.

"I didn't do it on purpose!" Lamar feebly protested.

Ken stood up and walked slowly toward Lamar, leaning forward to keep from clipping his head on the pulley system in the rafters. His eyes flashed menacingly, and a guttural growl in the back of his throat announced to the world that he had lost control once more. Guttural Ken was back, and he meant business.

"You let those things in here, you stupid son of a bitch!" guttural Ken roared, his voice drowning out the incessant chirping in the background. He cracked his knuckles aggressively as he strode forward.

Lamar took a step back. He looked to the others for aid, but none of them made a move. He looked around for his spear. He found it lying on his bedroll, which was on the other side of the teepee. He lashed out at Ken with the only weapon he had left.

"If you lay a hand on me, I'll tell the others all about the Series 7," he quietly threatened.

Guttural Ken stopped in his tracks. He paused just long enough for Lamar to think it had worked. Ken's knitted eyebrows slowly unfurled, and the downturned corners of his mouth slowly rose to form a grim smile.

"Fine," guttural Ken responded before turning to face the others. "Everyone, I have an announcement: I'm not a CEO, and I'm not a stockbroker. Lamar found out and has been holding it over my head since yesterday. He apparently thinks that exaggerating my professional accomplishments shields him from responsibility for nearly getting all of us killed."

Guttural Ken's admission yielded no more than a couple of raised eyebrows. As the others listened, their surprise at his confession slowly turned into contempt for Lamar. Even Coop looked disappointed in him.

"Satisfied?" guttural Ken asked before moving aggressively toward Lamar once more. "Because now I'm free to wring your ... useless ... fat ... fucking ... neck!"

He lunged at Lamar and tackled him to the ground, upsetting the rest of the log pile and sending the younger man sprawling. The wigwam was spinning and Lamar tasted blood. He dimly heard Gaby shout something like "No violence!" before his eyes focused on guttural Ken looming over him. Gone was the smirk of a bully showing the class reject where he stood in the pecking order, replaced with the bloodthirsty impulse of a predator that's cornered its next meal.

Guttural Ken stood over Lamar's prone form before dropping to his knees on top of him, rearing back and pummeling him in the face repeatedly. It wasn't until the sixth blow that Coop and Gaby managed to pry him off Lamar, who came up dazed and blood splattered. The skin around his swollen right eye looked like hamburger, and he was already sporting an impressive shiner on his left cheek.

"Hurting him won't accomplish anything!" Coop insisted as he struggled to hold Ken back, tugging on the hood of Ken's Patagonia jacket with such force that it split at the seam.

"It'll sure make me feel better!" Ken fumed, getting in one final kick before Gaby stepped between them. Ken was slowly coming to his senses now that his guttural persona had exacted retribution. He resisted less and less as Coop pulled him away from Lamar and over to the other side of the fire, where after much coaxing, Coop convinced him to sit.

Lamar rose unsteadily and tested the rapidly forming

shiner on his jaw. He flinched at the pain before slinking off to his sleeping bag without another word. No one came to check on how he was doing, he noted with a twinge of self-pity. Gaby, Coop and Beverly avoided eye contact with him, as though embarrassed to be near him. But Ken's eyes bored right through him, glaring at him from across the teepee like they were mortal enemies.

"So, whose shift is it now?" Coop asked drily.

"Like any of us could sleep now," Beverly replied.

"It'll be dawn soon," Gaby said wistfully, casting her eyes skyward, waiting for the pitch blackness overhead to slowly regain its coloration.

The iku outside seemed oblivious to the row, chirping impatiently as they swarmed along the exterior, desperate to get at the people inside.

As the minutes slowly ticked by, everyone retreated to their own little corners of the wigwam, keeping to their own devices as they waited for dawn. Coop stared at his faded picture of Johnny, as he had night after night, the anguish in his face visible in the firelight. Lamar brooded as he poked at the ground with his spear, imagining it was Ken's face. Gaby stared into the fire, her brow furrowed with worry. On the other side of the fire, Beverly fidgeted with nervous energy. Beside her, Ken was tracing lines in the dirt with a small switch.

Coop stood up to dump the last of the wood on the fire. All of them watched as it went up and secretly wondered what would happen if it burned out before dawn arrived.

Fortunately, small streaks of pink and purple had begun to appear in the sky overhead. The sounds of the iku gradually tapered off. After another 15 minutes, it was clear to all that one by one, the iku were retreating. By the time Lamar's watch read 6:18 a.m. and the sky was painted battleship gray, only the most determined and voracious iku could be heard outside, their chirps barely registering. The contrast with the painfully loud chirping of thousands of them not 30 minutes ago was breathtaking.

As the clouds overhead slowly became distinguishable from the sky, Ken stopped drawing in the dirt and tapped the ground to get Beverly's attention. She looked down at his scratchings and saw that Ken had written two words: "Phase 3."

Beverly looked around nervously. All the others were still lost in their own little worlds. She shook her head no as subtly as she could manage. Ken's expression quickly turned dark. He pointed to the message again. Beverly ran her right foot over the words, smearing them. She could feel his malevolence growing.

Ken hastily scrawled a new message, then tapped the ground impatiently with the switch.

"Do it," the message commanded. "Or else."

Beverly reluctantly met his eyes once again. He was positively radiating aggression. He lifted the switch to eye level, pressed it between his thumb and forefinger and snapped it in half. Beverly got the message, and after a moment's hesitation, nodded pitifully. She would do his bidding.

"Who has the food?" she asked in a quavering voice. "I'm starving."

"Come to think of it, none of us have eaten since lunch yesterday," Coop said, realizing that the gnawing sensation in his belly wasn't fear, it was hunger pangs. He looked around the wigwam and saw similar reactions in the others' faces.

"Well, we'll be able to eat soon enough," Lamar replied quietly, slurring his words slightly through his blood-swollen lower lip. "Once those things are gone, we can get the food bag back."

"What are you talking about?" Gaby asked with barely disguised contempt. "It's right behind you. I brought it inside after you went looking for Coop."

Lamar turned around and found his pack lying on top of the pile of discarded junk salvaged from the former shed. He had been so caught up in everything else that night that he never even noticed it. This was the first genuinely nice surprise he'd had in days.

"Let's dig in," Coop declared, salivating.

"Go easy," Lamar cautioned as he walked over to the pile. "There isn't much left."

Lamar hoisted the bag. It seemed strangely light. He peered inside. His expression changed from delighted, to confused, to horrified, all in the space of a few seconds.

"No, no, no, no, no!" Lamar cried out as he examined the bag. "This can't be happening!"

"I take it you 'miscounted' again?" Ken asked with a sneer.

"Lamar, what's wrong?" Coop asked, growing concerned.

Lamar turned to face the others, his mouth agape in astonishment.

"The food, it's … gone," he said, mystified.

"How much is gone?" Gaby pressed.

Lamar swallowed hard before holding up the bag for everyone to see. All that remained were two empty cans of soup and some leftover crumbs from the trail mix.

"All of it."

THURSDAY

The first rays of the sun were peeking over the eastern slopes, and the last of the iku had abandoned their siege when Gaby opened the door to the wigwam. She was glad to be free of its canvas constraints, even if it meant having to bundle up against the bitter chill in the morning air.

The overhead clouds' steel gray complexion perfectly matched the steaming ash piles covering every square inch of the campsite, with some of the piles nearly a foot deep. Just as disturbing was the sight of the wigwam coated in soot so completely that the fake animal skins decorating the exterior weren't even visible beneath their mottled covering, save for a few hairs poking out. Every surface of the pine tree looming over the teepee was likewise coated in ash, as far up as they could see.

But right now, all of these were ephemeral considerations. The group had more pressing concerns at the moment.

"I want an explanation," Beverly demanded as she exited the wigwam behind Gaby. "And it had better be a good one!"

"Don't say that like it's my fault," Lamar retorted, incensed as he ducked his head to fit through the teepee's narrow door. "Somebody obviously stole the food."

"Yeah, *somebody*," Ken sneered contemptuously.

"What's that supposed to mean?" Lamar shot back.

Ken balled his fists, and anger flickered in his eyes once more. Guttural Ken was about to make an encore appearance. Lamar didn't cower from him as he had last night; if anything, his indignation showed he was itching for a chance to redeem his masculinity, which was every bit as bruised and bloody as his face this morning. He glared at Ken through his one good eye.

Coop, who exited the wigwam last, immediately sized up the situation and stepped between the two of them, hoping to de-escalate things.

"Hang on," he said, pausing to look at each of them in turn. "Let's figure out what happened before we start assigning blame. Lamar, how much food was left when you last looked?"

"Six cans," Lamar responded, his eyes still boring into Ken. "After lunch yesterday, we had two cans of lima beans and four cans of soup."

On the other side of Coop, Ken paced back and forth restlessly, like a lion waiting for the right moment to strike.

"Have you had the food bag with you the entire time since then?" Coop asked.

Lamar seemed surprised by the question, and his focus on Ken faltered.

"What? I guess so ... I don't know," Lamar stammered, so flustered by the probing questions and Ken's insinuations that he completely forgot that he'd left it unattended when they went searching for Beverly at dusk.

"Why are you so eager to pin this on me?" Lamar demanded.

"He's not blaming you ... yet," Gaby said, joining the inquisition. "But you *are* in charge of the food, Lamar."

"That … that was a promise to keep track of the food, not guard it like it was Fort Knox," Lamar snapped, his face growing flush. "It was to stop Ken from taking extra helpings, remember?"

"If there's anyone here with a reputation for stealing, it's you," Ken replied darkly. "Gaby's bra and the canteen didn't crawl into your bag on their own."

"Hey! I told you I had nothing to do with that!" Lamar responded hotly.

Everywhere Lamar looked, he was met with suspicious stares. He was beginning to feel like he was surrounded by enemies. Even Beverly, who had been deeply withdrawn since her breakdown, stole questioning glances at him as she shivered in the cold.

"You can't really think he ate all the food he was supposed to guard," Coop said, finally speaking up for Lamar. "That doesn't make sense. Once the food ran out, he'd be busted."

"Stomachs don't obey logic. They just need," Beverly noted.

"And Lamar has the biggest stomach here," Ken added snidely.

Instead of addressing Ken's insinuations directly, Lamar turned to the others for validation.

"You see what he's doing here, right? This is a setup," Lamar insisted. "He wants to turn everyone against me, so he swiped the food. He probably planted that stuff in my bag yesterday, too."

Gaby face-palmed in disgust, while Coop looked away, embarrassed for his friend.

"You just said you've had the food bag with you the entire time, smart guy," Ken pointed out with a sinister grin. "So, how'd I take it or put that other stuff in there, huh?"

"I wasn't watching it the whole time!" Lamar erupted. "Maybe Ken took it while we were fighting the iku last night."

Gaby shook her head slowly.

"He was beside me the whole time," she said, her disgust with Lamar evident in her face. "First, using the bow drill, and then when I took over, he was holding the flashlight."

"Then maybe he took it while everyone was asleep!" Lamar shouted, throwing up his hands in frustration.

"You mean, when you were supposed to be keeping guard?" Ken needled him, not even attempting to hide his enjoyment.

Lamar glowered but held his tongue.

"It seems pretty clear that Ken didn't take the food," Coop said. "So, who did?"

"You already know who I suspect," Ken said. "I put it to you all: Has anyone actually seen Lamar count out the food? Or have we all just been trusting his math … and honesty?"

A quick scan of the others' faces showed that none of them had seen him do so. They'd just accepted whatever he'd told them when he was doling out portions.

"And would any of you say he's lost weight while we've been out here?" Ken asked cuttingly.

"Okay, that's enough," Gaby said, holding up her hand. "I think you've made your point."

"Someone here has to know something," Ken continued, looking at each of them in turn, with his eyes lingering on

Beverly. "All of us living so close together, one of you must have seen something off."

Coop noted the odd intonation in Ken's voice, almost like he was coaxing them into making an accusation. Beverly also picked up on it, and more importantly, the meaning behind it. Even in her weakened, sleep-deprived state, she recognized the signal. Time to complete Phase 3.

Gaby shook her head.

"I'm sure if anyone had they would have ..." she started, before Beverly interrupted.

"I did," Beverly said quietly as she stood over one of the steaming ash piles for warmth. The rising curtain of steam obscured and distorted her features, making her look mysterious and a little creepy. "Lamar, I'm sorry, but after what you just said, I couldn't stay quiet."

"Huh?" Lamar asked in bewilderment.

"When we were building the fence a couple of days ago, I took a break to ... you know, " Beverly started awkwardly, trying to tap dance around her bout with the bottle.

"Take a drink?" Gaby offered.

Beverly reddened, still embarrassed that they knew about her addiction.

"And when I get there, I find Lamar hiding behind a tree, inhaling a bag of trail mix," she continued.

The others looked disapprovingly at Lamar.

"What the hell?" he exclaimed indignantly. "She's lying!"

"I remember him wiping his hands on his shirt, like he does after meals," Beverly said, continuing as though she hadn't heard his emphatic denials. "He asked me not to tell, so I assumed it was a one-time thing."

"This never happened! She is making all of this shit up!" Lamar shouted, his eyes bulging in disbelief.

"Why would she lie?" Gaby asked. Her tone made it clear she believed Beverly over Lamar.

"I felt bad for him," Beverly continued. "He's so big, so I didn't say anything."

"**Shut up! Stop lying!**" Lamar screamed at her. He was so enraged that Gaby was afraid he might even attack her, so she inserted herself between them to protect Beverly. Her action shocked Lamar out of his righteous fury, and as he scanned the others' faces, he realized his outbursts were only convincing them of his guilt. He took a deep breath and willed himself to calm down.

"Folks, this is some half-baked scheme that she and Ken came up with," he said. "I heard them conspiring against me yesterday. It's all a power play."

"Paranoid much?" Ken replied cuttingly, with a nasty grin. Lamar winced, knowing that he was simply feeding Ken's false narrative.

Ken then turned to the others.

"There's a simple way to determine which of them is lying," he said. "Beverly, you said he wiped the trail mix off on his shirt, right? So that means the residue should still be there. Which shirt was he wearing?"

Beverly paused for several seconds as though she were struggling to remember.

"The gray one with the funny face in the center," she replied with a shiver. "Like a university logo."

Ken held up his hands like he were inviting the others to

bask in the magnificence of his deductive reasoning.

"So, somebody go get the shirt," he said. "Actually, make it two people, so Fatty Carbuncle here can't claim that we're framing him or anything. You cool with that, Fatty?"

The two stared each other down for several long, drawn-out seconds.

Ken had to have something up his sleeve, but Lamar hadn't the faintest idea what. And accusing Ken of shenanigans without proof again would only make him look guiltier. He had no choice but to play this out and hope Ken had made a mistake.

"Fine," Lamar said with an air of resignation that caused more than one set of eyebrows to arch. "Gaby, you'll find it in Coop's bag. He was carrying my clothes for me, since I had the food."

Ken nodded to Beverly, who shadowed Gaby as she walked to the wigwam. If he was thrown to learn that Lamar's clothes were in somebody else's bag, he didn't show it.

The men stood silently in a loose semicircle, waiting for the evidence, unsure what to say or do in the meantime. Lamar stared at his feet and racked his brains trying to work out what Ken had devised. Could he really have gotten to the food bag and Coop's bag, both on the same night? It didn't seem possible. He stole a quick glance at Ken, who was eyeballing him. The smirk on Ken's face had reached epic proportions. If his cockiness was anything to go by, Lamar could be in serious trouble.

Coop stood off to the side, his eyes fixated on the entrance to the wigwam, like a lawyer waiting expectantly for the jury to return its verdict. But the stakes here were almost certainly higher.

Seconds dragged into minutes. The wait was agony.

Just as Coop was about to go in to check on Gaby and Beverly, the two exited the wigwam. Gaby was holding Lamar's gray shirt. Their expressions were stony and unreadable.

They stopped just shy of the others.

"Well?" Lamar asked impatiently.

Gaby hesitated.

"Lamar ..."

"Just show us!" he snapped.

Gaby held up the shirt.

The right breast of the shirt had a light coating of grease on it, probably from when Lamar wiped his hands on his shirt after the fish dinner on their first night here. Several inches to the right was a smear of dried yellowish gunk; probably chicken corn chowder. And down the center, partially obscuring the troll face in the shirt's logo, was a deep brown smear that was unmistakably chocolate, just like in the trail mix. A half-dozen specks of salt — probably from the pretzels in the trail mix — decorated the chocolate stain.

Lamar stared at the shirt in utter disbelief, continually blinking, as though each blink would somehow erase what he was seeing. He felt like reality was melting around him. As he looked at the disapproval and disgust in his companions' faces, he could hear a ringing in his ears, and felt his heart jackhammering beneath his bubble jacket. As he looked over at Ken, the taller man mouthed the word "checkmate" before breaking into the most sadistic grin Lamar had ever seen.

"This can't be happening," he mumbled to himself, shaking his head in slack-jawed disbelief. "It's not possible."

"I knew it," Ken said triumphantly. "I'll bet you fatass has been sneaking food for days."

"But this is absurd," Lamar pleaded. "I didn't steal anything! I don't even like trail mix!"

His tone said what his words didn't: he knew he'd already lost.

"Just give it up already," Beverly said.

"Those two cooked all this up ... somehow," he feebly protested. "Gaby, Coop, you have to believe me!"

"Lamar, please stop," Gaby said quietly. "It's over."

He looked over at Coop, who turned away in embarrassment.

"I don't know what to believe," Coop said softly.

"I don't feel comfortable with him around anymore," Beverly said, still shivering as she hugged herself for warmth. "He eats all the food, he sleeps on watch, and he got us all hopelessly lost. Who knows what else he's done?"

Gaby noticed that droplets of a clear liquid were seeping through the cracks in Beverly's blackened left hand and oozing down into her gloves. She made a mental note not to touch anything Beverly owned, for fear of being contaminated.

"I agree," Ken said, lending his voice to Beverly's complaint. "I say he should go."

Lamar looked at Gaby and Coop helplessly.

"This is fucking insane! Don't you see what they're doing? They're trying to tear us apart!"

Neither of them was willing to meet his gaze.

"Let's vote," Ken said. "All in favor of Lamar staying?"

Lamar's hand shot up. After several agonizingly long seconds, Coop hesitantly raised his hand.

"All those in favor of expelling him?"

Beverly and Ken held up their hands. After several seconds, everyone looked over at Gaby, who was now the tiebreaker.

Slowly, reluctantly, she raised her hand. Lamar felt the pit of his stomach drop, and covered his mouth with his hand in shock. Tears began to well up in the corners of his eyes.

"No," he whispered.

"Lamar, I'm sorry. But they're right," she said, her voice heavy with remorse. "Because of you, we now have to spend the day foraging for food, instead of looking for a way out. I hope it was worth it."

"That's 3-2," Ken said with a smug air of finality. "I'll give you five minutes to say your goodbyes while we gather your belongings. If you return ..." he continued, but was interrupted by an anguished cry from Lamar.

"Why are you doing this?" he shouted. "Beverly, Ken, I've never been anything but nice to you all."

"If you return ..." Ken tried again, his tone sharper after being interrupted.

"Please!" Lamar interrupted again, clasping his hands over his chest. "There has to be something I can say! Don't leave me out here with those iku creatures!"

Ken suddenly snapped, grabbing Lamar by his jacket lapel and throwing him to the ground. The impact knocked the wind out of Lamar. When he got his bearings and looked up, he saw Ken holding the penknife inches from his throat. The blade glinted dully in the light, making his blood run cold.

"Because if you set foot in this camp again, I'll carve you up and serve you for dinner!" guttural Ken bellowed mere inches from Lamar's face. Now even interruptions triggered Ken's change.

Gaby made a move to intervene but Beverly held up her arm to stop her. Coop stood there like a deer in headlights, unsure what to do.

"Do you hear me?" guttural Ken demanded.

Lamar nodded hurriedly, terrified.

"Say it," guttural Ken demanded, running the blade along his thumb to illustrate his conviction. The parallels to Wade's conduct were eerie.

"I won't come back," Lamar mumbled, too scared to respond properly.

Guttural Ken leaned forward and pressed the blade against Lamar's face.

"Louder!" he shouted. "Or I'll carve the question into your forehead!"

"I won't come back! I swear it!" Lamar cried out, petrified.

"Ken, that's enough!" Gaby shouted. "You got what you wanted; now leave him alone."

Guttural Ken held the knife to Lamar's forehead for several more seconds, relishing the fear it elicited, before slowly standing up and pocketing the knife. He turned to face the others and they could see that his eyes had reverted.

"C'mon, Beverly, let's gather his shit," Ken said as he headed for the wigwam. After a moment's hesitation, Beverly joined him.

Once they'd entered the wigwam, Gaby and Coop came over to check on Lamar, who was still flat on his back.

"Lamar, are you all right? Did he hurt you?" Gaby asked, offering her hand to help him up.

Lamar sat up and batted her hand away, his mind a muddle of wounded pride, righteous indignation and naked fear.

"Don't you dare!" he insisted as he stood up unsteadily. "You've done enough to *help* today!"

"She was just worried about you," Coop scolded.

"Yeah, after she banished me!" Lamar vented. "She's perfectly fine sending me to my death, just so long as she doesn't have to watch!"

"That's not fair!" Gaby protested. "I'm not the one that stole all the food!"

"Neither am I!" Lamar bellowed in impotent rage.

"Gaby, you have to admit this all seems a little suspicious," Coop ventured. "I know the evidence against him is pretty damning, but look where it's coming from. Tell me you don't have doubts."

Gaby hesitated for a moment before answering.

"I've made my decision," she said firmly. "And if you're smart, you'll come around. Ken isn't likely to forget how you voted."

Coop stiffened. He looked from Lamar to Gaby and back again, seemingly indecisive, before turning on his heel and walking into the wigwam without another word to either of them.

Gaby watched him leave with a pang of regret. She may have convinced Coop, but she suspected he'd never forgive her for it. Lamar had an altogether stronger reaction, watching in stunned silence as the closest thing he had to a friend in this group — and his only remaining defender — turned his back on him. Lamar shook his head sadly as he clenched his knuckles in anticipation of the grim road ahead. While he had long felt alone in the crowd, and often sought out solitude, this was his first taste of true isolation, and its bitterness was more than words could express. He had never felt lower.

Several seconds after Coop entered the wigwam, Ken and Beverly exited it with Lamar's rucksack and spear in tow. Ken dropped both at Lamar's feet.

"I'd say 'have a nice life,' but I doubt you can do much with it in the 10 hours you have left," Ken sneered.

"I'll make for the abandoned nuclear facility," Lamar said ruefully as he slung his bag over his shoulder and hoisted his spear. "There may be radio equipment that I can get working. John said it was about five miles south of here, so I'll head there. Alone."

"No, not alone."

Everyone turned to see Coop exiting the teepee, his backpack slung over his shoulder and a spear in his hand. Gone was his usual happy-go-lucky grit, replaced with grim resolve. He walked past the others and stood shoulder to shoulder with a dumbfounded Lamar.

The others stared at him in disbelief, awestruck by the magnanimity of Coop's gesture.

"Coop, you can't ..." Lamar began, but was quickly cut off by Gaby.

"What are you doing?" she scolded.

"The same thing you should be doing: standing with your

friends," he answered bluntly.

Even Ken appeared impressed by Coop's conviction. Instead of mocking him or stomping down his mini-insurrection, Ken appeared content to let it play out.

"You sure?" he asked with a snort. "If you leave here with him, you can't come back. Ever."

"I understand," Coop replied. "So, I guess this is goodbye."

He nodded to Beverly, who was standing behind Ken.

"Beverly, good luck. Ken, drop dead."

Ken's expression grew dark, but he held his tongue.

Coop turned to Gaby, who gave him a pained look.

"It's not too late to join us," he said.

Gaby shook her head.

Coop drew closer and whispered so the others couldn't hear.

"I know you believe what you're doing is right, but don't let those two fool you. They're dangerous. Watch your back."

"If you change your mind, you know where to find us," Gaby said, trying to blink back the tears. "Regardless of what Ken says."

Coop shook his head no.

"I may be eaten alive by … whatever those things are out there, but I won't abandon Lamar. One for all and all for one, remember?"

Gaby sniffled as the tears flowed down her cheeks. In lieu of a hug, Gaby raised her arm for a fist bump. Coop smiled and obliged her.

"Good luck, Mouseketeer," she whispered.

Lamar patted Coop on the shoulder.

"It's time."

Coop nodded, and the two began the slow march out of camp, taking the dirt road that had brought them there five days earlier. It seemed like a lifetime ago.

The others watched as they departed, slowly ascending the southern lip of the enormous earthen bowl that defined their small sector of Quehanna.

Gaby watched them depart with a queasy feeling in her gizzard. As they slowly grew smaller on the horizon, she started to wonder if she hadn't made a terrible mistake.

She forced herself to look away and faced her remaining companions. Beverly was still shivering uncontrollably, her head pressed against her neck to preserve body heat. Ken was still watching Lamar and Coop depart. Impossibly, he was chuckling.

"Okay, that should buy us some time," he said.

"To do what?"

"To not get eaten," he replied. "We just handed those creatures two meals. Maybe that'll keep them off us for a night."

Gaby glowered at him.

"You can be a real bastard, you know that?"

Instead of answering, Ken headed back to the wigwam.

"Where are you going?" Gaby asked, exasperated. "We have a ton to do."

"Back to sleep," he replied dismissively. "I only got a few hours last night, and there's no reason to think tonight will be any different."

"Really? You don't care about finding food, escaping, maybe looking for a safer place? We have a ton of work to do."

"And how do you think we'll fare if we're dead on our feet?" he said. "We could all use a couple more hours of sack time before we get started."

He paused when he noticed Beverly wasn't following his lead. She stood stock still, shivering uncontrollably, seemingly oblivious to everything around her.

"Beverly, you coming?"

No reply.

Ken clapped his hands loudly, shocking the older woman out of her stupor.

"Rich bitch, party of one, get the lead out!"

Beverly nodded pitifully through the shivers and started toward the teepee. Gaby worried that her shivering might be a sign of something more than the early morning chill.

Gaby took one final, forlorn glance over her shoulder at Coop and Lamar departing before joining the others in the wigwam.

* * * Ten Hours Until Sundown * * *

The wind was picking up as Lamar and Coop crested the southern ridge leading deeper into the unexplored reaches of the forest. They were still following the dirt road, tracing its path as it snaked up and down a series of steadily shrinking hills before leveling out at the entrance gate. The deep indentations on either side of the entrance, where the giant totem poles once stood, were a stark reminder that nothing in this forest was what it seemed.

Lamar whistled low as they came across a beaver carcass in the middle of the road. Like all the other animal corpses they'd seen in the blight, this one looked untouched; understandable, since all the predators were dead along with their prey. Coop used his spear tip to shove the desiccated remains out of the way as they continued their journey in this barren, forsaken land.

Several yards past the entrance the pair spied the first fork in the road. The dirt path continued southward about 40 yards past the entrance before fading into an open field strewn with withered grasses and ankle-high ash piles, some of which were still steaming. It was the same field Ken had traversed when he had gotten lost on the group's second day in Quehanna.

On the other side, the road forked sharply west, wending its way around the field and gradually changing from dirt to gravel.

"Oh, I snuck something out of the wigwam when I was packing," Coop said as they walked, reaching into his pack and retrieving John's old flashlight. "Ta-da!"

"Nice!" Lamar said appreciatively.

"I figured it would come in handy if we ever find the research base," Coop said. After a moment's hesitation, he added: "Or for when it gets dark."

That observation cast a pall over things, and the conversation abruptly ceased. Lamar bit his lip nervously as they walked, thinking of the myriad hurdles they had to clear before nightfall. A distant rumble in the gray skies overhead alerted them to yet another potential problem.

As they reached the fork in the road, Coop started down the dirt path left, while Lamar turned right.

"Aren't we going south?" Coop said as he paused mid-step.

"No," Lamar answered as he leaned on his spear like a

walking stick. "We're headed for the lake. Ken said the nearest bank was on the southwestern edge of the floodplain, so if we follow the edge of the floodplain we should eventually find it."

"I thought you said we were going to the base, the one with the nuclear planes."

"We are."

Coop looked monumentally confused.

"But John said it was five miles south of camp."

Lamar wrestled with how to explain his thought process.

"John was giving us a general idea of where it was, not precise directions," Lamar said. "It could be south or it could be southeast. It could be four miles or six miles. We don't know exactly where it is, so if we just wander south and hope for the best, we might never find it, agreed?"

"With you so far."

"But we do know where the lake is," Lamar continued. "Ken told us all about it. So, if we follow its shoreline south, it'll eventually lead us right to the research base."

"And you know this how?"

"The base has to be beside the lake," Lamar explained patiently. "It's the largest body of water out here."

Coop ran a hand over his reddish curls, imitating a jet whizzing by.

"Whoosh! You went straight over my head."

Lamar cracked a smile, the first in some time.

"John said they were testing nuclear-powered airplanes and had a reactor on site. Nuclear reactors use water to keep the core cool; thousands and thousands of gallons of it. A creek or a stream wouldn't cut it, so it has to be beside the lake. Since Ken didn't mention seeing it, I'm guessing it'll be on the opposite bank."

Coop's eyes widened at Lamar's deduction.

"If you're right about this, I'm putting you up for a Mensa award," he said with a grin.

Coop joined him on the right fork, and the padding of ash-covered dirt beneath their feet quickly turned to the crunch of ash-coated gravel. The rumbling in the skies grew louder. Both of them kept a watchful eye on the rapidly darkening skies.

"I still don't understand why you're doing this," Lamar said. "Their beef was with me, not you. You could be luxuriating in a warm wigwam right now, instead of freezing your tail feathers off with me."

"And be goose-stepping for that prick Ken right now?" Coop said with a chuckle. "No, thanks! I'd rather be here with you."

Lamar stopped in his tracks.

"You're willing to die for friendship?"

Coop made a strange face, like he'd just bit into something sour.

"You make it sound so cavalier. I want to live, obviously. But if it's a choice between safety and friendship, I'll stand by my friends. Well, friend," Coop corrected himself. "After all, you're the only one I've got."

"You don't have any back home?" Lamar asked as they resumed walking.

Coop shook his head sadly.

"I'm a registered sex offender, so word gets out pretty quickly," he explained. "My coworkers only communicate with me by email, so they won't be seen talking to 'you-know-who.' My neighbors won't even make eye contact. Last week, I ran into one of them with her daughter in the supermarket. She literally scooped the kid up and ran out the store. I had to put steel bars over my windows because the neighborhood kids throw rocks at them."

Coop sounded almost wistful as he recounted the various indignities.

"You're not bitter?" Lamar asked.

Coop shrugged as he paused to clean his glasses with the sleeve of his robes.

"Sometimes. Then I remember what I did. Anyway, you're the only one who knows what I am and still treats me like a person."

Lamar gave him a sympathetic look and put his hand on Coop's shoulder.

"Since you're feeling so chatty, mind if I ask you something?" Coop said.

"Ask away ... friend."

"You didn't take the food, right?"

Lamar glowered at him and removed his hand from Coop's shoulder.

"Hey, I had to ask," Coop said with a lopsided grin.

The gravel road wound west around the open field before turning south. The pair left the road and continued west into the ashen remnants of the forest, following a gently sloping hill lined with desiccated maple trees down toward a football-field-sized dell. The thick lines of soot swirls that decorated the landscape had already turned Lamar's sneakers and Coop's sandals a dingy gray.

As they approached, they could hear a buzzing sound emanating from the dell. The pair exchanged confused and worried glances. After spending so much time within the blight's sound-dampening field, hearing external noises again was confusing and a little frightening.

They approached cautiously, flitting between the withered husks of the numerous beech, birch and oak trees that ringed the dell to avoid being spotted. Lamar was about to make for the next stand of trees when Coop tugged on his jacket.

"What?" Lamar whispered fiercely.

Coop pointed skyward. Lamar followed his finger, and through the withered branches of the trees between them and the dell's border, he saw something impossible. A beech tree 20 feet ahead of them, on the edge of the dell, was budding. Dozens of fuzzy green sprouts with reddish centers decorated the top branches of the tree. Lamar noted that the oak tree beside it was also blossoming, and was already growing leaves on some of its lower-hanging branches. And so was the one beside it.

All the trees in the inner ring around the dell were flowering and blooming, tiny markers of blossoming life amid a wasteland of death and decay. The pair quickly dropped the pretense of subterfuge and stepped forward into a dell bursting with life and greenery. The glade was awash with color, as dozens of thriving wildflowers dotted the thigh-high sea of grasses with white, pink, violet and orange hues. Sprouts, weeds and wild mushrooms grew lustily all around, seemingly impervious to weather so cold that Lamar and Coop could see their breath. As absurd as it seemed, springtime had come in mid-October to this one small patch of Que-hanna.

The buzzing noise came from a colony of bees flitting between the flowers, busy pollinating as many as they could find. The fragrance of the budding flowers was almost as intoxicating to Lamar and Coop as it was to the bees. Coop heard a bird's call overhead and spotted a small blue jay building a nest in one of the blossoming trees on the outskirts.

Lamar flashed back to yesterday, when they had found small pockets of wilderness untouched by the blight, but this was several orders of magnitude weirder. After all, it was still autumn in those regions. Here, Mother Nature seemed to have thrown out her Farmers' Almanac and leapt seven months ahead. He looked down at his feet and saw that there were traces of ash still on the ground, barely visible amid all the rejuvenated plant life.

In the exact center of the dell was a small, sloped mound that bore an enormous ash tree in full bloom, one that must have been seven stories tall. Hundreds of delicate white flowers decorated its numerous outstretched limbs.

Lamar and Coop stared at the strange scene for several long seconds before seeking confirmation in each other's eyes. This may have been surreal, but it was no dream.

They started toward the earthen mound, staring in slack-jawed wonder at this sudden burst of new life. Neither spoke, as if afraid it would shatter the mirage. As they ascended the mound, Coop noted the hearty brown tone of the earth, so different from the sickly gray dirt of the surrounding landscape.

At the base of the enormous ash tree they saw a network of exposed roots that twisted into pretzel-like shapes before plunging into the ground. In the center, at the base of the trunk, was a dark hole, possibly a badger's den.

"I can't decide which makes less sense: the blight or this," Coop said in an awed whisper, gazing around in wonderment.

"I think they're connected," Lamar responded, trying to process everything he was seeing. "Look at the ash in the dirt. The iku have been here."

"So why is this place *Appalachian Spring* and everywhere else looks like *The Road*?"

Lamar paused to think.

"I'm not entirely sure," he answered after a few moments. "But if I'm right, there'll be more patches like this springing up soon."

"I just hope we live to see it," Coop intoned.

Lamar caught a glimmer of something along the outer edge of the giant tree. He took several steps to his right to investigate. What he saw took his breath away, even in the midst of all this weirdness.

A crimson, eight-petalled talisman dangled from a nail on the other side of the great tree.

Coop stood beside him and leaned in for a closer look.

"Is that ..."

"Yeah," Lamar answered before Coop even finished. "It looks just like the one in the teepee."

"That can't be a coincidence."

The sound of distant thunder in the heavens broke their reverie. Lamar felt a splash of water land on his head. He looked up and saw that the skies were dark and menacing. Another drop fell. And another.

"Kinda wishing I'd brought wet weather gear," Coop said as he turned up the collar on his Patagonia jacket.

"Do you remember what John said about the mandala?" Lamar asked, still reflecting on the talisman in front of them.

"Something about it acting like a guidepost," Coop replied absently. "You don't think ..."

"I do," Lamar interrupted as thunder rumbled in the skies once more. "I'm starting to think the iku were summoned."

* * * Eight Hours Until Sundown * * *

Noise

    A metallic clattering

        Heavy breathing

            Feet stomping

Gaby opened one eye cautiously. Some kind of commotion. Bare feet shot past her. Gaby raised her head and tried to focus her eyes. Beverly was running around the wigwam in her slip, digging through the various piles of belongings, seemingly searching for something.

Gaby noticed that the Beverly's black mark had spread beyond her left arm to her shoulder and her left armpit.

A low-frequency rumble sounded in the skies above. Outside, she could hear torrents of rain pummeling the camp. She looked up hazily and saw little rivulets of water leaking through the hole in the ceiling.

Beverly continued digging through people's belongings

haphazardly, tossing objects to and fro as she shivered.

"Beverly, what's going on?" Gaby asked, rubbing her tired eyes.

The older woman didn't respond as she searched, her back to Gaby as she dug through the pile of knickknacks recovered from the former shed.

Beverly suddenly paused. She shuddered before hoisting something that Gaby couldn't see, presumably what she had been hunting for. Beverly made a beeline for the entrance.

Gaby propped herself up on one elbow, growing alarmed by Beverly's conduct. She started to wonder if Beverly was on the cusp of another psychotic breakdown.

"Beverly, what's wrong?" Gaby asked. "You're scaring me."

The older woman paused beside the entrance. She waited a beat or two before wheeling around.

Her eyes were wide and she was shivering uncontrollably. In her trembling hands she clutched the hatchet, holding it at the ready, as though she was prepared to attack the first thing that moved.

Gaby sat bolt upright and scooted backward, kicking her legs free of the sleeping bag as she did so. Her eyes scanned the room for anything she could defend herself with. Unfortunately, the spears were all by the entrance, right beside Beverly.

She forcefully shook Ken, who had managed to sleep through the commotion, while still keeping her eyes trained on Beverly.

"Urrhhmm, five more minutes," Ken mumbled hazily and rolled over.

"Get up!" Gaby cried and gave him a sharp kick.

"Oww! What the fuck?" Ken howled as he sat up. "What the hell are you ... hollleeey shit!" he exclaimed as he spotted the half-naked Beverly standing by the entrance, wielding a hatchet.

Ken held his hands up in front of him to show he was unarmed. Gaby quickly followed suit, breathing as shallowly as possible. No one spoke for several seconds as the pair locked eyes with Beverly. The older woman's wide, unblinking eyes betrayed fear, anxiety and pain, but not madness. Whatever this was, it wasn't a repeat of last night.

Beverly quivered once more, then slowly turned and pushed the wigwam door outward, running off into the torrent of freezing rain.

Gaby and Ken sat in silence for several seconds, dumbfounded, still trying to process what had happened.

"Explain," Ken demanded once they were both sure that Beverly was gone. "Was she about to go Lizzie Borden on us?"

"I woke up right before you did," Gaby insisted. "I have no clue what set her off."

"Whatever that was, it's not happening again," Ken said as he crawled out of his sleeping bag and tied off the door. He picked up one of the spears by the door and tossed it to Gaby.

"We keep these by our sides at all times now, got it?" he said.

Gaby nodded, still reeling from Beverly's inexplicable actions.

"Did you see how far the black spot's spread?"

"It was kinda hard to miss," Ken intoned as he tugged on the pull chain to close the flue overhead. The thin rivulets of rainwater trickling from overhead branches into the central firepit slowly ebbed into droplets.

"Maybe the black spot has something to do with last night's episode and whatever this was," Gaby said.

"What makes you think this wasn't more of the same?"

"I'm not sure," she admitted, biting her lip as she mulled it over. "Something in the way she looked at us. I think she knew who we were. Last night, she was hallucinating and thought we were all iku."

"Hallucinating or not, she pulled a hatchet on us," Ken said. "From now on, she doesn't get within 10 feet of any sharp objects."

"Agreed," Gaby said as she started rounding up anything remotely pointy and hid it all in Coop's empty sleeping bag beside hers.

As she worked, Gaby could feel a headache coming on, a dull throbbing in her temples that the storm only aggravated. Whether it was from a lack of sustenance, sleep deprivation, constant terror or all of the above, she couldn't say.

Partially due to her burgeoning headache, Gaby did little to hide her irritation with Ken as he quickly retreated to the warmth of his sleeping bag and zipped himself back up.

"How can you sleep after that?"

"I can't," he replied simply. "But I can stay warm."

"The least you could do is go hunting for some food," she nagged.

Fortunately, a couple of extra hours of sleep had brought Ken's volatility under control, and he didn't take umbrage at her cheek.

"In this weather?" he snorted. "The only thing I'd catch is pneumonia."

"But ..." Gaby started before Ken cut her off.

"We're going to wait the storm out."

His tone made it clear this wasn't a suggestion.

"So what's that mean for Beverly?"

"Not my problem," he responded callously. "We've covered enough for her. If she doesn't die of exposure, we can talk about letting her back in. But not until I'm sure she's sane."

Gaby harrumphed, not at Ken's new policy toward Beverly, or even at his increasingly controlling manner, but at something more ephemeral. Something in that phrase, "We've covered enough for her," bothered Gaby. Some nagging doubt that she couldn't quite put her finger on. Almost as if she had forgotten to cover something. But what was there ...

Gaby froze and her eyes opened wide with realization. She hadn't covered the log pile after chopping wood last night. She was sure of it. Their only means of defense against the iku was being drenched!

"Oh my God! Get up! Get up! We have to cover the woodpile!" she shouted in panic as she threw on a jacket.

"What?" Ken yelled, tearing himself from his sleeping bag.

"The wood's getting soaked!" Gaby fretted as she undid the upper and lower enclosures on the door and ran outside.

The temperature change was jarring. It was cold enough that should could see her breath, and the stinging rain had soaked her to the skin by the time she rounded the fence line to find the log pile uncovered as she had feared. The burgundy tarp lay on the muddy ground beside it, fluttering ineffectively in the wind.

Gaby upended the tarp to loose all the water it had collected just as Ken popped out of the fence line to assist.

"Why didn't you cover it?" Ken demanded through chattering teeth as the two struggled to right the tarp and set it in place as the wind threatened to rip it from their grasp.

"Like I knew this was coming?" Gaby shouted in frustration as they finally got two corners down over the log pile and smoothed the tarp out to cover the rest.

Gaby poked her head under the tarp to see what they had to work with. Ken quickly did the same on the other side. It looked like the logs on the bottom had escaped the worst of the storm, but everything above them looked soaked through. Worse still, the weight of the pile made it impossible to simply pull those logs from the bottom like they were Jenga blocks. The only way they could reach them would be to remove the logs on top weighing them down, which was virtually impossible without removing the protective tarp. It was a catch-22.

"It's soaked most of the way through on this side," Gaby called out.

"This side's not much better," Ken replied. "Let's unload the wet logs row by row. We'll stash what remains in the wigwam. You better pray there's enough dry wood left to get us through the night."

He added that threat at the end almost as an afterthought as the two worked furiously in the bone-chilling rain to salvage what wood they could.

* * * Seven Hours Until Sundown * * *

Sheets of rain pelted Lamar and Coop as they trudged through the mud, their eyes peeled for any type of respite from the storm. But the lake's shoreline remained stubbornly flat as they followed it south, offering up no shelter. The only constant feature as they walked, apart from the lake 100 hundred yards to their west, was row after row of dead and withered trees, none of which offered adequate protection without their leaves.

The two walked single file in brooding silence, their heads bowed low to keep the chill rain from seeping under their jackets. Lamar's bubble jacket kept his chest dry, but the rest of him was soaked to the skin. Rainwater trickled from the tip of his scraggly goatee like he was a human stalactite. Several paces behind him, Coop sneezed violently and breathed on his cupped hands to keep them warm. His jacket and robes afforded him virtually no protection from the elements, and as his shivering attested, he was suffering mightily for it.

The pair had been walking near the lake's edge for over 90 minutes with nothing to show for it. They hewed close to the tree line, reasoning that poor cover from bare trees was better than no cover. To the east, the ground rose a dozen feet to form a small ridge that ran parallel to the shoreline, with flatlands lying just beyond, but the ridge was graded and offered no protection. All it did was send small streams of icy water their way, where it pooled around their feet, numbing their toes as they walked. They had briefly considered walking along the ridge itself to avoid this, but it was narrow and slick.

As they walked, they made certain to maintain line of sight with the lake. They couldn't risk missing their quarry: the abandoned research base. But thus far, not so much as a single structure had emerged, let alone an entire base.

Coop wondered aloud if they were even still walking south. The lake's curve was so gradual, and its contours so inconsistent, that they could conceivably be on the opposite bank already, heading west instead of south. There was no way to be sure.

Lamar didn't respond. In fact, he hadn't said a word in over an hour. His expression was relentlessly grim, and the only noise he made was the squelching of his sneakers in the mud as they trudged onward.

Lamar's left knee buckled as he put his weight on it, sending him careening forward at a dangerous angle as his back foot struggled for purchase in the mud. Coop saw him slip and lunged forward to steady him, but Lamar caught himself in time, grabbing hold of a small poplar tree. The younger man clung to the tree as he righted himself, but even after his feet found purchase, he kept his grip on it, and made no move to continue the journey.

"You okay?" Coop asked cautiously.

"My legs are going numb," Lamar responded through chattering teeth. "I can barely feel them."

Coop could see that Lamar's lips were turning blue. Despite his many layers of insulated clothing and blubber, Lamar was clearly struggling with the cold and damp.

"Just think of how warm it'll be inside the base," Coop consoled him, while trying to gently pry Lamar's hand from its death grip on the tree. But Lamar refused to budge.

"C'mon, man, let's give it another 15 minutes," Coop said.

Lamar shook his head, like a stubborn child refusing to listen to reason.

"You said that 30 minutes ago."

"It's probably right around the next bend," Coop coaxed him.

"Just stop!" Lamar said in a raised voice, causing Coop to rear back. "We've been searching for almost two hours now, and we haven't found shit! There's nothing out here!"

He loosened his grip on the poplar tree as rain dripped off his trembling lower lip.

"You don't want to say it?" he shouted. "Fine, I will: I was wrong! We never should have come this way. I should have listened to you. And now, my fuckup will cost both of us ... our ... lives!"

With a shout of anguished frustration, Lamar hurled his spear skyward, sending it careening over the eastern ridge and landing out of view on the other side.

He collapsed in a wretched heap at the base of the desiccated poplar tree, sinking into the chilly mud as he struggled to blink back his tears.

"Go on without me," he insisted, refusing to look Coop in the eye.

Coop put his hand on Lamar's shoulder reassuringly.

"I told you before: I'm not leaving," he said quietly but firmly.

Lamar shrugged off his hand.

"Just go back; tell the others you made a mistake. You can

say I tricked you, or you had a change of heart. Tell them I'm the least dependable person alive; they'll certainly believe that!" he said with a snort.

"If you don't stand up and get your circulation going, you won't have that title for long," Coop said, half-jokingly.

But Lamar would not be mollified.

"You're just going to give up and die out here?" Coop asked, incredulous.

Lamar nodded, refusing to budge.

"And nothing I can say will change your mind?"

Another nod.

"Fine."

Coop sat down in the mud beside Lamar with a forceful splat that sprayed Lamar's hands and chest with mud. He crossed his arms defiantly and stared evenly at a rather surprised Lamar.

"Thanks," Lamar sulked. "Now I'll have your death on my conscience."

"If you don't want that, then get up and start moving," Coop said.

The two stared at one another for several minutes, each one silently daring the other to give in, like the world's most boring game of chicken. Coop's teeth started to chatter, and Lamar crossed his arms over his chest for warmth, but neither moved from their spot.

"Why are you so fired up to keep going?" Lamar finally asked, the question having been on his mind for some time. "I mean, if things are so shitty back home, shouldn't it be you giving up?"

Coop smiled faintly, but his downcast eyes showed it was

a smile born of pain.

"I have a lot to atone for," he said quietly. "And I can't do that if I'm dead."

Coop paused to clean the mud off his glasses, though his robes were so caked in it that he did little more than streak it. He held them up to the stinging rain, which gradually washed the muck off.

"I told you before that I came with you out of friendship," he said as he reseated his glasses. "But that's not the only reason. Whether you believe it or not, you are a natural-born leader."

Lamar snorted in derision.

"Think of the fence to keep Wade out. That was your idea," Coop reminded him. "The rest of us were prepared to build an earth wall around the wigwam. You convinced us to take up arms against Wade, and you fixed the C.B. How about the iku? If you hadn't figured out that they were afraid of the light, none of us would be here now."

"Uh-huh," Lamar said, unmoved. "And how was my leadership yesterday?"

"You were running on fumes," Coop said as he shivered. "Leaders are allowed to get tired. Look, the point is, I trust your judgment."

Coop looked out on the lake as he paused to reflect. Little by little, the storm was starting to let up. The needles of rain started to sting less and were slowly petering out.

"I practiced all kinds of different religions because I hoped my faith in them would cure me, make me like everyone else. None of them worked, but I kept my faith," he said. "When John abandoned us, I kept my faith, at least for a time.

When those things out there came for us, I lost faith in anything and everything ... except for you. I have faith in you."

Lamar looked at him, surprised and genuinely touched.

"And it's about time you start to have more faith in yourself," Coop said.

The storm had passed, leaving cloudy skies and only a few more droplets. A strong wind blew in behind the storm, chilling the waterlogged duo.

Coop stood up and brushed off his robes.

"Okay, I am legitimately starting to freeze," he said through his chattering teeth.

He leaned over and extended his hand to Lamar.

"Are you ready to go now? Or are you still set on quitting?"

Lamar stared at him, awestruck at his conviction. After a few moments, he nodded and took Coop's hand. He struggled to stand; the mud seemed determined to claim him, and his legs had grown numb from the cold. It took a minute or two of stomping in the mud to return proper circulation to them.

Another strong breeze blew past them, whipping up Coop's mud-spattered robes. He ducked behind Lamar's generous frame to avoid the brunt of its bone-chilling effects.

Lamar cracked his knuckles, signaling that he was ready to get back to work.

"Where'd I throw my spear?" he asked.

"Thataway," Coop said, pointing toward the ridge.

Lamar trekked up the ridge and looked out on the land beyond. Straight ahead was a large, open field that stretched out of sight, flanked on either side by the barren remains of forest. Dividing the field from the ridge was a curtain of shriveled and tangled vines, caught up in a row of withered hedges.

He found his spear near the base of the opposite slope, partially buried in the mud. As he pulled it out with a grunt of exertion, Lamar found his eyes wandering back to those hedges some 50 feet in the distance. There was something off about them. Six of them in a row, meticulously aligned, and too perfectly spaced to be nature's doing. Upon closer inspection, Lamar realized the vines weren't caught in the hedges; they actually hung behind them, their tendrils resting on top of the bushes. They were wrapped around something behind the hedges, something about the size of a person, but wider. It was hard to make out what it was due to the vine curtain covering it. Lamar approached, mostly out of curiosity. Even close up, it was still hard to make out what was beneath the vines. It had a deep brownish tone that made it difficult to distinguish from the withered vines, but he saw splotches of white peeking out from behind its vine prison. He raised his spear and swept away the vines before him.

It was a wooden signpost, painted brown with white lettering, with a row of rocks arranged around its base, like some kind of memorial or shrine.

"Lamar, how's it coming?" Coop called out from the other side of the ridge.

Instead of answering, Lamar leaned in, reading and re-reading the white lettering on the sign, trying to convince himself that it wasn't a mirage. But no matter how many times he read it, the sign spelled out the same message:

Former Site of Curtiss-Wright Nuclear Testing Facility

Lamar turned and shouted joyfully over his shoulder. "Coop! It's here!"

* * * Six Hours Until Sundown * * *

Gaby huddled under a blanket, shivering miserably as she and Ken checked the logs they'd brought in from the rain. After spending nearly two hours sifting through the wood-pile for salvageable logs, they'd found 30 prospective candidates near the bottom.

Meanwhile, the rain outside was actually starting to let up now that they'd finally carted all the salvageable wood inside. This bitter irony wasn't lost on Gaby, but she was too cold and despondent to care. Hardly any of the logs they'd inspected thus far were usable, and each time they discarded one, Gaby felt a pinprick of fear crawl up her spine. At this rate, they might not have enough dry wood to last the night.

Her fumbling fingers, numbed by the cold, struggled to obey her commands as they operated the penknife, peeling away layers of soaked bark to inspect the wood underneath. Ten feet away, Ken was on his hands and knees, ripping off the bark with his bare hands. His whole body trembled as it fought to stave off the chill. If neither one of them developed pneumonia, it would be a minor miracle.

"Shit!" Ken exclaimed as he tossed the log to the side. "This one's soaked clear through."

Gaby peeled back the inner layer of bark on her log to reach the wood underneath. It looked slightly discolored.

She ran her finger along the interior. Damp.

"Same here," she said in bitter disappointment as she pushed the unusable log aside and started on the next one.

"You really screwed the pooch here!" Ken exclaimed in frustration.

"Let's worry about how to make it through the night, first," Gaby insisted through chattering teeth as she peeled back bark on another log. "Worry about blame later."

"I'll worry about it whenever I damn well feel like," Ken snapped.

"This one's dry," Gaby said, grateful both to find a dry log and an excuse to redirect the conversation.

"Show me," Ken insisted, his tone suggesting that he didn't trust her judgment. Gaby peeled back the bark and held up the exposed wood for Ken to inspect.

"That's green wood," he said dismissively. "It won't burn."

Gaby tossed the log to the side and grabbed a fresh one.

"If only Beverly had helped us, we'd have more wood to work with," she said glumly.

"Exactly," Ken said, surprising Gaby by agreeing with her. "Baba Gaga isn't pulling her weight. Her 'senior moments' are getting weirder and more frequent. If she comes back, we should do something about it."

The casual way Ken said "do something" chilled Gaby far deeper than the rainstorm had. She didn't like the direction this conversation was going.

"We're not murderers," she said softly.

Ken snorted.

"I'm not talking about offing her, I'm talking about exiling her. She's been a lead balloon since Day 1. Between her running off, trying to kill herself, slowing down our escape and going schizo, it's a wonder we haven't talked about it before."

"Haven't we thrown out enough people for one day?" Gaby countered.

"Just think of it like tribal council on *Survivor*. You weed out the dead weight," he said.

"Except when people get exiled here, they get eaten," Gaby pointed out.

Ken shrugged to express his depth of concern. He finished examining another log and threw it on the all-too-small pile with the other dry logs. "This one's good," he said.

"I still don't know," Gaby said, vacillating as she weighed the pros and cons. "Banning her seems drastic. Wade and Lamar did terrible things to merit expulsion."

"She nearly burned down the forest and us along with it," Ken reminded her.

Gaby shook her eyes in astonishment. Things had been so crazy lately that she had nearly forgotten about that incident.

"Well?" Ken asked impatiently.

Gaby was torn. While she bore no love for Beverly, she didn't want to be as callous as Ken. She also wasn't comfortable about being alone with Ken, who was growing more volatile by the hour. But in the end, she concluded that having two unstable companions was worse than one.

"Fine," Gaby said reluctantly as she threw another log on the discard pile. "Just promise not to go as hard on her as you did on Lamar."

"I'm not promising anything of the sort," Ken said.

He peeled away the inner layer of bark on the last uninspected log and found it to be dry enough on the inside. He added it to the pile, which had only five other logs.

He stood up and wiped his hands on his jeans.

"This'll buy us maybe seven hours," he said glumly. "We need more."

"Only if those things come back."

"*When* they come back," he corrected her. "No reason to pretend at this point. Whatever it is they want, it's here, and odds are, it's us."

The pair stripped the remaining wet bark from the dry logs. They worked in silence, both privately fearing that this was their last day on Earth. The disquiet was punctuated by the occasional rumble of protest from Gaby's empty stomach.

As they were finishing up, the wigwam's door opened and Beverly stepped through.

She was drenched, with droplets still falling from her matted hair, which covered her eyes. The rest of her face was a mess; her mascara and eyeliner had smeared and run down her cheeks, giving the impression that her face was melting. Her slip — the only thing she was wearing — clung to her torso like Saran Wrap, doing absolutely nothing to protect her modesty. Ken looked away, not out of any sense of nobility, but from disgust. Gaby could see through the slip that the black mark had spread again and was midway down her waist on the left side.

In her shaking arms Beverly held a large bundle wrapped in colored plastic. Gaby recognized it as the remains of a target from the archery range down by in the floodplain.

The hatchet was nowhere to be seen.

No one spoke for several seconds. Beverly took an unsteady step toward Gaby. While her whole body was shaking, likely from the chilly weather, her knees undulated in an uncharacteristic way, like they were about to buckle. Beverly extended the bundle toward Gaby, who cautiously accepted it after a few moments of consideration.

"A peace offering," Beverly whispered, her voice barely audible.

Gaby realized what was in the bundle the moment she hefted it. The unevenness of its contents and the weight were a dead giveaway. She unwrapped the package and found two dozen freshly cut pieces of dry wood. Most were on the smaller side, but a few of the larger and more ragged pieces were nearly as thick as Gaby's calves. Ken leaned over her shoulder to examine the pile and did some quick calculations. There was enough wood here to last them another two hours, maybe three if they stretched it. Still not enough, but it left them in a much better position than they'd been just a few minutes earlier.

"I'm sorry we doubted you ..." Gaby started to say, but stopped when Beverly began swaying unevenly. Her hair parted mid-lurch, and Gaby could see Beverly' eyes rolling back in her head. The older woman lost her balance and fell onto Gaby, who reflexively dropped the bundle and caught her.

Gaby shrieked and immediately pulled away, as though Beverly were a hot stove. The older woman fell to her knees and then landed face-first in the dirt.

"What the fuck?" Ken exclaimed. "Are you that afraid

she'll infect you?"

"No, I mean, yes, but that's not it," Gaby struggled to explain. "Her skin was like ice!"

"She's been out in the freezing rain for the last two hours," Ken reminded her. "It's a wonder she hasn't turned blue."

He knelt down beside Beverly and pulled his hands into the sleeves of his leather jacket to avoid touching her. He put his coat-covered hand on her shoulder and rolled her over onto her back.

"Jesus! I can feel it through the jacket," he said with a low whistle of surprise. "I don't know what's worse than hypothermia, but whatever it is, she's got it."

Beverly wasn't moving. Gaby and Ken exchanged worried glances and leaned in for a closer look.

Beverly started coughing and spat up some dirt, causing them both to rear back. Her head lolled slowly from side to side, making a dirt angel under her. Her breathing was shallow and erratic.

"Help me move her to her sleeping bag," Ken said, putting on gloves to avoid skin-to-skin contact. Gaby quickly followed suit.

As they prepared, Beverly started waving her right hand in the air.

"Floodplain," she said deliriously. "Down there ... incredible."

Ken grabbed Beverly by the shoulder while Gaby took her legs.

"Ready?" Ken said. "One, two, three!"

With a grunt of exertion they lifted the older woman and carried her five feet to her sleeping bag, struggling to keep a grip on her as she shivered violently. Gaby stuffed a blanket down the front to warm her up and tried to zip the sleeping bag, but Beverly was making it difficult, continually moving her arms.

"Down there! See!" she said, motioning generally toward the floodplain. Gaby had to jerk her head away to keep from being touched.

"Look at her arm," Ken said with a head feint toward Beverly's infected left arm.

Gaby saw the skin of her blackened hand was starting to crack, with flaking and small fissures opening up all the way up to her elbow. A greenish-yellow puss oozed from the webbing between her thumb and forefinger.

"Whatever you do, don't touch it," he cautioned. "It looks necrotic."

Ken touched Beverly's forehead through his glove.

"You could cook an egg on her head," he said grimly. "Check her pulse. We need to know what we're dealing with."

Gaby hesitated.

"She's already touched you once, so what difference will it make?" he said impatiently.

Gaby saw the logic in this and removed her gloves. She placed her hands on Beverly's undamaged arm and resisted the urge to flinch at the cold and clammy skin. She pressed two fingers on the inside of Beverly's wrist.

"I don't feel anything," Gaby said after a minute.

"Press harder," Ken urged.

Gaby complied, and Beverly started to squirm.

"Don't! Darcy, stop it!" Beverly said, fidgeting and laughing. "That tickles."

Gaby dug her fingers in and concentrated.

"I had the oddest dream," Beverly said quietly with her eyes closed and her head still rolling aimlessly from side to side. "I was trapped in a forest with five other people. Ghastly, I know."

"Well?" Ken said impatiently.

"I don't think I'm doing it right. I'm not feeling anything."

As Gaby moved out of the way so Ken could take over, Beverly continued babbling.

"But one of them reminded me so much of you, Darcy," she said. "A Latin you, curiously enough."

As Ken removed his gloves, Beverly giggled to herself.

"I know, I know," she continued. "Sounds silly."

Gaby cocked an eyebrow at that.

"I'm guessing I should be offended," she said aloud, mainly to herself.

"But she was like you in so many ways," Beverly continued. "Around the same age. Strong, confident, fiercely independent. She knew her mind, like you. She also stood up for what she believed in, like you."

Ken made a face as he pressed his fingers against Beverly's icy wrist.

"You know, Darcy, I probably shouldn't even tell you this, but the day after the intervention, when you walked out, I was so proud of you, darling," Beverly said, her voice barely above a whisper. "It tore me apart, knowing that my drinking had pushed you away, but your refusal to back down gave me such a swell of pride. It means I raised you right."

"Her pulse is faint," Ken said after about 20 seconds. "And

really slow."

"I sometimes wish I were as strong as you, that I didn't need the bottle to feel things," Beverly said with a sniff. "Anyway, I just thought you should know that, here at the end," she concluded as she patted and stroked Ken's boot, mistaking it for her daughter's hand.

Beverly stopped stroking his boot after a few moments, and her hand slowly fell to her side. Her breathing deepened, but was still erratic.

"I think she's in real trouble," Ken said as he looked up from their patient. "She may have only ... Oh, come on!" he exclaimed as he saw Gaby tearing up at Beverly's confession.

"What?" Gaby said, waving her hands in front of her face to keep from crying. "That was really sweet."

Ken rolled his eyes in disgust.

"She needs hot water and a fire, two things we can't give her until nightfall," Ken said. "And I'm not sure she'll last that long."

Ken grabbed his leather jacket and boots.

"So, what do we do?" Gaby said, dabbing her eyes.

"For her? Nothing," he said as he laced up his boots. "But we can find out where she got dry wood and see if there's more of it. We're going to retrace her steps."

As Gaby zipped up her outer jacket, she noted that Ken hadn't asked her to join him; he'd ordered her to. At least he wasn't talking about throwing Beverly out anymore. Though if she was as sick as he said, it probably wouldn't make much difference where she died, Gaby reasoned as she upended the plastic target's wooden contents onto the pile of usable logs and folded it in her arms. It could prove useful if they found more dry wood.

Outside, the rainstorm had passed, but it was still misting. The woods were shrouded in light fog, making everything look mysterious and vaguely sinister. By the entrance to the fence line, they found the hatchet that Beverly had dropped, its blade buried in the mud. Ken hefted it and wiped the handle clean as they followed Beverly's footprints.

Despite the fog, the indentations were easy to follow. The rain had washed away most other footprints, and this set of tracks was unique in that Beverly had been barefoot. The footprints came from the south, disappearing into the fog back behind the showers.

As they followed the footprints south toward the floodplain, Gaby's stomach growled ferociously. Ken actually jumped slightly at the noise and looked back in annoyance.

"Sorry, but I haven't eaten a thing in 24 hours," she apologized.

"Neither have I," Ken lied, "but I can still regulate my bodily noises."

"The truth is, I can't stop thinking about food," Gaby admitted as they followed the trail.

"Then grab your spear and go hunting," Ken chided her as they reached the end of the path, right before the descent into the floodplain. "You can't expect Mother Nature to just provide ..."

Ken paused midsentence as he looked out over the floodplain. Even through the haze of mist and the rolling fog, they could see that the entire floodplain had been transformed overnight. In place of the blighted foliage and desiccated soil, they found a verdant and flourishing ecosystem. The rocky soil was awash in a sea of pastels, with delicate pink carnations budding beside fiery orange marigolds and sunny black-eyed Susans wafting in a gentle breeze beside trumpet-like tufts of bluebells. Wild grasses sprouted all over, while the few trees in the floodplain — all of which had been dead only last night — were now budding. Even the soil had been transformed; its pasty complexion of yesterday was now rich and brown. If the blight that had swept this area so rapidly two days ago represented winter's lethal embrace, this was surely the spring of renewal, and equally out of season.

"… for you," Ken finished, the words already forgotten as they rolled off his tongue.

The veil of mist and fog rolling across the lush landscape below made it appear almost mystical. This surreal impression was heightened by the fact that they were still standing in the blight, two feet from the edge. If they looked straight down, they could see the wild grasses growing right at the foot of the cliff, some 25 feet down.

Gaby and Ken followed the path down to the floodplain, paying virtually no attention to where they were walking as they soaked up the idyllic vista before them in slack-jawed wonderment. Gaby was convinced it wasn't real, like someone dying of thirst in the desert hallucinating about an oasis. But like that desert dweller, she felt compelled to investigate, even as she told herself it was just a mirage.

Partway down the slope, the dust and ash gave way to a carpet of burgeoning green, flecked with clover and budding violets. Glorious scents wafted tantalizingly past their nostrils as they descended. The moisture-swollen air seemed cleaner, too. It was like they were passing from the wasteland into the Garden of Eden.

The fog grew thicker as they neared the bottom, casting wild shadows in all directions and making navigation virtually impossible. Gaby took a deep breath before stepping into this new world. The grasses by the slopes were already ankle high.

As their eyes adjusted to the gray light of the mist, they spied a host of wild edibles nestled among the flowers and grasses: mushrooms, red sumac berries growing on the vine, fiddleheads curled tight above their thistled stalks, even wild onions buried in the dirt beneath their vine-like appendages.

Gaby dropped to her knees and started scarfing down a cluster of wild mushrooms, not even pausing to consider whether they were poisonous. She didn't care. Ken watched for a moment and then joined her, uprooting a clump of wild onions and eating them raw.

The pair fed for nearly 10 minutes straight without stopping, not even pausing to savor the taste or enjoy the texture of the food, just desperate to fill their stomachs. Only after Gaby had polished off the last of the fiddleheads within reach did she pause to consider the implications of their discovery.

"Like the phoenix," Gaby mumbled to herself.

"What?" Ken asked through a mouthful of berries, which he was shoveling in his mouth, stalk and all, before stripping the berries off with his tongue and discarding the stalk.

"The myth of the phoenix," she explained. "It would rise

out of the ashes of its forbearer. Kind of like those before-and-after photos you see of volcanoes. It blows its top and kills everything around it, but three years later the place looks like paradise because of all the nutrients in the volcanic ash."

Ken paused momentarily from his feasting to look down at his hands, which had been uprooting every wild edible in sight. He noticed that they were covered in dirt and smeared ash. He looked closer at the soil and could see the scattered remnants of the ash that had coated the landscape just yesterday.

"Except this took hours, not years," he replied.

The pair forsook their original plan of finding dry wood and used the archery target like a grocery bag, stuffing it full of all the wild edibles they could find. They had cleared out the area around the base of the slope and were foraging for more along the cliff's edge when they heard the clean crack of wood snapping underfoot in the distance. The two immediately tensed and scanned the perimeter for any sign of movement, but the mist and fog made it impossible to see anything more than 20 feet away. What had before made this place seem mystical now made it creepy and foreboding.

"What was that?" Ken hissed as he put his back to the cliff.

"It could just be an elk," Gaby said, though the lilt in her voice betrayed her doubt.

They heard another sound, like something heavy falling. It sounded like it was coming from their left, but it was hard to gauge in the mist.

"Or a bear," Ken said as he snatched the hatchet from Gaby's shaking hands and assumed a defensive posture.

Gaby knelt down, picked up a couple of palm-sized rocks and steadied her throwing arm.

As the seconds ticked by, the sound drew closer. They could hear the swish of grass and a shuffling sound as something drew nearer.

Ken cursed under his breath for leaving his spear in the wigwam. Gaby tried to steady her breathing as she felt her pulse quicken.

Before long, they could see motion in the fog to their left. Gaby reared back with her throwing arm and scrunched her eyes, trying to make it out. Fragmented images flitted before them, warped and distorted by the shadows in the fog. Formless and indefinable, these unconnected images slowly coalesced as the creature drew closer, combining into a monstrous and looming shape some 30 feet away. It looked like an enormous grizzly standing on its hind legs, but that could have been a trick of the light refracting off the moisture in the air.

When the creature was about 20 feet away, just outside their visual range, it stopped. Ken caught glimpses of brown fur through the wisps of vapor before the creature suddenly keeled over and splayed out on the grass before them.

He and Gaby exchanged confused and nervous glances, both wondering whether they should investigate or simply run for it. The creature was motionless. After a few moments, Gaby took a cautious step forward.

"Be careful!" Ken hissed. "It could be a trick."

Gaby nodded and stepped gingerly toward the unmoving creature, with Ken following several steps behind her.

Details started to emerge as they closed in on it. The creature was too large to be a coyote or a bobcat, but a bit puny for a bear. Thick, matted brown fur covered what they assumed was its back, with darker fur on its flank. The fur on its head didn't match the rest of its pelt; it was black, close-cropped and so thin it didn't look like fur at all. Ken spied blood on a splayed out appendage, which he guessed was its front right limb. Only the paw was pinkish and had fingers instead of claws.

It was human. A man, by the size of him, wrapped in various animal skins, while his own skin was coated in dried blood and caked-on mud.

Ken stood in front of the unmoving man, hatchet at the ready, and lightly kicked his head. No response.

Gaby knelt down and, with some difficulty, rolled him over.

He was emaciated — at least 25 pounds underweight — and much of his face was buried beneath a bushy black beard, but there was no mistaking the sunburned complexion of their former companion.

Wade had returned.

* * * Five Hours Until Sundown * * *

It was mid-afternoon by the time Coop and Lamar reached the other side of the ashen field bearing the Curtiss-Wright sign. The air temperature was still unseasonably cold, but had warmed to the point that their breath was no longer visible.

Waiting for them were three concrete bunkers, each the size of a small barracks. No control towers, no hangars, no runways; nothing to show that nuclear-powered jets had once been tested here. Either the base had been largely dismantled, or else this had merely been a satellite facility and not part of the main campus. Apart from the bunkers, the only sign of development was a long untended dirt road that wound around a hill behind the bunkers that marked the edge of the field. Lamar guessed that was Reactor Road, which John had mentioned when he first brought them here. It was hard not to feel disappointed by it all.

All the bunkers had five sides: exterior walls that reached only three feet above the ground before sloping inward and upward on either side before ending in a broad and flat roof.

This unusual design choice made each of the buildings wide but squat, with none of them higher than 15 feet; just three feet taller than the wigwam. It also lent them the appearance of octagons half-buried in the dirt. The bunkers on the left and right were layered with patches of moss, while the center one, which was a few feet smaller than the other two, was partially covered in rubble, courtesy of a rock slide from the hill behind it.

In the center of each was an imposing, seven-foot-high metal door that was double padlocked: one at shoulder height above the metal door handle and another at knee level. All the doors were reinforced with triple hinges nearly as thick as a man's arm that extended from the left side of the exterior frame halfway across the door. Both the doors and the hinges appeared scarred and aged but otherwise untouched by the elements.

Above each of the doors was a small placard identifying the building's function and security level. The building on the right was designated Curtiss-Wright Gen-1: All Access, while the one in the center was Curtiss-Wright Comm-1: Restricted Access. The left building had the most ominous designation: Curtiss-Wright Reactor-1: Code Access. A stylized logo of a C over a W in a small circle appeared beside each placard. After some thought, Lamar and Coop concluded that the one on the right was a generator building, the center bunker was a communications bunker, while the left one must lead to the decommissioned nuclear reactor.

"Where are the stacks?" Coop asked. "Those giant stacks you see on reactors in all those disaster flicks. And those big concrete domes where everything is stored in case of a meltdown."

Lamar, who was leaning heavily on his walking stick after walking all day, shook his head.

"I think this is just the entrance. They used to build reactors underground as a safety precaution, so I'm guessing the rest of it is far below us and probably extends all the way to the lake. I suspect that's where you'll find the discharge vents; the 'stacks' you're thinking of."

"Great," Coop replied. "So how do we get in?"

"No clue," Lamar answered slowly as he looked around. "To be honest, I wasn't sure we'd ever find this place." He looked back over his shoulder and noticed Coop's eyes were practically popping out of their sockets at this revelation. "C'mon, let's check the door," Lamar said, trying to stifle a laugh.

Lamar leaned against the door of the generator building and rapped it with the flashlight. It gave a startlingly loud metal clang that echoed throughout the interior of the deserted building.

"That sounded several inches thick," Coop exclaimed.

"At least," Lamar replied with a nod. He tested the padlocks; both were rusted clear through and wouldn't budge. "The front door is a lost cause, so we'll do what the best hackers do: start looking for back doors," Lamar declared.

The two started casing the perimeter of each building, looking for other access points. All of the bunkers were windowless, and they found no secondary entrances to any of them. They were starting to despair when they noticed the remains of a ventilation port at the base of the communications building. Part of the shaft was buried under rubble from a landslide, but the exposed portion showed a corroded metal plate had been bolted over it, probably when the facility was closed. More interestingly, part of the cover had been peeled back several inches, either by the rockslide or nosy tourists.

Jackpot.

Lamar and Coop exchanged a knowing look before dropping to their knees and scooping away rubble with their bare hands. After about 30 minutes of work, they'd exposed most of the vent. It was enormous, an industrial vent four times the size of modern ones, just large enough for them to squeeze through. It was held in place by two rusted bolts.

Coop shoved his wood spear through the exposed section of the vent cover and pushed outward, using it as a fulcrum to pry the cover loose. After several minutes of struggle, he peeled it back enough for Lamar to fit his spear in beside it. The pair alternated between pushing their spear tips toward their chests and away from them, trying to wiggle the bolts loose. It was backbreaking work, since neither of them had much in the way of upper-body strength, but after 20 minutes of pushing and pulling, their solid oak spears triumphed over the rusted bolts, which came loose with a wrenching noise of metal shearing against metal. Lamar leaned on his spear, exhausted, as Coop kicked the metal plate loose.

Coop activated the flashlight and aimed it into the vent, giving the pair their first peek inside.

A curtain of ivy and cobwebs blocked their view. Lamar brushed them away with his spear tip, revealing corroded flanges on the top and bottom of the vent, which probably once held an industrial fan in place. The rest of the vent was clear and every bit as wide as the cover suggested. However, time and the elements had not been kind to it, with the closest partitions badly rusted and partially warped. Coop could see jagged creases of compressed metal at several points where the seams collided. It looked profoundly unsafe.

"So, who gets to go first?" Coop asked, hoping that Lamar would volunteer.

Instead, Lamar balled up his right fist and placed it in the upturned palm of his left hand. Coop grinned and followed suit.

"Ready?" Lamar asked.

Coop nodded.

"1 ... 2 ... 3 ... Scissors!" Lamar said, holding his index and middle fingers out in the shape of scissors.

Coop looked down in disappointment at his choice of Paper.

"Fine," he said as he knelt down and faced the opening.

"But if I need a tetanus shot when all this is over, I'm sending you the bill."

Coop entered the vent headfirst, with the flashlight in his right hand and the hem of his robes in his left, to avoid snagging them on anything. Lamar leaned down to watch his progress. The flashlight backlit Coop's hunched-over frame as he carefully made his way on his hands and knees, trying to avoid touching any of the seams in the metal partitions.

Lamar took a deep breath and then followed him into the vent. The first thing he noticed was the musty smell, like old books left to decay in a metal tomb. He crawled forward and a shower of dust leapt into the sky, shimmering in the dim light as it slowly heeded gravity's call.

He paused after moving five feet in. It was the point where the outside light failed to reach; until he caught up with his flashlight-wielding companion, Lamar was effectively blind. From that point on, he tested the path with his gloved hands before moving forward, feeling for any sharp edges. It was a laborious process, one made all the worse by the claustrophobia-inducing darkness. He could see Coop's flashlight lightly bobbing up and down as he crawled forward, some 20 feet ahead. Out of nowhere the light began jerking wildly up and down. He heard Coop make a noise that was somewhere between a halted sneeze and a cry of pain.

"You okay up there?" Lamar called ahead, worried.

Coop's only response for several seconds was spitting noises. The flashlight gradually stopped waving.

"Just a cobweb," came Coop's voice, which sounded strangely distorted as it echoed off the narrow metal walls.

Lamar grinned and resumed crawling. While the going

was slow, he was gradually gaining on Coop. When the flashlight was 15 feet ahead of Lamar, it suddenly stopped.

"There's a metal grate here," Coop called out. "I'm going to try and open it."

Lamar heard the sounds of metal reverberating.

"Oww!" Coop said, more annoyed than injured.

Lamar was now 10 feet behind him. He watched the light judder and heard the metal ring out once again as Coop tried unsuccessfully to force the grate open once more.

"Hang on, I'm going to try something else."

Suddenly the flashlight spun and weaved, shifting between reflecting the walls and ceiling as Coop tried to turn around in the narrow space. Lamar realized Coop had succeeded when the flashlight shone directly in his face.

"You wanna lower that?" Lamar asked, turning his head and shielding his eyes.

"Here goes," Coop said as he reared back and donkey kicked the grate as hard as he could. The reverberations were much stronger this time, and they heard the whine of something metallic on the other side giving way.

"Harder," Lamar urged as he drew closer.

Coop exhaled loudly, held his breath for a moment, and kicked again. The metal whining sound was more pronounced this time.

"One more time," Lamar coached him, now just five feet away. The flashlight under Coop's chin distorted his face, the shadows turning his friendly mug into something hideous and unnatural. The ghastly face tensed up and then grunted in exertion as Coop kicked the grate hard as he could. The metallic whine turned into a wrenching clang as Coop knocked the grate loose from its moorings, sending it clattering across what sounded like a wooden floor.

"Way to go!" Lamar cheered, their faces now a couple of feet apart.

"I think I pulled something," Coop said with a grimace as he crawled backward out of the vent.

The light suddenly disappeared as Coop stood up to explore his new surroundings, leaving Lamar alone in the dark. The light returned and motioned for Lamar to come. He followed, holding up one hand to shield his eyes against the brightness.

Lamar crawled out of the vent and into a room that time forgot. As he stood up and stretched his aching back, images leapt out of the shadows at him, only to sink back into them as the flashlight's beam swept the bunker: a smiling face staring out of a framed poster, a rolled-up projection screen on the back wall, a pair of aviator sunglasses on a desk, an empty gun holster hanging over the back of a wooden office chair, an engraved cigarette case, an enormous stack of carbon paper.

The air tasted stale and vaguely metallic. A thin layer of dust covered everything. The room was enormous — too large for the light to reach from one end of the building to the other. A dozen or more desks lined both walls, separated by matching filing cabinets, with a wide open corridor in the center. Many of the desks had CB equipment on them with attached microphones. One had a reel-to-reel recorder, while another housed a projector.

The flashlight abandoned the furnishings to investigate the surrounding walls. A poster directly across from the pair announced that "Peace is Our Profession," written in the kind of billowy letters normally reserved for 1940s cartoons. One below it showed a blonde bombshell in a bomber jacket and Air Force cap winking in a coquettish pinup pose. The text beneath her declared: "Keep 'em Flying!"

Lamar tapped Coop's shoulder and pointed at a newspaper spread out on a desk to their right. Coop trained the flashlight on it while Lamar blew the dust off to read it. The paper was so old and brittle that his breath tore a corner loose, sending it flying into the inky ether. It was an old issue of Stars and Stripes, whose headline boasted: "DOD Hails Titan Missile's Ocean-to-Ocean Reach." Beside it was a story on Eisenhower revamping his New Look policy to address Cuba's relationship with the Soviets. A headline below the fold mentioned that someone named the "Big Bopper" and four others had died in a plane crash. Lamar looked at the date on the masthead: Feb. 8, 1959.

It was eerie being in here, seeing so many artifacts from an era that was nothing more than distant rumor to either of them. It felt less like trespassing and more like grave robbing.

Lamar and Coop slowly worked their way to the other side of the bunker, scanning their surroundings as they walked. On the opposite side of the building they found a large section of floor space — some 300 square feet — that was completely empty. Lamar didn't understand it until Coop pointed the flashlight at the pine-board floors to reveal long score marks, indicating that heavy equipment once stood there but had since been removed, probably when the facility was abandoned.

The beam of light dimmed momentarily. Coop smacked the handle and the light came roaring back, a stark reminder that they didn't have time for sightseeing.

"So, what's the plan?" Coop asked.

"Look for keys. We need to access the generator building. If we can get it running, maybe we can get some of this equipment working."

Coop cast a doubtful eye on the equipment Lamar planned to operate. The desk beside him housed a rusty microphone attached to a rig four times the size of John's C.B., with an antenna that reached six feet in the air. Its front panel was decorated with two dozen switches, buttons and knobs, some of which were unidentified because the lettering beside them had faded over the decades. Those that were still readable were indecipherable: "KLT455," "Distance 41-Plus," "RX/TX."

"And you think you can get this stuff working?" he asked dubiously.

"If you've got a better idea …" Lamar intoned.

Coop didn't, so he set the flashlight down on its base with the light pointing upward, giving them both just enough light to work independently as they started scouring the immediate area.

"Gotta say, this is not how I pictured my vacation when I booked it," Coop joked as he rummaged through a filing cabinet, getting a small chuckle out of Lamar. "If only I'd decided to stay home, I could be studying the I Ching right now. Maybe with a bottle of suds by my arm."

"Right now, Grammy's cooking for 15," Lamar said as he opened and closed desk drawers in search of keys.

"That's one big family!" Coop said with an appreciative whistle.

"Thursday is cousins' night in our household," Lamar explained. "The whole clan gets together to talk sports, TV, how much they hate their jobs, who's sleeping with who, and I'm just sitting in the corner, counting the minutes until they leave. I don't have anything in common with them; it's like I speak Java, they speak Perl. I never know what to say to any of them."

"That actually sounds pretty sweet to me," Coop said with a small smile that hid traces of bitterness.

Lamar looked at Coop like he was bonkers.

"My family rejected me after ... the incident," Coop explained, his expression souring as he reflected. "Nobody visited me in prison. My calls were refused. All my letters came back unopened. When I got out, I moved upstate for a fresh start. The first thing I did was write my folks a long letter telling them how I was getting on. Told them not to worry about me."

Coop paused pensively for several seconds. After a nod of encouragement from Lamar, he continued.

"A month later I get a reply," Coop said. "It was just one sentence: 'Don't contact us again.'"

"Ouch," Lamar said, wincing empathetically.

"Your family may not understand you, but at least they didn't disown you," Coop said before returning to work.

An awkward silence descended on the pair, which only accentuated their unease in this oversized time capsule. Lamar had cleared out three desks and was moving on to the fourth while Coop searched the ones on the opposite wall.

"You come up with anything?" Lamar asked after several more minutes of searching.

"Squat."

As Coop moved the flashlight over so they could check the last grouping of desks at the back of the building, a flash of color against the drab gray wall caught Lamar's eye. The shadows made it hard to tell what exactly it was, but it wasn't reflective like the framed posters and appeared substantially larger.

"Hey, Coop, can you bring the light over here?"

Coop aimed the flashlight in the direction Lamar signaled to reveal a four-foot map against the back wall, across from where the heavy equipment had once stood. Unlike a normal map, it was divided into quadrants, and featured no location or road names. Instead, it showed looping white lines across seemingly random parts of the terrain with numbers beside each swirl.

"What kind of map is this?" Lamar asked, mystified.

"It's a topo," Coop responded as he handed the flashlight to Lamar, who brought it in close so they could study the map together. "A topographic map. Instead of marking streets, it charts elevation. See these rising numbers here?" Coop asked as he pointed to a location in the center of the map. "That means this is a hill."

They both fixated on a red pin in the lower-left quadrant of the map. It was positioned just west of a sizable blue blob that Coop guessed was a body of water.

"So, I think this is us here," Coop said. "And that must be the lake." His finger glided up the map as he looked for more distinguishable landmarks. It paused near the center.

"See this area where the elevation dips? That's gotta be the floodplain." His finger moved right until it stopped on the western edge of the floodplain. "Which means the campsite is right around ... here."

"Forget the generator," Lamar said, the flashlight bouncing in his hands as his excitement grew. "This is our ticket out of here. Let's take it outside, where we can have a better look."

Coop nodded happily as he removed the pin from the map and gingerly peeled it off the wall. The ancient map was delicate but made of sterner stuff than the newspaper, and it held together as Coop folded it up and stowed it in his jacket's interior pocket.

He had started back toward the ventilation shaft when he noticed the light wasn't following him. Coop turned to see that something had caught Lamar's attention. He was aiming the flashlight at a desk to his left, staring at it intently.

"Lamar?" Coop said.

No reply.

In the center of the desk was a motivational desk blotter with two side-by-side images. The left side showed Elvis Presley in an Army uniform, saluting a superior officer. "Good Soldiers Follow Orders," the text below it stated. On the right side of the blotter was General MacArthur, puffing on a corncob pipe. "Great Soldiers Don't Wait for Orders. They Lead by Example," read the text box below it.

But what had caught Lamar's eye was a bit of impish graffiti on the blotter. Someone had drawn devil's horns on MacArthur's face and tried to cover it up with a Mickey Mouse sticker, which only partially obscured the doodling.

Lamar's eyes went from Mickey's smiling visage to the message below and back again, burning the combination into his mind.

"Mouseketeers lead by example," Lamar whispered to himself.

"Hey, you coming?" Coop called out from the shadows, snapping Lamar out of his musings.

"Sorry," Lamar mumbled as he followed Coop over to the ventilation port. Coop got on his hands and knees and proceeded to crawl back into the shaft. Lamar took one last look around the bunker before following.

As Lamar wriggled his way through the shaft's narrow confines, that phrase — "Lead by Example" — echoed in his mind, stirring something deep inside. While he had spent much of today's journey reflecting on his many mistakes yesterday — getting the group lost, falling asleep on watch, trusting Ken — Lamar now found himself lamenting his conduct instead. Each memory was more painful than the last, like a pinprick to his conscience. And after each one, that phrase repeated, louder and more insistent.

The times he had treated the others contemptuously for falling behind.

Lead by Example

Hiding Ken's tutelage from Gaby and Coop because he didn't trust them enough.

Lead by Example

Barking orders at the others.

Lead by Example

Threatening to leave Gaby behind for questioning his decisions.

Lead by Example

Lamar crawled out of the shaft, blinking at the sky. After spending so much time surrounded by darkness, the overcast sky looked blindingly bright. As his eyes adjusted, they focused on Coop, who was standing beside the ventilation shaft with the map opened in front of him, spread out across the exterior wall of the bunker.

"I think I've figured it out," Coop said, humming excitedly to himself as he studied the map. "This road on the map has to be that road right there," he continued, pointing to the dirt trail off to their left that looped around the hill above before disappearing from view. "That's gotta be Reactor Road. And it leads all the way back to the main highway. Now, if we follow the highway west for about …"

Coop paused to do some quick calculations, placing two fingers on either side of the distance converter in the map's legend to get a sense of scale, and then applied that to the road.

"…15 miles, it should take us to the nearest town," Coop continued. "I'm guessing that's what this Fawke's Mill notation means. Assuming it's still there, we can … Lamar?"

Coop paused again as he looked up from the map to see

that Lamar wasn't listening. Instead, he was staring at the field they'd crossed to get here, his eyes wide with surprise. Coop followed his gaze and saw tiny patches of greenery sprouting throughout the fallow field. When they had crossed that field nearly two hours ago, it had been nothing but ash and dust. Now they could see tiny flowers starting to emerge from the soil, and the trees along the edge of the field were beginning to bud.

The transformation wasn't as pronounced or jarring as what they'd seen in the clearing earlier in the day, but it had all occurred in the 45 minutes they'd spent in the bunker.

"Hollleeeey shit!" Coop whispered, giving a low whistle of admiration. He flashed back to Lamar's prediction hours ago in the clearing, that they might find more patches of greenery like it, and now it had come true.

"How did you know?" Coop asked. "What does it all mean?"

Lamar continued to gaze at the slowly morphing field, tugging thoughtfully on his scraggly goatee for several long moments before replying.

"Maybe the iku aren't what we thought."

* * * Four Hours Until Sundown * * *

Beverly struggled to pull on her fur-lined jacket with only one arm. Her blackened left arm hung limp and useless at her side, oozing yellow-green puss through numerous open sores. She found the sight repulsive, so she wore gloves to hide it. The rest of her shivered as she layered on clothes, but no matter how she bundled up, nothing seemed to stave off the chill.

Her entire body ached, and her breathing was raspy. She held her good hand to her forehead, testing it for signs of a fever. Both of them felt ice cold.

As she zipped up her jacket, the door to the teepee opened and Gaby backed through the entrance, carrying someone's legs. Ken came in behind her, lifting the unconscious man by the shoulders.

"What in the world ..." Beverly started to exclaim when she saw who they were carrying. Despite the layers of caked-on mud and a full beard, she immediately recognized the man who had nearly choked the life out of her a day earlier.

Gaby and Ken dumped Wade beside the firepit, tossing him on the ground like a sack of potatoes.

"Where did you find him?" she exclaimed, her voice strained and hoarse. "And why did you bring him here?"

Without a word of explanation, Ken exited the teepee just as fast as he'd entered.

"It's a long story," Gaby said as she rubbed her biceps, which ached after carrying him all the way from the flood-plain. Even though he clearly hadn't eaten in days, Wade was still heavy.

They heard an awful clatter outside, like someone banging pots and pans together.

Beverly rolled Wade over to take a closer look at him. His clothes were long gone, replaced by animal skins that looked like they'd been through a war. His deerskin kilt was torn and shredded in places, as was a rudimentary vest that looked to be made from a boar's hide. His fox-fur cap looked like it had been gnawed by wild animals, and the tail that used to dangle down the back had been lopped off. Everything was coated in mud and grime.

Wade's sunburned skin had all peeled away, leaving pink and raw flesh behind. His infamous knife was nowhere to be seen. And my God, did he stink.

Something about their prisoner's appearance was bothering Beverly. She zeroed in on his bare chest. He was so thin that his ribs were visible. But she was more focused on what wasn't there.

"Where are the scars?" Beverly asked, holding her nose as she leaned in for a closer examination. Shivering, she wiped away the gunk on his chest with a towel to reveal that it was unblemished. The scars he'd ritualistically carved into it to mark each kill were gone. Not healed, but wholly absent, without a welt or scar tissue to show that they had ever been there.

A thought occurred to Gaby, and she examined his right leg.

"Nothing here, either," she said, puzzled. "The bear trap got him right here, and there's no marks."

The two exchanged uneasy glances, afraid to vocalize what they were both thinking. Even the best plastic surgeons leave telltale signs, not that Wade was likely to run into one in the middle of nowhere. His miraculous recovery simply defied explanation.

The clatter of metal clashing against metal outside grew louder, and suddenly Ken was back, carrying a set of cans all tied to a long strip of plastic: the alarm system they'd set up three days earlier to warn them if Wade tried to infiltrate the camp. They no longer needed it now that they had him. Ken unhooked the cans from the string and tossed the length of plastic to Gaby.

"Tie him up," Ken commanded. "Tight as you can."

Gaby cocked an eyebrow; his imperiousness was getting out of control, but she recognized that he was also right: leaving Wade untied was dangerous. She took the length of plastic and rolled Wade over on his side so she could access both of his hands. She put them behind his back and started looping the plastic around his wrists. After two loops, she tied a bow, which she knotted with the remaining ends of the string.

"I said make it tight," Ken barked. "I don't want this lunatic getting free."

"It's already as tight as I can get it."

Ken rolled his eyes and walked around behind Wade, grabbed both ends of the knot and undid it. He pulled the bow as hard as he could, smirking as the bindings dug cruelly into Wade's flesh, and then double-knotted it, pulling both ends so hard that Gaby thought he might break the bindings.

"You'll cut off his circulation," Gaby protested.

"I don't care."

Ken sat the unconscious Wade up, and the group stared at him for a long while, still struggling to believe he was back.

"How did he do it?" Gaby asked in an awed whisper. "Three nights out there with the iku, and he's still alive."

"That's precisely what I intend to find out," Ken said tersely. "If he's found some hidey-hole that the iku can't reach, then he needs to show us where. We won't survive the night without it," he added, his eyes lingering over their pitifully inadequate wood supply for the long night ahead.

He walked up to Wade and smacked him hard in the face.

"Time to wake up, creepo!" he said. "Tell us what you know!"

Wade stirred but didn't open his eyes, so Ken smacked him again, harder.

Wade's eyes shot open.

"They're here!" he shouted after studying his surroundings for a few moments. "The visitors are coming again tonight! They're coming for you all!"

Far from the sullen, monosyllabic loner they all remembered, Wade was now remarkably animated. Only he didn't sound scared. If anything, he seemed excited, like a child on Christmas Eve dreaming of the presents to come. His eyes danced wildly with anticipation. He struggled against his bonds and tried to stand up, but Ken held him down, pressing against Wade's shoulders as he squirmed.

"Easy there, Wade," Gaby said, unexpectedly intervening. "Just take a deep breath and relax. We already know about these ... what did you call them?"

"Visitors!" Wade practically shouted. "They're the visitors and they're here for you! They're coming for you tonight, and they won't stop until every one of you is ... gwald wolkth bwe!"

Wade nearly choked as Beverly stuffed her makeshift eyeshade in his mouth to gag him. Ken gave a sadistic smile of approval.

"Wade, we need you to slow down," Gaby coaxed as he tried to talk through the gag, bouncing up and down like a hyperactive four-year-old. "We've met the visitors. We know what they do." She paused to cast a glance at Beverly's useless left arm. "And we're not going to let them get you.

But we need to know how you escaped. Can you tell us that?"

Wade nodded his head impatiently, his eyes positively manic in their boundless energy.

Gaby reached for the gag, but a sharp word from Ken stopped her.

"No," he ordered. "Not until he calms down. We won't get anything useful from him like this."

"So, I'm the psycho whisperer now, am I?" Gaby grumbled. "Fine."

She lowered herself until she was at eye level with Wade and tried to hold his attention. It wasn't easy, as his eyes darted to and fro. She had to lean in until their noses were inches apart before he got the message.

"I need you to calm down," she said deliberately and slowly. "I want to take this gag out, but I can't until you relax. Are you willing to do that?"

Whether it was from the eye contact, the soothing tenor of her voice, or a combination of the two, Wade's excited fidgeting gradually subsided.

"That's it, breathe," Gaby said, inhaling and exhaling in an exaggerated fashion so that he could follow along. "Think peaceful thoughts. Relax."

Wade followed her breathing, and little by little he calmed.

"Now, I'm going to take out the gag, okay?" Gaby said, still speaking slowly. "When I do, I need you to answer some questions. And I want you to answer calmly. Can you do that?"

Wade nodded slowly.

Gaby released the gag.

For a wonder, Wade remained silent, waiting for their questions.

"Now, can you tell me ..." Gaby started to speak when Beverly interjected.

"Do you know what they are?" she asked, her voice rising in anxiety. "Is their touch lethal?"

"Hold on!" Ken insisted, shouting down Beverly. "First things first. Where's your hidey-hole?"

"What about me?" Beverly shot back. "I deserve to know ..."

Beverly suddenly doubled over as a coughing fit consumed her. She covered her mouth with her good hand, and when the fit passed, saw it was splattered with black blood. Trembling, she held up her blood-splattered hand so the others could see, her eyes wide with terror. Ken made a face and took a step back in revulsion.

"Am I going to die?" Beverly asked Wade, trembling.

"Sick or not, you can wait your turn, Granny Badwill!" guttural Ken barked, irritated at her trying to monopolize the interrogation. "Because I have no intention of going out like that."

Wade began to reflect the others' anxiety, starting to bounce on his legs once again. Gaby saw it and moved to quash it.

"Enough, both of you!" she shouted. "You're agitating him. Wade, I need you to remain calm. Can you tell us how you managed to escape these visitors?"

Wade waited for a nod of encouragement from Gaby before speaking, like an obedient pet seeking permission from its owner.

"Yes," Wade said simply. As Gaby tried to prod him for more, he finally added: "Their touch is lethal."

Everyone turned to face Beverly, realizing he was answering her question rather than Gaby's. Wade gazed at the blood oozing from between Beverly's clenched fingers. "And you will die tonight."

Beverly inhaled sharply at the news. Tears started welling up in the corner of her eyes.

"I just … can't," she told the others with a heart-wrenching sob before stumbling toward the door.

"Probably just as well," Ken muttered under his breath. "She's as useless as a three-dollar bill."

Gaby recoiled at Ken's callousness, and considered going after Beverly, but Ken motioned for her to continue the interrogation.

"But …"

"If you don't, then I will."

"Fine," Gaby said with a sigh of resignation. She turned to face Wade once more. "If their touch is so deadly, then how did you escape?"

"I didn't," Wade drawled, his first calm words since they'd found him. "They found me and they freed me. And now they're coming to free you, and when they do …"

Wade was growing louder and more excitable with each syllable, and had already started bouncing up and down when Ken held up the gag again. The sight of it convinced Wade to settle down.

"Fine," Gaby said, starting over, the frustration evident in her tone. "If you didn't *escape* them, then tell us how you survived. Did you find some place the iku couldn't follow you?"

"I didn't hide," Wade insisted. "They came to me two nights ago. I tried to run, but they were so fast, so very fast. And always whispering. They whisper through their chirps, you know," Wade added matter-of-factly.

"That's super-fascinating," Ken deadpanned, rubbing his temples in frustration. "But we need to know how you keep them at bay."

"You can't," Wade answered plainly. "The visitors won't stop until they cleanse these woods, and they told me that you all are next."

"I've had enough of this!" guttural Ken roared, grabbing Wade by the sleeves of his crude boar skin vest and shaking him violently. "No more riddles! How are you still alive?"

"You're not listening to me," Wade said, growing anxious once more. "They're here to save you. When I first saw them, I was afraid, like you. The visitors cured me of that. They washed away my sins. Before they came, I was little more than an animal. I was a murderer. I even tried to kill you all. The visitors opened my mind and redeemed me, and they'll redeem you, too, and we'll all be … bwerry jere do hewp woo!"

Guttural Ken stuffed the gag back in Wade's mouth, jamming it in as far as it could go.

"This isn't working," Gaby said. "He's like a tent revivalist on acid. We should use our remaining time looking for food or dry wood."

"We need that intel," guttural Ken insisted, struggling and failing to revert to his normal persona. "And since reasoning with him didn't work, I say it's time we try other means of *persuading* him."

His emphasis on "persuading," unnerved Gaby. She had a terrible suspicion he was about to do something morally bankrupt again.

Guttural Ken walked behind Wade, lifted him by his bound arms and started dragging him toward the entrance.

"Bwgrh swub kwaprm!" Wade babbled through the gag as Ken manhandled him.

"What are you doing?" Gaby asked, growing increasingly alarmed.

"What needs to be done," guttural Ken insisted before brushing past her, which was as close as he came to reasoned discourse.

Wade was dragged out the door and around the fence, his heels leaving trails in the dirt behind him. Gaby followed closely, determined to stop Ken from going too far.

By the shower they found Beverly, weeping as she leaned against the cabana wall. She looked up with a sob at the commotion.

"Out of the way, Norma Demented!" guttural Ken barked as he dragged Wade, who was now kicking and flailing wildly, over to the showers. "You want to live? Then stop feeling sorry for yourself and help me."

Beverly dabbed her eyes and nodded obediently.

"We need to know what's in this fruitcake's head, and we don't have time for diplomacy," guttural Ken said as he dumped Wade in front of the shower stall and nodded skyward. The sun, whose dim outline could be seen behind the thick layer of low-lying clouds, was already dipping westward.

"Grab the water bucket and fill it," guttural Ken ordered.

Beverly grabbed it from its perch by the central firepit and carried it one-armed over to the spigot behind the shower.

"Ken, I don't know what you're thinking, but you don't need to do this," Gaby said, watching with rising panic as Beverly worked the old-fashioned pump, filling the bucket with creek water.

"We tried it your way," guttural Ken hissed. "Now we'll do it mine."

He righted Wade and set him on his knees, with his hands still tied behind his back. Wade watched anxiously as guttural Ken walked around him.

"Bring the bucket over," he ordered Beverly. With the water, it was too heavy for her to carry one-handed, so she dragged it behind her, sloshing water over the sides and wheezing as she complied.

Beverly set the water bucket down in front of Wade and hurriedly backed away, not entirely sure what Ken was about to do with it.

"We're going to play a little game, Wade," he grinned sadistically as he removed Wade's gag. "It's called: 'How long can you hold your breath?'" He walked around behind Wade and put his boot in the small of Wade's back, just above his tied hands. "If you don't want to play, then tell me everything I want to know, starting with how you escaped."

"I didn't," Wade protested in earnest, looking shockingly pitiable for someone who had threatened to kill them all only days ago. "Like I told you before, I ... bhwwgghh!"

Guttural Ken pushed his foot down, forcing Wade face-first into the water. Wade struggled as Ken held him under.

"This is wrong," Gaby protested as she watched pensively

some 15 feet away, wondering whether she should intervene.

"Hey, I warned him," guttural Ken said with a vicious
laugh.

After holding him down for about 30 seconds, Ken removed his foot from Wade's back. The Texan shot up out of
the water, sputtering and inhaling deeply.

"Feel like answering me now?" guttural Ken challenged.

"If you'd just listen to me ... ghhwwrrggh!"

"I guess not," guttural Ken snickered as he pushed Wade's
head back into the bucket.

"Ken, stop!" Gaby pleaded. "You're torturing him!"

Guttural Ken simply ignored her and pushed extra hard
against Wade, who was thrashing desperately in the water.
After several more seconds, Gaby decided she couldn't take
any more of this. She strode toward Ken, determined to stop
him, but Beverly suddenly moved between them. She tried
to walk around the older woman, but Beverly had anticipated this and blocked her again, holding her good arm out
to keep Gaby at bay.

"Out of my way," Gaby demanded.

"I know you can't see it, but this is for the best," Beverly
said quietly and with unexpected gravity.

"You're better than this," Gaby scolded. "Don't let fear
turn you into Ken."

"He tried to kill you," Beverly reminded her before being
overcome by another coughing fit.

Guttural Ken removed the pressure on Wade's lower back
after about 40 seconds.

Wade struggled to lift his head from the water, guttural

Ken's abuse having taken its toll on him. He gasped for air, taking huge lungfuls in a desperate bid to hold on.

"No more," Wade croaked between gasping breaths.

Guttural Ken walked around to face Wade, looming menacingly over him.

"Last chance, freakshow," he growled. "Tell us what we want to know."

"Please, no more," Wade pleaded.

Ken wheeled around behind Wade and dunked him again, pressing down hard on Wade's back.

"Wrong answer," guttural Ken said, biting his lip and shaking with violent glee. The sight disturbed Gaby, who finally recognized that Ken could no longer be reasoned with.

After 10 seconds underwater, Wade started flailing again.

"Dammit, Ken, let him up!" Gaby screamed. "Let him up!"

"He'll break this time," guttural Ken insisted. "And if he doesn't, who's gonna miss him?"

After 30 more seconds, Wade's flailing grew wilder, more spastic.

"He's drowning! Let him up!"

"He's faking it!" guttural Ken insisted, the glee in his voice evident.

"You're killing him! Haya paz!" Gaby shrieked.

Guttural Ken ignored her and kept pressing down on Wade. Gaby noticed to her horror that Ken's visceral thrill at torture had actually turned to arousal, as he was sporting a massive erection.

Wade's flailing started to flag. After another 10 seconds underwater, his whole body shuddered and went limp.

Gaby shot past Beverly and charged guttural Ken. He looked up from his handiwork just in time to see her lower her shoulder and slam into his left side. He was already off balance because one foot was planted on Wade's back instead of the ground, so Gaby's tackle sent him reeling, spinning end over end before landing several feet away in a crumpled heap, clutching his ribs in pain.

Gaby yanked Wade's head from the water and laid him on his side.

"Wade? Wade?" she called out.

He was unresponsive.

"Is he still breathing?" Beverly asked.

Gaby rolled him on his back and was about to perform CPR — despite only having seen it in movies — when water shot out of Wade's lungs and he gasped for air, panting and coughing as he clung to life.

"Please ... stop. Please," he begged, his voice barely more than a whisper.

The shadow of someone standing behind Gaby darkened Wade's face. She knew who it was by the heavy breathing.

"What's wrong with you?" she demanded as she whirled around to face guttural Ken. "You could have ..."

She was abruptly cut off when he coldcocked her with a roundhouse that sent Gaby sprawling face-first into a large ash pile. Gaby struggled to get up, but her head was swimming, and she gagged on the blood coursing down her throat. The best she could manage for several seconds was spitting out blood, which sent the ash skyward. Through the haze of gray, snow-like particles, she saw Ken walking away with his fists clenched.

"Your compassion just killed us all," she heard guttural Ken say, his voice sounding faint in her ringing ears as he stormed off.

Gaby struggled to raise herself off the ground. Her arms felt like rubber.

"Are you hurt?"

She looked up and saw Beverly kneeling beside her, still shivering fiercely despite the warmer weather.

Gaby gritted her teeth and rose to her knees. Her jaw was throbbing, and she felt warm blood ooze out of her split lip and down her neck.

"I'm … just a little dazed," Gaby insisted, getting one foot under her.

"What were you thinking?" Beverly admonished quietly, so as not to attract guttural Ken's attention. "You know better than to resist him when he's like … *that*. You're lucky he didn't kill you."

"I couldn't just let him drown Wade," Gaby said, finally standing up, leaning on the cabana wall for support.

"He was trying to save us! It was working! Wade was ready to talk!"

Gaby wiped the blood from her split lip. She couldn't believe what she was hearing.

"What's happened to you?" she asked, genuinely horrified at how fast the group had descended into *Lord of the Flies*. "I expected this from him, but not you."

To her surprise, Beverly looked genuinely hurt.

"All I wanted to do was live," Beverly said quietly, raising her left pants leg show that the black mark had spread to her calf. The skin near the ankle appeared mottled, with bands of inky discoloration that gave her skin a slightly bluish tint in this light. "You couldn't even give me that?"

Beverly walked off, shaking her head in disgust. Gaby watched her leave, still in shock. The Beverly she knew was vain and thoughtless, to be sure, but not cutthroat. She had even helped Gaby with the delicate matter of her splinter. This Beverly would never do that. She was a manipulative opportunist, groveling at the feet of a sadistic tyrant. Gaby didn't know — or want to know — this version. She had never felt more isolated in her life.

Gaby thought back to happier times with Lamar and Coop. She knew now that she had chosen wrong this morning, but had no idea what to do about it. She was so overwrought with guilt and fear that she didn't even notice Wade fumbling in the dirt, trying to claim a pointy rock on the edge of the campsite. He had rolled over on his side and was trying to pick it up with his hands still tied behind his back. Just as Gaby turned to carry him back to the wigwam, Wade's right hand snagged the stone, concealing it in his palm.

Now all he needed to do was wait for the right opportunity to present itself.

* * * Three Hours Until Sundown * * *

"You want to do *what*?" Coop fairly shrieked.

"I'm going back," Lamar repeated evenly as the pair stood on the edge of the hill overlooking the bunkers. It was now late afternoon, and the wind was picking up, sending them tantalizing scents from the fast-growing field just beyond the bunker.

"In the name of God, why?" Coop asked, stupefied.

"For the others."

Coop's face contorted as he tried to process this.

"They cast you out! You don't owe them anything."

Lamar smiled stoically, making it clear his mind was already made up.

"John was right about this place," he said. "It changes people. It's turned Ken into something he's not. And I don't think the others are far behind."

"What are you talking about?" Coop protested. "Ken was always a prick! And a bully."

"But not a sadist," Lamar pointed out. "You saw it last night and again this morning. His threat before we left wasn't empty. He genuinely wanted to kill me."

Coop tugged at his hair in frustration.

"That's all the more reason to stay away!"

"I think it's also magnified Beverly's worst tendencies, and now Gaby's starting to change," Lamar continued. "Do you think she would have just taken the word of those two before now?"

Coop could see he was getting nowhere and opted to change tactics.

"If that's true, then why haven't we changed?" he challenged.

"I think we have," Lamar responded. "Not so long ago the thought of speaking to a group or taking charge would have rendered me catatonic. And you stopped hiding behind the façade of a happy-go-lucky New Ager days ago."

"I suppose," Coop conceded. "John did say the process was different for everyone. But that still doesn't explain why you want to go back there."

"Because real leaders don't abandon their team," Lamar responded without a trace of irony. "They lead by example."

Coop gaped at him in wide-eyed astonishment.

"This isn't a Gilbert and Sullivan play!" he ranted. "Ken will kill you!"

Lamar flashed him a small smile.

"You're the one who told me to have faith in myself, remember?"

"There's a world of difference between faith and fool-hardy," Coop countered sternly. "And you aren't responsible for their terrible choices. None of this is on you."

Lamar simply shrugged.

"Maybe not, but if I'm going to be the leader you think I am, I have a duty to the others. I have to protect them ... even if it means protecting them from themselves."

Coop rolled his eyes skyward as though he were pleading for heavenly patience.

"Look, let's hunker down here tonight, leave at dawn, and then report the others missing to the first cops we see," Coop said pleadingly. "This is a job for the pros."

Lamar shook his head sadly.

"This is crazy!" Coop lamented. "We've got the map! We can follow it right out of this forest. Don't throw it all away now."

"I'm not asking you to come along," Lamar replied quietly.

"Good, because I won't!" Coop responded with a huff, crossing his arms defiantly. "I followed you before because I trusted your judgment. But this ... this is crazy talk!"

Lamar gave him a pained expression and extended his hand.

"Then I guess this is farewell."

"Don't do this," Coop implored him.

Lamar kept his hand out, waiting for Coop to take it. Coop could see the determination in Lamar's face, and after several long seconds, relented.

They shook hands as Coop gave him a bittersweet smile.

"If you're really going to go through with this, then let's leave it at 'so long,'" Coop suggested. "Farewell is too final."

Lamar smiled warmly at him as they shook.

"So long, then."

Coop tugged on Lamar's arm and pulled him in for a hug. Lamar reciprocated, and the two held each other, neither man wanting to break the connection, as they both knew this was likely the end.

"You really have no doubts?" Coop asked the younger man as he clasped him tightly, trying not to tear up.

"I have a metric fuckton of them," Lamar replied. "But it's what I need to do."

Lamar finally broke the hug and clapped Coop on the shoulder.

"Take care."

Coop swallowed hard and nodded, afraid that his voice would crack from emotion if he spoke.

Lamar started down the hill leading to the field. Midway down, he stopped and turned back.

"I'll be walking the shoreline up to the floodplain if you change your mind," he called out.

Coop waved in response.

"Good luck," he said quietly, his voice quavering as a single tear rolled down his cheek. "You're going to need it."

* * * One Hour Until Sundown * * *

Gaby sat on a small knoll overlooking the floodplain, watching as the harsh light of the fading sun bathed the land below in a fiery orange glow. It made the stunning growth there appear all the more miraculous.

The sight was a visual feast, but Gaby had no appetite for beauty. She knew what was happening in the wigwam right now. Almost on cue, she heard another muffled scream of agony. Ken had been torturing Wade for the past 40 minutes; she'd come out here seeking solace, but no matter how far she went, Wade's screams followed.

She clenched and unclenched her fists reflexively each time the cry sounded, feeling smaller and more impotent as Wade's screams turned more desperate. Because of her interference during the last interrogation session, Ken had locked her out of the wigwam to prevent another occurrence.

So here she sat, waiting for the end to come, trying not to think about what was happening in the teepee. Mostly she thought about Lamar and Coop. Wondering where they were, what they were doing; recalling how she had helped drive them away. This wasn't how things were supposed to be, and she realized with a burgeoning sense of regret that she was partly to blame. But the worst part was knowing that while she couldn't accept the status quo, she was also powerless to change it.

Another scream of pain echoed in her ears.

As she wallowed in guilt and self-loathing, Gaby noticed

Beverly sidling up to a desiccated maple tree some 30 yards to the northwest. Beverly's back was turned but she was instantly recognizable from her white jacket, frosted hair and constant shivering. Gaby noticed that she was favoring her left leg as she walked. Evidently, the black mark had worked its way down to her foot.

Beverly stopped at the center of the tree and leaned forward to peek into the large hollow in its center, no doubt hoping to find dry wood on the interior suitable for burning. Only she hadn't brought the hand ax with her.

"Your forgot the hatchet," Gaby called out as Beverly was reaching into the hollow. Beverly started, pulling her hand back like it had touched a hot stove. She looked around anxiously until she spotted Gaby on the knoll.

"What? I don't understand," Beverly said uncomprehendingly. Her facial muscles twitched nervously as the words tumbled out of her mouth.

"If you're looking for dry wood, you need the hatchet."

"Ah!" Beverly replied, finally understanding. "Given the hour, I think that ship has sailed."

She slowly climbed the knoll, struggling to find her footing before joining Gaby at the top.

"How's the jaw?" Beverly asked as she sat beside her.

In response, Gaby touched it lightly with her finger before grimacing in pain. Ken had done a real number on her jaw, and it was already beginning to swell. Just another bruise on a body that too many men had abused over the years.

"Still aches," Gaby replied glumly.

Beverly leaned in to examine the growing bruise with her

good hand. Gaby jerked away from her touch, afraid. Seeing Gaby's reaction, Beverly quickly retracted her hand.

"I keep forgetting," she said apologetically. "It's strange to think of myself as some kind of leper."

Gaby grimaced at the description but said nothing.

"I know you think Ken's a monster," Beverly said quietly, shivering as they watched the sunset together. "And maybe he is one. But he's doing this to save us."

Gaby sniffed as Wade gave another cry of agony in the distance.

"He doesn't give a damn about either one of us," Gaby retorted. "The only one he's trying to save is himself."

Beverly turned to face her.

"If that's what it takes to get us out of here, do the reasons really matter?" she asked coaxingly.

"They used to," Gaby said, blinking back tears of regret. "We weren't so ... ruthless before."

"Ken is in charge now," Beverly said firmly. "You need to come to terms with that."

Gaby lowered her eyes and traced a finger in the dirt.

"And what if I can't?"

In the distance, they could hear Wade screaming again.

"Then you know what happens."

Beverly doubled over as another coughing fit consumed her. She covered her mouth with a monogrammed handkerchief, which came away bloody. The blood shone dark red, almost black, under the fading sun's stark rays.

"Gaby, I know we've had our differences, but there was a time not so long ago that I thought of us as friends," Beverly said, wiping blood from the corner of her mouth.

Gaby lowered her gaze and allowed herself a small smile, recalling Beverly's assistance on the second day.

"So did I," she said quietly.

"Then one friend to another, you and Ken need to bury the hatchet, so to speak. At this rate, I won't be around to keep the peace for much longer."

The smile faded from Gaby's face, and her eyes unfocused as she reflected on something that had been troubling her for a while now.

"Hatchet?" she said to herself, recalling the start of the conversation.

"Gaby?" Beverly asked tentatively, watching her zone out but not understanding why.

"When I asked about the hatchet for cutting wood, you said that ship had already sailed," Gaby said softly, still working things out as she spoke. "Meaning, you didn't go to that tree for wood. What were you looking for?"

Beverly grinned nervously.

"Oh, this and that. Just exploring, really," she said.

Gaby's eyes narrowed in suspicion as she studied Beverly's reaction. She leapt to her feet and started down the knoll.

"Wait!" Beverly called out. "Where are you going?"

"Exploring," Gaby said over her shoulder as she made a beeline for the tree.

"But ... but I've already checked that one!" Beverly shouted frantically as she struggled to stand up with only one good arm and an increasingly useless left leg. "There's nothing to see, honest!"

Beverly's denials only fueled Gaby's suspicions.

"Then you wouldn't mind if I took a little peek myself."

"You don't want to do that!" Beverly cried out as she slid down the knoll's muddy edges. "Please believe me!"

Gaby reached the tree and stood on her toes to lean over and peer inside the tree's two-foot-wide hollow. She caught a glint of something metallic near the base and reached for it.

"Stop this foolishness at once!" Beverly demanded as she raced over.

Gaby's hand came up holding a round metal canister. She turned it over and saw that it was a can of beef barley soup, the same brand John had brought with them. And her fingers had brushed up against at least two other cans down there.

"I ... I found them by the tree," Beverly lied, shaking like a leaf. "Lamar must have dropped them when he was stealing all our food."

Gaby covered her mouth with her hand, her eyes wide with shock and horror as she tried to process her discovery. The can slipped from her numb fingers and fell to the ground.

"Lamar was right!" Gaby exclaimed, struggling to speak as she registered the depth of Beverly's betrayal. "He said you two were conspiring against him. I ... I didn't believe him; couldn't believe him. It was too absurd. But it was all true."

Gaby suddenly rounded on Beverly, furious.

"That whole thing with the missing cans, your story about Lamar sneaking food, was all that a charade?" she demanded, struggling to believe it herself. "Why? Just to get rid of him?"

Beverly looked away, quivering.

"Answer me!" Gaby shouted.

"Because there were too many people and not enough food," Ken said from behind, startling them both. He emerged from a withered thicket 15 feet away. Wade's blood dripped from his clenched fists.

"You abandoned Lamar and Coop to die in the wilderness just so you could stuff your face?" Gaby asked, indignant.

"*We* threw out Lamar because he was in the way. Count Fagula left of his own accord," Ken corrected her as he approached. "And if they hadn't gone, we'd all be starving now."

"What about Lamar stealing the water and my bra yesterday? Was that a lie, too?" Gaby pressed.

Ken smirked in response.

"And that thing with the directions? You fooled him into walking us in a giant circle?"

"I can't take full credit for that one," Ken admitted with a chuckle. "Sure, I told him that east was north for solar navigation, but I only expected him to get us lost. It never occurred to me that little shit would do it so many times we'd wind up back where we started. That was just icing on the cake."

"So ... when he got us lost, you could swoop in and save the day," Gaby said, a look of comprehension slowly crossing her countenance. "This was never about food. You wanted control of the group."

"And now ... I have it," Ken sneered.

"The hell you do," Gaby said defiantly.

"Gaby, it doesn't have to be this way," Beverly pleaded.

"You both tricked us, stole from the group, lied to banish two people and now you've escalated to torture," Gaby said, ticking off their crimes one by one. "Yeah, it does."

"Okay, playtime is over," Ken said menacingly as he strode forward. "Save your pity party for after you get the fire going."

"Fuck you."

Ken cracked his knuckles and leaned in, invading her personal space, but Gaby wouldn't be cowed so easily. She held her ground, watching as his eyes flickered with rage, knowing it wouldn't be long before guttural Ken made his appearance.

"It wasn't a suggestion," Ken hissed, his voice low and intimidating. "Unless you want to end up like Wade, get your ass in gear ... now!"

Gaby didn't bat an eye.

"Do ... your ... worst," she challenged.

A conflagration erupted in Ken's eyes, projecting liquid hatred as he raised Gaby up by the lapels and threw her to the ground like a rag doll. She landed flat on her back in a drying mud puddle, which absorbed some of the impact, but still left her breathless.

Gaby raised her head fuzzily and saw guttural Ken pull out the penknife and wave it in front of her, its blade glinting ominously in the dimming light. Her eyes went wide in fright, and she tried scooting backward in the mud.

"I should have done this days ago," he intoned as he approached, savoring the fear in Gaby's eyes.

Just as he was about to launch himself at her, Beverly jumped between them.

"Stop it!" she cried, waving her blackened left arm in the air to ward guttural Ken away.

He stopped in his tracks, confused and repulsed by the necrotic limb dangling inches from his face.

"Out of the way, you old bitch!" he bellowed.

In spite of his hollering, Gaby noticed that he made no move against the older woman. Even in this state, he was still afraid of being infected.

"We don't have time for this!" she shouted back at him. "Can't you hear them?"

Gaby listened intently. In the distance, she heard the faint sound of thousands of voices chirping in unison. The iku were awake.

The murderous rage in Ken's eyes slowly cooled. He looked from Gaby to the setting sun and back again, seemingly unable to choose between ending her life or safeguarding his own.

"If you want to live, then you need to make a fire ... now," Beverly insisted, trying to block Ken's view of Gaby to make the choice easier.

Ken seethed, his body shaking and his lower lip trembling with rage. He balled up his left fist and punched the nearest tree hard enough to break his knuckles. If he felt any pain, his face didn't betray it. Ken spat at Gaby's feet and walked away without a word.

Beverly hurriedly gathered the remaining cans from the maple tree's hollow and then turned to face Gaby, tears in her eyes.

"I begged you not to look in there," she said, shivering. "I was trying to protect you."

"I know," Gaby said as she slowly picked herself up. "But all you did was delay the inevitable. I was never going to trust Ken, and he was never going to accept anything other than total fealty. This would have happened sooner or later."

"Move it, Beverly!" Ken bellowed in the distance. "Unless you'd prefer to die out here with her!"

"I'm sorry, Gaby. I tried my best," Beverly apologized as she turned and hurried back to the campsite, eventually disappearing in the lengthening shadows.

Gaby wiped the mud from her raven locks and tried to steady her nerves as she waited for the end to come. She watched as the horizon consumed the sun, bit by bit. Only a narrow crescent of light remained as the shadows deepened with each passing minute.

She closed her eyes and took a deep breath, trying to calm her mind. Every instinct she possessed screamed at Gaby to run, but she knew it was futile. The iku were too fast and numerous to escape. She even started to rationalize this as one final act of defiance. She had run from her parents and their creepy traditions after college. She ran from her friends when they pressured her to leave her abusive boyfriend. And she'd come here for the express purpose of running from him. No more running, Gaby told herself, wiping away a tear. She just prayed that the iku would make her death quick.

The chirping was getting louder as the shadows slowly encroached. Gaby was thinking of all the things she would never get to do when a flash of light in the distance caught her eye. It projected upward, and reminded her of the mysterious pillar of light she'd seen on the top of the southern ridge two nights ago, right before the iku arrived. But while the original one was solid white and shot 40 feet up in the air, this one produced a yellowish light and was far weaker, diffusing after about 15 feet. Maybe the light and the iku were connected somehow. The light suddenly shifted and was now pointing parallel to the ground, flickering as it swayed to and fro. It took Gaby several seconds to realize it was a flashlight.

"Hello?" she called out uncertainly. The light paused and turned in her general direction.

"Hey! Hey, over here!" Gaby shouted, waving her arms and bouncing up and down to draw attention to herself. She could hear footfalls as the light moved closer. When the flashlight was 15 feet away, the footfalls stopped and the beam trained directly on her face.

"Gaby?" came a voice behind the flashlight. Gaby cocked an eyebrow. The voice sounded almost like …

The beam of light suddenly spun the opposite direction as her rescuer trained the light on his own face. It was Lamar, looking sweaty and exhausted. He was carrying the flashlight in his right hand and a spear in the other.

"Lamar?" she called out, uncertain whether to trust her own eyes. He nodded and smiled. "Lamar!" Gaby exclaimed.

He offered up his fist for a bump, remembering all too well Gaby's phobia about others touching her. But she was so overjoyed to see a friendly face again that she swept his hand aside and pulled him in close for a hug. It felt strange — alien, somehow — and yet comforting at the same time, even as her nostrils got their first good whiff of Lamar's rank body odor.

"It's me," Lamar said stiffly, unprepared for her outsized reaction. He cautiously put a sweaty hand on her back as she held him.

Gaby heard footfalls behind them.

"And me!" Coop said as he emerged from the shadows, resting his spear on his shoulder.

"Coop, too?" Gaby exclaimed, tears of happiness rolling down her cheeks as she hurriedly wrapped her free arm around him. She clutched them both fiercely, basking in the warmth of their embrace and giving silent thanks for this unexpected reunion.

"I'm so sorry about this morning," she said after a few moments. "You two were right about Ken and Beverly. I … I should have trusted …"

Gaby stopped midsentence and broke the group hug, her face a mask of confusion.

"Wait, why did you two come back? Especially now," she asked, motioning to the setting sun.

"Lamar thinks he can fix everything … somehow," Coop explained, his tone betraying lingering doubts. "I wanted to cut and run. And for about 15 minutes, I did. But he's one persuasive SOB, so here I am," he added with an uncertain grin.

Gaby began to wonder who exactly was rescuing who here.

"Ken and Beverly have turned against us and won't open the teepee door for anybody. You have a plan for fixing that?"

"Nope," Lamar admitted with a casualness that confounded Gaby. "But we'll figure something out."

"After all," Coop said, "we're the Three Mouseketeers."

He raised his arm skyward as though he were holding an

invisible sword.

"All for mice ..." he began.

Lamar raised his arm as well. Both looked to Gaby, waiting for her to join in.

"And mice ... for all?" Gaby finished doubtfully, raising her arm reluctantly after several seconds. Their joyous reunion was turning more farcical by the moment.

The sound of the iku drawing closer provided a curt reminder of the trio's present predicament.

"Uhm, maybe we should catch up later," Lamar said, drawing fervent nods from the others.

The group sprinted back to the campsite. The sun had already slipped behind the western skyline, and the heavy cloud cover overhead obscured the moon, making their flashlight the only light source available as they navigated the desiccated landscape. It flickered worryingly as it bounced in Lamar's hand.

They broke through the tree line and bolted into the campsite. Lamar and Coop ran around the central firepit while Gaby cleared it in a single leap. The iku sounded like they were right behind them. As they rounded the fence line, Coop accidentally clipped the fence with his spear tip, causing the fragile perimeter wall to shudder. They finally reached the door to the wigwam and tried it. As Gaby had predicted, it was already barred. Inside, they could hear tiny grunts of exertion, likely Ken trying to operate the bow drill.

Gaby pounded on the door.

"Open up!" she shouted.

The noise inside stopped.

"You made your choice," guttural Ken retorted from the other side of the door, which muffled his voice but not the sadistic glee in it.

Lamar sidled up to the door and leaned against it.

"You made the choice for her; kinda like you did for me," he called out.

Everything inside the wigwam went quiet for five agonizingly long seconds.

"Lamar?" guttural Ken responded in disbelief. "What the hell are you doing back here?"

Lamar opened his mouth to reply when Coop tapped him on the shoulder, nodding behind them. He spun the flashlight around and saw the ikus' vanguard were starting to spread along the perimeter of the campsite.

"We found a map," Lamar finally answered, raising his voice to be heard over the ikus' cries. "A map showing the way out."

"Bullshit!" guttural Ken spat from the other side of the door.

"What are you doing?" Gaby whispered fiercely at Lamar. "He won't fall for a cheap stunt like that!"

In answer, Lamar motioned to Coop, who hurriedly fished the folded-up map from his robes and handed it over. Gaby's eyes went wide with surprise as Lamar took the map and spread it out against the wigwam's exterior. Clearly they had spent their day more productively than she had imagined.

"Topographical Map for Quehanna Staging Area: Grid Reference System CW-15," Lamar shouted through the closed door, reading from the map legend in the corner. "Trademark: Defense Supply Management Agency, 1956. Now does that sound like something I just made up?"

Dead silence from inside the wigwam. Lamar strained to hear anything apart from the ikus' frantic cries, which were now coming from all directions.

"What if we kick in the door?" Coop asked.

"It opens outward," Gaby reminded him. "And if we busted it down, there wouldn't be anything to stop the iku from coming in."

Coop glanced nervously over his shoulder again. The first of the iku had entered the campground and were now congregating on the other side of the central firepit.

"Tell us where this supposed escape route is," guttural Ken shouted through the door.

"Twenty miles away," Lamar replied evenly. "But unless you open up, you'll never know which direction."

No response.

Gaby pressed her ear against the door. She could hear Ken and Beverly arguing, but couldn't make out what they were saying over the ikus' din. She looked up and didn't see any smoke issuing from the venting hole.

"How's the fire-making going?" she goaded. "Must be hard to do in the dark. Fortunately for you, we have a light source."

Lamar waved the flashlight in front of the wigwam, hoping enough light would seep in through the cracks in the door to prove their point. Coop snatched the light from his hand and aimed it at the fence line, where the iku were starting to congregate.

"You've got less than a minute to decide before the iku have us for dinner!" Gaby shouted through the door.

Coop swept the flashlight in a wide arc across the fence line. Everywhere his beam stopped, they spied new iku as reinforcements swarmed the perimeter, some trying to scale the fence while others tried to sneak through the entrance. A few tried to squeeze through cracks between the boards.

After several agonizing seconds of this, they heard the ties on the door being loosened. It opened outward, and guttural Ken's face appeared in the center, hateful and suspicious. He pointed the tip of the pocket knife through the door to underline his distrust.

"Don't try anything funny," he warned, waving the blade in front of them. "If either of you do, I'll kill you both."

Lamar moved the knife to the side and rushed in, followed quickly by Gaby. Guttural Ken was about to shut the door again when Coop forced his way in, catching him off guard.

"Him too, huh? Guess we can't get rid of any of you fuckers," he growled as he tied the door shut once more and the group hunkered down for the night.

* * * Twelve Hours Until Sunrise * * *

The teepee was engulfed in shadows. Coop lowered his spear and trained the flashlight on the central firepit, where it found Beverly, surrounded by dozens of logs. She was coughing, shaking like a leaf and feebly trying to operate the bow drill with her one good hand. Gaby made a beeline for the bow drill.

"Let me try," she said, taking the equipment from a grateful Beverly.

Coop handed the flashlight off to Lamar, who focused the light back on the entrance, where guttural Ken had finished tying off the upper and lower door enclosures. Guttural Ken shaded his eyes and hissed his disapproval. He looked almost primordial now, and reminded them of Wade back when the change was just starting to take hold.

"You little shits just couldn't keep away, could you?" guttural Ken groused as he bent down to pick up his spear, which he'd left beside the entrance. "I warned you what would happen if you returned."

Coop aimed his spear tip at Ken's midsection and held it at the ready, braced against his hip.

"You have to be able to make good on your threat, first," he warned.

Guttural Ken sneered with malice and stepped forward.

Before Coop could react, Lamar stood in front of him and shined the flashlight under his face for dramatic effect to get everyone's attention.

"No one is killing anyone!" he insisted and hastily motioned for Coop to lower his spear tip, which he did reluctantly. "We're not here for …"

A sound from the other side of the room distracted Lamar. He spun around, and the flashlight's beam found Wade on the opposite end of the teepee, sitting in the dirt with his hands tied behind his back and a gag in his mouth. He sported a nasty shiner and several fresh cuts to his forehead. Several feet away from him was the drinking water pail, which sloshed water over its sides as Wade bounced excitedly up and down.

"Whet whem whin!" Wade babbled through the gag.

"Wade's alive?" Lamar and Coop exclaimed simultaneously.

"No thanks to these two," Gaby intoned from the central firepit as she worked the bow drill feverishly back and forth.

"Is he still ...?"

"Nuttier than a box of Goobers? Yeah," guttural Ken said. He motioned for Beverly to move the water pail somewhere away from Wade. If given half the chance, that fruitcake would probably knock the water into the firepit, and then they'd all be fucked.

Beverly dragged the pail closer to the entrance, albeit with some difficulty. Coop observed that she was doing everything with her right hand and now walked with a pronounced limp.

Lamar studied Wade in the light. "He looks more excitable than psychotic. Has he said anything?"

"He never shuts up about how 'the visitors' saved him, and redeemed his sins, yada yada," guttural Ken replied dismissively. "He's clearly off his meds."

"I'm not so sure," Lamar said thoughtfully, approaching Wade. "Let me talk to ..."

Guttural Ken held out his spear to bar Lamar's passage.

"He's my prisoner."

The menace in his voice was palpable.

"Fine, you can take all the credit you want. If I could just talk to him ..."

Lamar started forward again until Ken turned the spear inward so its sharpened tip poked the young man in the ribs.

"The gag stays in," guttural Ken insisted. "Now, tell us about the map."

"It's a topo from the Air Force base. It's old, but I doubt the geography around here has changed much in the last 60 years," Lamar said, holding up the folded map as proof. "Coop and I found a way out. We can lead everyone out at first light."

"Let me see it," guttural Ken said, reaching for the map.

Coop batted the hand away, eliciting a snarl from guttural Ken.

"Your prisoner, our map," Coop said firmly. "It stays with us."

Lamar nodded and tucked the map back into his jacket.

Guttural Ken shook with fury at Coop's slight. He opened his mouth to threaten them again, but Gaby spoke first.

"Finish your pissing match later!" she insisted through gritted teeth as she sawed the bow drill in a furious side-to-side motion. "I need light to see what I'm doing."

Lamar and Coop backed cautiously away from guttural Ken before turning the light on Gaby.

Outside, they could hear iku skittering along the wigwam's perimeter on all sides. On the periphery of the flashlight's cone of radiance, they could see the lower sections of the teepee bulging inward as the iku tried to force their way in. Lamar pulled the beam away from Gaby every few seconds to focus on strategic areas, like the door and the venting hole above.

Gaby's efforts were starting to bear fruit, with tiny plumes of smoke rising from the fireboard, when the flashlight started to dim. Lamar smacked the battery case as always, but instead of the bulb roaring back to life, it simply went dead this time.

"Ohhh, shit," Lamar intoned as he flipped the switch on and off several times while repeatedly slapping the flashlight. Nothing worked. The triumphant sound of chirping filled the night sky. The rustling along the exterior of the teepee intensified as the creatures struggled to breach it.

In the darkness, Lamar noticed the smoke getting thicker as Gaby continued working, undaunted. He coughed and took a step back. A tiny pinprick of light sprung forth as an ember emerged at the base of the fireboard. Gaby gently upended the fireboard, and the glowing ember disappeared into a pile of kindling at its base. After a few seconds the ember reappeared, larger this time, as it fed on the combustible material. A tiny wisp of flame sprung from the pile, illuminating Gaby's face as she gently blew on the pile.

"You've gotten good with that." Lamar said, impressed.

The fire spread and gradually illuminated the room in a reddish glow. Guttural Ken's snarling visage appeared even more sinister by its light. The light repelled the looming shadows as it grew in intensity, feeding off the wood beneath the kindling. The pressure on the bugling canvas walls receded as the light continued to spread. Lamar noticed shapes wriggling in the far corners of the wigwam, hiding in the deepest shadows where the light couldn't reach. They were sharing the room with the iku once again, but unlike last night, they lacked a working flashlight to drive them out.

Coop took a deep breath and sat on one of the dozens of logs set in a wide circle around the firepit. He made a face as he sat on it, stood up again and ran his finger along the edge.

"It's damp," he complained.

"Most of the wood is," Gaby explained. "We thought we'd try drying these pieces by placing them near the fire.

"How much dry wood do we have?" Lamar asked.

Gaby pointed to a small pile off to the side, made up of six logs and dozens of branches and hacked pieces of bark.

"That doesn't look like much," he said, worried. "How long can we hold out?"

"It's 'we' now, is it?" guttural Ken sneered. "If we're careful, we could last nine hours. Ten, tops."

Lamar did a quick calculation and inhaled sharply.

"That only gets us to 5 a.m." he said, his brow furrowing in concern. "That's at least two hours we have to make up."

"You wanna chop some more wood? Have at it," guttural Ken said mockingly as he pointed toward the entrance. "Your imminent death is thataway."

* * * Eight Hours Until Sunrise * * *

After four hours, the two opposing factions had settled into a familiar, if still uneasy, rhythm.

Gaby kept the fire fed from her perch on one of the damp logs. She fondled the hatchet resting on her lap. To her right, Lamar sat stock-still as he stared impassively across the flames at guttural Ken, watching carefully for any further signs of aggression. His spear rested on his shoulder, ready to be lowered defensively at a moment's notice. Beside him, Coop alternated between pacing nervously in a tight loop like he was on patrol and trying to initiate a conversation with people who were in no mood talk.

On the other side of the fire, Ken and Beverly kept their eyes glued to the trio. Beverly looked sick, huddling under a blanket for warmth even as beads of sweat rolled down her face. Lamar noticed that the black mark had spread to her neck, and it appeared to be affecting her respirations, which were shallow and wheezy. Beside her, guttural Ken seethed with barely contained fury, just waiting for anything to set him off. Most people would grow fatigued after 30 minutes of constant rage, but not him. His hate seemed boundless, as though it were feeding off itself. That impression was heightened by the red glow of the firelight, which painted everything in a hellish light that made him look quite diabolical.

Wade seemed oblivious to the tension in the air, bouncing giddily up and down and straining against his bonds as he sought to welcome "the visitors."

Gaby eyed their rapidly depleting fuel pile. The iku were unusually aggressive tonight, slithering in frightening numbers right up to the edge of the light, as if its hold on them were waning. To keep the creatures at bay, they had been forced to keep the fire burning hotter and higher than on previous nights, and it was taking a terrible toll on their wood supply. It wasn't even 11:00 p.m. yet, and they'd already managed to burn through half their supply. At this rate, they'd be out of fuel by 4 a.m.

Lamar leaned in toward Gaby, while still keeping his eyes fixated on guttural Ken.

"How long have they been like this?" he whispered, nodding toward guttural Ken, whose left eye twitched disturbingly as he glowered at Lamar, and Beverly, whose quivering was so pronounced that the spear in her hand vibrated in time with the shivers.

"Beverly's been like that most of the day," Gaby whispered back. "Ken's been getting progressively worse, but I've never seen him this bad before."

"We can hear you, you know. Nothing's wrong with us," Beverly called out from across the fire before doubling over in another coughing fit.

Guttural Ken stood up, clenching his spear with such primordial fury it was a wonder the thing didn't snap in two. He was tired of waiting for something to set him off. Time to take the initiative.

"Enough fucking around!" he spat. "What did you really come back for? I want answers, and they better be good."

"We're not here for revenge," Lamar insisted calmly.

"Not for a lack of encouragement on my part," Coop chimed in, giving guttural Ken the nastiest look he could manage.

"I don't believe you," guttural Ken said, his voice dropping low with suspicion.

"That's your problem," Gaby retorted.

Guttural Ken lowered his spear until it was level with Gaby's head.

"I'm making it your problem," he threatened. Beside him, Beverly rose to her feet with difficulty and held her spear one handed.

Coop and Gaby stood up in unison, both of them itching for a fight.

"No, not like this!" Lamar shouted, throwing his spear down to the ground with such a clatter that it drew everyone's attention. "Gaby, Coop, stand down!" he glared at both of them until they reluctantly lowered their weapons.

"You want to know why we came back?" Lamar said to

guttural Ken. "It was to keep the rest of you from killing each other."

Guttural Ken burst out in condescending laughter.

"Wow, way to make him see the error of his ways, Lamar," Coop deadpanned, clearly uncomfortable with his pacifist approach.

"Self-defense is a last resort," Lamar insisted. "No matter how it looks, that's not the Ken we know. He's been changed."

"You can't hamstring us like that, Lamar," Gaby insisted, stealing an annoyed glance at him. "This is serious."

"As am I," Lamar answered sternly. "Everyone here is going to make it out alive. And once we're back home, those three ..." Lamar paused dramatically as his finger swept across guttural Ken, Beverly and Wade. "...will answer for their crimes."

Guttural Ken barked out in savage laughter again as Coop rounded on Lamar.

"We can't beat them by holding hands and singing *Kumbaya*!" he exclaimed, his eyes nearly popping out of their sockets.

"We don't have to beat them," Lamar insisted with an uncharacteristically self-assured grin. "They're going to surrender."

Gaby and Coop both looked at him like he was nuts.

"Really?" guttural Ken sneered, humoring Lamar for the moment. "And why would I do that, Martin Luther Ding-Dong? All I need is one good spear thrust and both you and your plan wind up in a ditch."

Instead of responding to guttural Ken, Lamar turned to

Coop.

"You remember the route to Fawke's Mill?" he asked.

"I think so," Coop replied, confused by the question.

"Good," Lamar responded as he fished the map out of his pocket and threw it on the fire. The ancient map went up like a Roman candle, briefly sending the flames two feet into the air and repelling the iku lurking in the shadows nearby.

"How about now?" Lamar challenged guttural Ken through the curtain of flames. "We're offering you a chance to surrender peacefully. We're the only ones that know the way out, and there's three of us. You can't take all of us down, and you can't escape without us. Accept my terms, and I give you my word no harm will come to you."

Guttural Ken spat into the fire in response. He quivered with rage, biting his lower lip so hard that it drew blood.

"You'll die for that," he promised Lamar.

Beverly, who was standing beside him and looked truly alarmed by the escalation of hostilities, leaned in and whispered in his ear.

"Maybe we should listen to him," she suggested timidly.

"Shut the fuck up, you stupid, wrinkly old bitch!" guttural Ken bellowed as she slinked away with her head bowed. "Do what I tell you, or you'll be the first to die!"

Off to the side, Wade began craning his neck at odd angles, trying to slip his gag. After several tries, he had loosened it enough on one side to talk out of the corner of his mouth.

"Let them in! Let the visitors in! They can save your friend, like they saved me!" he ranted, motioning toward Ken. "Before the visitors freed me, I was like him: little more than an animal, filled with so much malice I thought my heart would explode! It led me to murder my wife in a fit of rage! I buried her out in the Chihuahuan Desert and spent days wandering the wastes in confusion, not caring if I lived or died as the sun tried to burn the sin from my body," he proselytized at full volume, only his sermon was going a mile a minute. "But the sun wasn't strong enough. My sister found me and sent me up here to hide from the authorities. The sun had done its damage, but the rage persisted. It turned into self-loathing and finally, a rejection of my basic humanity. But salvation came! The visitors did in the darkness what the sun's light could not! They'll cleanse you as they did me! All we have to do is let them in! They will save you from yourselves."

Everyone gawked at Wade, still trying to process his bizarre confession. His conviction was absolute, and despite his erratic behavior, it evoked images of Cotton Mather rather than Hannibal Lecter. Wade didn't seem dangerous anymore, just overexcited, like a hyperactive 8-year-old. It was hard to imagine this was the same person who had tried to kill them all not three days ago.

That appeared to be the final straw for guttural Ken.

"You want salvation, little man?" he bellowed, the fire dancing in his eyes as Wade continued to ramble. Guttural Ken pushed past Beverly, nearly knocking her over in the process, and strode toward Wade with his spear in hand. "I'll give you a taste of my brand of salvation!"

Guttural Ken reared back and drove his spear deep into his prisoner's right thigh. Wade's sermon abruptly cut off, replaced with a shriek of agony. Guttural Ken started twisting the handle to maximize Wade's pain, wrenching it with such force that the tip snapped off in Wade's leg.

"Where are your precious iku now, huh?" he hollered, shaking with sadistic delight as he watched Wade writhe in unimaginable pain. "No one's going to save you from me!"

"Holy shit!" Lamar exclaimed as he stood up in shock. Gaby and Coop looked to him, wondering whether they should intervene.

Trickles of blood appeared around the edges of the jagged hunk of wood protruding from Wade's leg. The trickle quickly became a steady stream and started pooling at Wade's feet as he thrashed about in agony.

"Aggghhh! I suffer any atonement for my sins!" Wade shrieked through the pain. "Heed me, oh visitors! I will show this lost soul the way! Ggghhhhaaahhh!"

Guttural Ken examined his spear. It was now a foot shorter, and the new tip — the point where it had fractured — was jagged and fearsome looking. He aimed it at Wade's face, stopping just a few inches short. Wade instantly fell silent, his eyes wide with fear.

"If I hear so much as another peep from you, this goes in your eye," guttural Ken warned. Wade nodded his understanding as he grimaced in unimaginable pain.

"That goes for the rest of you, too!" guttural Ken declared, pointing at Lamar, who stood some 15 feet away. "This is my house now! You'll do what I say when I say, or no one will ever find your bodies!"

With that declaration, he sauntered back over to his former spot, causing Beverly to scoot fearfully out of his way, and sat cross-legged on the ground with a look of immense satisfaction on his face.

Lamar and Coop rushed over to Wade's side, while Gaby stood guard, hatchet in hand. Lamar tried to hold Wade still while Coop examined the wound.

The broken shaft protruded several inches past Wade's thigh, and a torrent of blood was seeping out from the sides. While the shaft sealed off much of the wound, the skin had torn around it thanks to Ken's twisting and jerking motions. Most of the blood came from those peripheral injuries.

"This is bad!" Coop exclaimed, making certain to keep his voice down to avoid arousing guttural Ken's wrath.

"Can you stop the bleeding?" Lamar asked.

"Maybe," Coop said doubtfully as he studied the wound. "It doesn't look like he hit an artery. The real problem is the internal bleeding. We need to stop it, or he could lose the leg."

"You're just going to keep that wood in his leg?" Lamar asked.

"Since that's the only thing keeping him alive at the moment, yes," Coop responded sharply. "Now give me your belt."

"What?"

"I need something to cut the circulation. Give me your belt," Coop repeated urgently.

Lamar hastily unbuckled his belt, handing it over to Coop, who looped it loosely around Wade's thigh, about five inches above the wound. He nodded to Lamar, who put the gag back in Wade's mouth.

"Bite down on this," he advised.

Coop grabbed both ends of the makeshift tourniquet and pulled tight. The gag muffled Wade's tortured screams as tears coursed down his cheeks. Coop buckled it into place as Lamar gently patted Wade's forehead to let him know that the worst had passed.

Wade's gasps of pain gradually eased until his breathing pattern was nearly normal. After a few minutes, he resumed his bouncing motion, only slower and without the enthusiasm of before. His previously giddy expression had been replaced with a mask of concentrated agony as the up-and-down motion flexed his mutilated thigh, sending shrieking nerve impulses up his leg. He was like a child that insisted on playing in a bouncy castle lined with spikes.

"No sudden movements," Coop advised him as he stood up and wiped his bloody hands on the hem of his robes. "Try to keep your leg still."

Wade nodded, although his eyes were squeezed shut with pain, and stopped bouncing. As Lamar and Coop returned to their seats, Wade resumed the motion, only now he was only using his upper body, alternating between hunching forward and sitting fully erect. Lamar and Coop exchanged confused glances as they watched him resume this masochistic display.

What neither of them knew was that Wade's bouncing had nothing to do with enthusiasm and everything to do with freeing himself. He'd spent hours using the bouncing motion as leverage to saw through his plastic wrist bindings. Every time Wade rocked up and down, the sharp stone he'd found during his water torture session would cut deeper into his bindings. He was already halfway through them.

Soon he'd be free, and then he'd show everyone the true power of the visitors.

* * * Three Hours Until Sunrise * * *

As the fire petered down to smoldering embers and a few wisps of flame, Gaby tossed the final log into the firepit. She grabbed Lamar's spear and stoked the embers with its tip, sending sparks into the air and producing additional trickles of flame that lapped greedily at the new fuel. The sudden burst of flames sent the iku lurking on the edge of the firelight scurrying away.

"That's the last one," she said dejectedly. All eyes went to the log as the flames began to eat away at its edges, trying to mentally calculate how much longer it would keep them alive.

Beside her, Lamar was stripping away bark from one of the dozen rejects they'd been warming beside the fire all night. He ran his finger along the interior wood, hoping for good news.

"Any luck?" Gaby asked him.

His crestfallen expression said it all: still too damp to burn. There was only one log in the teepee that he hadn't ruled out, and he wasn't about to examine it because of its occupant. Guttural Ken sat astride the final log, his back arched and legs splayed out like he was lord of the manor, except his ferocious gaze and bloodied spear reminded them all that this lord was not benevolent.

"What about the flashlight?" Gaby asked.

Lamar knocked on the plastic exterior and flicked the switch several times. Nothing happened.

"Either the battery's dead or the bulb burned out," he answered glumly. "Either way, no light."

On the opposite side of the fire, Beverly quietly suffered. Her shivering had progressed to full-on tremors so bad she could no longer hold a spear, a fact she tried to conceal by wrapping herself in a blanket. As she stared into the fire, Gaby noticed a dark liquid oozing out of the corners of Beverly's bloodshot eyes. It was hard to tell because of the firelight, but it looked like her tear ducts were leaking blood.

About 10 feet away from her, opposite the entrance, Coop tended to Wade. His patient had lost a lot of blood, and every time he adjusted the tourniquet to restore circulation, Wade's thigh spurted more of the precious liquid into the dirt.

Even in the reddish glow of the firelight, Wade looked white as a sheet. But that didn't deter him as he pleaded through his gag for the group to "whet whem win," a phrase he repeated incessantly. He grimaced in pain every time he raised and lowered himself, yet he persisted, to the bewilderment of the others. And with each downward thrust, his concealed stone sliced a bit deeper into his plastic bindings.

Lamar checked his binary watch: 4:38 a.m. The wood supply had lasted longer than they'd expected, but it was never going to see them through the night. And they had two and a half hours left to go.

Gaby stoked the fire with the tip of Lamar's spear, gently at first, and then with increasing fervor, until Lamar pulled it back for fear she'd break the tip.

"I never should have picked this place!" she lamented. "If only I had told Bill I was going to visit my folks! Or a yoga retreat! Better yet, I shouldn't have told him anything and just run the minute his back was turned! Literally anything would be better than dying here senselessly!"

"Was Bill your ..." Lamar gently probed.

"Yeah, my abusive boyfriend," Gaby cut him off, placing venomous emphasis on "abusive." No point in being coy about it at the end. "I told him this was a two-week trip," she continued, her head bowed low in despair. "I figured by the time he came to look for me, I'd have a weeklong head start. Why am I so unlucky?"

"Don't give up hope," Lamar said, awkwardly putting his hand on her shoulder as she sobbed. Gaby tensed at his touch but did not pull away.

"You seem to make a habit of bad decisions," guttural Ken remarked with a twinkle of malice in his eye.

Gaby's tears dried almost instantly. The only thing that could break through her despair was rage, something guttural Ken excelled at stoking.

"That's what they'll carve on your tombstone," he continued. "'Here lies Green Card Gaby. She died as she lived: A colossal fuckup.'"

Gaby raised her head, eyes blazing with fury, eliciting a smirk from guttural Ken. She reached for the small hatchet beside her. Lamar snatched it away first, putting it safely out of reach.

"Don't!" he cautioned. "It's what he wants. Don't let him goad you."

"That's right, girlie," guttural Ken said with a barking laugh of condescension. "Listen to your master."

Gaby clenched her fists so tight her knuckles had turned white.

"Don't fall for it, Gaby," Lamar insisted. "He's trying to

provoke you into making a mistake. We have to work as a team. The only way he wins is if he isolates us and picks us off individually."

"Do you really think so little of me?" guttural Ken asked with a throaty snicker, making it abundantly clear that was precisely his goal.

"The fire's getting low," Coop noted.

"You could always throw your spear on it," guttural Ken suggested, his maniacal grin stretching wide.

Coop looked at him evenly.

"You first."

As the fire gradually abated, the shadows closed in, as did their unearthly inhabitants. Lamar walked around the fire-pit and began collecting all the sleeping bags.

"Blanket fort?" guttural Ken scoffed.

"Fuel," Lamar replied, throwing his Voltron sleeping bag on the fire first. Flames leapt from the embers as the fire consumed the dense cotton material. The sudden brightness drove the creatures back, but the stench was truly awful. It also emitted thick black smoke that made everyone's eyes water. Charred fragments of the bag's exterior were swept aloft by the fire's updraft, pirouetting through the air as they exited the venting hole.

"You're just delaying the inevitable," guttural Ken chortled as Lamar threw the second sleeping bag on the fire.

"He's right," Gaby conceded as she coughed and tried to wave the black smoke away from her face. "Daylight's another two hours off. Even if we burn everything, right down to the clothes we're wearing, it still won't buy us another hour, let alone two."

"I'm not giving up," Lamar insisted, throwing a third sleeping bag on the fire. "Coop, start collecting anything burnable. Spare clothes, shoes, luggage, anything."

Coop started rifling through his luggage while Lamar did the same in his rucksack. Before long, the two had amassed a sizeable pile of fuel sources. Gaby didn't participate, preferring to remain vigilante, holding the hatchet at the ready. She knew full well that Ken would strike if all three of them were busy gathering burnables, so she kept her attention laser-focused on him, not even taking her eyes off Ken when she slid her backpack toward Lamar.

Lamar unzipped it and dumped the contents onto the pile, tossing away a few unburnable items, like toothpaste and a razor. Beside him, Coop added a spare pair of sandals and two extra robes to the burn pile. He fished his wallet from his robes, and after removing the picture memorializing his first and only victim, tossed the wallet on the heap with a sigh.

"What steams me is we can't even write out our good-byes," he said as he stared at his photo of Johnny smiling. "No paper or pencil, and any message we write in the dirt will be obliterated by those creatures when the fire dies." After a moment of bittersweet reflection, Coop added the photo to the pile. "It'll be like we were never even here."

Gaby nodded glumly as she fingered the hatchet's dull blade.

Lamar, on the other hand, appeared more reflective.

"Hmm. I'm not so sure," he said, stroking his goatee.

"There's nobody you want to say goodbye to?" Gaby asked, disturbed by his apparent ambivalence.

Her question shook Lamar out of his reverie, eliciting a guilty smile.

"No, that's not what I meant," he hastily explained. "I'm just not convinced this is the end. Are we really sure those things are trying to kill us?"

Gaby and Coop both looked at him like he was nuts.

"They are," came a distant, wheezing voice from across the room. Beverly raised her shaking head, revealing a steady cascade of bloody tears leaking from her eyes. The black mark was midway up her neck, now. "Just one touch did this to me," she reminded him before doubling over again in pain.

The others fell silent, cowed by her sobering message of what awaited them all. Lamar added the last of Gaby's belongings to the fire. Coop looked around and saw they had collected everything on their half of the wigwam. Without even thinking about the risk, he crossed the invisible barrier separating the two warring factions, making for Ken's metal suitcase. Guttural Ken slammed his foot on the suitcase and scooted it beside him.

"Come and get it," he challenged with a knowing smirk as he gripped the shaft of his spear, the firelight reflecting in his wild eyes.

Coop took an uneasy step back to his side of the demarcation line.

"Coop, it's not worth it," Lamar advised as he and Gaby took several steps forward to protect Coop if needed.

"What's wrong with you?" Coop unloaded on guttural Ken. "This isn't just for our sake! Don't you want to live?"

Beverly removed the blanket from her shuddering frame

and offered it up to Coop in her trembling hands. A withering glare from guttural Ken was enough for her to silently retract the offer.

"You just keep throwing your clothes on the fire," guttural Ken responded mockingly. "I'll take care of things on this side."

Gaby and Coop were aghast at his cavalier attitude, but Lamar nodded understandingly, as though he was expecting this.

"He wants to use it as a bargaining chip," Lamar explained. "Once we're out on our side, he'll demand something for contributing; probably our weapons. And that's when he'll strike."

A sadistic smirk from guttural Ken all but confirmed his theory.

Gaby's fingers tightened around the hatchet's shaft.

"You miserable, manipulative son of a bitch!" she fumed. "Don't you give a damn about anybody but yourself?"

Instead of responding, guttural Ken tested the jagged, broken tip of his spear as he stared Gaby down.

"Easy, Gaby," Coop cautioned, seeing how heated she was becoming.

"I say we fight them for it," Gaby whispered fiercely. "Why wait until he has the upper hand?"

"No! We fight in self-defense only," Lamar reminded her as he threw some spare clothes on the fire. "We can't become like those two."

"Whet whem win!" Wade pleaded off to the side, feeding off the group's tension as he bounced up and down. He had sawed through the first loop of his double-wrapped plastic bindings and was partway through the next.

Instead of responding to the others, guttural Ken turned to Beverly, who was fixated on the argument.

"See, Beverly? Didn't I tell you that Gaby would slit our throats the first chance she got? Here's the proof!"

"Quit distorting things, you pedazo de mierda!" Gaby warned him.

Guttural Ken continued toying with her as though he hadn't heard.

"She tried to betray you this morning, you know," he said. "When you took off to get more wood, she suggested we throw your ass out!"

"Shut up, Ken!" Gaby warned.

"She wanted to feed you to the wolves ... or whatever else is out there," he cackled gutturally.

Beverly seemed genuinely wounded by this news and stared quizzically at Gaby.

"Gaby, is that true?" she asked, virtually pleading with her to deny it.

"He's lying!" Gaby insisted. "It was all his idea."

"But you went along with it?" Beverly asked, crestfallen as she shivered under the blanket.

"Of course she did!" guttural Ken laughed cruelly. "Why save someone who's on borrowed time, right?"

"Stop twisting things right now!" Gaby screamed, raising her hatchet to eye level and taking a step forward.

"Gaby, don't let him goad you!" Lamar implored her. Gaby jabbed her finger in the air right in front of Lamar's face and glared at him until he fell silent.

She turned back to guttural Ken, her eyes smoldering

with resentment, practically daring him to continue. He dared.

"What else would you expect of someone who lets her boyfriend beat her like a dog?" he continued. "You act tough, but a couple of knuckle sandwiches are all it takes to put you in your place!" He leaned forward with a smirk. "Beneath your spitfire façade, you're … just … another … doormat!"

"¡Muere, tu maldito monstruo!" Gaby shrieked, spittle flying from her lips as she raised the hatchet and charged at him.

Guttural Ken smirked wickedly. This was the moment he'd waited all night for. He aimed his spear at Gaby and then rocked back on his log perch, preparing a thrust that would drive it right through her throat. But in his haste, he reared back too far and lost his balance as the log teetered beneath him. He swung his arms wildly as he tried to keep from falling over, sending the spear airborne. Just as he'd regained his balance, guttural Ken found himself face to face with Gaby, who was pressing the hatchet's blade against his Adam's apple. His spear landed on the ground with a ringing clatter.

Guttural Ken swallowed hard and took two steps back, which was far as he could go without entering the shadows and risking the ikus' touch. Gaby and her blade followed. Guttural Ken stole a glance over his shoulder and saw shapes writing in the darkness mere inches from his head.

Lamar rushed up behind Gaby, with Coop a few steps behind.

"Don't do it!" he pleaded with her.

"He deserves it a thousand times over! You know he does!" Gaby snarled as she pressed the blade hard against guttural Ken's naked flesh. A thin trickle of blood rolled down his neck.

"Maybe, but that's not our decision to make," Lamar said quietly. "If we appoint ourselves as judge, jury and executioner, then how are we any different from him?"

Gaby shook with fury, her breath coming in bursts as she wrestled with dueling impulses. She'd never have a better opportunity. He was completely vulnerable. All she had to do was rear back and …

"Please, don't hurt me."

It was Ken. Not guttural Ken, full of malice and impish cruelty, but the old Ken. The sudden reversion was spooky. He looked confused and more than a little scared as his eyes fixated on the hatchet. More than any words of Lamar, the fear she saw in his eyes — fear of her — disturbed Gaby, tempering her bloodlust. Little by little, she regained control, suppressing the primal voice inside her head demanding retribution.

"Dammit!" Gaby muttered, pulling back and slowly lowering the hatchet.

Ken smiled gratefully at her.

"Thank you."

As she continued staring into his clear eyes, she began to think that at long last the crisis was over. She even allowed herself to hope that they might still survive this night when she caught a glint of mischief in his eyes. They quickly narrowed, and the corners of his mouth turned downward, transforming his empathetic smile into a rictus leer. She had just enough time to let loose an "Oh!" before a gut punch from guttural Ken doubled her over. Before she could recover, the hatchet was lying on the ground and guttural Ken had her by the throat.

Lamar and Coop charged forward, ready to fight for Gaby, but stopped short when Ken whirled around behind Gaby, using her as a human shield while she was still dazed. He wrapped his left arm around her throat to hold her in place.

"Let her go," Lamar demanded. "This is your last chance to make it out of here alive!"

Guttural Ken simply smirked.

"You two want a piece of me? You have to go through her!"

The duo lowered their spears to eye level and stepped closer, training them on guttural Ken's head and shoulders, which were still exposed because he was so much taller than his hostage. Seeing they weren't deterred, guttural Ken pulled the penknife from his pocket with his free hand and pressed its blade against Gaby's temple.

"How about now?" he challenged.

The pair exchanged nervous glances, neither of them certain how to proceed. Gaby trembled in guttural Ken's iron grip, struggling to breathe through his chokehold. The terror in her eyes only magnified the sense of powerlessness Lamar and Coop felt.

"Don't make me choose between your life and hers," Lamar said as he took a hesitant step forward. "You know who I'll choose."

"*Now* it's a party!" guttural Ken laughed wickedly as he drilled the blade into Gaby's temple.

"Ngghh!" she groaned as the cold steel poked her, desperate to pull her head away, but unable to do so because of his chokehold.

Lamar and Coop pressed forward, side by side, trying to push guttural Ken back into the shadows, which were now within six feet of the dying fire. However, he turned and started backpedaling around the circle, dragging his petrified victim along with him.

As the two sides slowly circled the fire, Wade continued bouncing up and down on the edge of the firelight, insisting that the group "whet whem win." He was three-quarters of the way though the final loop of his plastic shackles.

Guttural Ken stopped backpedaling when he reached the pile of burnables that Gaby, Coop and Lamar had amassed. He stole a glance at the monstrous shapes wriggling in the darkness and kicked the top half of the pile over, cackling sadistically as the burnables rolled into the inky shadows, where they couldn't be reclaimed.

"Take another step forward and the rest of the pile goes, too!" guttural Ken threatened.

Lamar cast a sideways glance at the fire. It was already getting dangerously low.

"Don't listen to … ackk!" Gaby's words were abruptly cut off as guttural Ken tightened his grip around her throat.

As Lamar and Coop racked their brains for a solution, a voice from the other side of the fire shouted at them.

"Enough!" Beverly shouted raspily, tossing her blanket on the smoldering coals and standing up as best she could with one lame arm and one nearly lame foot. The blanket ignited almost immediately, and a burst of light filled the room. The older woman grabbed the drinking bucket with her shuddering hand and dragged it toward the stone-lined edge of the firepit.

"What the hell do you think you're doing?" guttural Ken demanded.

"This," she replied, as she knelt beside the bucket and tipped it toward the firepit, balancing it on her knees at a precarious angle until the water was sloshing along the lip of the pail. A single drop escaped and landed in the fire with a chilling sizzle.

Beverly looked up from her handiwork and saw the shock in guttural Ken's face, satisfied that he knew she meant business.

"Drop the knife and let her go!" Beverly ordered. "Or so help me, I'll do it!"

The pail shook violently in her quivering right hand.

"You're bluffing," guttural Ken sneered.

But the defiance in Beverly's twitching, bloody tear-streaked face suggested otherwise.

"As you already pointed out: I'm dead no matter what, so I've got nothing to lose."

"Well, well," guttural Ken replied, his voice betraying a certain admiration for her kamikaze tactics. "Looks like we have ourselves a genuine Mexican standoff."

Everyone stood stock still, waiting to see what would happen next. Gaby struggled to control her panicked breathing as she watched the flames recede and the shadows close in. From the corner of her eye, she could see hundreds of iku writhing within five feet of the firepit. Ken took a step closer to the center, dragging her along with her.

As the minutes ticked by, Lamar tried to divide his attention between Ken and Beverly, neither of whom appeared willing to bend to the other's demands. He held his spear fast, waiting. As the shadows drew closer, Coop — who had been standing shoulder to shoulder with Lamar — stepped behind him to avoid the ikus' touch.

No one spoke, except for Wade, who kept chanting "whet whem win" ceaselessly, like it was his personal mantra. The sound of the ikus' chirping was overwhelming as the firelight slowly faded.

"The fire's dying," guttural Ken observed with a vicious sneer. "You better feed it soon."

When the shadows were within four feet, Lamar shrugged off his jacket, making certain to keep one hand on his spear at all times, and tossed it onto the red-hot embers, which happily accepted it. Coop quickly followed up with his jacket.

Beverly locked eyes with the petrified Gaby.

"Are you scared, child?"

Gaby nodded, her eyes wide with fright.

"Good, that means you have something worth living for," Beverly said as she shook furiously. "'Fearless' is just another word for someone with nothing to lose. Don't make my mistakes. I lost everyone around me because of the bottle, and now it's going to cost me my life," she said, pausing to cough up more blood. "Make sure you live in my stead."

"I wish I'd known you better," Gaby said regretfully.

"You've spent so much time with me at my worst," Beverly mused. "Now you finally get to see me at my best."

Guttural Ken barked with savage laughter.

"This isn't an afterschool special, you dumb bitches!" he

mocked. "If those things don't kill you, I fucking well will!"

At a gesture from Lamar, Coop started walking around to the other side of the firepit, careful to watch his feet to avoid stepping in any encroaching shadows, which were now less than four feet from the outer rim of the firepit. Once he was on the other side, guttural Ken would be trapped in a pincer maneuver with nowhere to go.

"I don't know how much long I can hold this steady," Beverly warned, though no one could tell if it was a threat or if she was in earnest.

"Whet whem win! Whet whem win!" Wade shouted through his gag, bouncing up and down feverishly as he felt his plastic bonds start to give. Coop noticed that Wade was already sitting in the shadows, with the iku swarming all around, and yet they completely ignored him.

Coop walked carefully around Beverly and pointed his spear at guttural Ken. He and Lamar both pressed forward.

"Not so close," guttural Ken warned as the two spearmen converged on him. His eyes raging, guttural Ken grabbed Gaby by the wrist and guided her unwilling hand to the shadows and the congregating iku, which were only inches away.

"Whet whem win!"

"Drop your spears or watch her die!" Ken barked.

Lamar and Ken stood their ground, their weapons aimed at his head.

Ken pulled Gaby's hand further from the firelight.

The shadows were now within three feet of the firepit.

"Whet whem win! Whet whem win!"

Gaby shrieked as the tip of her index finger entered the

shadows and the waiting iku swarmed it. In the dying light of the embers, Lamar could see the tip of her finger slowly turn black, like Beverly's skin after her brush with the creatures.

"Sooo cold!" Gaby stammered, tears of pain streaming down her face. "Sooo cold!"

The black mark rapidly moved downward and started consuming the webbing between her fingers.

"Okay, you win!" Lamar shouted as he lowered his spear. "Just let her go!"

"Whet whem win! Whet whem win! Whet whem win!"

"Drop it on the ground, or you can pick up what's left of this cunt with a pair of tweezers!" guttural Ken growled.

Lamar dropped his spear to the ground, where it landed with a dull thud.

"Him, too!" guttural Ken demanded, motioning toward Coop.

The black mark had already consumed half of Gaby's hand. Her screams of pain and terror were deafening.

Coop reluctantly dropped his spear and kicked it toward guttural Ken.

"Whet whem win! Whet whem win! Whet whem win!"

Instead of pulling Gaby's darkening digits from the shadows, guttural Ken merely laughed at their capitulation.

"Did you really think I'd be stupid enough to let any of you live?" he asked mockingly as he raised his knife hand and aimed at Lamar.

Fifteen feet away, Wade's persistence was finally rewarded when the last of his plastic bindings snapped. He wrenched his arms free and tore the gag out of his mouth.

"I'll let them in! They'll save you all!" Wade shouted in rapturous delight as he struggled to his feet, blood spewing out of his mutilated thigh as he put his full weight on it. "No more monsters!"

Everything happened at once. Lamar watched in bewilderment as Wade barreled toward the entrance in slow motion, like he was running through molasses. Coop saw Wade running off to his left and gradually turned to face him, just as guttural Ken, who had been menacing Lamar with the penknife, spun around in response to Wade's shouting. Lamar watched, fascinated, as guttural Ken's face gradually changed from leering madman to startled intruder at the side of Wade bolting. In the confusion, his grip on Gaby loosened. Her foot rose up and then came crashing down on his foot, changing his look of astonishment to one of pain. Even over the screeching of the iku, Lamar could hear a bone in guttural Ken's foot snap. Beverly reacted to the clatter by lazily turning her still juddering head just as Wade barreled down on her, barely even registering her presence as he charged at the door.

"Lettttttt tttthemmmmm innnnnn!" were Wade's last words before he collided with Beverly. The collision knocked Wade into the shadows and upended the water pail in Beverly's lap, sending torrents of water crashing down onto the red-hot coals. The teepee quickly filled with steam and a terrible sizzling noise as the water quenched the flames. Lamar watched as the coals went dark, one by one.

"Oh, God!" he heard himself cry as the firelight snuffed out and the ikus' chirping reached a fever pitch.

He heard more than saw the teeming masses of creatures

outside force their way in, desperate to join their brethren for the feasting.

Lamar heard a scream off to his right that he recognized as Gaby's. In the dark, he could just make out her outline as the wriggling creatures swarmed her en masse. Her screams were quickly muffled as the iku enveloped her and then cut off two seconds later, replaced with a low choking sound.

The pulsating, heaving mass of creatures swamping Gaby suddenly exploded with light, transforming into a beam of such dazzling purity and brilliance that it hurt to look at it. The cone of white light extended in a five-foot-wide arc that shot straight into the night sky, passing through the wigwam's roof with no loss of potency. It was just like the light Gaby had seen pierce the night sky three days earlier, when Wade was still hunting them.

The radiant beam brilliantly illuminated the wigwam's interior. An impossible number of squirming black creatures were pouring through the venting hole in the ceiling and slithering over every surface imaginable. While the creatures had always run from other light sources — fire, flashlights, sunlight — this one, brighter than all of the others combined, had no apparent effect on them.

In the center of the cone of light was Gaby, her eyes closed like she was in peaceful repose and her face turned upward. She was hovering in the air, two feet off the ground, her arms outstretched as if in prayer. Lamar watched, fascinated, as Gaby's numerous injuries — the slash to her palm, her scalp wound, the black spot on her hand — all vanished.

A voice came from the light. It was Gaby's, but magnified so that it echoed throughout the structure, drowning out the ikus' cries.

"I can leave him," she boomed, her voice projecting an absolute serenity that Lamar had never seen from Gaby before.

The light slowly faded, and as it did, Gaby's body descended until it gently came to rest on the ground. Lamar was struck by how peaceful she looked.

As the light faded, the wigwam plunged once more into darkness. No sooner had the light gone than Lamar heard a shriek of terror from Beverly as the iku swarmed her. Light flooded the chamber again almost immediately as though there were less work involved in transforming her.

In the light, Lamar could clearly see all of his companions. Coop lay on the ground, five feet to his left, entranced by the light show, his mouth hanging agape. Guttural Ken was cowering away from the display, petrified of the light as he held up his arms to shield his face. Wade seemed delighted by the sight, his smile almost as brilliant as the cone of light. The iku thronged around all of them. Lamar looked down at his feet and saw they were gathering around him, too. He reached blindly for his spear, coming away instead with one of the river stones lining the firepit. His hand closed around it and he held it at the ready, prepared to bash any iku that came near him.

In the center of the light was Beverly, floating gently in the air, her arms outstretched like Gaby's had been. It wasn't the haunted, dying Beverly of recent days, nor even the irritating know-it-all Beverly they'd first met. She looked completely at peace with herself. All of the black marks on her body were gone.

"I don't need the bottle," she thundered.

Lamar slowly lowered the rock in confusion, trying to make sense of Beverly's pronouncement over the pounding intensity of his own jackhammering heart.

One by one, the others followed in the same fashion. Coop was consumed next, his assailants bursting into light as he levitated off the ground, transformed. In the dazzling brilliance surrounding Coop, Lamar could see the iku gathering around Wade's mutilated thigh, projecting a soft aura of light around it that appeared to be healing it. He happily ran his hands across the creatures, as though he were petting them, with no ill effects.

"I can forgive myself," Coop's voice proclaimed, echoing throughout the teepee.

In the fading light surrounding Coop, Lamar could see guttural Ken had located a spear, probably his own, and was swinging it wildly in the air, trying to keep the iku at bay as the light around Coop's body slowly faded.

"I'll kill you all!" guttural Ken snarled as the iku swarmed him in the darkness, his bravado replaced by screams of pain, followed by a sickening thud, and then a long, drawn-out exhalation.

The light reappeared and Ken was bathed in it, hovering off the dirt floor, eyes closed and arms spread wide. Because of his height, Ken's head was partially sticking out of the venting hole as the light carried him aloft.

"I don't need to live a lie," he announced before the light slowly faded and he was lowered to the ground.

Now it was just Lamar and Wade, and the creatures seemed to have no interest in the latter. Lamar took a deep breath and steeled himself as the room went dark. The sounds of happy chirping thundered in his ears, nearly out-done by the shuddering beat of his own pulse.

The strangest images flitted through his mind. He had heard how people staring down death always reflect on key moments in their lives, but all Lamar saw were images of their first day here in Quehanna as their guide John had lectured them on the truth circle, their coming transform-ations and the dark path Wade had chosen. John's words echoed in his mind.

"This is a journey of enlightenment."

"By the end of the week, you will be a changed person."

"Each of you must face your own truth."

"Spiritual rebirth."

*"Once the circle is formed, a sacred bond develops …
one that cannot be broken until the truth comes to light."*

"We call upon the weyekin — the spirits of the forest — for their assistance in the cleansing to come."

"The next time you see these welcome posts, you'll be very different people."

"It isn't the experience that shapes you; it's the truth."

"Discover your true selves."

Suddenly, it all made sense: the transformations, Wade's rants, the missing welcome posts, even the landscape that died and was magically resurrected. The iku weren't the enemy. They were the catalyst.

Lamar dropped the rock, closed his eyes and steeled himself for the inevitable.

The iku swarmed him, and each one's touch was like the prick of an impossibly cold icicle, thousands of them stabbing him over and over again, freezing him to the core. Lamar opened his mouth to scream, but no words came out. The pain was indescribable, setting every nerve ending aflame as the iku washed over his feet and legs and across his torso. Lamar's eyes shot open in agony. He saw black marks racing up his limbs and stomach toward his face as the ikus' venom consumed him from the inside out. He had just enough time to think how much this resembled Beverly's former condition — but massively accelerated — before the blackness consumed him utterly.

Lamar was awash in a sea of pain. He registered sickness, rage, fear, despair and unimaginable suffering, all at once. He could hear a gurgling noise as his lungs shriveled up and failed. Some dim part of his fading consciousness registered that he was dying. He wondered if this was what the others had experienced before the last vestiges of his mind slipped their mortal bonds.

Nothing.

Emptiness.

An all-consuming void of darkness, with nothing to see or interact with; not even the ground to orient him.

Something.

A tiny, flickering pinprick of light.

It spread and gradually pushed back the void.

Warmth.
Flesh.
A heartbeat.
The light grew stronger, more confident, becoming the purest, brightest light imaginable.

Lamar suddenly found himself floating in the middle of it, bathed in its warm glow as it radiated not only luminosity but also peace and tranquility. Lamar felt a joy welling up inside that he had never known. After so many years wasted in avoiding human contact, hiding his true self behind a computer screen and a hacker persona, he simply had no comparison for this sensation. His heart was so full he thought it would burst.

His mouth opened and words escaped his lips, impossibly potent and serene.

"I am equal to the task," he heard himself utter before the light slowly faded and gently deposited him to the ground. Lamar laid his head in the dirt and slipped into a sleep deeper and more blissful than he had ever known.

FRIDAY

Gaby opened her eyes slowly. It was late morning. A single beam from the overhead sun filtered through the teepee's venting hole, projecting a soft, diffuse aura of light across the firepit. She could see that the pine tree overhanging the wigwam was growing fresh needles after losing them all to the blight. Melodious chirping alerted her to the presence of birds nearby.

Gaby tried to orient herself and realized she was flat on her back. She raised her head and looked around the wigwam. The place was in shambles, with clothes and prone bodies scattered everywhere. She felt panic well up inside her until she saw their chests were rising and falling in rhythmic patterns. They weren't dead; they were fast asleep.

She turned her head and saw Ken lying beside her. He opened his eyes and smiled at her. Not a vicious smirk or fake grin masking cruelty, but a warm and inviting smile of genuine empathy. She reciprocated. It felt good.

All the animosity, all the distrust, all the ugliness that had passed between the two had been washed away by the iku in a matter of seconds. Gaby knew he wasn't the same man who had attacked her, who had threatened her life. Both of them were changed, complete.

Ken reached out his hand to her. She accepted it without

hesitation and squeezed his fingers lightly, enjoying the tenderness and the sense of belonging, something that would have been unfathomable scarcely 24 hours ago.

Neither spoke a word, but their eyes radiated the same indefinable sensation: wholeness.

They heard a noise behind them. Ken raised himself up on his elbow and craned his neck to see. It was Lamar, slowly stirring. Beside him was Wade, beaming with delight. The makeshift tourniquet that Coop had fashioned had been discarded. His thigh looked untouched, as though last night's madness had never even happened.

"Told you," Wade said with a quiet twang and soft smile. "No more monsters."

A distant hum broke their reverie. It sounded like a motor. All of them looked around for the source of the noise, until it became clear that it was coming from outside. After another minute or so the sound was unmistakable. It was accompanied by a crunching noise, like tires on dirt. A vehicle was approaching.

Lamar sat up and looked questioningly at the others, who were just as confused as he was.

The motor sputtered and died just outside the campsite. They heard a door slam and the sound of feet approaching the wigwam.

Coop and Beverly stirred at the noise, while the others looked to the door, pensively. Gaby wondered if she should try and bar it.

The feet stopped just outside the wigwam. Suddenly, the door opened and light flooded the small enclosure, blinding the group.

Gaby winced and turned her head away while Coop shielded his eyes from the brightness. A shape knelt down in front of the door, blotting out much of the light.

It took a moment for everyone's eyes to adjust from the blinding light to the darkness once more. As they did, the person kneeling before them gradually came into focus: reddish skin, weathered features, long, flowing silver hair. After a moment, they realized they were staring at the wrinkled visage of John Lightfoot.

There was the smallest hint of a smile on his face, and that irrepressible twinkle in his eyes was as bright as ever.

"So," he asked matter-of-factly as he scanned the confused faces in the wigwam. "How was it?"

Aug. 21, 2015 — Aug. 15, 2019

ABOUT THE AUTHOR

Cameron Ayers is a day-journalist and night-author who lives, works, and — on the rare occasions he has time — plays in the greater D.C. region. This is his first novel.

He can be reached by email (cameronayerswriter@gmail.com), on Twitter (@cameronayerswr1) or by opening the window and shouting *reeaaalllly* loudly.

Made in the USA
Middletown, DE
02 February 2020